BLACK DROP

Also by S.L. Stoner
in the Sage Adair Historical Mysteries of the Pacific Northwest

Timber Beasts
Land Sharks
Dry Rot

BLACK DROP

A Sage Adair Historical Mystery
of the Pacific Northwest

S. L. Stoner

Yamhill Press
P.O. Box 42348
Portland, OR   97242

Black Drop:
A Sage Adair Historical Mystery of the Pacific Northwest

A Yamhill Press Book

Cover Design by Alec Icky Dunn/Blackoutprint.com
Interior Design by Josh MacPhee/AntumbraDesign.org

Edition ISBNs
    Softcover   ISBN 978-0-9823184-8-5
    Ebook   ISBN 978-0-9823184-9-2

Publisher's Cataloging-in-Publication

    Stoner, S. L.
    Black Drop: A Sage Adair historical mystery of the Pacific
    Northwest / S.L. Stoner.
    pages cm. -- (A Sage Adair historical mystery)

    1. Northwest, Pacific--History--20th century--Fiction. 2.
    Labor unions--Fiction. 3. Detective and mystery stories. 4.
    Martial arts fiction. 5. Historical fiction. 6. Adventure stories.
    I. Title. II. Series: Stoner, S. L. Sage Adair historical mystery.

    PS3619.T6857B53 2013   813'.6   QBI13-600182

To the men and women of the
Amalgamated Transit Union, Division 757
for the opportunity
and
to George R. Slanina, Jr.
for being the center and the source of so many great things.

"The wise man's wealth lies in good deeds that follow ever after him."
—Tibetan Proverb

ONE

Late April, 1903, New York City

> *"The great corporations which we have grown to speak of rather*
> *loosely as trusts are the creatures of the State and the State not*
> *only has the right to control them, but it is in duty bound to*
> *control them wherever need of such control is shown."*
> —*Theodore Roosevelt (T.R.)*

AFTER SWINGING THE DOOR PARTIALLY OPEN, the man walked away. Dropping down into a plush armchair by the window, he surveyed his visitor with narrowed eyes.

Left to close the door himself, the visitor did so, but remained standing. Immediately his eyes began to sting from heavy cigar smoke, despite the window being wide open. Once his vision adjusted to the gloom, he spied a mound of cigar butts in a crystal ashtray. A match flared and a cheroot tip glowed red. Either his client was a nicotine addict or very nervous. Probably both.

"I rather like this vindow," said the man in the armchair, his exhale a billowing cloud between them. "The pigeons, they roost on the ledge above the awning next door, the one over the restaurant's outdoor terrace." An accent tinged the client's words, but neither Brit English nor French. Harsher. Maybe German since his "window" sounded like "vindow."

"Uh, you like pigeons?" the visitor asked, though he wanted the conversation to quickly reach the main point. It wasn't smart to stay here any longer than necessary. Since becoming a mercenary, his practice was to keep client meetings both secret and brief. So far, that practice had kept his risks to a minimum.

The other man had no such practice because he kept on about the damn birds. "No, I detest pigeons, you idiot," he snapped, sucking deep on the cigar and letting the smoke trail from his fat lips like some Eastern potentate. "As a matter of fact, I am conducting my own little eradication program from right here."

The mercenary suppressed a sigh, knowing he had to humor the man. "You poison them?" he asked.

"Oh, no, that vould present no challenge. I use this." The man brandished the Y of a large wooden slingshot, "And these steel ball bearings." The glinting spheres clanked as he shook his hand, just like a crap shooter about to throw dice.

"You're killing pigeons with a slingshot from the window?" The foreigner sure had an odd notion of entertainment.

"I must do something. My hunting club is thousands of miles away. And I haf strict instructions to be very discrete about my presence in New York. That means, I cannot hunt with my local acquaintances this trip. Instead, I sit here and eliminate the birds."

"The restaurant below doesn't object?"

The other man chuckled as he shook his head. "Because of the angle and the awning, no one can see me. That is the beauty of it. I am able to sit here and hone my targeting skills from the comfort of my armchair. When I am successful, the body slides down the awning to splat upon the terrace. You should hear the shrieking from below. Once, a table flipped over, dishes went crashing." He smiled at the memory.

The client tossed the slingshot back onto the antique table, not caring that he marred its polished surface. Likely the apartment was merely the client's temporary abode. Evidently, he cared little what its owner might think about the stink of cigars or damage to rare antiques. Flapping an impatient hand in the air, the fellow dismissed any further conversation about pigeons, saying, "Enough chatter concerning my simple pleasures. I vish to hear your report on the progress of our plan."

Momentary irritation fizzed through the mercenary. He hadn't been the one to delay the discussion. He swallowed the irritation, though, carefully keeping his face expressionless. The payoff for this job was too big for him to indulge in an honest reaction to the man's arrogance. Maybe later, when it was all over, after he received payment in full. So he kept his tone business like. "I've got most everyone lined up and in place, sir. The only slipup so far has been our Portland friend. He drinks too much when his nerves overtake him. Tends to wag his tongue more than he ought. It created a problem I was forced to fix. Things got a bit messy but I think I've corrected the situation."

"Humph, I trust you have explained to him the very terminal consequences should that tongue of his slip again before the deed is done."

"He knows now if he didn't before," the mercenary answered grimly. "I wish we didn't have to use him but, as you say, we have no choice since you've made him a key element in the plan."

"And aftervards?" The man's tone was silky, almost playful.

"Like you told me last week. Very shortly afterwards, there will be an accident," the mercenary said flatly. "A fatal one, unfortunately," he added a long second later.

The man in the chair bared his teeth in what the ignorant might deem a smile. Despite the surprisingly warm spring air, the mercenary shuddered but resisted the urge to twist the wall knob and light the dim room. "His tour, it is still on schedule?" the client asked, interrupting the mercenary's thoughts.

"They've not announced anything different. He still plans to visit Oregon, sometime in late May. My inside informant will alert me if that changes. He will also get me the exact dates once they're firm."

The other man's face turned from the window and he shook his finger, warning, "You must not fail. Millions of dollars depend upon our success in this venture. The entire future of an industry is at stake. Ve must make absolutely sure that the only vay our big-toothed friend leaves Oregon is inside a coffin."

Late April, 1903, Portland, Oregon

"That makes five this afternoon, six yesterday afternoon," Sage Adair grumbled to himself as he stood up to shake the cramps from his legs and the disgust from his mind. He looked away from the enameled red door and toward the other houses along his side of the street. At the street's end, a horse plodded past. The metal wheels of the trolley car it towed clanked every time they hit the steel joints. Soon the ugly spider webs of electrification would spread into this neighborhood just south of the city's center. Once that happened, that horse would be out of a job, Sage thought. Given the animal's drooping head, bony ribs and quivering shanks, he doubted that the horse would mind.

Sage stepped from beneath the cedar branches where he'd been squatting and headed toward a well-kept square house down the block. A wide front porch spanned its entire front and wrapped around one corner. Mounting the wooden steps, Sage knocked on the door. An apple-cheeked homemaker answered, drying her hands on a blue gingham apron when she saw him.

"Excuse me, ma'am." Sage said as he raised his hat politely. "I'm looking for an elderly gentleman I met near here last summer. He was small, frail, carried a cane. I have forgotten his name but I am certain that he lives somewhere nearby."

The woman's face lost its smile, and she frowned, saying, "Was he wearing a pair of square-framed spectacles, kinda thick?"

"Yes, that sounds like him," Sage answered, slowing his words because her expression and the crinkling of her forehead signaled bad news.

"Sounds like that was Mr. Compton who you met. I'm sorry to tell you, but he died just this past December. It was pneumonia, they said."

That discouraging information gained, Sage returned to squatting beneath the drooping cedar branches. This time though, he felt the heavy weight of guilt across his shoulders. He'd let that old man down. His ears recalled the sound of his confident voice promising Mr. Compton that the abominable house would be closed. Now the old man would never have the satisfaction of seeing Sage deliver on that promise. Sage had waited too long.

"I've got to believe you are still hovering about, like some well-meaning spirit," Sage said aloud, his words directed toward the bench where he'd last seen the old man sitting.

Time inched past as three more men entered the house just as two others left. Dusk began to fall and Sage finally rose to leave, his legs threatening to fail after all that squatting. The total lack of street lights meant that soon, he would no longer be able to see who was mounting that steep staircase to knock on the red door. Not that seeing their faces mattered all that much. Despite two such afternoon vigils, Sage still couldn't figure out how to deliver on last June's promise to the dead Mr. Compton.

The wind rose suddenly, setting the cedar boughs above him to creaking. Sage stepped out from under the tree's shelter. He glanced around the small park and froze, his attention caught by an abrupt movement in the second floor window of the adjacent house.

He squinted, trying to see into the room but he saw only window glass reflecting a darkening sky alive with wind-driven clouds. Possibly, his eye had simply caught the reflection of a cloud blocking the sunset.

Sage shoved his hands into his coat pockets and shook his head. He needed to get warm and eat something. It was nothing, just his mind starting to play tricks, he told himself. Because, otherwise, why would a man have been standing at that window, a pair of binoculars raised to his eyes?

TWO

Dispatch: *May 4, 1903, President Theodore Roosevelt's train arrives in Denver, Colorado, his tour of America's Far West is about to begin.*

> *"The demands of progress now deal not so much with the material as with the moral and ethical factors of civilization."* —*T.R.*

LINGERING OUTSIDE MOZART'S TABLE, Sage momentarily savored the contrast between the dark chill outside and the scene of warm normalcy within Mozart's interior. He saw his mother bustling about a dining room reputed to be one of Portland's most elegant eateries–second to only the Portland Hotel. No doubt she was wondering where he was. As the restaurant's official greeter, he should be already fully costumed and ready to perform as its gracious host. His role as John S. Adair, Mozart's well-to-do proprietor, was crucial to their work for the national labor leader, Vincent St. Alban. They were his undercover operatives in Portland. These last two days had taken him away from that role. Sage sighed, noticing that the weather had finally warmed to point that his breath could no longer make vapor clouds.

In an hour, Mozart's doors would open. Carriages would wheel up to the curb and the restaurant's well-to-do patrons would alight. Among those patrons might be one of the men he'd watched mount those weathered steps and knock on that damnable door. Such an encounter was inevitable because, from his vantage point beneath the cedar boughs, he'd recognized more than one Mozart's customer. Would he be able to hide his disgust? Would his gracious host persona crack, letting his contempt show through? And, there was a bigger problem. Now that he had confirmed that there was still a thriving business operating behind that red door, how could he put an end to it without revealing he was something other than Mozart's attractively shallow owner? Dare he jeopardize St. Alban's ongoing Portland mission that way?

Crossing the dark street with purposeful steps, Sage strolled through the front door. He quickly headed up the stairs to the third floor, not stopping to explain his tardiness despite seeing the irritated look Mae Clemens shot him as he crossed the foyer.

He'd barely begun to strip off his street clothes when his ostensible houseman, Fong Kam Tong, slid into the room, his face serene as always.

"Did you enjoy your day, Mr. Fong?" Sage asked in a mild tone he thought unlikely to trigger the other man's alarm bells.

"Most illuminating and very puzzling," Fong responded though his expression remained bland. Sage shot him a quick glance. Sure enough, those dark brown eyes were twinkling.

Sage stepped to the walnut bureau. "I saw you," he said to Fong's reflection in the mirror as he looped his bow tie into order.

"That is very good," Fong said, his smile revealing some teeth.

"You were that 'thick dark' in the 'thin dark' you're always talking about. The space between the those two houses is narrow but there is still just enough light to tell the difference. Since whoever it was stayed motionless for hours, I knew it had to be you."

"Ah, student is showing improvement." Fong's face reflected smug satisfaction. As Sage's teacher in a Chinese fighting style he called the "snake and crane," Fong had spent many patient hours training his Occidental student in the fine art of observation. Despite this effort, Sage felt his skills, if they were improving, were doing so at the proverbial snail's pace.

"Was it your idea or Mother's to follow me?"

"We both have same idea. I because important to keep senses sharp, yours and mine. She because you are 'up to something'."

Sage finished by quickly combing pomade through his hair and shrugging the fine suit coat onto his broad shoulders, "And, you going to tell her what?" he asked.

"That you are 'definitely up to something.' Not sure what. For many hours you watch house with a bright red door and you get very upset because you wiggle under that cedar tree like man sitting in ant nest." Fong's forehead wrinkled with some thought and then he said, "You better learn how to stay still, important skill."

"How'd you figure out I was up to something so quickly? I've only been watching that house for a few days."

Fong cocked his head to the side, the lines in his face deeper, giving it a bleak cast. "Past week," he said, "your smile never reach your eyes."

"So, what gave me away?" Sage asked his mother, Mae Clemens. The restaurant was closed and the three of them were sitting around the table in his room on the third floor. Her room also was on the third floor as was Fong's. But the Chinese man only used it intermittently. He preferred, instead, to walk the few blocks to his Chinatown provision store where he and his wife had their living quarters.

Mae didn't hesitate. "You've been acting like your mind is slipping gears. Once you called Horace by the wrong name even though he's waited Mozart's tables for nearly two years. Then there's your gazing into space like a cow chewing cud. I've had to ask you the same question more than once before you answer. Also, you've turned snappish as a roused bear in winter. Besides, it's your pattern. You always stir the pot whenever St. Alban doesn't have a job for us. It's been nearly four months. That enough reasons? You going to tell us what's going on or does Mr. Fong need to keep sticking to you like burrs on a bunny?"

Sage laughed. "It isn't a secret exactly. I was just gathering information. Matter of fact, I could use your help figuring out what to do."

Chair feet scraped across the wood floor as the other two scooted closer to the table, their faces alert. Obviously, he wasn't the only one yearning for some action. Sage explained what he knew and had seen.

"What do your Mr. Confucius and Mr. Lao think of such things?" Sage asked Fong once he'd laid out the situation.

"This is somewhat a problem for Chinese wise men. Two man pillowing together is yang and yang, instead of yin and yang. So, not in balance. But, if man also father children to keep up family line, nothing said. Not like Christ church that calls it 'sin' but people do it anyway."

"But what about 'pillowing' between a grown man and a young boy?"

Fong shifted in his seat, clearly ill at ease. "China still has slavery. Whenever someone can be owned, like cow, many bad things happen. Letters from home say maybe slavery end soon."

Now it was Sage's turn to shift uncomfortably. He looked into his mother's narrowed dark blue eyes, so like his own, and caught the warning. Fong's wife, Kim Ho, had been a slave in San Francisco's Chinatown until the day Fong had bought her freedom.

Sage cleared his throat. "Well, in this country, men with boys is definitely frowned upon."

His mother spoke, her voice quavering with indignation, "What I cannot believe is that the manager of the Boy's Christian Shelter is selling young boys. Are you sure?"

"That's what Lucinda told me last summer," Sage said, referring to Lucinda Collins, parlor house madam and his former lover. "And, from what I've seen the last two days, that house appears to have a ready supply of young boys given the number of customers going in and out."

Mae Clemens nodded. "Well, if that's what Lucinda told you, then it must be true." Left unsaid was Mae Clemens' oft-stated opinion that Sage had made a big mistake when he let inaction cost him the woman's affection.

"Anyway," Sage said with emphasis, hoping to derail that particular train of thought, "I recognized a few of the men but I don't know what to do with the information. I can't go public with it, or even be associated with it, because it would jeopardize our work for St. Alban. Not to mention I might get sued for defamation–right now, it'd be just my word against theirs." The other two nodded glumly.

"And, one other wrinkle. There might be someone else watching the same house. I thought I saw him. He was standing, with a pair of binoculars, at the second floor window of the house sitting next to the park."

"I not see that," Fong said, his tone slightly self-chiding.

Fong liked to think he saw and heard everything. Generally, his confidence was justified. Sage waved away the other man's concern, saying, "No way you could have, given the angle. But I am thinking he probably noticed me and will be very careful to stay out of sight whenever I am around. So, I was thinking that you, Mr. Fong, might work your magic and find out where he comes from and who he is."

Shortly after Mozart's noontime dinner hour the next day, Sage strode through *The Daily Journal's* door. Reporters with ink-stained fingers furiously clacked the keys on their type writing machines. Not one of them raised his eyes when Sage ambled past, heading to the publisher's office at the back corner of the large room.

Ben Johnston, however, looked up sharply when the door opened but not before Sage saw the publisher with his head buried in his hands.

"Something the matter, Ben?" Sage's question wasn't an idle one. He'd invested a significant amount of his Klondike gold into funding Portland's newest newspaper. Next to Johnston, he was the newspaper's largest investor. And, for good reason. Until Johnston arrived on the scene, city news was filtered through the pages of the establishment's conservative rag, *The Portland Gazette.*

Johnston's smile was little more than a rueful lip twist. "If you consider the threat of losing five percent of our advertizing a problem, then something could be the matter."

"You write an editorial one of the advertisers didn't like?"

"Nope, if only it were that simple. This," here Johnston tapped a letter on the desk, "is a letter from the Women's Christian Temperance Union. The lovely ladies are making threats."

Sage laughed. "I've been telling you that the whiskey still you've got operating down in the *Journal's* basement was going to get you into trouble," he chided.

Johnston didn't smile. "Hah! If I had a whiskey still down among the presses, it would be an easy fix. No, the good ladies of the WCTU are demanding that I refuse all advertisements for patent medicines that contain opiates. If I don't comply, they promise they'll launch a protest picket outside the *Journal's* front door."

That was sobering. The *Journal*, like all newspapers, did a brisk and significant business in patent medicine advertisements. "How many of them contain opiates?" he asked.

"There's the question. They don't print the contents on the bottle so how the heck am I to know?"

"Sounds like a fine query to make of the good ladies," Sage suggested.

Johnston's face brightened. "Why, so it does." He pulled a clean sheet of paper toward him and took up his pen–Sage's presence completely forgotten.

Sage cleared his throat. When Johnston looked up, Sage said. "Before you craft your letter to the ladies, Ben, could you take a moment to answer a question for me?"

"Ha, ha. Forgot myself, John. I suppose you didn't come here to solve my problem." Johnston was unaware that some called the restaurateur, John S. Adair, "Sage." Only Sage's mother, Fong, parlor house madam Lucinda Collins, and a few close associates in the labor movement knew him as "Sage." It was the diminutive of his middle name, "Sagacity." Ironically, the original Sagacity had gone to his early death as the advisor to a defeated Irish chieftain.

So, as "John Adair," Sage told Johnston about the house with the red door. Johnston's nose wrinkled and his lips twisted in extreme distaste but this reaction didn't affect his answer. "I know these things go on, of course. But, I haven't heard of it happening in Portland. Still, I've only been here a year. Problem is, this isn't something I can put in print until there's been an arrest. The risk of being sued is too great—you know they all will either flat deny it or they'll come up with some excuse about why they were seen walking through that door."

The next day, as he squatted once again beneath the cedar boughs, Sage had to admit that Johnston's refusal to publish the story was not unexpected. Ultimately, the publisher said he was willing to publish it but only if he could name the source of his information. Yet, there was no way Sage could have his own name associated with such public revelations. And, without the backing of Sage's credibility as an upstanding businessman, it would be foolhardy for Johnston to print it.

The breeze picked up and Sage shivered. Minutes later, overhead limbs creaked and snapped as a gunmetal gray cloud roiled up the valley pushing a curtain of spring hail. The ice pellets pelted tree boughs and ground, pummeling the newly opened crocuses. Their drooping stems made him recall that day last summer when he'd sat in this exact same place, watching the boys who lived in that house across the street. Sitting on those stairs, their shoulders drooped like those crocuses now being beaten down by hail.

He looked at that door. Today's severe weather failed to slow the foot traffic on those stairs. Seven this afternoon, one a repeat from the first day. Sage snarled low in his throat, torn between wanting to throttle the house's manager, Lynch, and craving a cigarette. For about the fiftieth time he snicked a covert glance at the second story window next door. Nothing was visible. The dark room hid whatever might lurk behind that glass. A person standing to either side of that window frame would be nearly impossible to see.

Mozart's supper hour was relatively busy, yet Sage per-formed his hosting duties absentmindedly. Mozart's genteel din-ing room, with its satiny, mahogany wainscoting, newly painted pale green plaster, snowy damask tablecloths, sparkling cutlery and lively, well-dressed patrons, did nothing to banish gloomy thoughts about that red door. Behind his ready banter and past-ed-on smile, emotion churned. He was going to fulfil his prom-ise to old man Compton. Lynch's business would be destroyed. Somehow he had to do it in a way that would not jeopardize their future missions for St. Alban. Maybe that meant acting through someone else. But, who?

Midway through supper, worry over Fong's prolonged ab-sence shoved aside all the other worries. The plan had been for Fong to hide between those two houses until Sage left. Then Fong was to follow the man who was using the binoculars to watch Lynch's house. And certainly, there was a man with bin-oculars. Sage had glimpsed him again. In the late afternoon, the sinking sun's slanted rays pierced the window, briefly illuminating a male figure. Sage had given the signal. And, shortly thereafter, he'd abandoned the cedar's sheltering branches, leaving the mys-terious watcher to Fong. But that had been hours ago and still no Fong. By the end of the supper hour, Sage alternated between telling himself that Fong was fine, just delayed, and thinking the worst.

THREE

Dispatch: *May 5, 1903, President's train arrives in Sante Fe, New Mexico.*

> *"We need to show in civic life the same spirit that you showed in . . . battle; what you cared to know about as to the man on your right and the one on the left, was not the way in which he worshiped his Maker; not his social standing or wealth; . . . What you wanted to know was whether he would do his duty like a man . . . it is the same thing in civil life now." —T.R.*

SAGE LOCKED THE DOOR BEHIND THE LAST CUSTOMER and headed toward the third floor, taking the steps two at a time. Fong had been absent way too long.

He was bent over tying his boot lacings when Fong slipped through the door.

"You've had me worried, my friend," Sage said, grinning. "Instead of stretching out over there," he nodded in the direction of his four-poster bed, "I was shoving my very tired feet into these heavy work boots."

"Not my idea," Fong assured him, taking a seat next to the stove and rubbing his hands in its rising heat. He gratefully accepted the whiskey shot Sage poured.

"The man stayed inside house for over one hour after you leave. When he leave, I follow. Not too hard, he never look behind. But he not go to another house. Instead, he go to a saloon. Of course, I stay outside. In the cold."

Fong's words carried the weight of an unspoken comment. They both knew that he'd had to stand outside in the cold because white men did not tolerate Orientals in their drinking establishments, unless, of course, those Orientals were washing dishes or standing over a cookstove.

"Sorry," Sage said, pausing to give the apology heft before continuing, "What did he look like?"

"He wore good business suit. Tall as you, only his hair is sand-colored. Smooth face, no mustache, round with square chin. Maybe your age." Fong sipped the amber liquid, closing his eyes when it hit his throat. He generally avoided spirits.

So the clean-shaven mystery man was six foot and around 32 years of age. Not a working man. A description fitting hundreds. They'd need more information than that to learn who he was. Before Sage could ask another question, though, Fong again took up his narrative.

"I wait two hours for him to come out. When he reach street, his feet tangle up stepping off curb. I grab his arm to stop him from falling. He said, 'Thank you.' After he looked into my face."

A considering "hmm" softly vibrated Sage's cranium. Politeness was not how intoxicated white men normally reacted when touched by a Chinese man.

Fong paused, sipped and, for a minute, stared at nothing, apparently seeing the scene once again. "His eyes not right. Drunk yes, but something more too. Desperate, I think." Sadness softened the Chinese man's tone reminding Sage once again, what a very big man Fong really was. Not in size, maybe, but in his capacity for compassion.

Neither man spoke. Sage gazed around the room thinking, not for the first time, about how its carefully staged prosperous appearance–polished furniture, flocked wallpaper and cheery rug–revealed nothing about who he really was. Same with Fong.

His room survey was interrupted by the rasp of Fong clearing his throat. "He did not go home. Instead, he enter new office building on west side of commercial district. I wait outside until I see light come on behind window on top floor in southeast corner of building. After that, I leave."

"If we're lucky, that will be where his office is. What building was it?"

That question made Fong smile. "It is same building, same floor, as Mr. Philander Gray," Fong said, naming the only lawyer in town that Sage trusted.

Gray wasn't in his office early the next morning, so Sage returned to help with Mozart's noontime dinner hour. An exuberant party of prosperous businessmen had taken over four tables pushed together. Their empty wine bottles meant more trips to the outside dustbin. Likely, that would be his job. The waiters would be busy enough making the room spotless for the supper hour. Meanwhile, the group's collective guffaws sounded more often and louder as the hour advanced.

Once the noon hour business trickled down to departures, Sage strode over to where his mother, Mae Clemens, was stacking plates on one of the walnut sideboards flanking the kitchen's swinging doors. "What's with the group in the corner?" he asked, nodding toward the men who'd begun standing up to take their leave.

"Those are our local Republican bigwigs," she told him. "They've just learned that the president will visit Portland at the end of May. Apparently he's coming for a parade and dedication up at City Park. Part of that exposition hoody-do they're cooking up."

Well, that certainly explained their high spirits. An event like that would be welcome news indeed for the city's Republicans. They'd won most of the open seats in the recent election except that of governor. But, they weren't happy about the outcome of the popular vote on direct democracy. The idea of sharing their power with the "rabble," through the mechanisms of initiative and referendum, had them predicting civic disaster at every turn.

Portland's Republicans also had to be nervous about the new Republican president. Theodore Roosevelt showed signs of turning maverick as a Texas range calf. His popularity was growing every time he lashed out against the big corporations. The common people were cheering him while the rich were gnashing their teeth.

What if McKinley's assassination had installed a leader into the presidency, someone who refused to serve corporate interests? The local Republicans doubtless had mixed emotions. So far at least, they could say that Roosevelt hadn't attacked big business as much as did the top democratic contender, William Jennings Bryan. Most likely the locals would suppress their reservations and go all out to take advantage of the political momentum Roosevelt's visit was sure to bring.

"The president's visit will keep our Sergeant Hanke busy, I expect," Sage commented aloud. More than once, the big policeman's aid had proved invaluable. So much so, that Sage had come to think of him as a sort of distant kin.

"I'm sure he'll be stopping in momentarily to tell us all about it," Mae predicted, her tone lacking any rancor. Her's was an easy prediction because Hanke himself was predictable. Having declared Mozart's Ida Knuteson an even a better cook than his own mother, the police sergeant usually walked through the kitchen door about the time Ida started puzzling over what to do with noontime leftovers.

Minutes later, Mae smirked as they entered the kitchen. The big German was sitting at the table digging into the last slice of meat pie. Hanke's wide face was placid as ever but his erect backbone telegraphed suppressed excitement. It took little urging before he confirmed that, yes, indeed, President Theodore Roosevelt would visit Portland and that the police chief had assigned him, Sergeant Hanke, to help develop the security arrangements. "No crazy anarchist will get a shot at T.R. like what happened to poor President McKinley," he assured Sage.

As Hanke polished off Ida's leftovers, Sage wondered whether the excitement over the president's visit would hinder their efforts to shut down the house with the red door. Probably won't make a difference, he concluded.

Certainly not to him. Sage didn't care all that much about the president's visit. It had no effect on his mission for St. Alban. Roosevelt was a Republican after all. He came from the monied class of New York City. The country was again being lead by yet another man born into privilege and wealth.

Like most progressives, Sage's choice for president had been William Jennings Bryan. Instead, they'd got corporate footman McKinley and now Roosevelt. Still, in the last year, Roosevelt had taken on and defeated J.P. Morgan when the Wall Street robber baron attempted to expand his railroad trust. And, Roosevelt had threatened intervention by federal troops in aid of the Appalachian coal miners' strike. Another defeat for Morgan since he owned the mines and wanted his henchman able to undertake any action necessary to defeat the workers. Thanks to Roosevelt, Morgan had been forced into binding arbitration. And, wonder of wonders, he'd lost.

People were starting to call Roosevelt the "Trust Buster." Still, Sage remained skeptical. He'd seen too many politicians play to the crowd while scheming with their corporate cronies behind closed doors. Whether Roosevelt's "square" deal was the "real" deal remained an unanswered question.

And then there was Roosevelt's warmongering. The corporations needed more buyers for the excess products they were wringing out of their workers. Another war would mean more blood soaking yet another country's soil just so the big corporations could sell to those expanded markets.

Hanke pushed back his chair, stood, pulled the napkin from his collar and shrugged into his heavy wool coat. Its polished brass buttons flashed before settling down into parallel rows. Beehive helmet tucked under one arm, he shook Sage's hand and headed out the kitchen door, only pausing to accept the paper-wrapped cookies Ida thrust into his big hand. "For later," she told him with a pat on his arm.

❀ ❀ ❀

Philander Gray apparently had just returned from court. A damp overcoat and hat adorned the office coatrack. He sat at his desk, directing a glowering gaze out the window, his big feet propped on an open drawer. Outside, the sky was a sullen gray blanket stretching low across the valley. But it didn't quite reach at the edges. To the west, a strip of pure blue promised afternoon sunshine.

Though lean and hollow-cheeked as Abe Lincoln, Gray was far hardier than he looked. Maybe that was because he could tuck food away faster than a mess hall of hungry soldiers. Mozart's food supply diminished noticeably whenever Philander Gray came calling. Yet, the lanky man never gained a pound.

The lawyer's long lips twisted wryly when he saw who'd entered his office. "Why, howdy, John. Think there's any hope of seeing spring this year? I had the wife crying her eyes out this morning over yesterday's hail beating down her flowers. You know how she dotes on them."

Indeed, Gray's wife set great store by her garden. Mozart's was sometimes the beneficiary of her blooms. "Well, you could remind her that if we were back East, it would be snow instead of momentary hail," Sage replied.

Gray grunted, removed his feet from atop the drawer and sat erect. "I guess it's too much to expect you to commiserate with me since, it seems to me, you've grown webbing between your toes these past months. I swear I saw you strolling down the street in the pouring rain just like it was a sunny day in May. Have you gone native? Turned web-foot?"

"I guess that, recently, I've come to appreciate the rain. There's lots of places in this country where folks pray for it, you know," Sage said with a silent nod of thanks toward the ragpicker, Herman Eich, who had given him this new perspective.

Gray waved a dismissive hand and changed the subject. "Do you have work for me? Is someone missing, soon to be lynched or maybe shanghaied onto a whaler? Goodness me, I don't know if I'm available to assist in such fine endeavors. After all, as you can see, I am so very busy on this fine, dreary day."

Sage laughed. It was Gray's way to be sardonic. Yet another reason why he liked the man. "No, this time I just need some information about one of the tenants in this building." Sage quickly described the man Fong had followed and the location of the office window where Fong had seen the light.

"McAllister. E . J. McAllister," Gray said flatly, his face turned stony.

"And just who is this Mr. McAllister?" Sage asked.

"Depends," Gray answered and then just stared wordlessly at Sage.

That response was puzzling. The lawyer ordinarily didn't guard his words or parse out his information so reluctantly. Sage mimicked Fong's tactic of staying silent but hoped his eyes showed sufficient inquiry.

It worked because Gray relaxed and said, "I am surprised you haven't heard of him before now, given your recent involvement with the carpenters' union."

When Sage merely continued looking at him, Gray explained. "McAllister is a new lawyer in town. Been here just about ten months. He's taken on cases for unions and has appeared on behalf of the ever-charming, if highly vocal, ladies of the Women's Christian Temperance Union. You may recall their recent heated engagements both in and outside various Portland watering holes. He rescued their righteous and august personages from our local jail cells by using some pretty fancy legal footwork."

"Sounds like you admire his lawyering skills," Sage observed.

"Well, whenever a new competitor comes to town, I like to visit the courtroom and watch him in action. Thus far, McAllister impresses me. He came by and introduced himself. We've met in the hall a few times. Seems like a decent enough fellow." This last was said with a tone of finality. Clearly, no additional information would be forthcoming.

Sage wasn't satisfied. "You're not being totally forthright about Mr. McAllister, are you Philander?"

Gray shrugged. "Let's just say I've told you what I know to be true. That which I suspect, I intend to keep strictly to myself."

When he left Gray's office Sage debated whether it would be better to confront McAllister directly or contrive to meet him by chance. He trudged down three flights of stairs because he refused to risk his life in the wheezing, creaking steam elevator contraption that Gray considered a grand invention. Stepping out the building's front door, he discovered that the air had turned ice-house cold. His fingers started stiffening before he thought to shove them in his pockets. Overhead, three seagulls wheeled in turbulent air, screeching their distress at being driven inland before a rising storm. Any sun break would be short-lived.

Sage started off, then paused in the middle of the sidewalk to think. Who was the mysterious McAllister? An able lawyer who represented both labor unions and the temperance women? Maybe that was it. McAllister was watching that house for the temperance women. Pedofilia was definitely a social vice guaranteed to make them bristle like cornered porcupines. That's it, Sage thought excitedly. That's what McAllister was doing with those binoculars. The same thing I was doing. Watching that God-awful house to see who was molesting those boys.

He wheeled around and resolutely entered the building once again. When he reached the third floor, only somewhat winded, he strode past Gray's office, looking for McAllister's. There it was, the new lawyer's name arching discretely across an opaque glass pane. He turned the knob and pushed the door open.

No one occupied the outer office. It contained a small desk, telephone instrument, typewriting machine and wooden file cabinet. In the far wall, a second door stood slightly ajar. It likely opened into the office that had the corner windows. Sage closed the outer door with a soft click and stepped across the room to the inside door. He paused, his ears straining but he heard only silence. Using two fingers, he slowly pushed the door open.

Inside, a man sat behind a desk. His head hung like that of the tired old trolley horse, his forehead propped up by his two hands. The polished desktop was empty except for a glass, a half-empty whiskey bottle and a black revolver.

At Sage's sharp intake of breath, the man lifted his head from his hands. His face was puffy and his eyes were blurry but his voice was firm when he demanded, "Who the hell are you?"

FOUR

Dispatch: *May 5, 1903, President's train arrives in Albuquerque, New Mexico.*

> *"There are good men and bad men of all nationalities, creeds and colors; and if this world of ours is ever to become what we hope some day it may become, it must be by the general recognition that the man's heart and soul, the man's worth and actions, determine his standing." —T.R.*

SAGE INVOLUNTARILY STEPPED BACK but stopped when McAllister didn't reach for the gun. After a long pause, Sage stepped forward again and slid into one of the two chairs opposite the lawyer.

"I am here to help. I am a friend," Sage said.

"I very much doubt that." McAllister's tone was bitter.

"Look, I know you've been watching Lynch's house, the same as me," Sage said.

McAllister nodded once but said nothing although his eyes behind rimless spectacles twitched even as the rest of his face remained rigid. This was a man confronting a potential enemy. His barricades were up.

Sage needed to establish a bond and quick. "We have to stop Lynch and close that damn house forever. And, we need to find safe places for those boys," he said. "Do you agree?"

The other man's face relaxed. "I wish it were that simple," McAllister responded, his voice bone-weary. He swiveled his desk chair around until he was facing toward the far window, his profile framed against a side window's rain-spattered surface.

For a long pause, the rain hitting the hard surface was the room's only sound. Sage studied McAllister who, indeed, looked to be in his early thirties. His face was rounded, even-featured, with a dimpled chin. His wavy light brown hair parted on the right, above a smooth, wide forehead. "Genial-looking" was the description that came to mind. A decent but wrinkled suit enclosed his somewhat bulky body. His topmost shirt button was open and his loosened tie draped his neck like a skinny prayer shawl. Despite a face puffy from a sleepless night, McAllister's countenance was kindly and trustworthy–the sort of person who'd talk the parties through a dispute and then celebrate eventual agreement by buying beer for everyone involved.

Since McAllister continued gazing out the window, Sage switched his scrutiny to the room. It contained the lawyer's desk and chair as well as two cushioned seats for clients. Behind the desk, stood a narrow table holding a neat stack of papers and a pair of binoculars. A short, glass-fronted bookcase against the wall beside the door, displayed thick law books. Framed diplomas hung on another wall. Sage saw that a few years prior, McAllister had obtained a law degree from the University of Virginia. This followed the award of an undergraduate degree from Syracuse University in 1895. Given that both were top schools, it meant the man was both smart and diligent as well as having a moneyed background.

A glance toward the lawyer showed pale gray window light washing across the man's face, catching on tears trickling silently down his cheeks. Sage shifted, uncertain how to give comfort. McAllister pulled a crumpled handkerchief from his pocket and blotted his face. The fact of that trembling hand, the tears, rumpled clothes, cleared desk, whiskey bottle and revolver all coalesced into a realization that straightened Sage in his chair. McAllister had been working up the nerve to kill himself. Maybe he would have, if Sage hadn't intruded.

"Perhaps I can help," Sage offered softly. No point in pretending he didn't understand what had been about to take place. People in such pain seldom had patience for conversational foreplay.

McAllister's laugh was harsh but his spine straightened. He wiped his face again before turning to look at Sage. Then he sighed and asked, this time without the sharpness, "Just who are you?"

Sage told him. No point in claiming to be one of his various other personas. McAllister was a likely Mozart's patron.

However, the lawyer said, "I've been to Mozart's once or twice. I don't recall seeing you there."

"Well, I have other activities so sometimes I have to leave the help in charge."

"And spying on Lynch's house is one of those 'activities'?" McAllister asked.

Sage had noticed that about lawyers. The really good ones had the impatient habit of plowing straight to the heart of matter. He rather liked it since impatience was no stranger where Sage himself was concerned.

"Yup. I found out about it last June but I couldn't act on the information until now," he said. "I've been sitting under that cedar tree watching the house. A couple of days ago, I happened to catch sight of you with those binoculars," Sage said, with a nod toward the table, "Quite frankly, I started hoping that you and I have the same goal in mind."

McAllister leaned forward, fierce intent erasing the despair that had bent his frame. "We do and we don't," he said. "You close down Lynch's house they'll just find another. As long as the boys are easy to procure, a house like that will exist in Portland. You've got to cut off the supply and instill terror in its customers' hearts."

"By cut off the supply, I take it you mean the Boys Christian Society?" Sage asked.

McAllister's eyes narrowed, as if he was recalculating his initial assessment of Sage.

"So, you know about the BCS," McAllister said, his tone matter-of-fact.

Sage nodded. "A friend told me that some of the boys come from the BCS. Except I don't know who in the BCS is involved. I know it can't be everyone in the organization. Some pretty prominent people sit on its board of directors," he said.

Pulling open the desk drawer, McAllister quickly stowed the whiskey bottle, glass and revolver out of sight. When he looked at Sage again, his eyes were steely. "What is supposed to be a safe shelter for orphan boys instead sends them down the path into a life of self-loathing. Men and boys mingle, inappropriately, inside the BCS facility, I know that much. And, I think it's the manager who sells the boys to men like Lynch."

"But why do the boys stay so biddable? Why don't they run away, tell the police?" Sage asked. It just didn't make sense. Young boys tended to be impatient, rambunctious and rebellious. He tried to envision a young boy, like Matthew, the nephew of Mozart's cook, tolerating such abuse and couldn't.

McAllister nodded. "That is the question. We have to figure out how their natural instinct to resist or flee is being suppressed. Shame yes, but there has to be something else. If we don't find out what that mechanism is, we could stop Lynch but find the same scheme springing back to life in another location. Just like that many-headed Greek hydra-monster."

Sage scooted his chair closer to the desk. He was relieved to see that McAllister's emotional distress had receded, pushed aside by his concern over the victimized boys. "You seemed to be well-positioned, as lawyer, to root out this evil. Why haven't you?" Sage asked.

The lawyer's face collapsed back into bleak despair. He again turned away from Sage to look out the far window and said, "Lynch knows my preference. If I try to go against him, he'll expose me. Exposure would utterly destroy my wife and family. My clients would be subject to derision, their causes degraded. In sum, I'd lose my practice, my reputation, and harm the people I care most about."

Sage forced his voice to remain level and without judgment as he asked, "You're one of his customers?"

McAllister quickly turned back around, his face twisted in anger. "Damn you! I would no more harm a child than you would! Men like Lynch and his customers are abominations. I damn well know that far better than you do," he said, his palm slapping the desk as if squashing a memory dead.

This exchange confused Sage. If McAllister wasn't a pedophile then what could a man like Lynch hold over him?

Light dawned. "Oscar Wilde?" Sage asked, naming the English writer who'd stood trial for his homosexuality in 1895. Sage had been deep in the Yukon when that trial happened. But, even there, its spectacular details gave rise to eager discussions around smoking fireplaces and pot-bellied stoves. The isolated Yukon territory, with its scarcity of females, was Sage's first inescapable exposure to the fact that some men preferred the company of their own kind. In that overwhelmingly male environment, men became a little more open–dancing together at the impromptu winter hoe-downs, partnering up in isolated cabins. Folks tended not to comment on such behavior. Still, you'd have to be denser than a tree stump not to see it. In the end, Sage decided he didn't care. When all was said and done, people needed to love and to be loved.

Over the years, Sage discovered that the existence of homosexuality had left him with one unanswerable question that had nothing to do with its practitioners. Instead, he wondered how some people reconciled their belief in God's absolute "perfection" with their condemnation of the people that "perfect" God had created. Sage concluded that his God, to the extent He existed, simply did not make mistakes. Instead maybe, by making human beings so different from one another, in such a variety of ways, God was providing His "faithful" with an opportunity to expand their capacity for empathy and compassion.

Sage shook loose from his metaphysical musings. When it came to McAllister and this situation, plain speaking was the best way move them past this awkwardness. "Okay, I get it. You're a homosexual and Lynch knows it."

The lawyer's nod was cautious, his short-lived assurance replaced by a look of painful vulnerability, his body bracing for an attack.

Sage sighed, deliberately relaxing before he smiled and said, "Okay, then, Mr. McAllister. It seems like we share a similar problem. I've got my own secrets that I can't risk exposing. Since we are equal in that regard, any chance that you might be up for figuring out how to destroy this damnable business without bringing our own lives down around our ears?"

After a moment of shocked incredulity the other man relaxed and grinned. "I am more willing than you can ever imagine. Or," he looked toward the drawer he'd just closed, "maybe you can imagine. The moral dilemma has been excruciating. No matter how I looked at the situation, I saw exposure and with that exposure, my utter and complete failure to save those boys and my own family and friends."

"Actually, the fact that both of us possess secrets and would be risking all, just might make us ideal conspirators." Sage said. "Neither one of us can tell on the other."

"You don't share my inclinations," McAllister said flatly.

"No, I don't. Not your sexual inclinations, anyway. But I do know, from your reputation, that you fight for the little guy against the monied elite. We're in perfect lockstep on that account. That's my secret. My ownership of Mozart's is just a front for my real work."

McAllister raised an eyebrow before he grinned again, flashing a row of perfect white teeth. "I am starting to think that it sure is a fine thing that you walked through that door when you did," he said.

"Yup," Sage agreed, letting the silence thicken slightly before continuing, "Listen, we're going to have to depend on others to help us. We don't have to tell them your secret, although the people I am thinking of certainly know how to keep secrets. The question I have is, can you keep theirs?"

McAllister rolled his eyes. "Ye gods, man. You're looking at a man whose life is like a damned iceberg. The real me is always and forever hiding below the surface. But, if it will make you feel more confident about sharing your secrets, hand me a dollar. That way, I will become your lawyer. Anything I learn through you, I can't talk about."

Pulling out a five dollar gold piece Sage slapped it onto the desk. "You hungry?" he asked, standing up and jamming his hat onto his head.

McAllister stood too, relief and hope in his face. "Starving," he said.

"Great!" Sage responded with a grin, "You're buying!"

Beyond the window, rain no longer fell and sunlight, shafting in through the glass, was near blinding in its intensity. Sage decided he'd interpret the sun break as a sure sign that the heavens approved of their deal.

FIVE

Dispatch: *May 6, 1903, President's train arrives at the Grand Canyon, in Arizona.*

"Women should have free access to every field of labor which they care to enter, and when their work is as valuable as that of a man, it should be paid as highly." —T.R.

JUST BEFORE THE SUPPER HOUR, Mae, Fong and Sage again sat around the table in Sage's third floor room above Mozart's. Fong said nothing, merely nodding thoughtfully, accepting McAllister's secret as a logical explanation for the man's actions.

Sage looked toward Mae Clemens. She responded with a look of mild exasperation. "Well, really, Sage. Don't you remember your father's brother, Alwyn?" she asked.

Beside him, he sensed that Fong had become more alert. John Adair, Senior, was a topic neither Mae Clemens nor her son ever discussed. For good reason. A Welch foreman in Appalachia's mines, Sage's father had turned informer. He'd delivered Mae's father and eldest brother into a murderous ambush carried out by the mine owner's private army of Dickenson thugs.

"I don't remember knowing anyone named 'Alwyn.' Yet, somehow, that name is familiar. What about him?" Sage asked.

Mae Clemens tilted her head to one side, bemusement softening the bold sculpted lines of her face. "Maybe you wouldn't remember him. You were only two years old when he went away. But, I bet you remember his oranges."

Oranges. A sparkling but elusive memory fluttered mothlike in his mind. That memory sent him far back into another place—one remote from this elegance of polished furniture, lace curtains and flocked wallpaper. He furrowed his brow at her, trying to sharpen the recollection.

Mae didn't wait. "Alwyn was the only one in your father's family who didn't condemn our marriage because I came from part-Irish stock. Alwyn stayed our friend. Even after your father . . . ," here she paused as a spasm of pain washed across her face. Starting again, she said, "When I left your father and moved to Carbon County, Alwyn helped me. Once you and I got settled, he left Pennsylvania. Said he was heading to New York City where there were more of what he called 'his kind'." She lapsed into silence.

"And the oranges?" Sage prompted.

"After that, at the end of every November or the beginning of December, a box of oranges would come on the train. Alwyn sent them. Surely you remember those oranges? They were from Brazil, each one wrapped separate in a corn husk."

Sweet scent, music, laughter, flooded back. "You would have a party. People would come. We'd share the oranges," Sage said.

She smiled. "Yes! Those oranges made us forget winter was coming. The neighbor women would arrive in the morning. We'd grate the peels and use the zest to make orange sugar rock candy. We'd scrape the white pith from the rind and set that atop the cookstove to dry. Then we'd store it in jars until summer canning time when we'd use it to thicken the wild berries. They smelled so good those oranges. Sundown come, our neighbors would bring whatever food they had to our two-room shack. There'd be a fiddle, a dulcimer and we'd sing and eat up those oranges. We called it our winter 'Orange' ceremony." She smiled. "We used to laugh over calling it that since every one of us was Catholic and a sworn enemy of the Orange Protestants."

As she spoke, he relived it. Again, the sweet, foreign smell of oranges, the laughter, the tapping of the boots and the voices raised in song.

"But what happened? Did Uncle Alwyn stop sending the fruit? I don't remember having any orange parties, there at the end." By "end" both knew what Sage meant. The end came when, at nine years of age, he'd saved the mine owner's grandson in a mine explosion and left to live as the mine owner's foster boy for the next twelve years.

Mae heaved a sigh. "The year you started to work in the mines, when you were eight, Alwyn died. Of consumption is what I heard. Up there in New York City. In the years since, I've thought of him so often. He was always good to us. That I never got to thank him personally for the gift of those oranges has always been a sorrow." Her voice trailed off before she straightened, her dark blue eyes snapping alert, her mouth a thin line of determination. "Far as I'm concerned, helping Mr. McAllister will be a way to pay Alwyn Adair back, to honor his kindness," she said. She reached out, picked up the teapot and began to refill their teacups. "So, what exactly is the plan?" she asked, leaning forward.

The rap on the door came five minutes after the last patron exited Mozart's. Sage let McAllister in, hung his coat and hat and ushered him to the table where Mae and Fong were waiting. McAllister's eyes widened at the sight of them, but he said nothing, merely nodded at both before taking a seat.

Performing the introductions, Sage deliberately didn't mention to McAllister that Mae Clemens was his mother. For safety's sake, that fact was their most closely guarded secret.

"These are the two individuals with whom I work most closely, E. J. Since you gave me permission to do so, I have told Mrs. Clemens and Mr. Fong why we must be careful in how we fight Lynch and his backers. In turn, I have told you about the work that we do for the labor movement so I think we can dispense with talking about each other's secrets. What we need to understand is Lynch's business."

McAllister slid a finger between his neck and collar before moving his chair closer to the table, his movements uneasy. He looked away as if ashamed to meet Sage's eyes and said, "As I am sure you can imagine, I move in circles where many people have secrets. That's how I heard about Lynch's house." He looked down at his laced hands with their white knuckles. He took a deep breath, relaxed them and rested them in his lap. "The idea of men assaulting a young child turns my stomach, so I tried to learn all I could about the situation. I've had to be careful, because if I'm discovered snooping around, Lynch and whoever he works with will take steps to expose me. That will hurt my wife and children."

He cleared his throat. Mae took that as her cue, jumping up and heading for a tea tray already prepared and sitting on the walnut sideboard. As she passed by McAllister, she paused, momentarily resting her work-roughened hand on his slumped shoulder. The lawyer blinked rapidly.

Tea poured, McAllister took a sip and spoke directly to Mae. "I am my wife's second husband. Her first husband died in a carriage accident. She has no living relatives. And when he died, my friend left her with three children to raise and no means of support. He died so young, just as his law practice was getting started. He was my boyhood friend and knew about my . . . me and always stood by me. Angelique, my wife, she has always known too. I owed them both so much. She loved James to distraction and says she wants no other husband. Real husband, that is. It was her idea that we wed and move here to get a fresh start. She's a fine woman and a wonderful companion."

Mae nodded. "It is an honorable thing for you to care for your friend's widow and children."

Once again the lawyer blinked rapidly before taking a deep breath and continuing, "There's going to be one other house just like Lynch's. Impoverished young farm kids are pouring into Portland. When they get hungry enough they become vulnerable to the tricks and enticements of men like Lynch. Some of them, of course, are probably like me but that doesn't make them want to prostitute themselves. Others, I think, are desperate or tricked into working for men like Lynch. Boys as well as girls."

He turned toward Sage. "Like we talked before, it seems that many of those boys working in Lynch's started out living in the Boys Christian Society building. Once I learned that, I began going there to the BCS to swim, taking note of the boys I saw there. It was very uncomfortable."

Disgust twisted his face. He looked down at his clenched hands, deliberately relaxed them once again and continued, "Anyway, next, I started watching Lynch's. That's why you saw me with binoculars. I have rented a room in the house across from Lynch's so I can see if the boys working in Lynch's house are ones I've seen earlier at the BCS." He gulped tea before saying, "I've recognized at least three of them as coming from the BCS. So, it appears the rumors are true."

Here Sage interrupted to tell Mae and Fong, "What E. J. and I can't figure out is why the boys don't just run away from either the BCS or Lynch's. Somehow, they are being forced to stay. Maybe their lives or, their families' lives, are being threatened."

McAllister cleared his throat. "I guess this is when I tell you that there's one additional piece of information I've managed to dig up concerning Lynch's little business. He's bragging about how he's about to open a second house. In Northwest Portland. That means he needs even more boys.

"The problem is, I think Lynch and his friends are getting suspicious of me. You saw me watching the house. Maybe he did too," McAllister said.

"What makes you think Lynch knows you're looking into his business?" Sage asked.

"As I told you, I've been visiting the BCS building, trying to find out how they were obtaining the boys. Well, last time I was there, people weren't friendly and I wasn't allowed anywhere but in the lounge, locker room, gym and swimming pool. Also, when I tried to do a little exploring, like up on the third floor, this unfriendly brute demanded to know where I thought I was going. He made no bones about the fact that he was there to make sure I didn't go snooping about. He knew my name."

"Maybe he just protecting boys," Fong said, speaking for the first time.

"Perhaps, but I got the distinct impression that it wasn't the boys he was protecting. A street thug is what he is. He doesn't act like one of the BCS staff and I've never seen him do any work," said McAllister.

Fong stood quickly, pressing a finger against his lips. In a few quick silent strides he was gone, leaving the three of them staring at the swinging kitchen doors.

"More tea, E. J.?" Mae asked. "Tell me whereabouts you were raised," she said as she refilled his cup.

McAllister caught on and answered smoothly. "I spent my youth in Delaware. Later went to various schools in Pennsylvania and Boston. Obtained my law degree in Virginia. One could say I had a privileged upbringing since there was always money enough to send me to the best schools. But my parents sacrificed to do it. I owe them a tremendous debt."

Sudden noise came from above them, followed by the bark of Fong's scolding voice. McAllister's face was a mix of puzzlement and alarm. "I better be going," he said, slapping his hat on his head and practically running out the door.

Heavy steps on the stairs, descending from the second floor, followed the thump of the front door's closing. The sight of the shamefaced, redheaded boy preceding Fong down the stairs was no surprise to Mae and Sage. Once the pair reached the ground floor Matthew paused, clearly reluctant to move any closer. Fong give him a stiff finger poke his back. The boy shuffled forward, albeit reluctantly.

Sage and his mother exchanged exasperated looks. Matthew, the cook's 16-year-old nephew, was proving to be a recurring problem. In less than a year, Sage had saved him from hanging for the murder of his brother's killer and then saved him from being shanghaied. During their last mission, it appeared that Matthew had finally learned his lesson about snooping because he'd done exactly as asked and stayed out of their business. But here he was again. A deep red, embarassed flush had swallowed up his freckles.

Matthew reached the table but remained standing even as Fong sat. Three pairs of eyes drilled into the boy, forcing him to clear his throat. "I was studying and, ah, decided to come down here to, ah, fetch a piece of Aunt Ida's apple pie. I saw the light on in the dining room. At first I thought, it ah, was, ah, thieves but then I heard voices. I listened a minute to make sure it wasn't . . . ," his words trailed away as he fidgeted on feet that were still too big for him.

"And you heard what we were talking about and decided to lurk on the stairs and eavesdrop," Sage finished for him.

Matthew opened his mouth to protest, then snapped it shut, clearly unable to deny the fact since he'd lurked there long enough for Fong to ascend to the third floor by the backstairs and then descend two flights to catch him in the act.

The boy's backbone stiffened and his chin came up. "What I heard was some man talking about the Boy's Christian Society. I listened because I know a boy who came from there. He said something bad is going on in that place but he wouldn't tell me what. I listened 'cause I thought I might find out." The boy's bright blue eyes searched the room for the man he'd heard talking.

Mae and Sage exchanged another look, and this time Sage grabbed a chair from a neighboring table and gestured for Matthew to sit. "Suppose you tell us exactly what this boy told you. Start with his name."

"His name's Ollie and he came here from a river-bottom farm up in Washington. I got to know him 'cause he made friends with Jimmy, my friend who works as the printer's devil. Jimmy let him stay overnight with him in the back of the print shop." Matthew's eyes widened in sudden alarm. "Crikey. Please don't tell Mr. Casey, 'cause Jimmy didn't get permission to keep Ollie there. It could get Jimmy fired and his ma needs the money."

"We won't. But, what about Ollie?"

"Something was real wrong with Ollie. He was jumpy as water dropped on a hot burner. He wouldn't tell us what happened to him at the BCS but it was something real bad. Once he started to tell us, then he started crying and wouldn't finish. That's how come Jimmy took him under his wing."

"How old is Ollie?"

"He's only fourteen." Almost to himself, Matthew added, "Billy's age." His brother's murder still pained the boy deeply. No one said anything for a beat, then Matthew returned to his explanation, "But see, Ollie's kinda slight, so he looks like he's only twelve or so."

The adults looked at each other, their faces grim.

"Where's Ollie now? We'd like to talk to him. Maybe help him, if we can." Mae said, her voice gentle.

Matthew leaned forward to say in a rush, "Mrs. Clemens, that's exactly why I was standing on the stairway listening to you all talking. Day 'afore yesterday, Ollie said he had to go help a friend. We ain't heard from him since. He's gone missing. He left all his stuff with Jimmy and just disappeared!"

"Oh Lord," Mae Clemens breathed. "We better move fast. Especially since now we know this boy, Ollie, has gone missing."

Sage's fingernail flicked his empty teacup, making it ping. The others turned their attention in his direction. "Maybe I should be the one to go investigate. They don't know me," he said.

Mae's response was swift and emphatic. "You walk through that BCS door and everyone in town will know about it. The last thing we need is for Mozart's owner to ever be associated with goings-on like that once they come to light." Because of Matthew's presence, she didn't say it would jeopardize their ability to carry out missions for the labor movement, but that is what she meant. So far, they'd completed only a few Portland missions for Vincent St. Alban, the man who gave them certain goals to reach. Still, she was right, they couldn't endanger those efforts.

A quick glance at Fong's steady dark eyes confirmed that Sage's other partner was in complete agreement with Mae Clemens.

Sage compressed his lips together before he sighed and said. "Okay, I accept that. But, E. J. sure can't keep snooping. Fong isn't even allowed in the door, and if I can't go in how the heck can we find out what is happening with those boys?" Sage asked.

"I go in, that's how," Mae answered. "A place like that always needs a cook or a cleaning woman. A few people might know me from here but I spend most of my time in the kitchen. And, I can make myself look a bit different. I'll get a job there and take a look around. The last thing they'll be expecting is a woman snoop."

"Me too! I can go in, they won't suspect me. Nobody at all knows me," Matthew said, clearly caught up in the excitement of the "hunt."

As one, the three adults turned toward him and exclaimed in unison, "No!"

Minutes later they sent a disgruntled Matthew off to bed with strict instructions. He was to forget everything he'd heard. He was to say nothing about Ollie to anyone. And, he was ordered by Mae Clemens to keep his "inquisitive nose to himself." Reluctantly, the boy promised to comply. Sage watched Matthew trudge noisily up the stairs and said to the other three, "So, which one of our instructions do you suppose that kid will disobey first?"

SIX

Dispatch: *May 6, 1903, President's train arrives in Seligman, Arizona.*

> *"In a country like ours it is fundamentally true that the well being of the tiller of the soil and the wage worker is the well being of the State . . . there can be no real general prosperity unless based on the foundation of the prosperity of the wage worker and the tiller of the soil." —T.R.*

SAGE WAS IMMERSED IN MOZART'S FINANCIAL RECORDS when the note came. He'd been putting off the book-work chore for weeks. Ordinarily, he found numbers work somewhat enjoyable because it engendered no emotion until that final calculation revealed overall profit or loss. Unfortunately, it took him five times longer to make things balance than it would have taken someone trained in the art. Still, Mozart's book-work would remain his chore since an accountant would ask too many questions about his odd expenditures.

He'd just double checked the final numbers and experienced a fizz of satisfaction over Mozart's modest profit, when Matthew's distinctive clumping ascended the stairs. Expecting a summons for his presence downstairs, Sage started tidying up his paperwork. But it wasn't a summons. Instead, it was a white piece of folded paper that the boy extended. Sage took it, noticing a blob of candle wax kept its flap secure.

"This just come for you by one of the messenger boys," Matthew said.

Sage dug in his vest pocket and tossed Matthew a coin. "Give this to the boy, will you, Matthew?"

The boy nodded but hesitated, curiosity welding him to the spot. Sage made no move to break the seal and unfold the paper. Instead, he stared directly at the boy, raised an inquiring eyebrow and asked, "Anything else, Matthew?"

"Uh, no. I guess not." He turned to leave, then turned back. "I was wondering if that note there had anything to do with the BCS, I guess?" he said.

The question wasn't unexpected. History had proven that Matthew tended to cling to his curiosity despite being strongly discouraged from doing so. Sage heaved a sigh. "Matthew, what did we tell you last night?"

The boy flushed, though a hint of belligerence stiffened his freckled chin for just a second before he lowered it and mumbled. "I'm supposed to act like I know nothing about it." There was an awkward silence. Then he heaved a sigh, rounded his shoulders, turned and clumped from the room.

"Poor kid, telling him to forget about his friend Ollie's situation is like telling him to not breathe," Sage told himself as his fingernail pried up the wax so he could unfold the message. What he saw jolted him erect. He smoothed the paper flat on the table and studied the line drawing at its center.

Depicted was a skilled sketch of a four-legged table angled so that the right-hand front leg was in the foreground. Only he and one other person knew the meaning of the sketch and the positioning of the table. It was their secret code. One chair meant wait to be contacted by someone acting on behalf of Meachum. Two chairs meant Meachum was going to be passing through and would have time to visit. But, a table? That meant business for St. Alban. Serious business. The right leg forward meant a meeting at twilight, that very day. Sage knew where. He had time.

It was last June when he'd first met Meachum in Seattle. Sage had immediately liked the man, trusted him and told him everything. About Mozart's, even that his own mother was one of his confederates in his work for St. Alban. So, Sage's first reaction was one of pleasurable anticipation. He wanted to see the silver-haired, craggy face leader of St. Alban's Flying Squadron once again. Sage admired how Meachum had chosen a dangerous way to protect the aspirations of working people. He and his men traveled throughout the West, riding the rails and living in railway hobo camps. Wherever the railroad bulls or the thieving roof crawlers on a line turned to violence, the Flying Squadron would materialize. A few threats and a toss from the train on a slow curve usually brought the thugs under control.

Sage's forehead wrinkled. Early May was a tad soon in the season for the Flying Squadron to be operating this far north. Until harvest time most bindle stiffs, the men comprising America's endlessly growing population of unemployed, usually stayed south or else hunkered down in the cities. Few braved the deathly cold by riding in a boxcar over high mountain passes sometimes clogged with snow. More than one dead man had been found curled up in an empty boxcar when the train rolled into a rail yard.

So, maybe this wasn't Squadron business after all. Maybe other business for St. Alban had sent Meachum from the comfort of his Denver home. Sage touched the drawing and felt his scalp prickle.

"But, what about the BCS and Lynch's new house?" Mae Clemens asked, her voice sharp with frustration, her body stiff-spined as she leant forward over the table in Sage's third floor room. "We can't let E. J. down, not to mention those poor boys."

"We won't," Sage promised her. "We've managed to carry out two missions simultaneously before and we will this time. I don't care what St. Alban wants us to do. There's Matthew too.

I don't think I could look him in the face if we didn't help his friend Ollie."

Mae Clemens leaned back in her chair, clearly relieved her son wasn't going to abandon their plan to stop Lynch and eliminate his supply source for boys.

Throughout this exchange Fong's face had remained blank. Only the sharp intent in his dark eyes revealed his interest in the subject. Once Sage and his mother had reached agreement, he smiled, as if he'd known the outcome was a foregone conclusion. "So we must divide up work, once we know what Mr. Saint wants. This time, though, we will have Mr. E. J.'s help," he said. "So, we have no problems," he added, sounding much more confident than Sage felt.

The hobo camp looked forlorn beneath the leafless trees. When it wasn't raining, men gathered here during the day to stretch toes and fingers toward the campfire's warmth and trade stories of the road. At night or when it rained, they'd disperse to whatever nook or cranny promised dry shelter. Warmth was a rarity unless they were one of the few permitted to sleep for free on the jailhouse floor.

Sage arrived in the camp bearing treasures snugly wrapped inside his blanket bindle. The hobos had water aplenty but the sight of an entire can of ground coffee perked up the ten men who sat on log rounds next to a fitful fire. Grubby, trembling hands reached for the flattened loaves of bread and paper-wrapped sausages as if the men couldn't believe their eyes. Sage countered questions about his generosity with the explanation he had a job helping a grocery move its stock and expected to work tomorrow so he'd have plenty to eat. They didn't question his story. Just slapped him on the back and laughed. In return, he received the pleasure of watching their bodies straighten and their expression lighten. One more day survived.

Around dusk, as men began gathering up their few belongings, another man walked into camp. Sage glanced at him, then turned back toward the fire, outwardly intent on hearing the last bit of a rambling story about how one of the men had lost his "sweet little farm."

"So's that last hail storm's what done me in. The golly durn bank foreclosed, even though there weren't nobody in the county rich enough to take it over. That good dirt's just a-lying there, growing weeds that can't nobody eat," the man glumly concluded.

"One day you'll be back farming. Once things settle down a bit," a man, young enough to still have optimism, tried to comfort.

An older, more experienced man, offered the farmer more coffee while another man, when he passed by to collect more firewood, silently touched the farmer on the shoulder. Across the fire, Sage met Meachum's bright blue eyes in mute recognition of the moment's poignancy.

When dark arrived, the air turned chill with a strengthening breeze. Once the dry firewood was exhausted, the camp disbanded. Each man shuffled off into the gloom to seek a place to bed down. Most knew that what lay ahead was a night of countless wakings as pain grabbed hold in stiffened joints.

Sage and Meachum ambled off together. Unlike the others, they didn't move toward the lights of the saloons lining the rail yard. Instead, they walked deeper into the alder clumps, trusting that tree trunks and a cloudy night would conceal their meeting.

"You have any trouble getting here?" Sage asked once they'd found a reasonably dry downed tree on which to sit.

"Nah. I rode the cushions all the way from Denver. St. Alban insisted on that comfort, thank the Lord," Meachum responded.

"I'm glad to see you, Meachum, but I must admit I am also more than a little concerned. From what you said last June, you're pretty adamant about staying with your wife and that wood shop of yours until early summer."

Meachum nodded in agreement as Sage talked. "Maybe you best suck on one of these machine-rolled," he said, handing a cigarette to Sage who took it, his forehead wrinkling with concern. There was no lightness whatsoever in the Denver man.

"Spit it out, Meachum," Sage said, after he'd expelled a lung full of smoke. "You know I'm going to help you so there's no reason for you to hesitate."

"I wish my only worry was whether you'd cooperate. I know you're going to. Fact is, this situation is so damn serious it never crossed my mind that you wouldn't want to help."

Sage shifted on the log. The prickling in his scalp had resumed and was now running up and down his spine. "Christ, man, spit it out. My guts are starting to churn like a Chinese laundry tub."

Meachum dropped his half-smoked cigarette and used his boot to grind it into the damp ground. Finished with that task he looked up, his face an intense mask of concern. "Someone's going to assassinate President Roosevelt. Here in Portland. This month. And they intend to do it in such a way that the entire country will blame the unions."

That statement froze Sage's cigarette just an inch from his lips. He stared at Meachum as the enormous and negative consequences of such an assassination blasted through his brain. Meachum was right, the matter was dead serious. He said the first thing that came to mind. "But, I just learned yesterday that Roosevelt's coming to Portland. The Republican bigwigs are in a tizzy about it. How could we have found out so fast?" he wondered aloud.

"Very few people know Roosevelt's itinerary yet. People in Roosevelt's inner circle know his schedule though, have known of it for some time now. He's scheduled to be here the end of May. Just fifteen days from now. St. Alban's sources have confirmed that fact."

"How do we know that the assassination plot is not just a rumor–some blowhard's wishful thinking?" Sage asked.

"We know too much about it and the source was reliable. A woman, a working woman, if you know what I mean. She got it straight from one of the conspirators. Apparently, while the customer was upstairs sleeping, she got a message to her brother. Her brother is a loyal union man. They met in the alley outside the whorehouse and she told him what she knew before going back inside."

"What do we know? What did she tell him?"

"The customer was mighty drunk and talked freely. He said he was in the pay of a big monied group. It seems the group has a representative here in Portland, someone important enough to be part of Roosevelt's local entourage. The drunk let on to the girl that his role in the plan is to make sure the assassination mastermind gets near Roosevelt. He also told her it was a complicated operation. He said some rowdies will create a distraction. In the uproar, his job is to make sure the plot's mastermind gets close enough to Roosevelt to trigger everything else. Once the deed is done, the actual assassin will be shot. It's that damn assassin who's going to get us involved. He's some poor deluded dummy who thinks the union movement is behind the plot and he's going to be helping us out. He has some kind of history being in a union. He also thinks that it's just a stink bomb he's going to be heaving at Roosevelt–a package containing ammonium sulfide–unpleasant but harmless. That's why he's signing on to the plot."

Meachum pulled out another cigarette and lit it up with dead-white fingers."But it's going to be a real bomb, filled with nitro. Deadly," he added once the cigarette was burning. "More people than the president will die."

"Who is he? Who is this assassin? Can't we find him? Tell him he's being used, tricked?" Sage asked.

"That's the problem. We don't know who he is. St. Alban's put the word out but, so far, nothing. The information came to us a bit garbled because the girl was afraid, in a hurry and the drunk had been trying to impress her at the same he was trying to be cagey."

Sage stared up into the alder branches, some part of his mind taking note that leaf buds were beginning to show. "Can't the woman find out more? There's still some time. Can't she ply her gabby customer with more whiskey, get him bragging again?" he asked.

Meachum's expression turned remorseful. "That's just it. We're certain this isn't just a drunk blowhard making himself sound important but an actual plan they intend to carry out. We're certain because, that night, right after she talked to her brother, the house burnt down. She didn't make it out. The fire chief said the fire was deliberate. It started in her room. They think she was already dead. Her drunk customer was gone."

For a while, neither man said anything, simply stared up through the tree branches at the pale roiling clouds blocking the starlight. Yet another life sacrificed.

"So we know someone will make an attempt and we know where. Here, in Portland. This month. May," Sage told himself then asked, "We know anything else, Meachum? Anything, at all?"

"One more thing, but it isn't of much help," Meachum said, "They've given a name to their little assassination plot. The drunk let it slip."

"What? What are they calling it?" Sage asked. Maybe the code name would provide a clue of sorts.

"They're calling it 'Black Hawk'." Meachum said. "She told her brother that the customer called it 'Operation Black Hawk'."

"Black Hawk? That doesn't seem to mean anything," Sage said.

"I know," Meachum said as he stood. "Hell, man. Let's go find ourselves someplace warm to get a beer. We've got too much to do in not enough time."

SEVEN

Dispatch: *May 7, 1903, President's train arrives in Barstow, California.*

> *"If we allow envy, hatred, anger to rule us. If we permit wrong to be done by any man against another, if we strive to interfere with the just rights of any man or fail to protect him in them, by just so much are we coming short of the standard set for us by those who in 1776 found this nation . . . ."* —T.R.

"I SAY, MISSUS, YOU'RE OUT AND ABOUT early this morning. You're my first customer. We're not really open just yet, but never you mind. What is it that I can I fetch for you?" the storekeeper said from behind a polished counter that contained neatly labeled glass-fronted bins, each one holding flour, grains, beans, dried fruits or sugars. The provision shelves rising against the wall behind the storekeeper displayed brightly labeled tins, boxes and bottles. The topmost shelf supported a variety of teakettles, lamps and empty canning jars.

"Take your time now, I've got to build up the fire in the old stove anyway," he told her as he lifted the counter gate. He crossed to the ornately chromed Ben Franklin filling the corner farthest from the door. Behind its mica-covered lattice, a banked fire glowed. Clangs and rattles sounded as the storekeeper opened the stove, deposited coal chunks inside, adjusted the damper and re-latched the door.

Once the storekeeper had resumed his post behind the counter, Mae was ready with her order. "One pound flour, one pound sugar, a dozen eggs, if they don't float stale, and one pound butter." The storekeeper bustled to and fro all while giving her assurances that, "Yes, all his products were fresh and weighed fairly."

"I can see that you are a man who puts value on honesty," she told him. He puffed at that observation as he opened a faded flour sack and placed her purchases inside.

"I suppose your store does quite a bit of business with the BCS kitchen next block over?" Mae asked as she handed him the coins.

He pulled the cash register's lever to make the drawer spring open. Collecting the change, he handed it over. "They get most of their supplies direct from the wholesaler, but there's some items they buy from me," he told her. "I maybe see them once or twice a week."

"I don't suppose there's any work over there? My niece is in from Chicago and she's looking for work. Typewriting work, that's what she does," Mae said.

"Hmm. From what I heard, that BCS don't hire females except in the kitchen. Leastways that's what I heard from Gussie. She's the kitchen runabout and scullery."

"My niece might want to work in a kitchen. Do you know if they have any openings?"

"Matter of fact, I believe Gussie said they'd lost another cook. They can't keep a second cook on because of the head cook, Mrs. Wiggit. She's a terror. Ain't nobody seems to please her."

The storekeeper's observation gave Mae momentarily pause. A terrorizing Mrs. Wiggit was not something to look forward to. That hesitation was chased away by the mental picture of pale, woeful faces. Boys just the age of Sage, when he'd had to leave her. Pain stabbed her heart.

She took a deep breath. "I expect that Mrs. Wiggit's the one who does the hiring?" she asked.

His head shake was rueful. "'Fraid so. Heard tell she in particular don't like young women. Thinks every one of them's spoilt. Not sure your niece would have a chance if she's young."

When Mae Clemens left the store, she paused to look south toward the four-story BCS building. Constructed of plain red brick, it occupied a quarter block. Most likely, the kitchen was quartered in the basement.

She looked down at the flour sack of provisions dangling heavily from her hand. She certainly couldn't apply for a job toting a sack of food. She'd look suspiciously well-to-do and not needy enough to be obedient. That wouldn't do, if she knew her Mrs. Wiggit. And, there wasn't time to run it back to Mozart's, meet the cook and still make the scheduled meeting.

As she stood on the sidewalk, uncertain what to do, she noticed a slender woman approaching. The woman's coat was too thin for the chill morning air and although her boots were clean and polished, the thick boot black couldn't hide the cracked leather. Mae raised her eyes to the woman's face. There she saw the strain of poverty, but also lips pursed in determination. Nearing the shop door, the woman paused. Her hand, encased in a darned glove, fumbled with the strings of the little bag she carried. Oblivious to Mae's scrutiny, the woman fingered the few coins she emptied into her palm.

Mae stepped forward. "Pardon me, ma'am," she said. "Would you accept these provisions? It turns out I can't carry them with me." She thrust the cloth bag at the woman who took it automatically, confusion crumpling her face as she tried to form a question.

"Sorry, I can't explain right now, I'm in a hurry," Mae said before turning and quickly walking north. The last thing she wanted was to hear words of gratitude. She knew what that sack of provisions would mean to the woman. She knew the gratitude the woman would feel for the unexpected gift. By the same token, she also well knew the shame that accompanied a gift of charity. No need to prolong the exchange.

Just before she turned the corner, Mae looked back. The woman's hand was deep inside the bag, exploring its contents as her jaw slackened and her mouth formed a small "o" of disbelief. The sight made Mae wish she'd bought a sack of dried fruit as well.

That was thanks enough. Mae nipped around the corner and strode on until she reached a café with steamy windows. Once inside, she ordered tea and sat down to plan the best approach to Mrs. Wiggit, the boss cook.

It had been Fong's idea that they convene in Herman Eich's lean-to at the edge of the Marquam ravine. Sage, Eich, Fong and E. J. McAllister were already there. Alerted by Fong, Eich had supplemented his seating arrangements. In addition to his work stool and sturdy cot, three ladder-backed chairs, likely borrowed from his next door landlady, crowded the floor space.

Sage looked around the room. It was snug and, as usual, the workbench under the only window displayed an array of chipped ceramics–bowls, plates and even a figurine or two. Stacked neatly beneath the bench were burlap bags, their contents no doubt gleaned from various dustbins across the city. Eich made his meager living by repairing ceramics and peddling dustbin finds at the city's back doors.

The ragpicker poet was bustling about, using a chipped graniteware pot to brew the coffee Sage had brought. Sage studied the man's tall, erect figure, his flowing beard and deep-set eyes and concluded that Eich had finally recovered his vigor after an ordeal a few months back that had nearly killed him. If the sad outcome of that experience had left its mark on the ragpicker, that mark was internal.

Mae was late. Sage knew it wasn't because she couldn't locate Eich's abode in this small working class neighborhood south of the city's center. She and Eich had stayed in touch. More than once, she'd left Mozart's bearing some fine delicacy only to return hours later, empty-handed but with a happy glow in her dark blue eyes.

Sage didn't mind. The man might be a ragpicker by choice, but he was also a fine human being. St. Alban's work made deep friendships difficult to form. He, Fong and Mae had too many secrets, too much they had to withhold from everyone. Herman Eich had inadvertently become a happy exception for all three of them. He knew their real business in Portland.

Fong squatted in one corner, his eyes hooded, his face impassive, immobile and seemingly looking at no one. Sage sensed, however, that Fong's attention was riveted on the fourth occupant of the small shack, E. J. McAllister. He was the least known person within their little group. A variety of past events had tested everyone else who would be meeting today.

E. J. perched on the edge of one of the ladder-backed chairs, "awkward as a cow at a hen party," as Mae would say. He kept repressing the crease in his suit pants. When his fingers weren't on his pants, they fumbled at his bow tie, as if checking to see that it hadn't unraveled.

Pleasantries about the weather and an explanation of Eich's ragpicker activities hadn't relaxed the man. Maybe getting started would. "E.J, we're waiting on two other people. But you need to know that something has happened. St. Alban has given us a crucial mission." An expression of dismay flooded the lawyer's face in response to this statement.

Sage hurried to reassure him. "Don't worry, we still intend to stop Lynch and the selling of boys from the BCS. But we're small in number. We need your help, maybe for both missions. You're already helping with the Lynch matter. Maybe you can help with the other matter as well."

E. J. seemed to relax slightly for the first time. "When Mr. Fong came last night and said it was urgent and we were meeting sooner, I thought you had changed your mind or that Lynch had already made his move. That they had taken more boys from the BCS. We'd already planned to meet tonight so I figured the early meeting meant bad news." Sage wanted to kick himself. Fear had kept the poor man tense, fear that he had started the ball rolling too late.

"What's this other mission?" E. J. asked, leaning forward, eagerness sending a flush across his rounded face.

"We have to wait for the two other people before we talk about it. One is Mae Clemens whom you've already met. The other is a man whose name I am going to withhold. He's the one who's going to explain what's going on."

The shack door creaked as it was eased open. Mae stepped inside. Eich jumped up to take her cloak and hang it on a wooden peg. Her first smile was for him. He returned the smile before ushering her to a chair and thrusting a mug of hot coffee into her hands.

Not for the first time, Sage admired his mother's high cheekbones, sculpted face, large dark blue eyes and generous mouth. As usual, her dark hair, lightly streaked with silver, lay tightly coiled against the nape of her neck. Not a pretty or beautiful woman but certainly a handsome one.

A glance to his side revealed that Eich seemed to be regarding her with similar admiration. She, however, was oblivious. She sat on the cot beside Sage, sipped the coffee, made a soft "mmm" sound and looked at all of them, smiling wide as she announced, "I've landed a job in the BCS kitchen and rented a room in a house nearby."

Before they could respond to her news, a sharp rap sounded on the door. Sage jumped up from the cot before Eich could slide off his workbench stool. Sage opened the door so Meachum could step into the hut. Outside a fine rain had intensified to the point it hazed the daylight.

Once over the threshold, the Flying Squadron's leader paused to survey those inside. Then he smiled, "Well, Adair, you certainly have pulled together an unexpected conglomeration of folks." The obvious pleasure in his face blunted any sting his words might have carried.

Sage took Meachum's coat, saying "That's exactly what works to our advantage. No one will imagine that we're working together."

Sage glanced in E. J.'s direction and saw that the lawyer was smiling. Apparently he was glad to be considered part of the "conglomeration."

Meachum settled into his chair and Sage introduced him as "Mike." Without any further social to-do, Meachum related exactly the same story he'd told Sage the night before. Mae and Fong had already heard it from Sage but Eich and E.J expressed alarm that someone planned to assassinate Theodore Roosevelt when he was in Portland.

"Before we discuss this situation further, Mike, you need to know about another problem we are in the midst of tackling," Sage said and swiftly laid out the problem of Lynch's house and the BCS's possible role in supplying boy prostitutes. Once done, Sage looked at his companions, letting his gaze linger on E. J.'s wrinkled forehead and drawn-together eyebrows." The lawyer clearly realized that it was critical that Meachum agree to their BCS plan.

Sage had to admit he was also anxious about Meachum's reaction. The other man couldn't stop their plan to put an end to Lynch and his suppliers but his willingness to support their efforts in that direction would make life much easier.

"Damnation!" the Squadron leader said. "Just when you think you've heard about the most venal thing one American can do to another, something else comes along to top it. What can I do to help?"

With a collective hiss five people released held breath. Sage grinned, reached across to cuff Meachum on the shoulder and said, "Thanks! Your offer is much appreciated. First, however, let's see if we can figure out which group is behind the plot to kill the president."

EIGHT

Dispatch: *May 7, 1903, President's train arrives in Casa Blanca, California.*

> *"A man who has never gone to school may steal from a freight car; but if he has a university education, he may steal the whole railroad." —T.R.*

NO ONE SAID ANYTHING. Sage looked toward Fong who responded promptly, "To unravel tangled threads do not grasp the whole knot."

The others simply stared at Fong. Sage, however, raised an eyebrow and asked, "Another saying from Mr. Confucius? "

"Idea comes from ancient Chinese warrior, not Master Confucius. Means we must look at each group as the end of thread and follow thread to separate from tangle."

Mae nodded vigorously. "That's exactly right. We look at what groups could assassinate the president and decide whether it is likely that they would. Like the suffragettes. There's enough of them, they are big enough to launch a national operation. But what is likelihood they'd do it?"

McAllister jumped in. "Not likely at all. First, and foremost, Roosevelt has made it clear he values women's opinions. Jane Addams, the Chicago Settlement House leader, is one of his advisors. And he positively hates wife beaters. He says they ought to be branded. So, the suffragettes have nothing to gain and everything to lose if Roosevelt dies."

"Chinese not like Roosevelt very much," Fong said, speaking softly as if to himself. Their heads turned until all were looking at him. "Roosevelt speak up for immigrants but not for Chinese. In many speeches he say 'exclude Chinese'," Fong said.

"Still, I've never heard of the Chinese mounting any sort of attack on Americans," Meachum said. "Even when sorely provoked."

Fong flashed them his toothiest grin. "That because we out-numbered and easy to spot. We are small but not stupid."

Meachum laughed in response, saying, "Besides, it's hard to imagine a monied white man bragging to a prostitute about how he's a front man for a bunch of powerful Chinese."

"Well, it sure isn't any Negro group who'd want to kill him," Sage said. "Roosevelt showed where he stood on racial equality when Booker T. Washington was one of his first dinner guests at the White House. The white southerners went crazy. One sena-tor said they'd have to lynch a thousand Negroes to undo the damage done by that invite. Hasn't stopped Roosevelt, though. Do you think it's possible that it's a group of Southern whites?"

There were nods all around.

"What about all that land Roosevelt wants to tie up in na-tional parks and such?" McAllister asked. "Could the ranchers and farmers be after him?"

Eich shook his head. "No, I've been watching Roosevelt's conservation actions. There's no groundswell of opposition. He's cleverly walking a narrow path. He's giving the Muir conserva-tionists their wildernesses by proposing national parks while giving the exploiters Gifford Pinchot and Pinchot's 'wise-use' forestry policies. They'll get to fall trees and run their sheep." More than a little bitterness laced Eich's prediction.

"Well, how about them snooty aristocrats? I read in the newspaper that both the Republicans and Democrats aren't hap-py about Roosevelt giving so many Catholics important positions in his administration. They call them the president's 'incense swingers,'" Mae said. Although not a practicing Catholic, she remained touchy about the prejudice her Irish Catholic family had experienced in the Appalachian coal fields.

Meachum made a face. "Nah, the parties will make Roosevelt's presidency hell, but they won't try to kill him. They plan to outflank and outmaneuver him legislatively. If all else fails, they'll combine forces and back his opponent come the 1904 election," he said.

McAllister cleared his throat before offering, "Roosevelt has kicked up quite a bit of dust with his civil service reform. The grafters hate losing their patronage power."

Meachum nodded his head. "No question some of them would like to see him in a coffin. I am sure they're afraid he's going to take what he learned in New York City and apply it nationally."

Eich shook his head. "But, the prostitute's customer said it was a big-monied 'group'," he observed. "Hard to see municipal grafters ganging together in a 'group'. Their rivalry would get in the way." The others, including McAllister, nodded their agreement.

Sage stood up and rubbed the small of his back. "That gives us one more likely direction to look. Money is their goal and power is their game—the Trusts," he said and watched their faces turn grim. The Trusts were the country's biggest financial gorillas and they were out of control—living proof that there was no limit to some people's avarice and thirst for power.

Mae's tone was bitter. "You might as well say house flies are going to kill him. Those trusts are everywhere. Just about anything a body tries to do runs up against some rich old men who already control things." Mae said. "Just how many Trusts are there, anyways?" Her question was sobering. How could six people possibly figure out, in such a short time, which Trust, if any, was involved?

McAllister leaned forward eagerly, speaking up. "Happens, I actually recently tried to identify the biggest ones. There are trusts controlling Sugar, Insurance, Meat Packing, Mining, Timber, Steel, Banking, and of course, the biggest one of all, the

Railroad Trust. Practically, his first day in office, Roosevelt ordered the U. S. Attorney General to move against the J.P. Morgan railroad monopoly. You want to talk about big monied groups, that one's the biggest."

Meachum rubbed his chin. "Hmm, the guy told her that the "group" has a representative here in Portland. How likely is it that Sugar, Mining, Meat Packing, or Insurance Trusts would have a representative here in Portland?" he asked. Sage watched as the question energized them all. Spines straightened, and a lightening of spirit seemed to wash through the small shed. Meachum's question thankfully narrowed down the number of trails they'd have to follow.

"Mozart's feeds everybody who is anybody in this town," Sage said. "I think I can safely say that only the Railroad, Timber, Banking and Utility Trusts have official representatives in this town."

"You and Mr. McAllister, are best ones to investigate local Trust people," Fong observed.

"And, I can wiggle my way into the good graces of any southerners new in town who could be involved," said Meachum in a southern accent that sounded authentic to Sage's ears.

"I'll chat up the various servants on my rounds," Eich offered. The ragpicker visited the dustbins of the rich on a regular basis, pausing at back porches to offer household servants his refurbished wares. Sage felt a rush of gratitude toward the hawk-nosed, bearded poet, with his soulful dark-brown eyes.

"I do same. Ask the cousins to be on lookout for visitors in rich houses." Fong said. His cousins were uniquely placed to make such observations since they tended to blend into the background even as they kept clothes clean and lawns exquisitely groomed.

"Mr. Solomon could be big help," Fong added.

"Good Lord, he'd be a great help," Sage agreed. Angus Solomon was the maitre'd at the Portland Hotel. In that capacity, he also had the opportunity to observe the activities of Portland's elite and their guests since the Portland Hotel housed the city's most exclusive restaurant. Moreover, the enterprising

Carolinian was also the part owner of the only decent hotel in Portland that catered to Portland's black community and especially to the railroad porters.

"These outsiders are almost certainly going to arrive here by train," Sage said. "If Mr. Solomon could have the porters on the lookout we might be able to identify the assassination group faster."

Fong silently rose from his squat in the corner, drawing all eyes toward him. "Mr. Solomon says Roosevelt second best president for for his people. He will help us," he told them.

Sage nodded. He shared Fong's confidence that the black man would step forward to assist. Angus Solomon had proved to be a resourceful and willing ally in all their endeavors.

As one, the men in the room looked toward Mae Clemens. She gave them a bleak smile. "I guess it's up to me to get to the bottom of what's going on at the BCS."

"Do you mind carrying that load?" Sage asked her.

"No, I know you'll all be here if I need you."

"I will come to back door of your rooming house two times a day," promised Fong.

"So, Fong, you'll be the one to keep the rest of us on top of what's happening at the BCS." Sage was grateful that Fong had volunteered because he'd been trying to figure out how he was going to single-handedly run the restaurant, ferret out those likely involved in the assassination plot and still manage to keep an eye on his mother.

She summed up the situation neatly, "We already know what's going on at Lynch's. And, Mr. McAllister's done a good job of identifying Lynch's source for boys and discovering Lynch's next step." McAllister stirred and flushed at Mae's praise.

"What's left is figuring out how they are getting the boys to cooperate and who at the BCS is behind it. That can only be done from the inside. Once we have those answers, we'll know what needs to be done," she said. "So I'd say, right now, it's a one-woman job."

Sage looked at the faces of his co-conspirators. Not one of them had expressed a moment's hesitation–not even McAllister.

Sage blinked away a sudden stinging behind his eyelids even as warmth spread inside his chest. He glanced toward Fong. The Chinese man smiled gently back at him.

New York City, May 6, 1903

The mercenary paused outside the apartment door, aware his shoulders were tight, as if readying to endure a blow. "Buck up, boy," he admonished himself. "After all, you're the one who takes the risks, makes the kills."

The door swung open after a single knock. Once again, the only light in the room came from the uncurtained windows facing the park, and even that was murky given the heavy layering of cigar smoke.

The client waved him in and took his customary chair next to the window. On the table at his side lay the slingshot and steel ball bearings. Same as before.

"What is it that you want to talk about?" the client demanded. "Don't stand there before me like some chastised schoolroom miss. I was forced to cancel an important appointment, thanks to your 'urgent' request. And don't ask us for more money. My principals are already expressing dissatisfaction over the amount you are making us spend."

The mercenary bit back a retort. He knew, from other sources, that his payment was a mere fraction of the funds this man controlled. In all likelihood, much more of it was going toward booze, cigars, women and elaborate dinners in fancy downtown restaurants. He said nothing because this boor, after all, was the customer he had to deal with. He lacked access to the men who were behind the man who sat in the window chair.

"A union man, St. Alban, knows an attack is planned against Roosevelt," he said.

A minor explosion sounded from the depths of the chair. "How stupid and incompetent! How the hell did he find out? You were supposed to be controlling the situation. If we haf to call off the operation because of your inability to carry it out, we'll vant all our money back or else," the man in the chair punctuated his threat by throwing a glass ashtray against the wall where it shattered.

"He found out because of the man you forced me to use in the operation. The man you selected because you said he was living in Portland and would be invaluable. Like I told you before, he got drunk and he blabbed to the whore."

"You told me you took care of her. You told me the whore was dead." The client remained on the attack. He was a shifty fellow, always on the offensive.

"Apparently not soon enough. Before the fire started, she talked to her brother."

"So kill the brother!"

"It's too late. He went straight to St. Alban."

"Wait a minute. How do you know all this? Who told you? How do I know this isn't just your ploy to get more money?"

The mercenary twitched as anger shot through his body. The fool sitting in that chair with his silly slingshot and pigeon-killing games didn't know the danger he was in at that precise moment. Maybe he did, though. The client shifted uncomfortably as if sensing, somewhere deep in the recesses of his primitive mind, the danger he was in.

The mercenary thought of his promised fee, swallowed, breathed deep and said mildly, to take the sting out of his words, "Never mind how I know. You want your money back, what hasn't been spent, you can have it. I'm not telling you my sources of information. That's my business, not yours. I'm not about to risk future work." He clapped his felt hat onto his head and turned toward the door.

The client's next words were spoken without his customary hectoring tone. "Just who is this St. Alban character?"

The mercenary turned back and said, "Vincent St. Alban started out with the mine workers' union, out in the Colorado Rockies. Became a hero to the miners when he went back inside after a cave-in and saved a bunch of miners. Lost an eye doing it."

The man in the chair lit a new cigar off the smoldering end of the old one and sucked deep before saying, "You know, I hate unions. If God wanted the average swine herder deciding how to run the world, he would have set things up differently. But, the fact is some men are born to rule others and some men are born to serve them. It puts everything out of kilter when the workers get above themselves. Makes nothing but trouble for everybody–even them."

"Most of the men I take jobs from don't like unions either," the mercenary observed.

"Just exactly what does this St. Alban know?"

"Near as I can find out, St. Alban knows that someone will try to kill Roosevelt somewhere in Oregon and try do it in such a way that the blame falls squarely on the unions."

"That's too damn much knowing! What's he planning to do, have you at least figured that out?" The nasty tone was back.

"I know he's already sent someone out to Portland. So, one would think St. Alban intends to disrupt our plans," the mercenary said, his sarcastic tone matching the other's.

Feistiness did the trick, because the next words spoken by the man in the chair were sly. "Vell, in that case we will make a deal, you and I. There is an additional five hundred dollars if you make Portland the last time St. Alban's man does an errand for his boss. Actually, make that a thousand. I also want you to take care of that big mouth drunk who blabbed to the whore. Do it the instant the bomb explodes."

NINE

Dispatch: *May 8, 1903, President's train arrives in Riverside, California.*

"Much can be done by organization, combination, union among the wage workers, and finally something can be done by the direct action of the State." —T.R.

ALTHOUGH MISTING RAIN drenched her shawl-covered head, Mae Clemens lingered outside the kitchen door. "This is not going to be easy. That harridan inside will try every smidgen of patience in my bones," she muttered to herself, adding, "Lord knows I got shorted when they handed out the patience." The interview with Mrs. Wiggit had been mercifully brief the day before. Merciful, because their exchange was not pleasant.

"You look a might long in the tooth to be starting this kinda work, Mrs. Clemens," the cook said once Mae explained she sought employment as the assistant cook. Mrs. Wiggit sat with her arms crossed over her ample bosom, her brown eyes cold and suspicious, her face set in a prove-it-to-me smirk that Mae's hand twitched to slap away.

Mae swallowed her retort in order to meekly agree, "Yes, ma'am, but I've worked hard all my life and don't know any other way to be."

Meek worked because the cook nodded and said, "Well, then. I'm sick to death of the young ninnies I've had to fire lately. Never saw such a bunch of lazy preening gadabouts. They think everything's supposed to drop right in their laps. And, despite me telling 'em different, they had to poke their nose where it didn't belong."

Mae's eyebrows rose of their own accord. Where had they been "poking?" This was definitely the kind of information she wanted to hear.

The other woman saw Mae's interest because she said, "If you want to work here, you got to listen better than they did. That's a male establishment overhead. They do not permit women above the basement level for any reason whatever," she declared, as stern as a schoolroom nun. "For *any* reason, you understand?" she repeated, her eyes narrowing.

That was yesterday. Now Mae was about to start working in the BCS kitchen in the hope that she'd get an opportunity to learn more about a monstrous criminal scheme. Somehow, she had to do a good enough job and remain meek enough for Mrs. Wiggit to keep her on. The vision of a submissive dog, lying on its back with its throat exposed, slid into her mind.

Fong once told her that a person's mental attitude becomes the mirror of their universe. She wasn't quite certain what he meant but she thought she knew. Anyways, she was done with the light rain soaking her through. Mae stepped down the cement step to the basement door and turned the knob. "Woof," she said softly as she stretched out her neck and stepped over the threshold.

Inside Gussie, the scullery maid, was washing pans and crockery in the tin sink, her small hands dipping periodically into a bowl of creamy, homemade soap. Evidently, Mrs. Wiggit ran an economical kitchen where excess lard was converted into soap.

Mrs. Wiggit was stirring a pot of gruel on the top of the huge black cookstove while simultaneously checking bread toasting in its oven. She expertly slid the done toast onto a platter sitting in the cookstove's warming oven. A deep dish also sat in the warming oven, already brimming with crisply fried bacon. The smell of it filled the air, making Mae's mouth water. She'd eaten only buttered bread and cheese for breakfast since the rooming house landlady didn't start serving until 6:30 in the morning.

Momentarily, Mae wondered if she'd arrived late to her first day of work. She glanced at the clock. No, it was ten to six, and Mrs. Wiggit told her to arrive at six.

Mrs. Wiggit dipped a practiced hand into a box of salt, scooped some out and dribbled it onto the gruel before glancing in Mae's direction. "Hang your wet garments over there." She pointed with her chin toward a row of pegs next to the outside door, where some outerwear already hung.

Mae quickly did as told, wrapping the long skinny strings of a spare white apron twice around her waist before knotting it snug. She turned back toward Mrs. Wiggit and asked, "Are you needing more coal for the stove?"

At the cook's abrupt nod, Mae crossed to the coal bucket, filled a scuttle full, carried it over to the cookstove, raised the heavy cast-iron lid and carefully spread the lumps across the burning embers.

"You're early," Mrs. Wiggit observed sourly. "Don't think by coming early, you'll get paid any more. I told you a dollar a day and so it will be, not a penny more." She was a tidy, sturdy woman of average height who coiled her dull brown hair atop her head. What made her unattractive was the sour downturn in her mouth and the hard pebble brown of her eyes.

Mae shook her head. "It's my habit to get places early. I couldn't sleep any longer anyways."

"Humph, I guess we'll see. We need rolls baked for lunch and dinner. After that some apple pies, though the apples are more rot than ready–it being the season's end."

So, Mae stirred and kneaded and rolled. That done, and the small mounds rising on the warmest, least drafty part of the kitchen counter, she took up a paring knife and went after the huge woven basket of last fall's apples. As peels curled and brown spots dropped away, Mae had her first opportunity to study the kitchen and its other two females.

It was a large room, maybe thirty by twenty, with a small alcove on one side where Gussie's washing up was done. The floor was clean, covered with white tile that had deep blue ceramic diamond shapes anchoring each corner. Dishes washed, the wafer-thin Gussie was down on her hands and knees mopping up the few dribbles her washing had left upon its surface.

The kitchen itself ran the length of the building on the side where the door opened to the outside. Full-size windows allowed light in on that long side while two smaller windows provided light on each of its shorter walls, one of the windows being situated over a sink that was in a small pantry-like alcove.

In the main room, black iron skillets of every size hung from hooks on the rear inside wall next to the massive stove. On the stove's other side, open shelves held boxes of salt, glass jars of various powders and sugars, pots of honey and jam. A long counter below had glass-fronted bins displaying a variety of dry staples like flour and oats. A number of woven baskets, the open tops showing onions, potatoes and other root vegetables, crowded one corner of the counter. Opposite the scullery on the other end wall, next to its single window, stood floor-to-ceiling shelves. These held dishes, glasses, cups and bowls of many different sizes.

Two sturdy wood chairs stood on each side of the rectangle work table where Mae sat. Glowing electric globes dangled above the red-checked oil cloth covering the table, providing a level of light far superior to that shed by the single globe in Mozart's kitchen. "All and all," Mae thought, "This is a well-organized space—I wish our kitchen was this open and bright."

Besides stove, shelves, pans and bin counter, the back wall also sported a doorway. Mae was eyeing it, wondering what was on the other side, when she realized that the door was slowly opening. A thump sounded and a boy of about seven years, limped through. The crutch he held hit the tile floor once again. He panted with the effort to move his twisted body across the floor toward the table, his right leg seeming to trail behind. As he neared Mae, he looked up from beneath long, sand-colored bangs. His eyes were a startling clear blue, guileless as an infant's.

A thread of drool was dribbling from the corner of his slack mouth.

Mae grinned at him. "Well, hello there, young man," she said. "Would you like a bit of apple?" She held out a peeled hunk of fruit.

He nodded and reached out with the hand that wasn't clutching the crutch. "My name is 'Andy'," he told her, carefully enunciating each word before biting into the apple.

From over by the stove, a slow exhalation sounded. Mae looked toward the cook and saw that the woman had eyes only for the boy. Her stern face had softened and her brown eyes glowed.

Ah, Mae thought. Trapped is what you are, Mrs. Wiggit, and mighty bitter at your caging. Mae smiled at the boy. "How about one more bite, Mr. Andy?" she asked him, offering a second piece. The boy giggled and took the apple eagerly.

The apple pies were near done when a heavy-set man lumbered into the kitchen. Noting the lusty stare he directed toward Gussie's backside, where the girl bent over the tin sink scrubbing the breakfast pots, Mae knew there'd be no liking him. She forced her face to relax into blandness and dipped her head submissively when Ms. Wiggit introduced her to "Cap'n Branch, the manager of the BCS."

"Guess we can't be calling you the new 'girl'," he said with special emphasis on the last word. He attempted to take the sting out of the words with a toothy smile.

"No, sir," Mae said and clamped her lips tightly shut.

She noticed Mrs. Wiggit watching their exchange closely. The other woman's chin lifted as if in satisfaction, though why Mae couldn't tell.

The Cap'n turned toward the cook. "This evening, I am expecting a few extra gentlemen in for dinner at six o'clock. See that there is extra grub on the table in the small dining room. Make it good. The doc's one of them so I don't want to see smears on the brandy snifters. Hmm, is that apple pie I smell?' The cook nodded. "Great. Just make darn sure it finds its way to our table in the small room." With that admonition, he turned on his heel and headed for the door.

"Oh," one hand on the doorknob, the Cap'n turned. "Kevin will be serving. Just make sure that the trays are ready on time and he'll bring them up."

"Yes, sir," the cook's voice followed the man out the door.

Mae glanced toward the cook and saw an expression of venomous hatred flit across the woman's face before she turned back toward the stove, "Make sure, just you make sure," Mae thought she heard the woman mumble.

A slight rustle came from the vicinity of Mae's feet. She looked down just as the oil cloth twitched and the wide eyes of the boy peered out. For the first time she realized that, when the Cap'n had entered the kitchen, the boy had slipped under the table and out of sight.

"Curiouser and curiouser," Mae Clemens muttered to herself. To the boy at her feet she mouthed, "He's gone." Her reward was a wide grin.

McAllister looked in a bad way when he entered Mozart's at the dinner hour's tail end. Sweat beaded his brow, deep creases pinched a tight-lipped mouth as his shaking hands fumbled with his hat. Sage seated the man quickly and signaled the waiter for a glass of house wine, Mozart's not being an establishment that sold hard liquor.

"E. J., something bad happen?" he asked, once the glass appeared in front of the other man.

"Not yet, but two bad things are about to happen." E. J. said before taking a gulp and making a face. "I prefer whiskey myself," he said, "but today, this is better than nothing." He drew in a shaky breath.

"We just found out that Lynch plans to open the second house within a week, not six weeks like we thought," McAllister said. "Up in the northwest, near Twenty-Third Avenue."

"Do you know where? And, who is this 'we' you're referring to?"

The corner of McAllister's mouth twitched, as if Sage weren't as up to snuff as he should be. "Some of my kind, of course. You think I'm the only one of us that can't bear to see those boys used by Lynch?" His face seemed to blank with memory and he said slowly, "More than one of us got used by men when we were boys. Sometimes, I wonder . . . ." His voice trailed off.

Sage looked at the man, thought of him as a small boy and felt his stomach tighten. If what he suspected McAllister meant was true it explained why the man was so distraught. Empathy can stab painfully deep when the hurt is one remembered instead of one imagined.

"Okay, so we know where the house is. That's a beginning," Sage said matter-of-factly, hoping to reassure McAllister that he wasn't going to be the one solely responsible for halting Lynch's moved-up plans.

McAllister didn't look relieved. If anything, his anxiety lines deepened. "That's just the point. The others . . . ." again his voice trailed off.

"The others what?" Sage prompted.

This time the lawyer sighed heavily. "The others are planning to set fire to Lynch's new place later tonight," he said.

He reached across to clutch at Sage's wrist where it lay upon the table. Then, seeming to realize that his behavior might draw attention, he abruptly let go. Forcing himself to sit back in his chair, McAllister said dully, "I can't let them do it, Adair. They could get caught. Other people could get hurt. I have sworn duty, an ethical duty to stop them. But, if I go to the police, good men will get hurt. It will ruin their lives, their families . . . ." He rubbed his face with both hands. "Dammit, Adair. If we don't stop Lynch, he'll have that damn house filled with new boys in just a few more days." McAllister fell silent, as if the dilemma had grabbed ahold of his throat and squeezed it shut.

TEN

Dispatch: *May 9, 1903, President's train pulls into Los Angeles, California.*

> *"It is far more difficult to deal with the greed that works through cunning than with the greed that works through violence. But the effort to deal with it must be steadily made."* —T.R.

THROUGHOUT THE NIGHT, the third floor of Mozart's felt empty. It was as if some corner of Sage's sleeping brain remained aware that his mother was not in the room next door and it could not rest easy. Her absence nibbled at him until the sound of the metal mail flap clanking three stories below roused him fully awake. He slid from bed, started the corner stove, fetched the newspaper, settled into the rocker near the window and began reading the paper by the growing sunlight.

A short time later Fong entered the room. A woven basket filled with various dried herbs dangled from one hand. Sage dropped the newspaper to the floor and gestured Fong toward the teapot on the table.

"Mr. Fong, the tea's hot. Just got it boiling myself," he said and waited while Fong poured and drank before asking, "Did you see her? Is she alright?"

Fong nodded. "I sold her herbs from basket when she came out door of rooming house. She took them to work." He swallowed again. "She say everything going like planned. She met boss. Says he is a bad man. She will try to explore more today."

"But is she doing okay?"

Fong smiled. "Lady Mother would nip your nose if she heard you ask that question. Still, I think she not sleeping enough."

Sage used his stockinged toe to flip the newspaper over so the headline showed. "Tragedy Averted in House Fire."

"You're the "oriental" man referred to in the story?"

Fong picked up the paper. "Must be," he said after a few minutes.

"What happened? You didn't spot them soon enough?"

This time Fong shrugged his shoulders as if the fire getting started was of little concern to him. "Turns out, Mr. E.J's friends enter house more than one way. I only one person," he said. "I see one man crawl through open porch window with gas can. I go in right away. Another man already inside, upstairs. He start fire before I get to him."

"What did you do to stop them?"

"I screech like angry temple monkey. Man upstairs jump onto porch roof and slide down post to ground. Man below run right out back door. Not even shut it after himself. Then I run and knock on house next door. Neighbor sent boy for fire brigade."

"And you?"

"I ran back inside burning house and straight out back door. Poof! I am smoke," From the glitter in his eyes, Fong appeared quite pleased with his adventure.

"It says in the newspaper that nobody saw the arsonists and they couldn't find the oriental man who raised the alarm. And that it's going to take some weeks to fix the damage."

"That is what I thought too. Fire burned walls upstairs and stairway but did not spread to whole house or to next door houses."

"Thank God. Hopefully you scared those fellas enough that they won't try that again. From what E.J. said, they were having to screw up their courage as it was."

"Man, downstairs, he fling gas can up to ceiling and shriek like mouse run across bare foot. He not come back." Fong's grin said he enjoyed remembering the moment.

"I wish that house had burned to the ground."

"Yes."

"I wish it had burned to the ground with Lynch in it."

"Yes."

"I hate Lynch and men like him."

"Hate is a bad attachment to have," Fong said, and stood abruptly. "Time for training. You getting flabby."

"What do you mean 'attachment'?" Sage asked an empty room–empty because Fong was already gone.

Sage climbed the attic stairs in a buzz of mild irritation. Just once it would be nice if Fong would spit out what he meant instead of being so mysterious. This time, by gum, I'm going to tell him that.

He didn't. Fong was already gliding across the varnished hardwood floor in the flowing movements of the snake and crane. On white walls hung the only ornamentation, narrow scrolls of Chinese calligraphy, the flowing black script a single column upon a white silk panel that was trimmed with red. Overhead, sunlight filtered through the skylight Fong had installed. New leaves on the rooftop's potted plants made shadow patterns across the floor. That sight gave him satisfaction. Those were his very own plants, ones he'd planted the summer before and carefully bedded down for winter. It was like moving art, he thought as he watched the leaf shadows flutter.

Sage pulled his shirt from his pants and stepped out in his bare feet, ready to follow Fong through the 108 movements. Fong said nothing. His only acknowledgment of Sage's presence being the fact that he closed the form and began it again with the first move, one he called "begin form, greet the sun."

Sage lost his place in the movements more than once, always when his mind snagged on thoughts of Lynch. It was strange,

how the movements cleared the head until only the consequen-
tial thoughts distracted. When they did, the body hesitated, like
a hummingbird unsure of its next target. Today, thoughts of
Lynch acted like a white-hot snare. Enough. Sage mentally shook
himself and tried to concentrate on the form, "Step Up, Grasp
Bird's Tail, Single Whip, Fair Lady Work Shuttle . . . ." When his
mind was focused on the movement, that elusive power Fong
called "chi" seemed to grow, making his palms feel like they
held a pulsing magnetic field and his feet seem anchored to the
earth's core. But it never lasted. Always his mind strayed and the
chi feeling dissipated like smoke before a sudden breeze.

"What did you mean about 'attachments', Mr. Fong?" Sage
asked again, once they had finished the routine.

Fong looked at him, his brown eyes radiating a teasing light.
"You have some trouble staying with form today, Mr. Sage," was
all he said and left Sage standing in the middle of the room wondering whether Fong had just answered his question or ignored it.

Mae Clemens stood at the tin sink, her large sturdy hands
scrubbing turnips clean. Outside the window was a small courtyard, surrounded on three sides by buildings and on the street
side by a brick wall six feet high. Two benches provided a seclud-
ed place to sit and enjoy the spring day. A few tendrils of deep
green English ivy crawled up the sides of the buildings, but otherwise the space was bare of nature. As if to refute that thought,
a robin landed atop the wall and even through the rippled glass
she could hear its cheerio celebration of spring, its song sweetly
pure in the crystalline air.

The birdsong stopped abruptly and seconds later a young
boy wandered into view followed by others. There were five of
them, all around the age of nine. Like old men, they shuffled
over to the two benches, slumped down and turned their faces
up to the sun. There was no lightness in their bodies, no anima-
tion to their limbs.

Mae heard a sound like a suppressed moan of pain behind her. Turning, she saw Mrs. Wiggit standing behind her. The cook said nothing. She shrugged and moved back toward the stove but not before Mae had seen the features in the woman's face momentarily collapse, as if in grief, before restoring themselves to their customary mulish expression.

Mae looked out the window. The boys had not moved. Maybe they were sick. Certainly, their pallor was like a consumptive's. But surely, the BCS would not let seriously ill children live midst the healthy ones.

A man strode into sight. He went straight up to the boys, radiating vigor, carrying a black leather satchel. With a jolt, Mae realized she knew the man. It was Dr. Harvey, a frequent patron of Mozart's. Reassurance was her first reaction. The boys were getting medical care from Dr. Harvey who had the reputation of being a competent doctor. Alarm replaced this easing of concern. Some of Mozart's patrons were oblivious of her and the other staff as people. But not Dr. Harvey. He always greeted her by name and engaged her in conversation. He'd even recently brought her a tin Miss Liberty trinket. So, he would certainly recognize her. She stepped back from the window. She needed to make herself scarce if he entered the kitchen.

She looked around the big room. Nowhere to hide. There was the toilet room, but that would mean crossing the kitchen to the internal door—an action likely to draw his attention to her. That left her the option of rooting around in a lower cupboard, her tail hanging out like that of a skittish dog's during a thunderstorm, until he had gone.

Her plan made, she relaxed and watched the doctor go through the paces of feeling each forehead, palpating each neck and otherwise examining each boy. Despite the man's patting of shoulders and ruffling of hair, the boys remained sullenly unresponsive. The doctor didn't seem to notice. At last he packed up his bag and left the courtyard. Mae tensed, ready to shove her head into a lower cabinet. When the kitchen door stayed closed, she relaxed and went back to watching the listless boys even as her hands scraped away the turnips' skin.

A few minutes later, the gate in the brick wall swung slowly open and a brown-clad figure stepped into the courtyard. Eich! It was Eich. Mae almost rose on her toes at the sight of him. He went to the dustbin and began rummaging through it without acknowledging the boys' presence. They reacted by turning their heads to watch him, showing the most life she'd seen them display since they'd entered the courtyard. Eich looked toward the window, caught her eye and raised one shaggy eyebrow. She gave a little nod, glanced around the kitchen and saw Mrs. Wiggit exit out the inner door. Gussie was dreamily smearing tarnish remover on the bottom of a silver coffee urn reserved for use in the Captain's private dining room. Mae grabbed the pail of vegetable peels and made a beeline for the door. When Gussie looked up, Mae waggled the pail and Gussie nodded in understanding.

When Mae entered the courtyard to dump the peelings, she saw that Eich had finished his rooting and was over by the boys. As she watched, his gnarled hand reached into one of his commodious pockets and retrieved a paper sack. He deposited a hard peppermint candy into each upturned hand. Touching his cap to her, he went out through the gate. She quickly followed.

"Herman, it is so good to see your face. Is something wrong?" she asked.

"No, Mae. Everything is fine. Just thought I'd add your dustbin here," he nodded at the brick building, "to my daily rounds unless you think it a bad idea."

She looked up into his warm brown eyes and smiled, "I think it's a great idea. This place gives me the crawlies. What's wrong with those boys in there do you think?" she asked, tipping her head in the direction of the courtyard.

Eich shook his head. "I know what you mean. They seem lethargic for being as young as they are. I do have another reason for being here. Have you a minute? Remember when we all put our heads together and figured out what trusts might have representatives here in Portland? Fortunately, it's not New York City or the task would be too daunting."

Mae glanced at the closed kitchen door. She began to worry that Mrs. Wiggit might appear to call her in. "I have a minute. What do you need to know?"

"I'm thinking I'll start visiting some key dustbins in the city. See if the household help tell of any new visitors from back East. So, I was hoping you might know, for example, who are the representatives of the timber, railroad, investment and utilities trusts. Those seem to be the big ones in Portland."

Mae knew, rattling the names off quickly, "William Fenton for timber and railroad, Cyrus Dolph also for the railroad, Abbot Mills for investment banking and, probably, Fred Holman for utilities."

They both turned quickly when the door swung wide and Gussie poked her head out to whisper, "Mrs. Wiggit's wanting to know what's taking you so long at the dustbin."

Herman Eich picked up the shafts of his cart and began trudging up the street. His voice floated back to her:

> I was born to work and laugh and play
> I am the future of my race
> I am the cheated child.

Mrs. Wiggit's disapproving frown greeted Mae when she entered the kitchen. "You want to buy off that ragpicker's cart, that's fine. But, next time, be quick about it," the cook snapped before turning back to the stove.

"Yes, ma'am," Mae said, returning to her turnip preparation. Beyond the window the courtyard was emptying as the boys meekly filed back into the building, even though the street gate stood open. Mae watched them, her eyes blinking away tears as the words "cheated child" echoed in her head.

ELEVEN

Dispatch: *May 9, 1903, President's train arrives in San Luis Obispo, California.*

"There should be relentless exposure of and attack upon every evil practice, whether in politics, in business, or in social life."
—T.R.

MCALLISTER'S FACE WAS RED and his expression eager when he opened Mozart's front door and stepped inside to shake the raindrops off his hat and coat. Sage seated the lawyer at a small table facing the room. Directly in the lawyer's line of sight was a much larger table in the opposite corner where a confabulation of Republican bigwigs was underway.

"Thanks for getting here so quickly," Sage said, taking the seat opposite the lawyer and signaling the waiter who arrived within moments with two cups of coffee.

"Mr. Fong said it was important," McAllister said, "Hey, is he the man who raised the alarm about the fire?"

"Yup, that'd be Mr. Fong all right."

"Thank God, that fire didn't burn down the house and take the whole neighborhood with it. One of the fellows stopped by this morning. He said they all realize now that it was a crazy thing to do. Maybe, I suppose that ethically, I should report them. But

I'm not going to since the damage was minor and they've vowed that they won't do anything like that again."

McAllister chuckled before saying, "They learned their lesson. Your Mr. Fong scared the holy bejesus out of them. They still think it was a ghost that screeched." McAllister's blue eyes twinkled. "But enough of the Lynch business, unless that's why you called me here."

"Nope, not Lynch, although things are still progressing satisfactorily. Mrs. Clemens is working inside the BCS and both Mr. Eich and Mr. Fong are staying in close touch with her. Today, though, I asked you here so I could point out the men who are most likely to give shelter to the mastermind of the assassination scheme."

McAllister dipped his head at the corner table. "I'm betting you mean it's one of the men who are sitting at that table over there."

Sage nodded, gratified McAllister was so quick on the uptake. "Exactly. I thought maybe, as a new man in town, that you might not be acquainted with our biggest frogs."

"Well, you are right on that point," McAllister said. "The only one I know over there is Fenton and that's just because he's my landlord and a fellow lawyer. Friendly man. We've tipped a few together. Didn't know he was a 'big frog' though."

"One of the biggest. Besides owning your building, he's in tight with a group who recently ran a timber fraud scam on the federal government. They got indicted for it a few months back. He's their defense lawyer." Sage decided he wouldn't tell McAllister of his own role in obtaining that indictment.

"More important," Sage continued, "he's the one providing the legal grease for the Southern Pacific Railroad. It has misused the law to finagle over a billion board feet of raw timber from the federal government for itself. At the same time his client works with the other railroad companies to fix rail transport prices so high that the farmers can't afford to ship their products. Way too many of them are losing their farms because of it."

Sage didn't bother to suppress his bitterness as he said, "Yup, those railroad men are real admirable human beings, one and all. I know you lawyers claim you are just doing your job but to me, that's an unacceptable excuse for being part of something immoral."

"And, yet, Fenton is such a congenial companion." McAllister's tone was sardonic. "And, you're right, Adair. Some lawyers have no problem leaving their moral scruples at the door. I just don't happen to be one of them."

Sage smiled warmly at McAllister. Here was another man who recognized the unrelenting hypocrisy of the rich and their hired lackeys. "That white-haired man to Fenton's left is Cyrus Dolph," he told the lawyer. "He's also big into transportation. Owns a couple of wharves. Lately, he's been dabbling in railroading. He's a front man for the railroad trusts, but Dolph also owns a big piece of the Portland Hotel. If he's involved, then he might be the one providing housing for some of the conspirators."

"That dark haired man, with the thin face on the other side of Dolph, looks very familiar," McAllister said.

"Ah yes, Mr. Abbot Mills. He's familiar because you see him everywhere with anyone who has money. He's got eastern connections in the banking industry. If anyone in town speaks for the financial trusts, it is Abbot Mills. He just came off the city's public works commission. He was its chairman and in that capacity he oversaw the letting of contracts for hay, hardware, sawdust, street paving, sidewalk building and such, as well as those lucrative utility franchises."

"Graft?" McAllister asked.

"Nothing so crude as dishonest graft. I suspect Mills is expert at what my friend, F. T. Merrill, likes to call 'honest' graft. Don't know how he lined his pockets but I figure he had some kind of angle going on."

"And the other two?" McAllister prompted.

"The one with the red hair is Fred Holman. He's another lawyer. His area of expertise is utilities, franchises and regulations. He's one of the founders of Portland General Electric. Most days, you see the smoke of their coal-fired steam plants down near the river. What's odd about him sitting at that table is that he's the only Democrat. But, he's so important to the city's financial picture, I guess he's welcome anywhere.

"The last guy is also an odd addition because he's not really involved in the economics of the city. He's a doctor. Name of 'Harvey.' I guess you could call him a doctor to the elite, since he seems to spend most of his time with them. He's got a summer cottage south of the city at that Waverly golf course that they built not long ago. I've heard tell that he's particularly skilled at the game. That probably accounts for his presence."

"So, now that I know who they are, what did you want me to do?" asked McAllister.

"Well, E.J., since you are the new lawyer in town, I was hoping you would have entreé into their circle and might be able to find out whether any of them are planning to entertain an out-of-town guest. It is certain that every man at that table will hobnob with Roosevelt when he gets here. So, they will be perfectly situated to provide the assassin mastermind with access to the president."

"You actually think one of those men might be in on the assassination plot?"

"No. I don't think they'd be knowingly involved. But, I think the plotters could find a way to make use of them. Remember, that murdered gal back East told her brother that the mastermind behind the whole plot, the one making sure the assassin gets signaled, also plans to be visiting someone here in Portland."

"Well, I guess I better start taking Fenton up on his sociable offers. You know, I play a pretty good round of golf myself."

When Sage raised an eyebrow, McAllister said, "It was either golf or rowing in college, I can't swim, so there you have it."

McAllister stood up. "Guess I might as well start now," he said and ambled over to the other table. He was well received, each man raising slightly from his seat to shake the lawyer's hand. After McAllister had gone on his way, Sage also approached the table.

"Good afternoon, gentlemen," he greeted them. "Everything satisfactory with your meal?"

Dolph replied, "It was quite good. Your kitchen is a real competitor to our hotel."

"I am flattered that you think so, Mr. Dolph. And, delighted that you favor us with your custom given the excellent food served in the Portland Hotel's dining room."

"Well, I guess I don't have to tell you that it's always good to see what the competition's up to. Besides," here Dolph leaned forward and winked, "sometimes a man gets tired of the same food day after day no matter how good it is."

Fenton entered the conversation. "I see that you've made a friend of my tenant, E. J. McAllister. You two seemed to have quite a lot to say to one another."

Sage was prepared for this bit of probing. "He attended Syracruse University the same time as a close friend of mine. Turns out he knew my friend. So, we had stories to swap about the various escapades of our mutual acquaintance," he told Fenton.

"McAllister? Isn't he the lawyer working for the unions?" asked Mills, his voice sharp with suspicion, his mouth pursed in distaste.

Crap. It sure would have been nice if they didn't know about that, Sage thought but he said, "McAllister was telling me how he's been forced to take their cases, since he's just starting up his practice here in Portland. You fellows throw some work his way, and I'd be willing to bet the unions will have to find some other lawyer. Maybe one not half as competent as Mr. McAllister seems to be, if you know what I mean."

They knew what he meant because they exchanged speculative looks. Might as well goose the idea further along, "Besides, McAllister tells me he's a pretty good golfer. That's something you fellows appreciate, I hear."

The group laughed and their mood lightened. Sage had done his best. Now it was up to McAllister to reel them in.

Three o'clock brought Sergeant Hanke to the kitchen door. Sage was waiting for him. "Thanks for coming, Sergeant," Sage said in greeting. He gestured the policeman toward the kitchen table near the back door and farthest from the kitchen help who were busy with supper preparations.

"Your note came early enough so that I could plan my day to be here at three. Oh, thank you, ma'am. You're looking in rosy fine health," Hanke said to Ida when she put a hefty slice of canned cherry pie down in front of him. She laughed easily, patted his broad shoulder with a plump hand and went back to her stove.

Hanke turned back to face Sage, his face expectant. "Well, Mr. Adair, I suspicion that you didn't call me here to feed me. Although you are always darn generous in that direction. Is there something besides Ida's cooking on the boil?"

Sage laughed. "You've got the right idea. Tell me, first, how are the security plans for the president's visit coming along?"

Hanke rose taller in his chair and his chin lifted. "I'll have you know Chief Hunt has put me in charge of one of the details that'll be guarding him."

Perhaps Fortune was starting to smile on their efforts to save Roosevelt, Sage thought. But getting information out of Hanke would be tricky. The man took his police responsibilities seriously, unlike many in Portland's police force.

Out loud Sage said, with an admiring smile, "That's quite an honor for you, isn't it? I would think he wouldn't assign a police sergeant such an important job."

Hanke tried but couldn't control his grin."I'm the only one out of the sergeants. Mostly because of you and Mr. Fong, of course."

Now here was an opening. Play him carefully, like fly fishermen play the stream trout. "Oh, I'm sure there's more to it than that."

"Well, I dunno. Thanks to you, the new chief, Charles Hunt, thinks that I've solved more murder cases than all the detectives put together. And, he's fed up with most of the men, anyway. Hunt thinks they're more crooked than a dog's hind leg. He tells me that I'm 'smart' and 'honest.' I'm thinking that, if I do a good job on this presidential detail, maybe I'll make lieutenant next go-a-round."

Sage took his time adding more coffee to Hanke's cup. The big man took advantage of the pause to fork in another bite of the deep red pie.

"Sergeant, I need to take you into my confidence but I have a dilemma. If I tell you something, will you keep it to yourself? No matter how serious it is?"

Hanke carefully laid his fork down on the plate, his pie only half eaten. He cleared his throat and his wide Germanic forehead acquired an earnest crease. "You know, Mr. Adair, I trust you and Mr. Fong more than anyone I know. Three times now you have fought crime right beside me and every single time you've made me take all the credit. Couple of those times, some of the things you did made me nervous, but they worked out all right in the end. I guess that's a long way of saying I trust you and your intentions and that you can trust me to keep mum. But," here the policeman raised a cautionary finger, "don't ask me to do anything downright illegal 'cause I won't, no matter how much I owe you."

His response was pretty much what Sage had expected. "I wouldn't ask you to compromise yourself that way. I know better. If I did, you'd probably walk out that door and never come back." Hanke nodded, his shoulders relaxing a bit.

"The problem is, what I want to ask you, well, it involves something you're going to want to speak to Chief Hunt about and that won't do."

Hanke interrupted, "I'd trust Chief Hunt with my life. It's the men around him I don't trust."

"Exactly," Sage said.

"So you want me to tell you something but you want me not to tell anyone else you asked? Why ask me at all?"

"Because you have information I need. I can't tell you any more right now, but you must believe me when I say that it is urgent that I know exactly what steps will be taken to protect the life of the president while he's in town later this month," Sage said.

Hanke's ruddy face drained of color and his mouth dropped open.

TWELVE

Dispatch: *May 9, 1903, President's train arrives in Del Monte, California.*

> *"This country will not be a permanently good place for any of us to live in unless we make it a reasonably good place for all of us to live in . . . The welfare of each of us is dependent fundamentally upon the welfare of all of us." —T.R.*

SAGE THREADED HIS WAY among the humanity crowding the North End's sidewalks. The mild spring night had drawn roughly dressed men outdoors to mill about, lean against brick walls or squat down to toss pennies in a friendly game of chance. Sage mused about how the milder weather animated everyone, even here in the North End, where the unemployed made every nook and cranny a place to bed down. Overhead, stray pots of budding red geraniums perched on windowsills while, below them, aggressive bright green weeds shoved skyward from pavement cracks. Every living thing seemed to be heralding the end of winter's dark, wet days.

Sage joined the herd of men pushing their way into Erickson's saloon. Inside, smoke layered the air as alcohol-loosened voices created a hubbub of sound that made thought and conversation hard. Adding to the din were the tinny notes of the piano that accompanied the four girls who were caterwauling a ribald tune and kicking their feet into the air.

A dense line of men toting mugs of beer packed the stairway leading to the balcony. Once he gained the top, Sage moved a few paces toward the railing and paused to gaze down at the saloon's ground floor. Below, a mass of bowler and other hat-covered heads bobbed and shifted like the surface of an agitated sea. Casually, Sage glanced around the balcony. It ran along three sides of the block-sized room. Behind him, rented booths snugged against the balcony walls, each one concealed behind faded, velvet curtains. The saloon's "hostesses" were having a busy night. Tables and chairs crowded the railing. Here and there sat well-dressed toffs. They swilled Erickson's most expensive liquor as they engaged in bawdy exchanges with the roving women and ridiculed the antics of their social inferiors below. Tucked into the balcony's dim corners were the less desirable tables. Meachum sat at one of these, his head down, his hands wrapped around a mug of flat beer.

Sage took a seat, facing the wall so that his back was to any passerby. He was wearing nondescript workingman's clothes, the streak in his hair was blacked, his now limp moustache concealed his mouth while his floppy-brimmed hat kept the light off his upper face. But, he wasn't taking any chances. Some of those sitting at the railing tables frequented Mozart's as well. Only when they did so, they arrived impeccably dressed and with a haughty wife on their arm rather than a laughing saloon tart.

Meachum looked up at the scrape of the chair being pulled out. His hat was pushed back so that his swath of silver hair glinted in the oil lamp's light. The last few days had been hard on Meachum. There were black shadows beneath his bright blue eyes and the lines in his craggy face had deepened. Still, he gave Sage an easy smile as the two shook hands across the table.

"Jeez, Meachum. You look like you've been three days trailing cougar through the brush," Sage commented as he sat down.

"Humph, I wish. You aren't looking all that great yourself, Adair. Your eye holes look like they're sporting war paint," Meachum returned.

Sage leaned forward, lowering his voice even though the din around them guaranteed privacy. "There's a lot going on. Mother's working at the BCS. Eich and Fong are keeping an eye on her. McAllister's going to play golf, I hope, with the trust crowd and find out whether any of them might be harboring the assassination's mastermind. I'm about to head over to the Portland Hotel and talk to Solomon, the maitre'd there. Fong's already filled him in and he's on board."

"Well, I've called the entire Squad together and they're all here in town now," Meachum said. "I've got them watching the rail yards, flophouses, watering holes and prostitute cribs–on the lookout for a gang of newcomers to town. It's not easy since we don't know how many or how far in advance they plan to get here. After all, their part is relatively small. They just need to create a distracting commotion. Not a lot of planning needed to make that happen."

"No, but they'll need to meet with their leader and coordinate both the when and the where of their distracting rumpus. And, I suspect one of their number is going to make sure they stay together until the time comes. That should make them easier to spot," Sage said, aware that he sounded more confident than he felt.

Meachum sighed, clearly not buying the confidence. "Yup, that's about what we figure. Still, there's only eight of us and we can't be everywhere," he said.

"That's where I've got some good news. You don't have to be everywhere. Apparently Police Chief Hunt is taking his job very seriously. My police contact tells me that the money men have loosened the purse strings. They don't want Portland to be like Buffalo–forever known as the city where our president got assassinated. Bad for business, you know."

His lips twisted. "So every man on the city's force as well as the secret service men traveling ahead of the president are combing the streets looking for suspicious characters. The city is also importing detectives from other towns all over the West. And, they're using Dickenson men, Theil's agents, railroad detectives and even deputized men from other city bureaus. Everybody's watching the arrival of men on trains and steamers. The police station walls are plastered with the pictures of every known criminal and 'anarchist crank' in the country. That last description is his label, not mine," Sage added.

"I'm glad to hear it since I count some of those 'anarchist cranks,' as close friends of mine," Meachum said. "So long as they're not into the bomb-throwing approach," he added.

"Yah, me too. Although, I have to tell you, when I think of what men like Lynch and his backers are doing to those boys, the idea of a little educational violence seems mighty attractive," Sage said, his tone glum.

"I'm with you on that," Meachum agreed. "Especially, whenever I look into a widow woman's eyes, her hungry kids clutching her knees and I know that some greedy, arrogant bastard–who already has way more than he'll ever need–is responsible for her despair. I swear, my hands itch to get around his throat."

"Somehow it's worse, you know? It's worse that they destroy men's lives, families, so thoughtlessly, without considering the harm they are inflicting. A man gets mad at another man, they come to blows, one of them dies. Somehow, that is understandable–human. But, to casually destroy another man's livelihood or life, with just the scratch of a pen or an order to a minion and then put on your hat to go to the club or to the golf course . . . that's . . . ." Sage's voice trailed off.

"That's inhuman," Meachum finished for him.

Once again, the picture of those drooping boys on Lynch's stoop flashed into Sage's mind. It was chased away by a sudden fierce burning in his core. "Sometimes," he said, "I just hate them. I just hate them all. More than anything, I want them to feel, just once, the full measure of pain that they cause their fellow humans," he said.

In contrast to Erickson's, the atmosphere at the Portland Hotel's dining room was one of hushed decorum. Angus Solomon returned to the mahogany podium after seating a patron and gave the waiting couple ahead of Sage a friendly smile that warmed his deep brown eyes. As always, Sage found himself admiring the man's smooth walnut burnish and high cheekbones. Fong had told him that Solomon had an Indian chief in his background and Sage thought that if regal beauty was an indicator, the story had to be right. Gradually, Sage's ruminations gave way to the realization that an altercation was building between Solomon and the couple before him.

"I said, boy, that I wanted that table right over there," the man said, stabbing his finger toward a table snug against the window.

Even from this distance, it was easy to see that the white placard resting against the table vase displayed the word "Reserved."

"I am most sorry, sir, but that table is reserved." Solomon sounded sincerely regretful.

The man was having none of it. "Well, I can see the damn sign on it. But nobody's sitting there and I promised my wife the best seat in the house." At this, the woman at his side stirred, making demurring sounds that he ignored. "First that train porter refused to carry our bags and now you're refusing to seat us. And, don't look down your nose at me, boy. Where I come from, you would do as I tell you or else!" The man's face splotched puce with anger.

Sage stepped forward only to halt when Solomon flashed him a warning look.

"Sir," he said. "I am most sorry for the inconvenience. But, my dilemma is that the gentleman who reserved that table is my employer." Solomon paused a beat to let the impact of that fact sink in. The man seemed to calm and his wife softly touched his forearm.

Into the pause, Solomon said, "I know that it will not take away your disappointment at not dining at that table, sir, but may I offer you and your wife complimentary glasses of champagne by way of an apology?"

The man looked at his wife who nodded eagerly. "Well, all right," he said, "But I don't know what kind of hotel owner would take the very best seat in the house."

Solomon nodded, picked up two leather-covered menus and began to walk toward a very good table in the center of the room, the couple trailing along behind.

On the other hand, the table to which Solomon ushered Sage was easily the worst in the house. Near the kitchen door, behind a potted palm. Once he'd seated Sage, Solomon said, "You look a bit thrown together, Mr. Adair," he said, fingering his own hair at the right temple.

"Damn, didn't get all the blacking out?"

"Nope, afraid not."

Sage pulled out a white handkerchief and rubbed vigorously at his streak. "Better?" he asked.

"A bit, but I'd stay away from bright lights."

"It's been a busy day. You and Fong have a chance to talk?"

"Yes. I understand that I am to keep an eye on misters Fenton, Mills, Dolph and Holman to see if they have any out-of-town guests. I am also to ascertain if anyone staying in the hotel might be a mastermind assassin." At this, one corner of Solomon's mouth quirked up.

"Well, I can see that the last task might be a bit more difficult than the first."

Solomon laughed but immediately sobered. "You know Roosevelt was the first president to ever invite a Negro to dine at the White House? And, that Mr. Washington was one of Roosevelt's first guests?"

Sage nodded.

"Well, then, the least I can do is try to keep him safe when he's a guest in our city." Solomon glanced around, saw that no new patron waited at the podium and stepped closer. "You know Roosevelt's going to be staying here, of course?"

"Actually, I figured he would since it's the best hotel in town. But, I didn't know for sure."

"We have had the police and secret service crawling all over the place."

"I expect you are taking precautions too?"

"We certainly are. Our group has met and agreed on a procedure for sharing information." By "group," Sage knew

Solomon meant the black men and women who worked in the dining room and as the hotel's cleaning staff. Together they saw more of what went on in the hotel than anyone else. More than once, their willingness to help and share information had proved invaluable.

Solomon picked up the menu. "The Special as usual?" he asked.

"Mr. Solomon, before you go, how can you put up with that," Sage nodded at the couple seated in the middle of the room, "day after day?"

Solomon's eyes softened. "Well, Mr. Adair, I would be less than truthful if I said it was easy."

"Don't you hate people like that, the ones who treat you and the others that way?"

The other man's forehead wrinkled, then he shook his head. "No, I do not hate him. I feel anger, any man would. You see, where my people are concerned, we'd have cause to spend every day of our lives hating. And that hate would destroy us, wall us off from the succor to be found in this world."

"Succor?"

"A loving family, delicious food, beauty, God and," he nodded toward Sage, "good friends, like Mr. Fong and you, Mr. Adair," he said, before flashing a wide smile and walking away.

As Sage watched, the dignified maitre'd paused beside the couple's table to exchange a few words. Whatever he'd said left the couple smilng once he'd moved on.

THIRTEEN

Dispatch: *May 10, 1903, President's train arrives in Monterey, California.*

> *"Wise factory laws, laws to forbid the employment of child labor and to safeguard the employees against the effects of culpable negligence by the employer, are necessary, not merely in the interest of the wage worker but in the interest of the honest and humane employer who should not be penalized for his honesty and humanity by being exposed to unchecked competition with an unscrupulous rival." —T.R.*

MRS. WIGGIT WAS IN A FOUL MOOD. She slammed pans down on the iron cookstove like she was killing a mouse, all the while muttering to herself in fits and starts. Gussie was scuttling around the edges of the kitchen, gently putting clean dishes and cookware onto shelves so as to not draw attention to herself. Mrs. Wiggit's boy, Andy, sat at the table, watching Mae roll out pie crusts, cringing and sliding down in his seat every time another bang sounded from his mother's direction. As Mae finished pinching the last pie dough into a baking dish, Mrs. Wiggit took up a skillet, this time to fry up some onions for a soup. Andy slid further down in his chair as that pan hit the stove with an unnecessary bang.

Mae picked up a basket of scrubbed turnips, a paring knife and an empty bowl. "Mrs. Wiggit," she said to the cook, "would it be all right if Andy came outside and kept me company while I peel these turnips?"

The cook paused in her muttering to look at her son. Her face softened and she sighed. "Would you like to go outside with Mrs. Clemens?" she asked him. At his eager nod, she said to Mae, "Long as he's no trouble to you, I'd appreciate him getting a bit of sun."

Mae held the door open while Andy and his crutch hobbled through. A few paces down the sidewalk, they entered the gate and passed into the building's courtyard. It was empty. She picked the bench hit by the sun because the springtime shade still chilled. Andy scooted next to her, laying his crutch at his feet. He turned his face up to the sun, and one side of his mouth curved up in a smile.

"The sun is happy today," he said, his words coming out slow and slightly distorted by a thick tongue that seemed hard for him to control. Still, Mae was finding his words easier to understand the more she listened to him talk. She was beginning to think that his mind worked just fine, it was only his speech that lagged a bit behind. Otherwise, he was like any other seven-year-old.

"'Happy' is a good way to put it," Mae agreed, as she began paring the skin off a turnip.

"My mama is not happy," he said, turning his face toward her, the happy glow gone from his eyes. "She's mad at me. I was bad."

"I don't think you could be bad, Andy."

"But I was bad." He leaned closer, as if to tell a secret. "I went up to the third floor."

"You're not supposed to go up to the third floor?"

Andy's eyes widened and he shook his head. "No. Cap'n says I can be only in the basement and on the first floor. Now Mama's mad."

"Sometimes, mamas get angry, but they get over it. And, they always and forever love their sons," Mae said, thinking of all the time she'd spent regretting her own bursts of anger in those days after the rich mine owner had taken her boy from her life. Water under the bridge, she told herself. Sage had survived. They were together again.

"I don't like this place anymore," Andy said, more to himself than to Mae.

Mae shifted, uncomfortable at the thought of what she had to do. But, the opportunity was here. Andy was the only one among those in the kitchen who might know what occurred in the building above their heads. He was a little boy after all, so the Cap'n apparently tolerated his presence on the floors above the basement level.

"What don't you like about it?" she asked.

"The Captain is mean and some of the other kids, they are funny."

"Funny, what do you mean by 'funny'?" she probed, hoping Andy had the answers she sought stashed away in his innocent mind.

"They stay together in one room, like they are sick. They just lie on their beds. They don't talk to me."

"Maybe they are sick."

"They sleep a lot but they don't have spots or anything."

Mae thought back to the boys she'd seen in the courtyard the day before. "Does the doctor come see them?" she asked.

"Yes, Dr. Harvey comes to see them almost every day. He gives them medicine."

"There, you see, if he gives them medicine maybe they are sick," she said.

"Maybe," he echoed but he didn't sound convinced.

"What else don't you like here?"

He put his fist up to his chin, thinking. "The Cap'n. He gets mad and then he makes my mama mad."

"Is that what happened today?"

"Yup. He yelled and my mama yelled."

"What about?"

The boy lowered his eyes and said, "Me."

Mae felt a surge of anger toward the obnoxious Branch. "Why, Andy, what did you do that made him mad?"

"Like I told you, that Mister Growl caught me up on the third floor."

"Aren't you supposed to go up on the third floor?"

"Nah unh," the boy said, shaking his head.

"What were you doing up on the third floor?" she asked, looking at her hands peeling the turnip skin off in one long strip.

"Well," he said slowly, drawing out the word. "That's where those sick boys are. But I went there 'cause I heard a thumping noise and someone yelling. I thought maybe it was one of the sick boys that needed help."

"So, you wanted to help?" she asked.

He looked up, his face showing earnest. "That's just what I told Mr. Growl. That I was going to help the sick boys."

"Was it a sick boy that was yelling?"

He shook his head. "Nope, they was all sleeping when I looked in their room. I don't know who was making that noise."

"And that's why the Cap'n was yelling at your mama?"

"Yup. But he was mad already and not about me. I heard him shouting at Mr. Growl afore they caught me."

"Mr Growl, what does Mr. Growl do? What's his job?" Mae asked.

Andy started giggling, in little gasps, his eyes twisted shut. "It's funny to hear you call him Mr. Growl. That's not his real name."

"What is his real name? What does he do?"

"He walks around and growls at the boys," Andy said, the laughter drained from his voice. "I don't know his whole name but Cap'n calls him 'Giff'."

A rattling sounded outside in the street and then the court-yard gate squeaked open. Herman Eich stepped into view. He paused upon seeing the courtyard's occupants. Then he nodded gravely and advanced on the dustbin. Andy slid closer to her on the bench.

Mae quickly finished peeling the turnips. Once Eich was done rummaging through the bins and replacing their lids, she stood up. "Come on, Andy, we should go back inside."

Andy slid off the bench, and they followed the ragpicker out onto the sidewalk where Eich started stowing objects beneath the tarp he kept spread atop his pull cart.

"Mr. Eich," she called. When he turned toward them, she said, "Andy, this is Mr. Eich. He goes around and finds good things in dustbins. Things other people can use."

Andy hobbled forward and stuck out his right hand. Eich smiled and took the small hand into his own and shook it. "Pleased to meet you, young Andy. Are you helping Mrs. Clemens here with her cooking?"

"Ah, no, sir. But I was keeping her company." Although the boy's words were slurred and came painfully slow, Eich understood them because he said in that low, warm voice of his, "That is kind of you. It makes the time pass quicker when a body has company."

Andy gave the ragpicker a lopsided grin but said nothing.

Eich looked at Mae. "Looks like turnips are on the menu tonight," he observed.

"That's not all," she answered.

He nodded and glanced down at the boy whose attention had fixed on a horse-drawn trolley rolling its way toward them. Eich looked at Mae. "About eight tonight?" he asked her, in a low tone.

"Yes," she replied and tapped the boy on his shoulder. "We'd best get inside now, Andy. I've got a passel of apples to core and peel for all those pie shells I made."

They turned toward the basement door and Eich picked up the shafts of his cart and trudged up the road after the trolley.

A preoccupied Sage seated Mozart's early supper patrons. Earlier, he'd seen Eich's cart rattle past the front windows. That was Sage's cue to make for the kitchen door. Opening it, he'd found Eich bent over, going through his dustbin routine. Sage had stepped out the door, pulling it shut behind him.

"You saw her? No problems?" he asked, hearing the tension in his own voice. It was frustrating. If he wasn't in the midst of trying to stop the assassination plot, he would never leave the contacts with his mother to just Eich and Fong. The goings-on at the BCS were worrying. Men who'd exploit children were men without any moral restraint. The idea of his mother all alone in their midst, without him nearby, scared the hell out of him and he didn't care if Eich knew it.

"She's fine," the ragpicker assured him. "But, she's discovered something. We couldn't talk so I'm to see her again at eight tonight. Outside the back door of her boardinghouse. We planned that out before she started working at the BCS. It's the safest place. A high board fence surrounds the yard and there are two ways in and no one can see the back entrance from the house."

Sage could think of nothing more. He asked Eich to tell his mother to be very careful and to leave the BCS at once if she felt in any danger whatsoever. Eich smiled gently. "Your mother's a resourceful woman," he said. "And, she's smarter and tougher than most men, even if she has a gentle heart."

Their exchange two hours ago hadn't done all that much to reassure Sage. Mae Clemens could also be heedlessly bull-headed when her mind was set on a course of action. He heard her likely reply to that observation ring clearly in his head, "Yup. That makes you one apple who didn't fall far from the tree, right, Sage?"

Mozart's front door opened, intruding on this inner dialogue. In stepped McAllister with another man. The lawyer's companion was neatly dressed, clean shaven, average in height and weight and unremarkable except for vivid green eyes that sparkled with humor.

Sage led the two men to a table. McAllister seemed to be bristling with an air of suppressed excitement and his smile reached his eyes. After being seated, McAllister gestured across the table toward his companion. "Mr. Adair, I'd like you to meet a very good friend of mine, Robert Clooney. He's debating whether to make Portland his home." McAllister grinned at his companion who grinned back at him.

Sage shook hands with Clooney, noticing, as he did so, a white bandage on the back of the man's hand.

"Looks like you've injured your hand, Mr. Clooney. Hope it's nothing serious."

The other man smiled ruefully. "It's not too bad. I learned that I shouldn't try to light a fire with gasoline. Burns like the holy dickens."

Sage sent a sharp questioning glance at McAllister. The lawyer's blue eyes locked on his with an intensity that affirmed Sage's unspoken question.

Sage laughed, "I've concluded fire starting is an art form. It takes plenty of practice to master it. Luckily, it's not often that I'm called upon to do it. Otherwise, I might have to resort to using gasoline myself."

McAllister interrupted. "Robert here is staying with my wife and me until he can find appropriate lodging in a boarding house. Angelique is delighted that he is considering actually moving here to Portland. She's known him for many years also. James, her first husband, Robert, and I, were all in law school together. Before that, all three of us were in the same grade at a boys' preparatory school." The lawyer and his friend exchanged glances once again.

"Portland may acquire another lawyer?" Sage asked.

Clooney lifted his shoulders, saying, "Yes, well, I'm thinking about it. But I'm not one to enjoy the rough and tumble of litigation. My practice focuses more on wills, estate planning and business contracts. If I decide to move here, I'll leave the litigation side to E.J."

McAllister interrupted. "Say, Adair. I don't know what you said to Fenton but he's showered me with invitations. I am having dinner with him and his companions at the Portland Hotel tomorrow night. And Friday afternoon, I'll be golfing with him and a few others at the Waverley club. I expect to learn quite a bit. Maybe, I'll drop in here on Friday night."

The lawyer's meaning was clear. By Friday night, he intended to know which of the city's power brokers would be entertaining a guest during Roosevelt's visit.

The waiter arrived with menus and Sage returned to the front door to greet and seat a large party. Over the next hour, he kept an eye on McAllister and his guest. He observed the intensity of their conversation, the way they leaned toward each other across the table, McAllister's air of suppressed elation. When the lawyers' meals arrived, Sage gestured for Horace.

"Please serve a bottle of champagne to Mr. McAllister and his guest. Compliments of the house."

Sage watched as surprise, then pleasure, brightened the men's faces. McAllister flushed and grinned widely as both men saluted Sage with their flutes of champagne.

Sage smiled back, aware of a twinge of sorrow tightening his throat. Living a secret life is hard when it's a matter of choice. Being forced to hide the essence of who you are, that has to be worse. Much worse.

He gave himself a mental shake. Enough of his brooding. His mother was right; if you can't do nothing to fix it, no point in dwelling on it. Better to put some thought into their mission instead.

By Saturday, thanks to McAllister, they should know which trust representatives might be entertaining an assassination mastermind in the bosom of their home. With that information, they could narrow their search down to the guests of just those men. There wasn't much time left. In eleven days, Roosevelt's train was going to be pulling into Portland.

FOURTEEN

Dispatch: *May 11, 1903, President's train arrives in San Jose, California.*

> "*. . . it is for us to stand for the indivisible nation, for liberty under and through the law and for brotherhood in its widest, deepest and truest sense, the brotherhood which will not suffer harmful wrong and will not inflict it.*" —T.R.

HIS CLIENT MUST HAVE DECIDED to get a little exercise because, this time, they met outdoors in New York City's Central Park. He was easy to spot. It was a warm night, yet he was wearing a black cashmere overcoat and long white silk scarf.

"Right on time, I see," was the client's greeting and he gestured to a nearby park bench. The words carried that look-down-his-nose arrogance calculated to set a man's teeth on edge and ball up his fists. Maybe the arrogant so-and-so was a duke or something back in the old country.

Still the mercenary said nothing. He perched on the edge of the bench until he realized that his toes were clenching the ground through his shoes, as if preparing to propel him toward the client's throat. Slowly, he released his breath and eased himself backwards until the bench hit his shoulder blades.

"I am afraid I don't have all good news," he said, as the client pulled a paper sack from a capacious coat pocket. Long fingers, clad in thin leather gloves, dipped into the sack and emerged holding a handful of dried corn kernels that he began casting to the pavement.

"Spit it out. Vhat is the news?" said the client without looking at him. He seemed mesmerized by the small herd of pigeons, sporting pink, gray and green iridescent feathers, stepping eagerly toward the corn.

"Well, the Dickenson agency has a man planted inside St. Alban's camp."

"St. Alban, the labor leader you told me about last time?" This time the client turned the full effect of an icy stare on his companion.

"Right, St. Alban. Also known as the 'Saint' by his followers."

His client nodded slowly, "Yes, I see. And so, I suppose you haf managed to recover some information about this so-called "Saint" from the spy in the labor organization?" The client mispronounced "have" as "haf." Definitely Austrian, German or Swiss raised, the mercenary mused. Out loud he said, instead, "Well, information not from the spy himself but from someone very close to him. My informant has always been very reliable."

"Are you telling me you haf managed to insert a spy into the Dickenson operation?"

For the first time, confidence straightened the other man's spine. "Had him on my payroll for some time now. I never know when I'll be working on the same project as the Dickensons and the monthly retainer to my inside fellow doesn't cost all that much. He's been worth it more than once," he added.

His client said nothing, merely cocked an eyebrow and jutted his face forward in irritation, "Get on with it, sir. This isn't one of your American penny dreadfuls, where you must prolong the suspense to keep my interest," he finally snapped.

The mercenary continued, "Like I told you last time, St. Alban knows about our plans for the president. Unfortunately, what I learned is that he knows more than we thought–but only that our action will happen in Portland. He is also certain that we've figured out a way to put the blame on the unions." What color there was drained from his client's face.

"Not as bad as it sounds," he rushed to reassure. "Yes, St. Alban now knows someone is planning to hit Roosevelt while he's in Portland and that more than one player is involved. But, St. Alban doesn't know who, when or how our men will act. And, my Dickenson informant will keep me apprised. If St. Alban learns more, my informant will tell me."

The mercenary crossed his arms and stretched out a highly polished boot. He waggled it back and forth as if admiring its sheen. "The good news is that the Dickenson agency is not taking the St. Alban information seriously," he said. "They're hearing about so many plots all across the country that they aren't giving St. Alban's report any special attention. I've done my best to spread rumors of numerous assassination plots everywhere but in Portland. With Roosevelt traveling 14,000 miles, I've got plenty of places to send them looking. Besides, the Secret Service is using Dickenson agents already as part of the presidential advance team in every city. I expect they're confident that they're already situated to stop any attack on Roosevelt no matter where it happens."

The client was not reassured. "To hell with the Dickenson company. What are St. Alban's plans? He's the one to worry about. He knows too much of our plan and those damn union sympathizers are everywhere. Has he conveyed his information to the Secret Service?"

"My contact doesn't think so. St. Alban is skeptical of the Secret Service's willingness to treat the threat seriously or to handle it correctly even if they do believe it exists—which is justified since the alert would be coming from a labor union leader," he said, taking out a slim cigar and lighting it. "And remember, St. Alban doesn't have any proof to show them. Just secondhand information from a dead prostitute." The memory of those wildly rolling eyes in the moments before the woman died seized hold of the mercenary's mind before he could blank it away.

His client shifted on the bench. "What are St. Alban plans? Spit it out. I don't appreciate getting my information piecemeal.

Like I said, this is not one of those penny dreadful booklets you Americans waste your time on." His snippy tone managed to convey irritation, insult and threat.

The mercenary found that he'd slid forward on the bench again. He stayed there, saying with forced calmness, "Like I told you last time, St. Alban has sent one of his trusted lieutenants out to Portland. He's supposed to work with some of the locals out there to find our local contact and prevent the assassination."

"Who is this lieutenant of your so-called Saint? Do you know any more about him than you did five days ago?" Anger made the client's accent more clipped, guttural and imperious.

"I know a lot more. All I need. His name's Meachum and I've got a good description. My men are already out there. We wanted them in place long before the Secret Service and local police went on the lookout for unsavory strangers. I telegraphed them his description so they are already hunting for this Meachum character. They'll find him and put him out of action. Maybe they already have."

"Vell, they damn well better find him and stop him. I'm not afraid of the police or the Secret Service. They won't suspect a plot involving so many people. They're going to be on the lookout for a single, crazed fanatic. But St. Alban and his man know different. They are the real threat." That word hung between them, midst the sound of a barking dog and a playing child's shrieks.

The client turned to face the mercenary straight on. "We cannot fail in our mission. The men at the top, my bosses, will not accept failure—mine or yours," he said. For the first time, the mercenary detected fear in the man's voice.

They both rose to their feet. The client carefully stripped off his gloves and shoved them into the empty paper sack. He looked at the pigeon flock and smiled.

"I thought you didn't like pigeons," the mercenary commented.

"I hate them. They are disgusting vermin." Then awareness sharpened the client's eyes. "Do not be a fool. There vas strychnine on that corn," he snapped, turned on his heel and strode off without looking back, pausing only to drop the empty bag with its leather gloves into a trash can

"Thought you said it wasn't 'sporting' to poison them," the mercenary mimicked the guttural accent in a low voice. "Don't know why you think you can come here and kill our birds," he said a little louder, braver now that the client was beyond hearing range. Then he thought of how much money the client was paying him for this job.

"On the other hand, they are just vermin," he told himself as he stepped off in the opposite direction without a backward glance at the doomed birds.

Portland, Oregon May 11, 1903

"Hey, this beer is way better than usual," Sage commented to the barkeep as soon as the man had moved close enough to hear over the din. The saloon had invested in a row of electric globes that lit up the room. It was a good commercial decision since the place was packed. Many customers were taking advantage of the brighter light to play card games.

"Glad you like it. My uncle makes it in the cellar of his saloon out Silverton way."

"Bet your uncle's name is Einar. I thought this had a familiar taste."

"You know my uncle?" The barkeep looked pleased.

"I had the pleasure of drinking his beer last summer. Spent the night there with him and your aunt."

"That'd be my Aunt Pru. She rules the roost. Hey, my name's Mike." The barkeep switched his rag to his other hand and shook Sage's with a firm, friendly grip.

"All I can say about your Aunt Pru is she sure can cook."

Mike rolled his eyes. "You have any of her pie?" When Sage shook his head, Mike said, "That's too bad. My mom always says Pru is the best cook in the family and Ma's cooking is pretty damn good."

His chitchat with Mike the barkeep postponed his worry over Meachum's failure to appear. But even so, their conversation ran dry before the beer was gone from the mug's bottom. By midpoint in his second beer, Sage was shifting on his feet, trying to ease the building tension in his limbs. A minute later, Meachum walked through the door and Sage exhaled his relief with a whoosh.

He signaled Mike for another beer and once it arrived, Meachum took a gulp, wiping the foam off his lips with his sleeve.

"Where've you been, Meach?" Sage asked. "I was starting to get worried. How come your face is red?"

"It's red because I just crawled over the back fence. Whew, I must have ate too much this winter."

"Was there a particular reason you climbed over the fence? Or are you just practicing your freight-hopping skills?"

"It felt like someone was following me but, when I looked back, I didn't see anybody in particular. I decided to act like I was being followed, just in case. Didn't want to lead them to you."

Sage straightened, took a look at the other patrons in the saloon and tried to remember if anyone had followed Meachum in.

Meachum shook his head. "I've been watching that door ever since I got here," he said, nodding at the huge mirror behind the bar. By looking straight ahead, it was possible to watch the saloon's front entrance. "Nobody followed me in."

"Why did you think someone was trailing you?"

Meachum took another gulp. "It's this feeling I get. Like my tail bone's suddenly sat itself down in a mound of snow. I've learned to pay attention to it."

"Mister Fong says that's about knowing, without the knowing why."

"It's kept me ahead of the fox hounds more than once," Meachum said as he rolled the glass between his palms. He looked up, cleared his throat, and said in a stronger voice, "Anyway, we haven't had much luck tracking down any small group of would-be assassin accomplices. Tomorrow we're going to hit the public baths, the cheap food places and some of the boarding houses. We figure that wherever they are, they're likely hanging out together."

Sage told Meachum about the happenings at the BCS and also about McAllister's plans to infiltrate the group of trust representatives who were busy planning Roosevelt's visit. Sage stayed silent about McAllister's private life. Meachum was no innocent. Men being with other men wasn't all that unusual in this part of the country where males outnumbered females fifteen to one. Still, that was McAllister's secret to tell.

Sage waited a minute after Meachum left before following him out the door. He reached the sidewalk just in time to see Meachum turn the corner. Sage picked up his pace. He intended to follow the man all the way to his hotel. When he reached the corner and looked up the street, Meachum was nowhere in sight. Yet his hotel was at least three blocks farther on.

Sage began stepping softly along the edges of the boardwalk, staying close to the front of the brick building that housed an outfitter's store. Reaching the front door alcove he paused to listen. Nothing. Only silence. He peered through the glass door into darkness, seeing nothing to indicate Meachum had been forced inside. He quickly moved along the boardwalk. As he reached the building's corner, he heard the distinct sound of a bottle smashing. Someone was there in the dark, alongside the building, back where the only light came from the street.

He slid around the corner, keeping his back pressed against the brick. Stepping with great deliberation, he tried not to alert those at the rear of the building to his presence. His eyes at last dilated so that he could make out three human figures. He froze. They couldn't help but see his figure outlined against the brighter light out on the street. But they didn't rush toward him. Straining to see, he realized that all three were facing away from him. They were looking instead at a man they'd trapped at the alley's end, only the pale outline of his face visible. Meachum, it must be Meachum. A high wooden fence was at his back. His hand clutched the end of a broken whiskey bottle. As Sage watched, that same hand moved awkwardly to press against his other arm that dangled limply at his side. Meachum was hurt. "You mugs are real brave, aren't you," the injured man taunted, "three against one."

"Don't take it personal, Meachum, just doin' our job," said one of the three.

Sage silently stepped toward the middle of the alley and advanced on the tableau. He wasn't worried that Meachum's attackers would turn to see him. Their attention remained fixed on their prey with all the intensity of cats studying a cornered mouse.

Wordlessly, the three men stepped apart until they stood evenly spaced across the alley. Their movements were relaxed, calm, practiced.

Sage moved soundlessly forward. He could hear Fong's words whispering in his head, "Surprise is very important strategy. Make best of it."

The man in the middle staggered, whirling away to crash against the wall, when Sage's heel kick landed in the center of his back. He recovered quickly, however, because in the next instant, the man's left hand held a knife. Steel glittered in the faint light bright as a newly minted coin dropped into an empty coal bucket.

FIFTEEN

Dispatch: *May 12, 1903, President's train arrives in San Francisco, California.*

"No people is wholly civilized where a distinction is drawn between stealing an office and stealing a purse." —T.R.

SAGE QUICKLY STEPPED BACK. The man's knife was a bear sticker, not a potato peeler. The blade looked nine inches long and needle sharp. Fear gripped him momentarily only to be edged out by a vivid memory. There'd been a session with Fong where they had practiced with wooden knives. Fong's calm words were part of that memory, "Mind must control body. If mind sticks to knife, knife will cut you. If mind freezes at sight of knife, body freezes too. Keep mind moving past knife, to opponent's body. You stop body, you stop knife."

That thought cleared the fear from his mind, just as if a door opened to let in a blast of wind. Sage looked beyond the blade at the attacker's stance, the balance of his body. It showed an unpreparedness, a sloppy over-dependence on his weapon.

His attacker lunged forward, knife point aimed at Sage's stomach. Sage twisted his body to the left. With his left hand he grabbed the attacker's knife wrist and pulled down. The blade flashed past Sage's belly and kept on going. Sage stepped forward, placing his right foot behind the man's left leg just as his right arm shot up to shove against the man's left shoulder. Sage's right leg flexed against the back of the man's left leg, uprooting him. The attacker was down on the ground, his knife clattering away into the dark. A passable "slant flying" maneuver, Sage noted.

His attacker didn't stay down. He regained his feet, but now had no knife. The man began shuffling warily towards Sage. At the edges of his vision, Sage registered that the two other bad guys stood immobile, whether in shock or merely to wait for their friend's eventual triumph wasn't clear. He also saw that Meachum had slid down the fence to sit on the ground, his good hand pressing against his upper arm, the top of the broken whiskey bottle now at his side.

The only near sounds breaking the silence were the scrape of the attacker's boots as he cautiously advanced and his labored breathing. Sage noticed that his own breath was deep and steady. Good. Fong would approve.

The other man's hat had fallen off his head so that, for the first time, Sage could see his face. It was expressionless, cold, professional. But a glittering from the heart of his deep eye sockets telegraphed anger.

"Good," Sage thought. "Easy to fool an angry mind with fake action. Surprise is weapon." Another of Fong's sayings. Sage moved his left foot forward to rest softly on the ground. He extended his left arm in front of his face, as if readying to block a blow. His attacker saw this as an opportunity. He grabbed Sage's wrist and reared his right arm back to increase the power of the punch he planned to deliver into Sage's face.

Sage's mind imagined and his body reacted. His left hand raised and rotated until his palm faced upwards. The first move in "step back, repulse monkey." That action reversed the grab. Now it was Sage's hand gripping the other's wrist even as Sage's left leg lifted and stepped back, sinking his weight to the rear. Once again, the attacker fell forward, out of control. A firm right hand into his armpit and he hit the ground once again. This time, it took him longer to gain his footing. There was a rustle as the other two attackers shifted their weight. Still, they didn't move forward, they seemed uncertain about whether to join the fray.

This time the attacker staggered when he regained his feet. His left swing was so clumsy that Sage easily intercepted it with his right forearm. Even as he did so, he rolled back, pulling the attacker down and to the left. Sage's left knee snapped up into the man's groin as he held the man's arm low. As the man sagged toward the ground, Sage twisted the arm sharply and heard a crack as the elbow dislocated. The man dropped to the ground with a guttural scream. He was out of commission. His cry finally spurred the other two men into action. They began cautiously advancing.

Sage glanced toward Meachum who slumped motionless but his eyes were open and alert. Sage switched his attention back to the remaining two attackers. He stepped back. Maybe a "Sweeping Lotus" kick could drop one of them quickly if he managed to hit a knee. His own breathing was heavier but he released that thought. A clear mind. That's what he needed.

The attackers were on either side now. This was going to be tricky. He couldn't watch both of them at the same time. "No" Fong's voice said, don't just "watch." Instead, "open all senses." Sage flicked away all thoughts of the pain that might come and once again, Fong's voice was there, "Be brave, do not hesitate."

Just as he stepped back, loosened his waist and lowered his shoulders a puff of air hit the left side of his face. Even as he whirled to meet this new threat, the moving air had transformed itself into Fong. He swiftly glided past Sage with the grace of a fish through calm water. In the dim light, the Chinese man's impassive face conveyed a warrior's intensity–his half-lidded eyes focused on nothing, seeing everything as he stood in front of the downed Meachum and faced the two men. Then Fong was a black blur, every limb slicing through the air. Hard flesh smacked soft, followed by "oofs" of expelled air and finally high-pitched screams as bones cracked. All in less than a minute.

Now all three attackers were writhing on the ground. But not for long. Each man struggled upright, using only three sound limbs. Seconds later, the three had staggered out the alley's end and vanished from sight. Sage and Fong watched them go.

"Lord have mercy," came Meachum's weak voice from where he still sat on the ground. "Mr. Fong, I have never seen the like. You nearly killed them with one blow. And you, Adair, I thought you were a gonner. The guy with the knife was fast. He got me before I ever saw it."

"Yes, he is not bad student," Fong said, giving Sage a pat on the shoulder.

Sage rolled his eyes at his teacher, who merely smiled at him before commenting with smug satisfaction, "One has broke arm, two have broke foots. Should be easy to spot."

Meachum closed his eyes. An inspection of his wound in the dim alley showed that blood still flowed from a cut in his coat sleeve. He was only partially conscious as Sage and Fong hefted him to his feet. Like three drunks they shuffled, their arms wrapped about each other, down the alley and toward the street. Meachum's toes trailed more than stepped.

Fortunately, the New Elijah hotel was just a few blocks away. When Angus Solomon wasn't seating privileged white patrons in the Portland Hotel's exclusive dining room, he was at the New Elijah. That hotel provided bed and board to a steady stream of black porters whose railroading work regularly took them through Portland.

While Sage waited outside with Meachum, in yet another North End alley, Fong slipped into the hotel's kitchen. Minutes later, Fong opened a side door, stuck his head out and beckoned them inside. A few steps more and they were in Solomon's apartment on the hotel's ground floor, just to the left side of the front desk. Solomon guided Meachum to a brocade divan and covered him with a blanket.

Like an angel of mercy, Miz Esther immediately appeared. She carried strips of torn but clean cotton cloth and a tin basin of warm water. The touch of her hands looked gentle as a mother's with her newborn babe. Her rich voice kept up a soft murmur as she cut away Meachum's coat and shirt. Meachum groaned when she finally freed his arm. She began to carefully clean the stab wound that slashed a long tear down the thick part of Meachum's upper arm. Thankfully, the blade had missed both bone and major artery. Satisfaction surged through Sage at the thought that he'd probably torn that knife-wielding thug's elbow apart. It would be a long time before the man could stab someone else using that arm. Maybe never. Sage hoped the dirty rat was suffering even more than Meachum.

Sage, Solomon and Fong soon retreated into a corner of the hotel dining room where they drank hot coffee and filled their bellies with newly baked bread and raspberry preserves. They told Solomon about the attackers and their own efforts at defense. The room was empty. All the train porters were fast asleep in their upstairs rooms. Only a few hours remained before they'd be up and ready to mount the steel steps of the train cars heading north, south or toward the rising sun up the Columbia River Gorge.

Solomon, in turn, explained to Fong how he had met with the hotel staff and everyone was now on the alert for a hotel guest who entertained rough visitors. "You and Mr. Adair have now made our job much easier. Men who have broken arms or who limp down the hotel's corridors will be much more noticeable."

Sage had a thought. "Mr. Fong, how did you manage to find us back in that alley?"

"My cousins and I search North End for men who might start fuss in crowd around president. I tell cousins, if they see you, they should follow. Make sure you get out of North End safe. One of them saw you go in alley. Ran to get me."

"I am glad he did. I wasn't sure I was up to fighting off both of them."

Fong tilted his head to one side, studying Sage. "You did good job with first man. Nice start with Slant Flying."

"You were there? Right from the beginning?"

"I was less than block away when you went into alley. My cousin run fast, so do I," he added.

"Why didn't you come help me right away?"

"Chance to see if you learn Snake and Crane properly."

"So why didn't you wait until I really got into trouble?"

"Saw Mr. Meachum slide to down on ground. More important we finish fast. Find him help."

Solomon cleared his throat and they both looked at the South Carolinian. "The attack on Mr. Meachum concerns me," he told them, his face somber. "We best conclude that someone is aware of our intent to thwart the Roosevelt assassination."

Sage and Fong exchanged perplexed looks that turned considering. Sage spoke first, "Nah, it was just a mugging. Rough boys looking for someone to rob." Even as he spoke, he knew his words were no more than whistling in the dark.

Solomon shook his head. "Think about it, Adair. It was three men against one," he said. "There was no need to first stab Meachum if their intent was simply to rob him. Besides, you said when you came upon the scene, you heard one of them call Meachum by name. I fear that the only conclusion one can draw from the attack on Mr. Meachum is that they planned the attack and that they intended it to be fatal. It would be foolish to conclude otherwise."

Silence followed this pronouncement. Drunken shouts in the street outside drifted into the empty dining room. "Mr. Solomon is right," Fong said, his voice calm and sure. "Opportunity of surprise now lost. Assassins know we are looking for them."

SIXTEEN

Dispatch: *May 12, 1903, President's train remains in San Francisco.*

> *"I wish to see the average American take, in reference to his fellows, the attitude that . . . scorns injustice by the strong or doing injustice to the weak." —T.R.*

MAYBE HE SHOULDN'T HAVE DRUNK that third cup of coffee. His fingers twitched to grab something and choke the life out of it. He knocked, the door opened and he entered even as the client crossed the room to fling himself into the armchair by the window.

His lordly way hadn't improved. He made no attempt at civility. "I can see from your mealy-mouthed expression that our plans are running into problems out there in that backwater town," was the man's snide remark. "You must get control, right away or else," he added with a biting hiss.

The mercenary had removed his hat and was twirling the brim round about with his hands.

"Stop playing with that damned hat and tell me what is going on!" Now the client's voice was a near shout.

The mercenary cleared his throat and, as the man in the chair stiffened, he hurried on to say, "We didn't get Meachum.

The telegram didn't say much more except something about getting jumped, hurt and that the Chinese are involved."

"'Chinese!' There's no way the Chinese are going to be involved with this. Stop trying to get more money out of us with these outlandish excuses."

The mercenary's chin raised and, for just a moment, his eyes held an unholy glitter that sent the other man back against his chair cushion. When the mercenary spoke, however, his voice was mild, level. "I am leaving New York City on the train today so I will arrive on the scene in just a few days. I don't know why my men failed to get Meachum. He had help that's for sure. I plan on finding out just who is helping him and take care of them too. Roosevelt will die in Portland." With that, the mercenary clapped his hat back onto his head, turned on his heel, opened the door.

Behind him a querulous voice said from the depths of the chair, "We want him dead. You better make sure that happens if you know what's good for you!"

The mercenary said nothing. He just stepped into the hall and pulled the door softly closed, leaving behind the smoky room and the spluttering man.

"Damn foreigner gets mad and forgets how to talk, 'Ve vant him dead,'" the mercenary mocked once he'd moved well down the hallway.

Portland, Oregon, May 13, 1903

Eich's cart rolled down the middle of the cobbled street in the residential area that lay northwest of downtown. He had only one more house to visit on 20th Street. It had been one of those changeable days. Sometimes, he kept his head bent low to avoid the fine but dense drops of a sudden spring squall. Then a breeze would stir up to shove the clouds aside and he could enjoy warming sunlight on his upturned face. The glistening droplets seemed to intensify the beauty of the flowering trees. Portland's grandest springtime offering were its trees blossoming into gigantic, scented bouquets of color.

"Old man! Looks like you took a wrong turn! This isn't the North End," came a jeering, pipsqueak voice off to Eich's right. Hoots of derision followed. Eich looked toward the well-to-do residence. A boy of about twelve stood on its wide veranda, hands on his hips, his upper lip raised in a sneer. Standing beside him were two other boys. One of them, his voice even more reedy than the first's, raised his voice to call, "Maybe he's hunting for a bush to set up house under! Is that why you're rolling your garbage down our street, old man?" The three guffawed again.

Eich said nothing, his tired feet trudging forward at the same steady pace but his hands tightened on the cart shafts. Boys in the North End have better manners, he observed to himself.

The door of the house opened and a shrill woman's voice called out, "Rupert, don't you be talking to bums like that! He could be crazy. You boys come inside!" There was grumbling but the three obeyed and the door slammed shut.

"Why is it that petty cruelty flourishes strongest in those whose lives are the easiest?" Eich asked a red-breasted robin. The bird paused in its worm hunt to gaze at him with one bright black eye, its head cocked to the side as if contemplating the ragpicker's question. Eich laughed aloud. "Maybe I am crazy. Because, for a minute there, Mrs. Bird, I actually thought you might answer."

The alley privet hedge was abloom with small white flowers midst shiny dark leaves. The opening into the kitchen garden was wide enough for his cart to roll through and up to the kitchen porch. This was the last house he had to visit. That was a blessing. He must have walked at least six miles today and his feet within his worn boots were sending up painful protests. And, he still had two miles to make it back home. But, if he could learn something here at the Holmans' mansion, his pain would be worth it.

He lifted the dustbin lid and carefully dug among its contents. Just as he finished his unsuccessful inspection the screen door on the porch slapped shut.

"Oh, Mr. Eich, you didn't need to dig in the rubbish. I've set aside all the good stuff for you." Eich turned to see the housemaid, Sarah, standing on the porch nodding toward a burlap bag on the porch floor. In her hands she held a gold-edged plate and a small bowl. He moved to the bottom step, picked up the burlap bag and tucked it into his cart. "Thank you," he said and tenderly took the dishes in his rough hands. The bowl had a hairline crack that probably let its contents seep. A significant chip marred the plate's rim. He could fix both.

He looked up at the expectant housemaid. Repairing damaged things and returning them to use, especially chinaware, was both his skill and his offering to the world. "Things of beauty must always be treasured and preserved—handmade plates, majestic trees, the human spirit," he thought. "She recognizes that, I think."

"My, my," he said, studying the objects he held. "These are quite beautiful. French, I think."

She smiled happily. "Can you fix them? The housekeeper told me to toss them out. But, if you can fix them for me, I would be ever so grateful. My sister is getting married and she has barely nothing to decorate her rooms and these were so pretty before they got broke."

Eich returned the smile. "Why, Miss Sarah, I think these are easily fixed. What do you say to twenty cents each?"

"Oh! That would be great. Me and Edgar, we don't make all that much working here and I so want to give Sally something she will treasure as a wedding present."

Eich nodded. "Call it done then. I can return them to you about six days from now. I'm somewhat busy at the moment. Will that be soon enough?"

"Six days is plenty early. She's not getting married until next month."

"You keeping pretty busy?" Eich asked, as he carefully wrapped the dishes in a length of cloth and stowed them away.

"Lordy, yes. The master is all in a dither because President Roosevelt is coming soon and Mr. Holman is helping to plan the events." Sarah's pride at working for such an important man was always readily evident. And, fortunately, her pride was un-tainted by any hint of the abuse that so many household servants endured.

"Mr. Holman probably has out-of-town guests who are hoping to meet the president I suspect."

Sarah nodded her head. "Only one couple, though, is plan-ning to come stay."

"Oregonians or from Seattle maybe?"

"No, they're coming from all the way back East and plan to stay for at least two weeks. We've been airing the guest room and beating the rugs."

"Oh, relatives. That will be nice for the Holmans."

Sarah shook her head, "No, not relatives. And, I'm glad of that. The Holman kin from back East are more than a bit snooty. The missus even gets upset at their bad ways. Nope, the man who is coming is an important financial man. His coming's got Mr. Holman in one heck of a tizzy, I tell you," she said.

Mae Clemens stood at the kitchen sink with her back to everyone else. Behind her came the thump of the rolling pin as Mrs. Wiggit rushed to get her meat pies in the oven. Gussie was at the table peeling and chopping the vegetables and Andy's slurred chatter described the bugs he'd discovered in the courtyard.

"Don't have a choice," Mae grimly told herself as she stuck her finger in her mouth to tickle the back of her throat. She heaved again.

Mrs. Wiggit appeared at her side. "Good God, woman. You sure you ain't sick with something? That's the third time you upchucked."

Mae shook her head, "It was the bacon I ate back at the boardinghouse this morning. It tasted a bit off," she lied. "It's given me the devil of a headache. I am sure I'll be over it in an hour or so."

"Well, you're no help to us now. And, listening to you throwing up is not my idea of a good morning," came Mrs.

Wiggit's unsympathetic response. She strode over to a cupboard, opened the door and took a small vial off the top shelf. "Here," she said handing the vial to Mae, "that Dr. Harvey left this lying about. I picked it up so Andy wouldn't get into it. Laudanum. Should help kill that headache." Mrs. Wiggit turned back toward the kitchen, "Andy! Come take Mrs. Clemens to our room so she can lie down." To Mae she said, "You ain't no good to us, puking all the time. And we are really going to need your help for supper. It's another one of the Cap'n big to-do's for his men friends. Take the laudanum, lie down and I'll come check on you in an hour."

Mae allowed Andy to escort her from the kitchen, their exit accompanied by Mrs. Wiggit's admonition to Andy that he was to "come right back and not bother Mrs. Clemens with all his chatter."

The cook's quarters consisted of just two rooms, their concrete walls painted white. A gloomy light filtered in through two windows tucked inside deep window wells. One room was a sitting room with a large rocker, a small rocker, an end table, a few oil lamps and a book shelf.

Andy ushered her into the other room. It held two twin beds standing close enough together that their occupants' hands could touch. A wooden bar, suspended from the ceiling rafters, supported a few dresses and boy-sized shirts. A scarred highboy dresser stood in the corner. A conservative black felt hat sporting a large purple silk flower was the room's only spot of color.

"You can lay down on my bed," Andy offered shyly and gesturing to the bed occupied by a stuffed rabbit of faded blue gingham. "Rabbie will help you sleep if you hug him tight. That's what I do," he solemnly advised.

Once Andy had headed back to the kitchen, Mae got up from the bed and put the laudanum on the dresser out of Andy's reach. She didn't need it. The only thing that hurt was her raw throat and swallowing the liquid opium wouldn't do much for that. It would only make her woolly-headed. She stepped back into the sitting room. Here, some effort had been made at decoration. There was a braided rag rug of bright hues. And two rockers sported matching braided cushions. Mrs. Wiggit's work, without a doubt. There was a picture on the wall, hanging from a nail driven deeply into the concrete. It depicted a country scene where rosebushes lined a dirt path that wound toward a neat little cottage tucked beneath towering chestnut trees. Given its place of prominence, this might be Mrs. Wiggit's most prized possession. After Andy, that is.

Mae stepped closer to the bookshelf and ran her finger along the spines. A well-worn Bible was the biggest. After that, all the rest were children's books–"Happy Hearts and Lively Times," "Picture Book Garden," "The Big ABC Book" and even that brand new one called "Puss in Boots." Books were obviously Mrs. Wiggit's one indulgence. No surprise that it obviously involved Andy.

Mae stepped to the door, opened it a crack and listened. She could hear sounds in the kitchen accompanied by murmurs of conversation between Andy and his mother. Mae hated deceiving the woman. Despite Mrs. Wiggit's rough manner, she was a good, fair boss who never asked anyone to work harder than she did. That was a rarity.

But deception was necessary. As she'd approached the BCS that morning, Mae had spotted the Cap'n and his thug, Mr. Growl, hurrying away down the sidewalk toward the downtown. When she'd mentioned it to Mrs. Wiggit, the cook had replied, "Yes, once a month the two of them take off for the whole morning. I don't know where they go but I suspect it's some kind of business meeting. The Cap'n was more than grumpy this morning and with this big supper coming up, I'm glad he'll not be underfoot."

Those words had given birth to Mae's pretend headache and subsequent finger down the throat antics. Mae had read Mrs. Wiggit right. The woman needed help for the supper. But, her gruff exterior was wrapped around a core of basic kindness. The outcome was just what she hoped. An opportunity to be out of the kitchen and closer to the door upstairs. She figured she had no more than thirty minutes for a look-see.

Mae stepped into the corridor, listened again and pulled the door shut behind her so that the latch clicked softly. On tiptoes, she moved toward the closed door in the opposite direction from the kitchen. Beyond that door was the stairwell that rose up from the basement to the top floor. And, that's where she intended to start snooping, the top floor. From what Andy had told her, there'd be fewer people wandering the hallways up there.

Sage was standing at the podium, marveling that his body felt no ill effects from the night's adventures. Unfortunately, Meachum couldn't say that. Miz Esther had refused to relinquish her patient, insisting that she needed to watch him closely to prevent infection. Solomon said Meachum was welcome to stay and so Sage and Fong had left him in the nurse's capable hands. Now, Sage was rethinking the fight of the night before, wishing he'd caused the knife-wielding attacker greater harm. The door opened and McAllister walked in.

"Good day," said the lawyer. "I cannot stay to eat. I'm on my way to meet Fenton. We're going to ride out to the country club together. I wanted to know whether we might meet sometime soon?"

"Mr. Fong and I were talking about that very thing this morning. We had a bit of a dustup last night that we should discuss. What about tomorrow night, say seven o'clock, at Eich's place?"

"That sounds good. Um, I also wanted to thank you for your kindness to myself and Mr. Clooney last night."

Before Sage could answer, a couple entered and McAllister stepped aside. Once Sage had seated the new arrivals, he returned to where McAllister stood waiting. Sage had been glad of the interruption. He'd needed time to think out his response because he felt that the air needed to be completely cleared and in a way that did not offend McAllister.

"E.J.," Sage began, "what matters to me is that people are kind to each other. What I hope for everyone, including myself, is that we find love. It's none of my business who a person finds to love as long as no one is hurt. I figure God, if one exists, doesn't make mistakes. And some of us, for reasons I will never fathom, are given harder roads to walk than others. Who knows, maybe those Eastern religions are right. Maybe some of us actually chose to walk harder roads than others. Maybe those who do are the most courageous spirits of all. So, that champagne last night was my way of saying 'congratulations.' I am glad that you have someone."

McAllister's face relaxed and for the first since he arrived, his smile was easy. "I'll thank you for that fine speech, Mr. Adair. It means a lot to me. More than you can know." With that, he shook hands, clapped his homburg onto his head and left.

Sage mulled over the speech he'd made to the troubled lawyer and thought of Lucinda Collins, the woman who'd slipped out of his own grasp. "Of course, you have to be smart enough to recognize that someone when you see them. Otherwise, all the pretty words in the world won't make a damn bit of difference," he told himself bitterly.

SEVENTEEN

Dispatch: *May 13, 1903, President crosses the Bay to visit Oakland, California.*

> *"What counts most is the honesty, the courage, the common sense, and the capacity for hard work of the average man. Nothing can take the place of those qualities in the average man." —T.R.*

MEACHUM WAS TELLING THE TALE of how his arm came to be bound up in a neat white sling. Miz Esther's handiwork without a doubt. Sage did not join the conversation. Instead, he paced the fir floorboards of Eich's tiny shack. "Where was she? Those three words kept silently repeating in time with his steps. She knew we were supposed to meet here at 7:00 p.m.. He slipped his pocket watch out. Seven thirty already. She was never late. She knew how they'd worry. Sage reached the door. This time he opened it and stepped out into a mild May evening. He stepped along the side of the shack and attached house until he could see up the dirt road in the direction of downtown. There were people out and about but no Mae Clemens. He pulled out the pocket watch again. Seven thirty two.

When he stepped back inside, Eich's eyes met his own. Sage shook his head. The ragpicker poet frowned in concern. Sage felt his anxiety strengthen, ready to spin out of control.

Slowly the room stilled. Everyone was looking at him. He realized that he and Eich weren't the only ones worrying about the missing Mae Clemens.

Fong eased upright from where he'd been leaning against the shack's back wall, near the potbellied stove that had a small fire burning to keep the dampness out of the room. "Maybe we should go looking, Not like Mrs. Clemens to be late," he said.

Sage's hands rubbed his upper arms as if they'd felt a sudden, intense chill. "I knew it was a mistake to let her go into that place all by herself," he told the room at large.

Just then, the door latch lifted and the door was pushed open. Mae Clemens stepped into the room. She paused, seeing every face turned toward her.

"A bit late, I expect," she noted, matter-of-factly. "Couldn't be helped. Big luncheon for the donors tomorrow and the cook needed help with the pies. Did I miss anything?"

Sage felt recriminations bubble up and was about to give vent when Eich caught his eye. The ragpicker gave a small shake of his head. Sage relaxed. Eich was right, and besides, she'd probably make the point that he'd kept her waiting and worrying more than once.

"Glad you made it, Mrs. Clemens. We were beginning to get worried," he said mildly.

His effort to sound calm didn't fool her. She sent him a sharp look, opened her mouth to say something but must have thought better of it because she compressed her lips instead.

Meachum cleared his throat. "I guess I could make my report first," he said. All eyes turned in his direction so he continued, "I'm a little too noticeable with my wing here all bunged up. So, I'm going to have to rely on the Squadron for help. More men arrived this morning. If it meets with your approval, I want them to fan out to all the watering holes where a union man might wet his whistle and suck up a bit of courage."

"There's legions of single men drinking in the saloons. How are they going to find him among all them?" asked Sage.

"Well, we had a little meeting among ourselves about that very thing. Best approach we could figure is to strike up conversations and work in that we don't think much of President Roosevelt. Most people in those saloons, that will stir up a contrary reaction. But, the fella we're looking for, he might act like he's found a friend. 'Course, if you have any better ideas, we'll listen to them." Meachum looked around the room.

"If you can match a man's dislike of Roosevelt to the same man being in a union, that might narrow down the likely number of candidates for being our bomb-throwing friend," Sage observed. "I think it's a fine approach. How about the rest of you, do you agree?" There were nods all around.

"Once you have the group of likely suspects narrowed down, your men can try to interest each one in working a job and earning some money on the day of the president's visit. If the individual turns down the invitation, that could narrow the field further," Eich suggested.

"That's a good idea," Meachum said, then lapsed into silence as gloom deepened the crags in his face. He pushed a rough hand through his thick silver hair before leveling his bright blue eyes at them and saying, "You know, it is more likely than not that the assassin is going to slip through our fingers. Christ, I hate to think of what will happen if a union man kills Roosevelt. All our work will be for nothing. The Trusts and bosses will use it against every single union in the country. They and their buddies in Congress will pass a slew of anti-union legislation laws, see if they don't. All in the name of national security."

"That's why we're all here Meach," Sage said. "There's more than one approach to foil this plot. It's not all on your shoulders."

Meachum straightened and nodded but his expression stayed glum.

Sage turned toward the lawyer in the group. "McAllister, any luck on finding out if our representative of the Timber Trust has an out-of-town visitor?"

McAllister sat forward on his hardbacked chair. "I spent a rather pleasant afternoon with Mr. Fenton at that fancy new golf course south of town." Irony lay heavy on his words. He knew none of them, with the exception of Sage, would ever be allowed to stroll the course's grassy expanses.

McAllister cleared his throat. "So, I played a round with Fenton, Dr. Harvey and the good doctor's brother-in-law. I can state, with assurance, that Fenton has no house guest other than his wife's mother and father. They are quite elderly and I am sure cannot be involved."

"I guess the good news is that's one Trust down and three more to go," Mae observed.

"I have information on another one." Eich said. Their attention switched to him. "Our utility friend, Fred Holman, will be entertaining a guest from back East. Someone attached to the Financial Trust." They listened closely as he told them what the housemaid Sarah had said.

"Okay, that means we have to learn more about Holman's house guest. Is he already staying there?"

"No, Sarah said they aren't arriving until three days before the president does, on May 18th. They're coming by train."

Mae straightened, her face alert with a thought. "I know, how about Mozart's hosting a private party for the local planners of the president's visit, say, on the 19th. Maybe you can pick up something then?"

"The 19th is cutting it close." McAllister said.

"Yes, but it's still a great idea," Sage said. "If we're lucky, we'll know all the players in the plot by then. But, if we don't, a supper party will give us one more chance to find out which local man is involved." There were nods all around.

Sage looked toward his friend, "Well, Mr. Fong, it appears it's time to hear your report."

The Chinese man stepped forward as all faces turned in his direction. Sage felt a surge of affection for his Asian friend and teacher. "I have not much to report. After Mr. Meachum's fight, I tell cousins to look for limping men in North End," he said, a

sly smile the only indication of his pleasure at the injury they'd
caused Meachum's attackers.

"Jeez, that's like saying 'look for a man with two eyes',"
Meachum grumbled, "Men are always getting hurt one way or
the other."

Fong took no offense. "Yes, it is not easy but Mr. . . . ," Fong
paused as he quickly assessed who in the room didn't know
Sage's nickname, "Mr. Adair here, he break one man's arm and I
break two men's right feet. They stay together in group, cousins
will find them. If they still in town."

"Humph. We didn't think of that. You're right, Mr. Fong,
it's the combination of injuries that will set them apart. Of
course, there's the danger that the mastermind of this damnable
plot will order them out and send in replacements. There's still
enough time," Meachum said.

Sage shook his head. "No reason to. Their job is simple.
They only have to stand in the crowd around the president and
cause an uproar. They can do that with gimpy feet and a broken
arm. Besides, Sergeant Hanke tells me the police, the secret service, Dickenson's operatives and even men lent to Portland by
other police jurisdictions are watching every entrance into the
city. It would be risky bringing in new men now. Better for them
to use the ones already in place, even if they are injured." Sage
turned toward Meachum.

"Which reminds me. You better tell your men to be ex-
tremely careful. We don't want them picked up for saying bad
things about Roosevelt. They're not the only ones hanging out
in the saloons looking for malcontents."

McAllister cleared his throat. "I guess I should keep pump-
ing Fenton for information. He's asked me to be his guest at the
Cabot Club for dinner on Monday."

"Perfect, that will be another opportunity for you to see
who else, associated with the Trusts, might be entertaining guests
from back East." Sage said.

McAllister nodded in agreement but he didn't look happy.
He remained slumped in his chair with an air of defeat.

Eich's deep rumble sounded, "If we are finished with the assassination plot, maybe we could move on to the problem with the children." Eich's words straightened McAllister's spine.

The transformation made Sage realize the lawyer had been afraid the children's plight might be pushed aside. "Yes, Mrs. Clemens, have you learned anything? And McAllister, is there any more about the house in the Northwest?" Sage asked.

McAllister gestured toward Mae, suggesting she should go first.

Mae told them about her ruse to gain access to the BCS's upper floors. "Nearly got myself caught," she told them. "I was pushing open the stairwell door and stepping into the basement hallway just as the kitchen door started opening. I nipped into the water closet, pulled the chain and came out just as Mrs. Wiggit was going into her rooms. One minute later and she would have caught me."

She looked directly at Sage. "I'm sorry that I worried you by arriving late. I had no choice. After taking time off to be 'sick' I really owed Mrs. Wiggit the time. Besides, I wanted to help her. She's got more bite than a dill pickle but somehow I find myself liking the woman. Well, maybe 'like' isn't the word. Let's say I admire her."

Sage's smile at his mother carried a rush of warmth that he didn't try to hide. What he said, however, was, "Dill pickle, huh? Do dill pickles like to crock together?"

She waved a dismissive hand in his direction while Fong grinned widely. "Anyways," she said with enough emphasis to let him know that she was refusing to be nettled by his little jab, "I made it to the top floor. I climbed straight up there because little Andy tells me that's where peculiar things are taking place."

Everyone was leaning toward her, intent on her next words. She didn't keep them waiting, "The top floor is a hallway with rooms on either side. Most of the rooms were open. They looked like they were used as either storage or overflow bedrooms for when the place gets too many guests. There is also a door leading to the attic. I didn't go up there. Not enough time. There was also one locked door and the key was missing. The room behind that locked door is on the side of building that's away from the street. Someone in that room, looking out the window, would see only the brick wall of the building next door."

She took a breath, "Anyways, I got down on these bony knees of mine to take a look through the keyhole. Sure enough, there were boys inside. They all seemed to be sleeping. I couldn't see their faces, but I bet they're those boys that I saw the other day in the courtyard. Maybe they're so bored being locked up they can't do nothing but sleep." A sudden thought seemed to flit across her face. "Say, do we know what Matthew's missing friend, Ollie, looks like?" she asked.

"I never thought to ask Matthew," Sage said. "I'll do it tonight. As soon as I get back to Mozart's. Mr. Fong could meet you in the morning with a description of the boy."

McAllister spoke up, "Well, the bad news I have is that Lynch has put two crews on repairing that damn house. And, it's being guarded at night by at least one watchman," McAllister said. He took out a handkerchief and wiped his forehead that had become damp, even though the room was on the cool side. "Some folks—no, my friends, are still determined to stop that house from opening. They're also talking about doing something to Lynch's house, the one south of downtown. It's only the presence of the boys living there that's giving them pause. I've been talking but they aren't listening. I don't know how long they're going to hold off." He looked toward Sage. The direct, intense gaze of those blue eyes informed Sage that Robert Clooney, McAllister's special friend, was one of those the lawyer was trying to restrain from doing something foolish.

EIGHTEEN

Dispatch: *May 13, 1903, President visits Berkeley, California.*

"*If we allow envy, hatred, anger to rule us. If we permit wrong to be done by any man against another, if we strive to interfere with the just rights of any man or fail to protect him in them, by just so much are we coming short of the standard set for us by those who in 1776 found this nation . . . .*" —*T.R.*

THEIR MEETING IN EICH'S SHED had ended about 9:30 p.m. when Mae Clemens announced that she had to "skedaddle." Her land-lady, refusing to have any "spirit-drinking doxy" living under her roof, locked the entry door promptly at 10:00 p.m..

Twilight had deepened into full night while they'd been in Eich's shack. Outside, the air was warm, still and sweet with the smell of spring flowers. After months of spewing wood smoke into the air, household stoves were cold.

Sage and his mother walked toward her boarding house, Mae's hand resting lightly on his forearm. He glanced down at her, admiring as he always did, the strong planes of her face. She glanced up at him.

"You doing all right, son?" she asked softly.

He put his hand on hers and squeezed. "Yah, Ma, I'm doing fine. Just a bit frustrated. It's like there is a big clock ticking in the back of my head. We're only seven days away from Roosevelt's arrival and we haven't identified a single man involved in the plot. Not even those with the busted wing and broken feet."

"Sage," she paused in her steps, making him stop and look down at her. "I feel the same way about those young boys. I can't think how to free them and stop what's going to happen to them. It feels like that day the tailings pond dam broke and sent that filthy water roaring down the holler back home. I can hear it coming but I am powerless to stop the disaster."

"I know," Sage said. "And, McAllister is beside himself with worry. One of those men who want to move against Lynch is a special friend of his."

"I figured as much," she said and started walking again, "I've been thinking, and this is just an idea, but anyways, I was thinking maybe we should have Matthew help us out."

"No!" Sage said, "He's been in danger too many times this last year. Ida would skin me alive. She gets to worrying whenever he's even a little bit late coming home from school."

Sage didn't have to add that he found Ida's concern justified. The summer before, during a train-hopping trip to Portland, Matthew's brother Billy had been murdered. The youngsters had planned on starting a new life in the city, using Ida's apartment above Mozart's as their home base. Instead, Billy had died and Matthew was jailed. Sage, Mae and Fong had sorted that mess out, only to have to rescue Matthew from shanghaiers a few months later. It had taken Mozart's normally cheerful cook a long time to recover her equilibrium.

"Ida starts worrying again," Sage told her, "and Mozart's will be serving burned pies, scorched potatoes and lumpy gravy. Besides, I just can't put her through that again."

Mae had been nodding all the time he was speaking. "I know all that, Sage. Remember, I was the one left holding Ida's hand while you and Fong gallivanted around after the boy."

"Well, if you knew that already, why did you even suggest the idea of using Matthew?" The sharp edge to his words drew the attention of a man passing by, because he glanced at them before stepping up his pace.

They'd left the neighborhood of small, closely-packed houses on the southern edge of the city and entered the city itself. Here the streets sported hard surfaces edged by good sidewalks and tall brick and wood-frame buildings.

Surprisingly, Mae didn't take offense at his tone. Instead, she asked, "Where does Ida think I am?"

"Down river in Linnton, nursing an old friend whose been having pains in her chest," Sage answered promptly. Sometimes he wondered whether Ida and her husband Knute didn't see through their ruses. After all, for a woman new to Portland, Mae Clemens certainly had an unusual number of close friends needing her assistance now and then.

His mother was ready. "That's right," she said. "So, I was thinking I could tell her I need Matthew for a few days, to help me fix up my friend's house. You know, nail down a few boards, patch the roof, clean out the weeds and gather the limbs winter brought down."

"It would mean him missing school."

She had an answer for that also. "He's a smart boy, getting real good grades. He can spare a few days off from book learning."

"Yes, but, every time Matthew gets involved in our missions, I end up having to rescue him." The sight of Matthew's desperate, pale face and blurry eyes staring out from between the bars of the shanghaier's holding pen was a sharp memory.

"Not last time, you didn't. Not when the bridges were falling and you needed him to find that messenger boy. Last time, he did exactly what you asked. And, he stayed out of trouble. He's older now, more experienced. And he wants to help. It's not like he doesn't know that we're always up to something. He had that figured out the first month he moved in with Ida and Knute."

Every word Mae spoke was the truth. Sage thought of the awkward, earnest red-haired boy. He was more mature and had proven himself to be responsible as well as smart.

"Okay, tell you what. I'll see what Fong thinks of the idea. If he's agreeable, then I'll ask Matthew what his friend Ollie looks like. While we're talking about that, I'll try to find out if he'd be interested."

It was a concession and they both knew it. Matthew was always "interested." In fact, his interest in their affairs was one of their nagging concerns. It was hard to carry out secret missions when the inquisitive sixteen-year-old scrutinized their every movement.

They walked along in silence until they were a block away from Mae's boarding house. Mae stopped and turned toward him, "Sage, something is troubling you, son. What is it? Can I help?"

The unexpected tenderness in her voice disarmed him. He spoke without thinking, right out of the sore spot that hung near his heart. "Fong says I shouldn't hate. He says it's a 'distraction.' But these days, I feel consumed by it. I look at the ugly things men do to other people and I hate those men. I want to stop them, yes. But, I also want to make them hurt like they make others hurt. It doesn't seem fair that they keep getting away with it, even thrive from doing it. But what I do for the labor movement–well, I like to think that I do it because I love my fellow man. But hating and loving humanity at the same time seems to be one heck of a contradiction."

Her blue eyes, dark and changeable like his own, filled with tears and she looked away, down the street. He knew she wasn't seeing the buildings, the nighttime strollers or the horse and buggies rattling over the cobblestones. The expression on her face said she was staring into a painful past.

She turned back towards him. "I don't need to tell you that I have cause to hate. We've both plowed that rocky field more than once. And, I've never been a big enough person to forgive. But I have found a way to put hate aside. What I do is write down the name of the person I hate on a piece of paper. I folded that piece of paper up and put it in that wooden box on my dresser. Then I shut the lid, tight. That's where they stay and that's where my hate for them stays." She looked at him then, the faint gaslight showing spots of red on her cheeks. "Kinda silly, I suppose, but it seems to work," she said.

❀ ❀ ❀

Fong had been waiting for him on the third floor. A plain white teapot sat in the middle of the small alcove table. Fong was sipping from his handleless cup and staring out the window when Sage opened the door.

Despite Fong's appearance of ease, Sage sensed tension in the other man. "What's happened?" he asked.

Fong smiled. "Good news. Cousins find three hurt men all together . . . one arm, two feet."

"Great! Do we know where they are staying yet?" Sage asked.

"No. But cousins sticking to them like rice grains in cook pot. We soon know where the three pillow their heads. After that, we will follow everywhere. See who they meet. Follow that person too."

"The cousins will do that for you?" Sage asked. He didn't know why Fong commanded such respect from the silent Chinese men who were always available to help out. Maybe it was Fong's skill with the snake and crane fighting style, maybe it was because Fong owned a small provision store in Chinatown, or maybe because they belonged to Fong's fraternal "tong" organization or maybe–a thought sent a shiver rippling across Sage's shoulders–maybe their loyalty had something to do with their admiration for Fong's skill with a hatchet. Whatever the reason, the cousins had proved themselves invaluable more than once.

Fong flicked the window curtain aside to gaze down at the wood block street. "Yes, they said they will help," he said. He turned back toward Sage. "Cousins do not like Roosevelt because he call Chinese men 'heathens.' Thinks we all belong back in China. But cousins like Trust men even less."

Hot shame flooded Sage's face. He'd assumed that the men of Chinatown neither cared nor knew little about white men's doings. It had never occurred to him that Fong's Chinese foot soldiers, searching throughout the night, might be well aware of the stakes. So aware that they were risking their own safety just to thwart a plot against a man they disliked. Slinking around the city's dives after dark was a dangerous activity for Chinese men. According to city ordinances, once the sun went down, they were supposed to retreat to those few areas that comprised Chinatown. The ordinance wasn't strictly enforced, but its existence made them fair game for any surly drunk who decided to act out his frustrations.

"Be sure to let them know that I will make up any lost wages and then some," was all he could think to say.

"Already done that," Fong assured him, with a sardonic twist to his lips. "But, not every Chinese man wants to return to China," he said. "Some of us think we are Americans."

The next morning, Sage found Matthew on his hands and knees scrubbing the restaurant's white marble floor. No doubt, Matthew would prefer pedaling his safety bike around town with his gang of friends, but Ida required Matthew to work for his bed and board. The boy never seemed to mind. Instead, he was a diligent and cheerful worker. He'd once assured Sage that nothing could be worse than standing ten hours a day in a cannery gutting ocean fish. From this emphatic statement, Sage surmised that Matthew had left the Marshfield canneries behind for good.

Other than Matthew, the dining room was empty. Sage went into the kitchen, fetched two cups of coffee, black for himself, heavily milked and sugared for Matthew. Returning, he gestured to a table. Matthew rose and took a seat, perplexity creasing his freckled forehead.

"Matthew, I need you to give me a physical description of Ollie."

Matthew scratched his head. "Well, let's see. Ollie is about five inches shorter than me, so, about five and a half feet. He has yellow hair that's sort of curly but not real curly. Wavy like."

"Unfortunately, that description could fit a lot of boys in this town. Is there anything about him that is unusual?"

The boy thought for a bit, then answered, "I guess the thing a person might notice about Ollie is that he has really big feet and his eyes are green. Real green, like bottle glass."

"Now, that is helpful. Average height, big feet, green eyes and wavy yellow hair. That's a very good description."

Sage could tell the boy wanted to ask questions. But, instead, Matthew turned his mug of coffee round and round about, staring into its depths, his lips clamped shut. The boy had taken to heart Sage's instructions to stay out of the matter. Such restraint was a good sign.

Sage cleared his throat and the boy looked up eagerly.

Sage exhaled loudly, trying to let loose the feeling that he might be about to make a very big mistake. He looked sternly into the boy's face and said, "Matthew, I need to have a little discussion with you. A discussion you must keep to yourself. You can't be telling your friends or anyone else. Do you understand?"

The boy nodded, somehow managing to slosh his coffee onto the table top at the same time. Lurching to his feet to fetch a rag, he jostled the table, causing Sage's coffee to spill as well. A few minutes later, the boy'd wiped up the coffee spills and was settled back into his chair. This time, he held himself rigid, his freckled cheeks flaming red.

"Don't worry, you'll grow out of the clumsiness," Sage assured him.

The boy nodded but didn't look reassured. He mumbled, "I'm clumsy and that is that. My ma sez that I came into the world with two left feet, it's just my toes that got put on right."

Sage smiled, thinking Matthew's mother must be a fine woman given the quality of her son. He pushed that thought aside and picked up where he'd left off. "So, as I was saying, this talk has to be kept secret. Even from your aunt and uncle. Can you agree to that?" He hated asking the boy to keep secrets from his aunt and uncle. But, that's the way it had to be.

Again, the boy nodded. He said nothing but Sage could see the excitement building in the bright blue eyes. So, he made his voice stern, "This is serious business, Matthew. Not some lark. You could get hurt and you could cause other people to get hurt."

The boy's eyes widened and this time his nod was solemn. "I understand, Mr. Adair. I will keep my mouth shut. I won't tell nobody, not my friends, not Aunt Ida or Uncle Knute. Is it about Ollie?"

"Yes, it's about Ollie and the boy he was worried about and it's about other boys like them. I told you we would try to help find Ollie, right?"

"Yes, sir, you did. And I thank you for it. Do you want me to help? Maybe ask some questions of the other street boys?"

"No, you shouldn't talk to anyone about Ollie. I need you to do something more difficult and more dangerous. It would mean you taking a few days off from school. Are you at a point in your studies where you can do that?"

Matthew thought for a moment. "I got an essay due tomorrow but I am almost finished with it. Another boy could take it in for me. After that, it's just book reading I got to do. I'm pretty fast when it comes to reading." Pride tinged the boy's words.

Sage took a deep breath, then he told Matthew where Mae Clemens really was, why she needed his help and the ruse they'd devised so Ida would let Matthew out of her sight for a few days. Not surprisingly, the boy eagerly agreed to their plans.

Sage didn't try to hide the misgivings he felt when he said, "Don't be so damn eager. This is no lark. You must promise me that you will only observe and report to Mrs. Clemens. You will not go exploring. You will not stick your nose into unusual places in the BCS building. You will tell her what you observe Captain Branch and others doing and you will do absolutely nothing else. You promise?"

"I promise, on my honor, I will only do what you tell me to do." Matthew said, struggling to keep his face solemn even as the sparkle in his eyes gave away the excitement that had taken over.

Once the boy returned to his floor scrubbing with renewed vigor, Sage carried their cups to the kitchen sink, hoping that Matthew really comprehended the dangers that lay ahead. Mae planned to turn up later in the day to ask Ida the favor of her nephew's help with her ill friend in Linnton. If Ida agreed, Matthew would be checking into the BCS that evening, a simple farm kid looking for a warm bed. Hopefully, the boy's advanced age meant he'd be considered too old for Lynch's house of child prostitution. Matthew's face had blanched when he heard of the suspected fate of the BCS's younger residents. He'd swallowed hard, his new Adam's apple bobbing, but he hadn't shied away from the scheme.

The night before, it was Fong's observation that had finally convinced Sage to chance using Matthew's help. "Many boys Matthew's age are already doing man's work. Some travel across country by themselves with nothing but wits. Some, like my nephew, Choi Ji, travel half way around world. Matthew is young man. No longer a boy. He will rise to trust we place in him."

Sage wished he had Fong's complete confidence in Matthew. But, he didn't. As he passed Ida's door on his way to the third floor, the memory of her tear-streaked face sprang into his mind, sending a gush of guilt and fear surging into his belly. He forced himself to again envision those wan-faced boys sprawled atop those steps that led to that accursed red door.

NINETEEN

Dispatch: *May 14, 1903, President returns to San Francisco.*

"Justice consists not in being neutral between right and wrong, but in finding out the right and upholding it, wherever found, against the wrong." —T.R.

SAGE STEPPED STEALTHILY DOWN the third floor hallway toward his mother's room until he caught himself doing it, then he paused. "There's no one but me up here. Besides, she wouldn't have told me where to look if she didn't expect me to look. She knows me too well," he told himself out loud.

He pushed open her door. The room was spare and spotless. She hadn't wanted her room to display trappings of wealth like his room did. Not just because adornments wouldn't be suitable for Mozart's sometime hostess, cook and general all-around helper, but also because luxury made her uncomfortable. "Froufrous and geegaws cluttered about make me feel silly as a milk cow wearing tail ribbons," she'd once told him.

Inside the room, her rocking chair sat with its back against the window so as to capture the best light, a wicker basket of mending close by its runner. Her single bed stood against one wall, a patchwork quilt snugged up to the headboard, an extra one folded neatly across its foot. Old and tattered, the quilt was a possession from those days she rarely talked about.

The plain, pine-top dresser was his focus. He'd seen that wooden box atop it before but had thought nothing of it. Now the box seemed to have grown in size, capturing and holding the light streaming through the room's only window.

He walked to the dresser and lifted the box lid. Inside were three small pieces of folded paper. He picked one up and carefully unfolded it. The angular slant of his mother's handwriting spelled out the name of the mine owner who'd forced a Hobson's choice on her those many years ago: "Raise your only child in dire poverty or, relinquish all contact with him, and I will raise and educate him alongside my grandson."

She'd made that sacrifice for the remainder of his childhood. It had been a childhood tainted by that mine owner's scarcely concealed resentment over Sage's survival of the mine explosion that had killed the mine owner's only son. But, he'd persisted in raising Sage because of the debt he owed the kid from Appalachia who'd saved his grandson from the same explosion.

Though Sage had experienced all the privileges and trappings of wealth, there had been a persistent undertone of derision coming from the mine owner and his friends. Sage had felt like an organ grinder's monkey. Still, he did not hate the mine owner. Neither did he feel overwhelming gratitude or any strong favorable emotion toward the man. Sage carefully re-folded the paper and placed it back in the box.

The next name was no surprise. It was that of the Dickenson supervisor whose gang of agent thugs had swarmed over Mae's Appalachian hills and hollers those many years ago. They'd used their guns and fists to crush the Irish miners whose only crime was wanting to give their families lives free of hunger and uncertainty. Those Dickenson agents killed Mae Clemens's father and brother after they'd been betrayed by a man close to them. It was that man whose name was written in bold strokes across the third piece of folded up paper—"John David Adair." Sage's father.

❀ ❀ ❀

"Thank you for coming so promptly, Sergeant," Sage said as he entered the kitchen and clapped a friendly hand onto Hanke's broad back. The police sergeant, who was sitting at the kitchen table, made as if to rise.

"No, no. Finish your dinner." Sage poured himself a cup of coffee and sat opposite the big man.

Holding up a massive paw, Hanke shook his head. "It's okay, I can talk now, Mr. Adair. I know you're busy out front what with it being the dinner hour and all." He began pulling the napkin out of his collar.

"We don't have a problem there. We've promoted Horace to the position of fill-in maitre'd whenever Mrs. Clemens and I have to be absent. Got him fancied up in a new suit. He's having a grand time and doing a very good job of it," Sage assured him. "Go ahead and finish your meal and then we'll talk."

Hanke chuckled but still demurred, "Really, Mr. Adair, I might be stuffing my face like a farm hand but, my ears work fine. What's the problem?"

Sage glanced around the room. The two kitchen help girls were jumping to Ida's orders and the two waiters were bursting through the doors at a steady pace, stacking up empty plates and snatching up full ones. Good, Ida's new special of the day was being well-received. They'd debated adding the Italian noodle dish but it seemed that people liked it.

He shook his head. "No, Sergeant, we'll need to go upstairs for this talk. Too many folks busy around here. We should get out of their way." He cupped his ear as if scratching it.

The sergeant's blue eyes widened but he said nothing. He cleaned his plate with a few rapid forkfuls. And, for once, he didn't look around expectantly in the hope of seconds. Mozart's owner had never before invited the sergeant to his private third floor quarters. The policeman rose to his six-three height, tucked his beehive helmet under his arm and let Sage precede him from the kitchen.

They climbed the stairs to the third story. Sage saw Hanke shoot a quick glance around the room but the man's broad face betrayed nothing. Sage gestured toward the small table standing within the window alcove.

Once Hanke got settled, Sage took a deep breath and began, "Sergeant, you've known me for over a year now. We've worked together on three cases and every time, I've made sure that you were in the right place, at the right time. Isn't that so?"

That question brought a cautious nod as Hanke's blue eyes narrowed. His big face, with its wide forehead, might suggest the passivity of a contented bovine but anyone who thought him stupid would be in for a surprise. There was a reason the sergeant's men would follow him anywhere. Hanke could be both commanding and decisive. And, although Hanke might chow down a free meal now and then, all it purchased from him was an open mind and a willingness to do anything that wouldn't compromise his sworn duty. Although the outcome of Sage's escapades usually made Hanke look good, the man had also advanced out of the patrolman's ranks on his own merits. He was a rare bird on Portland's underpaid police force. Fortunately for the city and their current mission, the new police chief had valued Hanke's attributes and given him a promotion.

"Here's my problem, Sergeant. Someone who is close to the city's planning for the presidential visit is involved in a plot to assassinate Roosevelt."

Hanke stiffened in his chair and his jaw dropped. "Who?" he demanded, all geniality gone from his face.

"We don't know. That's the very problem Mr. Fong, myself and some other people are trying to solve. But, as of today, we don't know. All we know for certain is that more than one person here in Portland intends to carry out the plot."

The big policeman started to rise, declaring, "I've got to tell the chief . . . ."

Sage reached out a restraining hand and gently tugged at Hanke's forearm until he settled back down onto his chair.

"That's just the problem. Until we know who, we can't tell the chief. Because the traitor could very well be someone in whom the police chief would confide. That is even likely. But, I trust you, Sergeant, and I think we can help you prevent the plot from being carried out. That's why I needed to talk to you."

Hanke remained unconvinced. His forehead wrinkled into his brow and he pursed his lips. "I don't know, Mr. Adair. Chief Hunt's a good man. Most honest police chief we've had since he was chief before."

Sage shook his head. "Think about it, Sergeant. You've got maybe a hundred men trying to make this city safe. How many assassination plots have already come to their ears? Why would Hunt consider this one to be any different?"

"Well, because the information's coming from you," Hanke said, but even as he said it, his words slowed making it clear he'd spotted the problem. "You don't want it known that it's coming from you, right? You want your involvement kept secret, like before?"

Once again Sage nodded his head. "Not only must it be kept secret but we don't have enough specifics yet to enable the police to stop it. So, I am thinking you and I can put our heads together, share information and see if we can figure out when and where the attempt might take place. That way, you can start taking steps so that you, and the men you trust, are ready to act if we're right."

"You're wanting me to share secret police information, aren't you?" Hanke's tone was dryly matter-of-fact, not accusatory.

Again, Sage nodded. "I want us to make our best guess about where this attack will take place and then make sure you and I are both situated to stop it."

Hanke sat back in his chair and turned his head to stare through the lace-curtained windows into a drizzling spring day. The silence of the room was broken only by the tick of the clock atop the dresser and the steady raindrops outside the window.

"Sure hope it doesn't rain on that day," the policeman muttered. He turned back to face Sage and said, "Okay, Mr. Adair, I'll go along with you, but only for now. But the information has to travel both directions. By now, you should know that I am trustworthy. My word is my bond. But, I'm not going to give up my secret information unless you give up yours'."

Sage had expected this response. Hanke was right. He'd always done his best to aid their efforts, often without asking why or demanding any explanation. He'd earned a greater level of trust. Sage told the sergeant everything he knew, except that he named neither McAllister nor Meachum. As he laid out what they'd learned of the plot, he watched Hanke's face turn pale.

"Great God in Heaven," Hanke said softly once Sage's story was finished. "We got men watching every train, steamer and stable and there hasn't been a hint of a group of strangers like that in town. Fact is Chief Hunt just told the newspaper reporter that no dangerous characters are in the city."

"Your folks didn't spot them because we think they came in way early. If they have someone helping them inside of Roosevelt's inner circle, then they've known for longer than you that Roosevelt was coming to Portland—probably even on what date. We suspect they've likly been here for a month or more." Sage said.

Hanke huffed out a deep breath. "The president will be going to all sorts of places while he's here in Portland. How can we figure out where they plan on trying to kill him?"

"That's what I hope you and I can do today," Sage said. "We need to think like they do. What location is most likely to give them the best chance of success? If you can tell me where Roosevelt will be, maybe between the two of us, we can figure out what will be the most likely place."

"Well, his train is pulling into the Union train station. From there, he'll climb into an open carriage and travel through town on 3rd and a bunch of other streets until he stops in the South Park Blocks for a children's rally."

There was a pause as Hanke tried to recall the rest of the planned route. "Let's see, after that, his carriage will roll around downtown, until it reaches Everett and 23rd," he finally continued. "Next, the parade heads south on 23rd Street until it reaches Washington Street where it will turn due west. They'll travel uphill to City Park. That's where Roosevelt is going to mortar in the cornerstone of that new Lewis and Clark monument. They've built a platform and all up there. Once he's done there, he's supposed to go to a gathering of some fraternal organization but his advance people tell us he's been canceling the side events, so that one is less certain. That night, he's attending a smallish fancy dinner party at the Portland Hotel. That's where he's staying. Next morning, his train pulls out at the crack of dawn, heading north."

"So tell me, how will he be guarded?"

Hanke hesitated his eyes narrowing.

"Sergeant, we can't figure out where they're going to try to kill him if we don't know where the holes in his defenses might be," Sage prodded, keeping his voice calm.

Hanke twisted his lips as he thought, then he made a decision because his next words came without restraint, "When he comes out of the train station, eighty mounted calvary soldiers from the Eighth Artillery will be there to make an arch out of their sabers for him to walk under. Then they will mount and ride in advance of his carriage. From on top of their horses, they'll keep an eye on the crowd. Closest, on either side of the carriage, two columns of men, made up of the Grand Army of the Republic, will march in close formation. Between those two columns and the sidewalk, on each side, there will be a column of twelve mounted policemen. There's also going to be mounted policemen following behind the carriage."

Now that Hanke had evidently decided to completely trust Sage, the information continued to flow easily. "Also, along the route from the train station to the park, we'll have other police officers from our force, as well as every other local police force near Portland, walking along the curbs, keeping up with the carriage. They'll keep people on the sidewalks and be on the lookout for someone who might jump out with a gun or a bomb. Mingling with the crowd, but also keeping pace with the president, will be forty-two specially sworn-in plain clothes detectives, secret service men and some hired Dickenson men. They'll be watching for bad characters, too."

"Where will you be?"

Hanke reddened with bashful pride, "It looks like Chief Hunt's assigning me to lead a team of officers ahead of the whole shebang. We're to be the parade scouts. Our job is to look for problems in the buildings overlooking the route, among the people lining the route and catch signals from everyone else. If we see something suspicious, I am authorized to stop the whole parade."

Sage thought for a moment. "I don't think it will happen during the parade. For one thing, with all that protection, it would leave too much to chance. Also, remember, that drunk told the prostitute that his job is to make sure the bomb thrower has access and that another group will create a diversion. That scenario doesn't fit a parade situation very well because a parade is always on the move."

"But, it sure does fit the celebration at the monument site," Hanke mused. "There will be a gaggle of dignitaries on that platform, including the governors from Oregon, Washington, Idaho and Montana and all the folks who came with them. That means strangers. There'll be a lot of strangers on that platform," he said and paused before continuing, parsing out his words as he worked through the idea. "And we can't have policemen encircling the president when he's speechifying because then nobody could see him. And, the area around the platform is so small, what with the trees and all, that folks will be packed in tighter than canned salmon. It'll be a chore just to keep people from climbing onto that platform. So, that's the only time Roosevelt won't have people between him and the crowd," he concluded slowly.

"That's exactly what I'm thinking. They'll attack him at the monument," Sage said.

The sergeant nodded, his lips a grim line.

TWENTY

Dispatch: *May 14, 1903, President's train readies to leave San Francisco in the morning.*

> *"The principle of which I have spoken must be applied to each individual case according to that case's nature, . . . by the law, not in spite of it, under and through and by it, a spirit of genuine brotherhood, the spirit which looks to one's neighbors's interests as well as one's own, which thinks it a shame to impugn the rights of anyone else." —T.R.*

HER HANDS MIGHT HAVE BEEN STEADILY MOVING through the task of mixing and rolling pie dough but Mae's mind was wandering down the upstairs hallways. Matthew had been in the building, on his own, for nearly nine hours and she hadn't seen neither hide nor hair of him.

Mrs. Wiggit was more surly than usual as Andy played with a wooden wagon out of sight beneath the table, obviously doing his best to make no noise. Mae didn't like it. She debated with herself. Should she just break loose, throw the whole scheme to the wind, open that door to the hallway and go look for Ida's nephew? Or, should she be patient, something she had to admit was not an easy thing for her? Her rolling pin slammed down so hard on the dough that the sound jarred Mrs. Wiggit's from her morose stirring of a sauce pot.

"Mae, you keep beating on that dough and it will turn tough as a cow hide. Get on with making the pie," the cook snapped.

Just then doorway to the hall opened and Matthew stepped through. Mae had to look away for fear that relief would show in her face.

"Who might you be, busting into my kitchen with no introduction?" the cook asked sharply. At Mae's feet, Andy scooted out from under the table, his eyes bright with interest. Matthew caught sight of the boy and gave him a wink. Mrs. Wiggit saw the wink and her face softened.

"You one of the boys earning your keep upstairs?" she asked.

He dipped his head respectfully, explaining. "Yes, ma'am. I'm to fetch coal for the parlor stoves in the evening, wood for the fireplaces and anything else that needs to be done. I figured, since the Cap'n is putting on a special supper tonight, you might be needing extra coal for your cookstove."

"Why, that's real thoughtful of you, boy. The coal scuttle's over there in the corner," Ms. Wiggit pointed, "and we are running low for sure. We've already worked a hard day and now we have this supper to fix. When you're done, there's some cornbread that needs eating. You could use a little meat on those skinny bones of yours," the cook added.

Matthew flashed his full-on grin, grabbed up the scuttle and trotted back into the basement hallway. In a few minutes later he was back, the heaping scuttle skimming low to the ground. He quickly emptied it and returned to the basement furnace room where the coal was stored. Five trips later, the coal bin was full. At Mrs. Wiggit's gesture, he took a chair at the table. Andy shyly crawled out from under it and took the seat across from him. Matthew looked at the slack lips and lively eyes and said, "I bet you're a boy who likes to see a top spin."

At Andy's eager nod, Matthew pulled a bright red top from his pocket and started it spinning. As the top twirled, Matthew asked, "You know how to count?"

Andy began to count, surprising Mae. His enunciation was muddled but still clear enough to prove he was correct. Mae glanced toward the cook. The woman's face shone with pride. Mae felt her eyes sting. "Git ahold of yourself, girl. You can't go barmy right now," she chided herself.

Matthew and Andy were still playing, the boy's eyes focused on the spinning red top.

"So, I start it spinning and we'll see how long it stays up. You count it out. We'll see what will be the best out of three times. Do you think you can do that?" Matthew asked.

Andy said, "Yes, I sure can." Matthew spun and Andy counted. Mrs. Wiggit turned back to the stove and vigorously stirred her sauce. Mae set aside the rolling pin, pulled a pie dish closer and laid in the dough.

When Matthew finally stood to leave, at least three pieces of cornbread were no longer in the larder. Mae waited for a count of ten before announcing that she had to visit the "necessary." Once inside the hallway, she found Matthew standing in the gloom near the stairwell door.

"My hair was turning gray waiting for you to show up," she said to the boy, her voice a mix of chiding and cheerful.

"They had me making beds, sweeping out. I had no reason to be heading toward the basement. Besides, that tough fellow you said Andy calls 'Mister Growl' was following me everywhere."

"How'd you get down here then?"

Matthew's long lips twisted up at one end. "They got chilled 'cause of the rain and they wanted fires. The wood and coal are down here in the basement," he said.

"Who's coming to the supper upstairs?" Mae knew their time was short. She needed to get whatever information she could before Mrs. Wiggit decided to investigate her assistant's absence.

"They're already here. A bunch of men I don't know. I'll keep my ears open in case they drop names. They're going to have me fetch and carry for them while they're eating. One funny thing though, that doctor who goes to Mozart's is there, he seems . . . ."

The rest of Matthew's words were cut off by the frozen silence that fell on both of them when the outside kitchen door opened. In the distance, there was the scrape of a metal bucket on concrete and then of the door closing. Both of them relaxed. Gussie dumping her mop water into the street gutter.

"You better get going," Mae said, a sudden premonition sharpening her words.

He silently touched her arm, opened the door to the stairwell and eased it closed behind him. No sooner had the latch clicked than the inside kitchen door started to open. Mae Clemens quickly stepped into the toilet room and then stepped back out.

Mrs. Wiggit was moving purposely toward her. "Glad to see you're all right. After that scare we had the other day with you, I thought maybe I should check." The edge to her voice said she'd come looking for more than that one reason.

"Why, thank you, Cook. Certain things take a bit longer than others, I fear," Mae Clemens said dryly.

The cook chortled before she could choke it off, turned on her heel and headed back toward the kitchen with Mae Clemens following behind. "Tarnation, and I really did need to use it," Mae muttered to herself.

"Thank you for the invitation, Adair. My wife likes dining here," said Abbott Low Mills, when he returned from using Mozart's wash room. "You might want to get electric lamps installed in there. That gas lamp can make it a bit close." His cocked eyebrow and a quirk of his lips took all sting from his words.

Sage laughed and said, "Mr. Mills, much as I hate to admit it, it's beginning to look like I will have to give in fairly soon. I hate to add to the mess outside. Between the electric trolleys, electricity lines and telephone wires draping the streets, its starting to look like we live in some old lady's yarn basket."

"Just think of it as progress. That's the purpose of the human race." Mills said before getting directly to his point. "Like I said, I appreciate the invitation but I am sure you had a reason for issuing it. I thank you for not trying to pitch it to me at the table during dinner," he nodded to where his perfectly groomed wife sat surveying the room with an idle, contented gaze.

"It's more like an offer I'd like to make you," Sage acknowledged. "I'm still one of the new men in town. Mozart's is doing well, but it could do better. I know that you and other gentlemen are very involved in planning for Roosevelt's visit. That is a daunting task."

Sage watched his words wash over Mills and melt the other man's cool reserve into pink-faced pride as Mills said, "Yes, indeed. It was hard for me to tear myself away from the planning tonight. But my wife," here he nodded at the waiting woman, "can be very determined."

"What I would like to propose is that you and your associates plan to meet here at Mozart's one last time before the big day. I'll reserve a large table and, of course, the cost of the meal would be totally on me," Sage said. When Mills looked like he was going to protest, Sage added. "Think of it as a way for me to market my restaurant to the very people I desire to see as frequent patrons. Besides, I am a loyal Portlander, too. I want the president to see us put our best boot forward."

Mills grinned. "Lucky for us, Roosevelt is a 'boots' sort of guy. Fact is, I heard he's coming here after spending four days in the wilderness. He's camping out with that wild man, John Muir, down in the Yosemite Valley. If we're not careful, Muir will convince him that we need to build everything out of bricks just so we can save all the trees. As if we weren't awash in the damn things. It'd take centuries to cut down the forests around here.

"Well, Mr. Adair," Mills continued, "the answer is that we would be most delighted to accept your kind invitation. Will the evening of the 18th be suitable? That gives us two whole days to discuss and fix any remaining difficulties with the visit. There would be about ten of us. You also are welcome to join in. Maybe you'll think of something the rest of us haven't."

Sage agreed verbally even as he mentally smiled in response to Mills's last statement, thinking that an honest answer would be, "Mr. Mills, I guarantee that most of my thoughts are ones you and your associates will never have."

The Mills couple soon prepared to depart. Sage made sure he stood at the door. He had one more task to perform.

"Mrs. Mills, I am so delighted that you came out tonight. I know the weather is not at its best just yet," he said to the woman whose exposure to the weather that evening would consist of five paces from her front door to the enclosed carriage, followed by five paces to the restaurant door and back again. He doubted that when she'd looked out her carriage window she'd even notice the rag-wrapped figures huddling in every doorway.

"Mr. Adair, it was a perfectly delightful evening. I know Mr. Mills has thanked you, but please, let me add my gratitude to his," she responded graciously, extending her hand.

He bent over it, continental style, saying as he straightened, "I imagine this is a busy week coming up for you, with the president's visit."

She laughed gaily, "I am spending a surprising amount of time with my dressmakers. I use the Kimberly sisters, you know. I am so looking forward to attending the banquet."

Of course, Mrs. Mills would have a new gown for such an important event.. And, of course, the Kimberly sisters would sew it since they were the pre-eminent dressmakers for the rich women of Portland, be they high society and low. "I imagine any number of ladies are attempting to obtain new gowns for the presidential visit," Sage observed.

"Oh, lah, isn't that the truth. But, of course, I don't need to worry. My last name opens every door. No one wants to annoy the bank president's wife." She chuckled and patted her husband's hand where he had taken hold of her forearm.

Sage spoke quickly, seeing his opportunity escaping as Mrs. Mills began turning toward the door. "I expect you are also going to be busy with out-of-town guests as well–so many people are."

The woman paused, looked puzzled and then her face cleared. "Abbot must have told you that my sister planned on traveling over from Boise. But no, she had to cancel the trip. Her children came down with the measles and her husband did not want to come by himself. Thank goodness. I am busy enough as it is." With her swish of skirts and a hat tip from Mills, the couple went out the door and into their waiting carriage.

Sage sucked in a deep breath and let it swoosh out. That eliminated a second Trust representative from the plotting. Only two men remained who might be potentially involved: Dolph of the Railroad Trust and Holman of the Utility Trust. Holman certainly had a guest from back East coming to town to see the president. Whether Dolph would be entertaining an out-of-towner was still unknown.

Sage looked around the room for Philander Gray. The lawyer had slipped in through the front door just as Sage started talking to the Mills couple. Gray sat at his favorite small corner table underneath the musicians' balcony. Not for the first time, Sage thought how the lawyer's tall, ungainly figure brought to mind both Ichabod Crane and Abraham Lincoln. Sage strolled over.

"I see you are late staying in town today," he commented to the lawyer.

"Well, the wife's visiting her sister across the river in Vancouver, so I thought I'd try out Miz Ida's supper-time cooking for a change."

"And, what do you think?" Sage asked.

"It's second only to her dinner-time cooking," the lawyer assured him. Then he fell to silently pushing food around his plate.

"What is it, Philander?" Sage asked. It wasn't like the lawyer to stop eating for anything. As Mae Clemens liked to say, "Philander Gray could eat the Fifth army under the table and still not burp."

Gray laid his fork down, took a swallow of water and looked directly at Sage. "It's not my place to tell you who to associate with, John, but Abbott Low Mills only seems like a nice guy."

Sage leaned forward. "I don't know all that much about him except that he's the president of First National Bank, sits on the board of a few other banks and used to be on the city's franchise committee," he said.

"That certainly describes the civic wrappings around Mr. Abbott Low Mills," Gray said, "But, let me tell you a little sto - ry about a former client of mine. For years my client, his son and son-in-law have been running a nice little paving compa - ny. They employed about ten other men pretty much full time. Summertime, they lay down new streets and convert the rotting wooden boardwalks into sidewalks. Wintertime, they do their best to repair other streets and boardwalks. Nobody's getting rich but at least thirteen families are eating pretty well. You fol - lowing along okay?" Gray asked.

At Sage's nod, Gray continued. "Mr. Abbott Low Mills, he gets appointed head of the city public works commission. Under his leadership, the committee decides to cut the street work into much bigger slices. And, at the same time, they also decide to re - quire high dollar performance bonds from the contractors bid - ding on the work. Still with me?"

Sage nodded again and Gray went on, "To qualify for these high dollar performance bonds, there are two things the bidder must have. The first is enough assets to pay for or back the bond, and second, their bank must be big enough that it can afford to offer the bond. That leads to another requirement. Your paving firm has to be one of the two biggest in the city, both of which just happen to be customers of banks owned by Mr. Abbott Mills."

Sage screwed up his face. Gray saw it and nodded. "That's right, it's disgusting. But it's worse than that. My client loses his city work because he isn't big enough to qualify for the bond. He, his son, son-in-law and some of his workers are now left doing low paid day work for one of those two big outfits. Thirteen families have gone from making a comfortable living to living hand-to-mouth."

"I guess that's what City Commissioner Fred T. Merrill would call the fruits of 'honest' graft," Sage said.

"Bloody rotten fruit, in my opinion. There's not a single thing honest about what Mills and his cronies do," Gray said and took a hefty swallow of wine.

"Yup, that's Fred's view too," Sage agreed.

"I told you that story because I hate to think of you tangled up financially with Mills and his ilk. I'm not a superstitious man but I've got to believe that the taint on that kind of money rubs off on a fellow's life."

Sage stood, clapped his lawyer on the shoulder and said, "Don't you worry about me, old friend. You, Mrs. Clemens and Mr. Fong will never let me stray too far off the narrow. Besides, when it comes to Abbot Low Mills, he's the one who needs to worry." Sage leaned down and said softly into the lawyer's ear, "Trust me, the 'game's afoot'."

TWENTY-ONE

Dispatch: *May 15, 1903, the President's train arrives in Raymond, California.*

> *"Of all forms of tyranny, the least attractive and the most vulgar is the tyranny of mere wealth, the tyranny of plutocracy [the wealthy class that controls the government]." —T.R.*

McAllister was the first Mozart's customer the next day. "I'm just here for coffee. I have to be in court in a few minutes," he told Sage during the seating ritual.

Sage moved the china plate and silver cutlery to one side of the two-person table and hand-signaled to Horace for coffee.

"Big case?"

McAllister laughed and, for the first time, Sage could see the light-hearted boy he must have once been. "Fun case is more like it. Our temperance ladies got themselves arrested and my job is to fulfill their expectation that they will spend no more than one night in jail. They consider themselves to be 'conscience criminals' to which a different set of rules must apply, as compared to the rules governing other criminals."

"You disagree?"

"I'm afraid the question of what is 'criminal' is a bit more fuzzy for me. A man can steal to feed his family. Or because he's addicted to a substance that is making other men rich. Or, maybe, because he's seen the cards he's been dealt and they're all blank. On the other hand, the corporate robber barons destroy countless lives every day with complete impunity. The question is, where does one man's criminality begin and another's end? You start looking and, in most cases, there's a long sequence of events that leads to a single act of lawbreaking, you know?" Sage merely nodded, figuring McAllister didn't expect an answer.

"Oh, thank you," the lawyer said when Horace arrived with silver coffee pot, cup and saucer, sugar and cream.

Sliding into the chair opposite McAllister, Sage asked, "Another war at a saloon?"

"An apothecary, can you believe that? They are demanding the man remove a good thirty percent of his stock."

"Sounds like you are representing the wrong side," Sage said.

"No, not really. You've got to have people like these women making noise on the fringes. They draw attention to problems the rest of us need to consider and resolve. That's a good thing. But, enough philosophizing. I had dinner with Fenton last night at the Cabot Club. Smoky place. Angelique insisted I hang my clothes on the back porch to air when I arrived home. That said, I managed to talk to Cyrus Dolph. He will have a guest in town, starting the 17th, three days from now. The fellow will be staying at the Portland Hotel. Because Dolph is one of the hotel's principal owners he always has the use of a suite. When the president is checked into the hotel, Dolph's guest will already be there."

Sage shifted uneasily. Had he and Hanke gotten it wrong? Was the assassination attempt going to take place at the hotel instead of at the monument?

"I couldn't get any information out of him about the guest because just as he told me, the club's steward called him away and Fenton was ready to leave. As his guest, I had no choice but to leave with him."

"I will try to find out who is staying in Dolph's suite at the Portland Hotel. I have a friend working there," Sage said.

McAllister's face turned glum. "They're starting to paint the new house inside," he said. "They'll have it mostly done to-morrow. Probably start moving in the furniture the next day."

"Mrs. Clemens is in the BCS and so is our young friend Matthew."

A deep wrinkle appeared between McAllister's eyebrows. "I don't know that I would have sent the boy in there. There's more to worry about than the fact that someone involved with the BCS is stocking Lynch's houses."

Sage hadn't thought about that. But surely, if Matthew felt threatened, he could just run out the door or jump out a window. The place wasn't a fortress after all. But there was that strange, submissive behavior of the boys at the BCS. What could they do to make Matthew act like that? Sage looked at McAllister, "Ah . . . ," he started to raise that question but McAllister interrupted.

"I've got to leave now or I'll be late. Can't have either the judge or the ladies getting mad at me. But, I'll head over there to the BCS just as soon as my court hearing is done. In fact, I think I will step up my patronage. A daily swim and an afternoon card game might be just the thing," McAllister told him before swallowing the last of the coffee and grabbing his hat from the table. "What's he look like? How will the boy know I am a trusted friend?"

Then Sage had it. "Tell him Adair said 'the Blue Beauty misses him,'" he said. That bicycle was Matthew's most prized possession. If Sage knew the boy, he was missing that wheeled contraption as well. Then he described the sixteen-year-old's unmistakable deep red hair and freckled face.

"Mr. Fong, we only have five and one-half days before the president's train pulls into Portland, I'm not sure running through the exercise is the best use of our time," Sage said, even as he stepped into the attic and began removing his shoes.

Fong smiled, assumed the starting position and intoned, "Begin form."

Sage shrugged, put his stockinged feet shoulder width apart, breathed deeply, relaxed his shoulders and slowly raised his arms forward and up to shoulder level, resigned to the fact that, until the exercise was completed, all 108 movements, there would be no talking. It was hard to follow along at Fong's slow pace. Thoughts of the imminent danger to both the president and the young boys gave a vigor to his movements that made him move too fast. So, he concentrated and did as Fong always told him. Slowed, breathed deep again, and lowered his shoulders, which always seemed inclined to crawl upwards as if to protect his ears–particularly when he was tense. At last, the movement caught him up, his mind emptying to a point where thoughts snagged only briefly before moving on and out. That intangible something began flowing through him, warming his palms and swirling between his hands whenever they passed near each other.

"Now, we talk," Fong announced, breaking the motionless peace that signaled the exercise's end. "We follow the three men. They are staying in one place. Chinese man who work in yard next door say they live there almost one moon."

"It's just what I thought. That's how they got past the police and detectives watching the trains and steamers. They were already here when the city found out about the visit." Sage's conclusion meant only one thing. Someone who was privy to the president's schedule was working with the assassins or, at least, someone was being indiscrete with the information. Still, how the assassins obtained the president's schedule early wasn't as important as stopping them.

"Are they meeting with anyone?" he asked.

Fong shook his head. "The one whose arm you break, go to telegraph office. But otherwise, they spend time looking for Meachum, I think."

"Damn, they haven't given up on that? Is Meachum safe?"

A vertical crease appeared in Fong's brow as he answered, "Meachum takes many chances. Only one of his men guards him. I have only six men. It is hard to guard Meachum and follow bad men. Sometimes bad men split up."

"Mr. Fong, I don't know what to do. We have to keep them always in sight. Time is running out. We don't know who is going to signal the assassin. We don't know who the assassin is. It could all happen so fast that we won't be able to stop it."

"I did have idea," Fong said, his words hesitant. Sage knew from experience such hesitancy meant Fong feared Sage wouldn't like his idea.

"Mr. Fong, I am desperate. We need more information. Trust me, I might not like your idea but since I don't have any of my own, I want to hear it."

Puffing out a little breath, Fong said, "Of three bad men, one is boss, one is soldier and one is stupid. I have told my cousins to get stupid one and take him to cell."

"Cell?" Sage repeated before the light dawned. "Oh, the underground cell!" That explained Fong's hesitancy. It was the one thing Sage and Fong never agreed on. After Matthew's imprisonment in that underground shanghai cell, Sage had wanted the cell destroyed. Fong had not complied. A good thing too, since the cell had come in handy last fall. Besides, Fong had promised to make sure that shanghaiers stayed away from that part of the underground.

"I long ago decided you were the wise one when it came to that cell, Mr. Fong. I agree wholeheartedly with your plan to capture the stupid one and put him in the cell."

"That is good. It took one whole day but now stupid one is in pen, guarded like round pig in hungry village," Fong said, his big teeth showing in a wide smile.

Late that night, Sage slipped down the hidden staircase into Mozart's cellar, moving along the tunnel to the alley trapdoor and surfacing behind a row of empty dustbins. Sage slipped from the alley's mouth, pretending to button his trousers in the well known way of men who'd had too much to drink and needed the alley's privacy to achieve relief. The few passersby didn't cast a second look at him, in his shabby clothes and slouch hat.

There was a soft rustle at Sage's side and he looked over to see Fong moving past him. They couldn't walk together, not in that part of town. So Sage trailed Fong until they reached the side door into a building. Fong put a finger to his lips, pulled the door open and slipped inside. Sage followed, tugging the door shut behind himself. At the end of a dingy hallway a Chinese man leaned casually against a wall, a dirty white apron tied around his middle. He nodded at Fong and pointed toward another door. Fong and Sage went through that door and down some wooden steps into a cellar. Bags of flour and other provisions used by the restaurant overhead were stacked high against the walls. Across the room, an open padlock dangled from a door hasp. For a moment, Sage reveled in the realization that he no longer feared exiting out that door into the underground. Not anymore. He'd conquered his fear of the dark. At least as far as the underground was concerned. The darkness of a mine, well, that was likely another kettle of fish.

The sight on the other side of the door was not the dusty blackness of the underground. Instead, like some strange Renaissance painting, a man sat on an upturned wooden box, the smoky glow of a kerosene lantern at his feet. The man's back was toward them, but as they stepped into the cellar the man turned his head and a swath of thick silver hair caught the light.

"Meachum!" Sage said, as he eagerly stepped forward to grab the other man's hand.

"Ouch, careful there! That's the sore arm," Meachum said without any heat, a wide grin splitting his craggy face.

"Sorry, I'm just glad to see that you are still in one piece."

Meachum smiled but then nodded grimly. "Let's have a little sit before we head out. Thanks to Fong's men, I got here early and found a box for each of you."

Sure enough, two other upturned wooden boxes faced the lantern as if it were a campfire. Once seated, Sage couldn't help but notice how the light at their boots shot spooky shadows up their faces.

Not beating around the bush, Meachum said, "I got more information about the bomb-throwing fellow we're looking for.

St. Alban sent word that he thinks our duped assassin is a former union member who used to work in the government printing office."

"So, our union dupe is a former government printer hoping to embarrass Roosevelt with a stink bomb?" Sage said.

"Yup. We think he's the one. He's the best we've been able to come up with. And, he hasn't been at home for some time now. Before he disappeared, he bragged that he was heading out West and Roosevelt was going to be sorry. It all fits. Whether it's really him, we don't know for sure. But, so far, he's the mostly likely person. His name is Obediah Perkins."

"So what's his story?"

"He lost his job when Roosevelt put a non-union printer back to work in the print shop. He got bumped off the job by seniority. St. Alban describes Perkins as tall and gangly. Best of all, he's missing the tips of three fingers on his left hand–little, ring and middle." Catching sight of Sage's raised eyebrow, Meachum elaborated, "He was working on a letterpress that had no safety guards, of course. God forbid any extra money goes to protect the workers. Anyway, his fingers got smashed and they had to amputate. My men are out scouring the town for him. So far, he's the only fella we've learned of that could be our assassin."

"Do we have any other information about him besides the missing fingers?" Sage asked.

Meachum's pursed lips did a sideways twist before he said, "Unfortunately, the description we have of him right now is not very useful. When last seen, he was very thin, near six feet tall, with scraggly black hair and beard. What he looks like now, who can tell?"

"Still, at least we know not to look for someone short and round. And the fingers will help us weed through the tall, skinny ones," Sage said. "Do you mind if I tell Sergeant Hanke about Perkins?"

"Heck, no. We need all the help we can get. My men are doing their best but I'm not much help with this gimpy arm and having to watch out for those fools who tried to take me down."

"Cousins will look too," Fong said and stood. "Time we go question the stupid fella. He's been in dark all day." Having made that pronouncement, the Chinese man picked up the lantern and headed deeper into the underground.

Meachum cast a startled glance at Sage who both grinned and shrugged before jumping to his feet and following Fong. The scuffling sound at his heels told him Meachum was close behind.

TWENTY-TWO

Dispatch: *May 16, 1903, President is camping in Yosemite Valley with Scots-born naturalist, John Muir.*

"The conservation of natural resources is the fundamental problem. Unless we solve that problem it will avail us little to solve all others . . . Leave it as it is. The ages have been at work on it and man can only mar it . . . ." —T.R.

ONCE AGAIN, Sage was heading toward the underground cell that Fong and he had seized from the shanghaiing land sharks. Ordinarily, it was vacant and padlocked shut so no one could use it.

Portland's underground was a confusing, tricky place. Arches, installed between foundation walls, connected the buildings on many of the city's blocks. The dirt floors, never exposed to the elements, sent dry-as-bone dust flying upward with every step. It was different in the street tunnels connecting each block. Here and there, water seeped through the brick ceilings and walls, creating underground potholes waiting to soak the unwary.

Fong said it was possible to travel underground almost two miles upriver and a half-mile to the west. The Chinese knew the underground well. They had to. Above ground, the few city blocks where they were permitted to live were "filled to the gills," as his mother liked to say. That meant that many Chinese were forced to live in the underground. Usually in rooms walled off by scrap lumber, with candles and oil lamps their only light.

And, there were less benign uses of this inky maze–opium dens were down here, allowing customers an escape through the underground during police raids. Same for gambling dens, where the air was thick with yearning, bitter disappointment and tobacco smoke. All this varied activity created such a clutter of walled rooms, arches and tunnels that, even with a map and kerosene lantern, Sage rarely entered it without a guide.

After two blocks of basements and the wet muck of a two street tunnels, Sage heard the familiar chorus of squeaks and low chirps. It sounded like a swarm of ravenous rodents filled the black space. In fact, the noises signaled that they were nearing Fong's cousins who were manning posts around the shanghaiers' cell. Because scared people usually talked more, they would have insured that the "stupid one" was treated to endless hours of squeaking and scrabbling animal sounds.

Sage caught at Fong's sleeve. "Why not the leader or the other one? Why the 'stupid' one?"

Fong lifted the lantern so that it illuminated their three faces. Fong's eyes were mere slits, sparkling with a puckish confidence, "The stupid one best," he assured Sage. "He not know what important. Also, his mind slower so he not lie as good. You will see."

Sage pulled his hat brim low, took the lantern from Fong and stepped toward the cell, gesturing for Meachum to follow him. They moved to stand in front of the cell bars. The figure that had retreated to the dark rear of the cell cautiously limped forward. When he'd shuffled close enough to see Meachum's face, he stopped.

The lantern light shone on their prisoner's broad forehead, wide-spaced little eyes and a pair of ears that stuck out like jug handles from a round head. "Who . . . why, what the heck are you doing here?" he demanded of Meachum in a quavering voice.

Meachum's smile was almost kind. "Well, now. That just happens to be my question too. Just what exactly are you doing here?"

Even in the dim light, it was possible to see their prisoner's eyes shift first left, then right, as if the answer to Meachum's question hung in some corner cobweb.

The man stalled for time, "I don't know what you mean. The Chinks put me in here."

The kind smile turned cold as Meachum slowly shook his head, "No, what are you doing in Portland? You're not from this city, are you?"

For some reason, that question seemed to relax the other man because his shoulders dropped and he stepped closer. "No, I ain't. I'm up from 'Frisco and I wish I was back there. My cousin talked me into coming up here."

"What did he tell you was going to happen, once you got up here?"

"That lowdown buzzard lied to me. He said there was going to be a party, we were going to cause a to-do and then go home. We been here three weeks and no party's happened. And, they got me chasing after you, mister. I'm sorry about that fight in the alley. I had to protect my cousin but I weren't the one that stuck you."

Meachum nodded slowly. "I know. The one that stuck me was wearing a plaid coat. That your cousin?"

The man nodded.

"He the leader of the three of you?" The prisoner nodded again, this time more cautiously.

"There's more than the three of you in town, isn't there?"

"Yup. I haven't done met them all but there's another group like us living somewheres else."

"Who is the boss of both the groups?" Sage tensed and held his breath at Meachum's question.

"Well, it was some fella back East."

Meachum caught it too, "What do you mean 'was'?"

The other man's little eyes squinted in obvious calculation, "You going to let me go if I tell you?"

Meachum shook his head slowly. "Well, now, I can't let you go so you can cause me more trouble, can I?"

The calculation disappeared from the other man's expression. Slack-mouthed, big-eyed fear took its place. "You're not going to leave me down here, are you? You wouldn't do that to me, would you?"

Meachum said nothing, simply looked at the man who'd started whimpering low in his throat. Meachum heaved a sigh, "You really mean it? Do you wish you were back in 'Frisco?" he asked.

"On my ma's grave, I swear that's the truth." The man's little eyes widened with entreaty and he moved closer to wrap his pudgy hands around the bars.

Meachum cleared his throat, then said, "Okay, I can't let you loose here in Portland. But, if I got you a berth on a ship to 'Frisco, would you work your passage down?" Meachum asked.

The man's face answered the question. For the first time he smiled, showing them a wide space between his two front teeth. Then the smile was gone, replaced by a worried look. "How do I know you won't send me to China?"

That brought an approving nod from Meachum. "That's a smart question. Let me ask another one of you before I answer it. Did your cousin tell you that the so-called 'party' was to be for President Roosevelt?" he asked.

The other man froze, his face scrunched up as he added whatever else he knew to the information supplied by Meachum's question. They saw the moment that everything snapped into place for him because his face blanched and he stepped back from the bars, his mouth in a horrified "O." "The president, why would we cause the president trouble?" he quavered but before they could answer, he muttered, "My ma always said Dickie was the no-good black sheep of the family."

"What's your name, son?"

"It's Terrence Lincoln O'Connor, the Third," he said with obvious pride. "But, most folks call me 'Terry'," he added.

"Well, Terry. I think you know what I said about your cousin's plan fits right in with what little he's told you."

That comment sent Terry back to recollecting and left him staring at nothing, his mind seemingly caught by a realization.

"Terry," Meachum continued, speaking softly, "if your cousin is planning on doing harm to the president and he also wanted something bad to happen to me, what do you think that means?"

The man's hand tightened on the bars and he shoved his face forward. "It means you fellows are helping the president."

Meachum straightened and leaned closer. "So, if we're helping to protect the president, do you think you can trust me to put you on a ship sailing to 'Frisco and not one to China?"

Terry took some time thinking that one over. Then he raised his shoulders, jutted his chin forward and said, "I am an American. I support the president. If I'd known what Dickie was planning, I would have stopped him. I'm gonna tell you everything what I know. You send me to 'Frisco, I'll be grateful. If you send me to China, well, my ma warned me to stay away from Dickie. So it's my fault, whatever happens."

Meachum and Sage exchanged a look. It was seldom that they encountered a bad guy who really wasn't a bad guy. This Terry seemed to be an exception.

Meachum stood and reached his right hand through the bars, Terry responded likewise and they shook as Meachum said, "I believe you, Terry. I believe that you would never knowingly cause the president harm. I promise you that the ship I put you on will sail straight south to the Golden Gate and right into 'Frisco bay. It sails tomorrow with the early morning tide. I'll need to have you stay here until then. You got enough blankets?"

"Yes, sir," came Terry's subdued answer. "Is Dickie going to get killed?"

"I don't know, Terry. I hope not. My job is to try to make sure that nobody gets killed. But I can't promise you. You understand?"

Terry nodded solemnly, then said, "I said the man 'was' back East because he's coming here to town tomorrow. So, I figure he's on a train or a ship or a coach or horse or something by now."

Sage and Meachum exchanged another look. "Tell me everything you know about this man, Terry," Meachum said.

❀ ❀ ❀

Mae was at the kitchen sink, scrubbing down carrots, when the door to the basement opened. This was followed by the sound of Matthew's cheerful greeting and Andy's answering shout. Matthew had arrived with another bucket of coal. That dumped, he sat at the table across from Andy, who began pulling various bits of stone and wood from his pocket, explaining the origin of each one.

Looking at Matthew over the top of the little boy's head, Mae saw a gleam in Matthew's eyes that meant he had news for her. She reached for the garbage pails, gave a sharp yip of pain and clutched at her back. Matthew jumped up and grabbed the pail handle, "Please, ma'am. Let me help with that." He quickly picked up the pails and headed for the outside door, with Mae trotting in front of him to open the door. Within seconds, they were both outside on the sidewalk heading for the dustbin before Andy or anyone in the kitchen realized what was happening.

"What is it, Matthew?" Mae asked.

"A man has come. His name is McAllister. He claims Mr. Adair sent him and he says that he's here to assist me. He told me my bike, Blue Beauty, misses me."

Mae felt relief wash over her. "Oh, that is good news. Yes, McAllister is certainly on our side. I am glad there is someone above stairs in case you need help."

"He said he'll be coming every day."

"Anything else? We don't have much time."

"I'm to serve at one of those dinner parties tomorrow night. The Cap'n seems a bit excited, he's running around bossing us boys more than usual."

"You'll keep your ears open?"

"Of course, I will. And, my eyes too."

Mae clutched at his arm. "Don't you go above the second floor."

Matthew said nothing for a minute, "I won't unless I see cause for it."

"Now, Matthew," Mae started to say only to be interrupted by the side door opening to let a curious Andy poke his head out.

She quickly raised the dustbin lid so Matthew could empty the garbage pails.

The Portland Hotel was a beehive of activity as preparations were fully underway for the presidential visit. Gardeners were busy clipping the grass and bushes that formed a tidy green island in the middle of the circle drive. An army of industrious men was polishing the U-shaped hotel's windows. Other men were stringing wires from one window ledge to the next. From these would hang yards upon yards of patriotic bunting. Inside, the activity was just as frenetic.

Standing at his customary place behind the dining room podium, Solomon appeared to be the only calm soul in the building. For some reason the maitre'd always recalled to Sage's mind those stately redwood trees in Northern California—imperturbable and firmly rooted in some ancient, elemental wisdom.

"Mr. Solomon, I see that preparations are well underway for Roosevelt's overnight stay," Sage said in greeting.

Solomon rolled his eyes to the ceiling but smiled. "May I show you to your customary table, Mr. Adair?" His question was code for "do we need privacy to talk?"

Sage answered in the affirmative so Solomon led him to the table nearest the kitchen door, behind the drooping palm. Solomon stood with his back to the rest of the room, his tall muscular body shielding their exchange from curious eyes.

"I presume I am to go a-hunting once more among the hotel's guests?" he asked.

Sage chuckled. "Before I ask another favor of you, I wanted to thank you again for taking care of Meachum. Please thank Ms. Esther, too."

"I am grateful for the opportunity to assist President Roosevelt. He has done more to raise my people's hopes in one year than all the other presidents put together, save for Mr. Lincoln, of course."

"I just wish he'd show the same open mind toward our Chinese friends. It has to be hard for Fong and his cousins. They are taking a lot of chances for a man who calls them 'heathens' and tries to ban them from the country."

"Yes, Mr. Fong and I have discussed Mr. Roosevelt's ignorance on that score. But, Mr. Fong and I, we believe it is necessary to consider the big picture. Whatever moves people in the direction of decency will eventually open their hearts to other compassionate possibilities. On balance, Roosevelt is leading the country in the right direction."

"You and Mr. Fong are bigger men than I am," Sage said and added, "and, in your case, not just in size."

Solomon shrugged, "We need hope to survive as men, so we both look for it. Some find it by dwelling on the hereafter, but that is a little too distant and uncertain for my liking. Although I do find a small measure of comfort in those thoughts as well." He glanced over his shoulder toward a couple who were waiting to be seated.

"It appears I am needed, Mr. Adair. What is it that can I do for you?"

"Starting tomorrow, Cyrus Dolph may have a guest staying in Dolph's suite here in the hotel. He may be the man we're looking for. We just learned that the leader of the assassination scheme is due to arrive tomorrow as well. It may just be a coincidence but, it's the only lead we have right now. We need to know more about Dolph's guest. Do you think you or your folks can find out about him?"

"Obtaining that information will be easy as a swamp turtle slipping off a log," Solomon said with a smile. "It just so happens that it is my duty to personally call on all of Mr. Dolph's guests to offer them the services of the dining room and its staff. I will send a message to you and Mr. Fong when I have learned something of note. But, now, I must return to my post." With a dip of his head, Solomon turned and glided away.

TWENTY-THREE

Dispatch: *May 17, 1903, President remains camping in Yosemite Valley, California.*

> *"There is not a man of us who does not at times need a helping hand to be stretched out to him, and then shame upon him who will not stretch out the helping hand to his brother." —T.R.*

MAE ONCE MORE STOOD AT THE SINK, this time paring age spots out of turnips. Springtime, most of the stored root vegetables got spots and turned woody. That meant a menu change. No more young turnips with a glacé sauce for the Cap'n and his guests. They'd be eating turnip mash just like the boys in the dining hall. That's what Ms. Wiggit had proclaimed and Mae thought she'd seen a grim smile of satisfaction cross the cook's face as she'd turned away.

Outside the window she saw the same sad little scene take place as it had every afternoon since she'd started working at the BCS. The same boys sat or stood near the courtyard's bench, their faces slack with disinterest. "What is wrong with them?" she asked herself, yet again.

The sound of the inner kitchen door opening turned her eyes away from the window to glance over her shoulder. Matthew entered the room, his frame vibrating with energy–the exact opposite of the boys she'd been watching. His bright blue eyes locked on her own and the intensity of his gaze told her he needed to talk. With swift steps, he reached the coal scuttle, dumped his burden and turned to ruffle Andy's hair, a touch that made the little boy pink with pleasure.

Swiftly bending to lift the garbage pail, Mae dropped it, giving yet another yip of pain and clutching the small of her back. As she hoped, Matthew was at her side in a second, reaching for the pail. "Here, ma'am, let me get that for you."

"Why, thank you, boy," Mae said, aware that Mrs. Wiggit had turned from the stove to watch their exchange. Mae forced herself to speak offhandedly, "That pail you're holding and the other one over there, need carting to the dustbin. Do you have time to carry them out?"

Even as she spoke, Matthew was lifting the second pail and she was striding toward the outer door, yanking it open so he could pass through. He was at her heels, the both of them stepping over the threshold as Mae called back over her shoulder. "I'll be right back. Just going to open the dustbin lid for him so the pails don't get mucky bottoms from being sat down in the mud." She didn't wait to hear Ms. Wiggit's response before firmly closing the door. She pushed from her mind the fact that their little subterfuge had been obvious as a donkey's nose sticking in a window. The courtyard was paved with bricks so it was not likely there'd be any mud in sight.

Once they were on the sidewalk, Mae halted to ask, "What is it, Matthew, what have you learned? Talk quick because we can't dally. Lord knows what Mrs. Wiggit is making of our exit. This is the second time I've used the crook in the back excuse." The cook was a smart woman with a suspicious nature.

Matthew wasn't thinking about Mrs. Wiggit. "Mrs. Clemens," he said, "I'm near certain sure they got Ollie or someone else locked up there on the third floor or in the attic."

"What makes you think that? What's happened?"

"I been staying here three days now. Them boys they take out to that courtyard every day, I've been counting them. Seeing how many they are. Five of them is what I count."

They passed through the gate into the courtyard just as those very same boys exited the courtyard, using the side door into the building's stairwell. Mae looked at the kitchen window. No one seemed to be watching.

When they reached the dustbin, he passed one of the full pails to her. He lifted the dustbin lid and Mae held it up so he could tip the pail's contents into it. "Yes, there's five boys, " she confirmed, wondering what the number of boys had to do with anything. The way it was looking, they'd made Ms. Wiggit suspicious for no reason.

He must have sensed her impatience, because Matthew stood holding the empty pail, his face earnest with the need to make her understand, "Every day, at noontime, Mr. Growl takes a tray upstairs to the third floor. That's because those boys never come down to the dining room to eat. So, I started counting. Two days now, there's been six plates on that tray."

"Maybe one plate's for Mr. Growl. His name, by the way, is Norris Grindstaff. Could be he stays and eats with them."

Even before she'd finished her sentence, Matthew was shaking his head. "No," he said. "I thought of that but he comes right back down. He doesn't stay up there long enough to eat. When he goes back up, he comes back with six empty plates. Oh, and I learned his name, all right. I just think Andy's name fits him better. Every time he speaks, it's like he's fixin' to take a bite out of you."

Mae studied the boy's freckled face, thinking that behind those innocent country-boy eyes was a clever, fine mind. "Best be dumping that other pail. We've been gone a mite too long."

Matthew hefted the pail and flung its contents into the metal bin as he said, "It's Ollie. I know it's Ollie up there eating off that sixth plate. I'm going to get him out of there somehow."

A glance at the boy's profile showed a set jaw. "Let's get a move on. We'll talk on the way back to the kitchen," she said.

Once they got through the gate and out of sight of the kitchen window, she grabbed his forearm and pulled him to a stop.

"I think you might be right, Matthew. If he's up there, he's being held in the attic. The one time I was up there, I noticed a door with a key in the lock. That might be the attic. I know he's not on the third floor because I managed to look in every room. But we have to be careful and smart. We have two missions here at the BCS. We must save Ollie but we must save those five other boys too. That's what Ollie wants. You understand?"

His mouth compressed and his chin jutted out, but Matthew nodded. "They don't take Ollie out into the sun like they do the other boys," he said.

Worry sent a twinge through Mae. He wasn't about to delay his rescue of Ollie for very long. She tried to get Matthew's mind back on track. "That's because they have different plans for those boys. They can't have them looking too peckish." Mae studied a puff of white cloud drifting leisurely toward the east as she fought to control a sudden roiling of disgust.

She glanced toward Matthew, saying, "Listen, I agree with you. Somehow, we have to get Ollie out of the building right away. But, we've got to do it without anyone suspecting you or me."

"They're having that dinner party tonight. A friend of the Cap'n is coming to stay and the Cap'n wants to impress him. That would be the best time," he said. "They'll be carousing and drinking and won't notice me going up the stairs."

Mae was already shaking her head. "No, that's too soon. It can't look like you're involved and it would take too long for you to break him out. And once you got him out, then what? Once he's out of the building, do you just leave him standing on the sidewalk? He has to be taken away and, if you do that, then they'll for sure notice you're gone. You couldn't come back and we need you here to help save those five other boys."

They stood in silence. When Mae spoke, her words came slowly, as she tried to parse out the glimmer of an idea. "We need Mr. McAllister's help and Mr. Eich's too. He'll be coming later. We'll send him to talk to Mr. McAllister. You said they drink alcohol at the Captain's parties?"

"Yup, when I wait on them during the dinner hour, one of my jobs is to make sure their glasses stay full to the brim."

"What time do the two of them get up the next morning?" Mae asked.

A grin spread across Matthew's face. He'd caught on to her plan. "They usually crawl out around ten o'clock or so."

Mae grinned back at him. "So, long about eight a.m. tomorrow morning they'll be dead to the world?"

Matthew nodded.

In a flash, like a solitary bolt of lightening hitting a mountain top, the plan details clicked into place. She ran them through her mind one more time. They fit together snug as a flour bin lid. She swiftly laid her plan out, "The BCS doors open at eight o'clock. That's when we'll have McAllister come in. Is there an out-of-sight place for him to wait?"

"In the back stairwell that goes down to the swimming pool room. Nobody goes down to the pool that early."

"Can he get out of the building from there without going out the front door?"

Hope and eagerness lighting his face, Matthew said. "Yes, there's another door out of the basement right near there. It unlocks from the inside."

Once again, Mae felt respect surge for the boy's ingenuity and foresight. "You've done a pretty thorough investigation," she observed before asking, "So, can you get up to the third floor, break open the attic door where they're keeping Ollie, or whoever that sixth person is, and get him down to Mr. McAllister in the stairwell?"

The boy's brow furrowed. "I better make it look like he broke out his own self," he said.

"You think you can manage all that?"

It was clear from the boy's scrunched face that he had some misgivings but then he set his jaw. "You betcha," he said.

When they entered the kitchen, it was to encounter the thin-lipped gaze of a suspicious Ms. Wiggit. Without looking at Mae, Matthew dipped his head in the cook's direction and exited the kitchen, grabbing up the empty coal scuttle on his way. Mae saw the look of disappointment on Andy's face as Matthew exited and felt a momentary pang before she turned her attention to the cook's disapproving face.

"We got to talking about growing up on a farm." she told the woman. Her own ears told her the excuse sounded flimsy as a cobweb across an outhouse door.

"Humph," was the cook's response before she turned back to the stove. In the following silence, Mae heard Mrs. Wiggit add under her breath, "I thought that boy told us he came from fishing folk."

Mae kept her mouth shut. She'd already made one blunder. No sense in adding more salt to the shaker.

When he made his customary four o'clock visit to the BCS dustbin, Eich was surprised that Mae failed to appear. She usually finagled an excuse for leaving the kitchen just in time to catch him as he left the courtyard. He stood for a moment on the sidewalk, uncertain what to do, but finally he shrugged his shoulders, picked up the cart shafts and trudged down the street. "When clouds appear, wise men put on their cloaks," he quoted to himself. Shakespeare might have been talking about a different situation but, if Mae didn't return to her rooming house tonight, he would raise the alarm.

Almost like notes of music in his ears, he heard her voice behind him, calling "Herman, wait!"

He knew the smile he turned on her was bright with relief. "Ah, Mae, you gave this old heart of mine a fright. When you didn't show, I was afraid . . . ."

She put her hand on his forearm and grinned at him. "That's because I was telling another big lie to Ms. Wiggit so I could get more time away to talk. Let's keep walking toward the rooming house. I don't want to run into anyone from the BCS."

Curious stares were cast in their direction but the ragpicker with his cart and the dowdy middle-aged woman at his side were too busy talking to notice.

Mae quickly filled him in on what she'd learned from Matthew. "So, I was thinking that you could watch the door and cover the boy up in your cart when McAllister brings him out.

That way, McAllister can drop off the boy to you, stay in the BCS and act as if nothing's happened. And, Matthew could stay pretty much in their sight the whole time too. They couldn't blame him for the disappearance either. If McAllister and Ollie haven't exited in a half-hour or so, maybe you could go in and create a commotion. Give them time to escape or something."

"That sounds like an admirable plan. I suppose you would like me to inform Mr. McAllister of his role in this escapade?"

"Well, I can't exactly justify being gone that long just to pay my landlady the rent I forgot to give her this morning," Mae said with a just hint of snap to her tone.

Eich threw back his head and laughed. When he saw her stiffen, he hastened to reassure. "I will be happy to pay a call on the lawyer. You sure are the one for coming up with imaginative excuses at the drop of a hat."

Her indignation gave way to a rueful smile, "My mama always said I was the fanciful one. I try not to think she was calling me an easy liar."

"Mae, you are a clever, wonderful woman," he told her and had the pleasure of seeing her blush.

She looked away from him and said, "Herman, stop your blathering and get to talking with E. J. We've got a boy to rescue."

"I presume my cart's final destination will be Mr. Fong's provision shop?" he asked, permitting her effort at composure and distraction to succeed.

"Lordy, I hadn't even given a thought of where to hide him. But that sounds good. Poor Mrs. Fong, every time she turns around we're dropping yet another person on her doorstep."

That caused Eich to chuckle. "You don't worry about Mrs. Fong," he told her "She might be no bigger than a minute, but she is tougher than a rawhide rope. She knows exactly what is what. Besides, it gives her a chance to practice her English and study us European-types up close. She likes that. Our Mr. Fong chose his wife well."

❁ ❁ ❁

When Eich reached McAllister's building, he tightened down his canvas and left his cart snug against the building's front. If anyone wanted to steal his bits and pieces, they were welcome since it meant they had a greater need for them.

Eich entered the building and stepped into the elevator. He enjoyed the novel experience of being hoisted upward by a clanking and huffing steam elevator, marveling at the ease with which he reached the third floor. All that way without a single twinge in his knees or a pause to catch his breath.

Fortune smiled on them all. McAllister was alone in his office. When he saw Eich, he jumped up, grabbed the ragpicker's outstretched hand with both of his and shook it, smiling all the while. "You have news? You must have news, otherwise you wouldn't take the chance of coming here."

For a moment Eich felt a sharp pang that he wouldn't be able to ease the lawyer's mind about Lynch's new child prostitution house. But then he let the regret go and explained the situation before laying out Mae's plan for rescuing Ollie from the BCS.

The lawyer controlled his disappointment well, stating crisply, "I can be there promptly at eight. I know where that stairwell is and the door into the alley. They might think it peculiar that I am swimming so early in the morning but the man on the front desk is a stupid fellow and he might not say anything. Besides, you say the Cap'n and Grindstaff should still be asleep."

"That's my hope. Mae is certain they will be. The only thing is, we don't know anything about the Cap'n's friend. We don't even know if he's spending the night. We'll just have to hope that all of them get drunk as lords and have to sleep it off."

TWENTY-FOUR

Dispatch: *May 17, 1903, President remains camping in Yosemite Valley, California.*

> *"I think there is only one quality worse than hardness of heart and that is softness of head . . . Character, in the long run, is the decisive factor in the life of an individual and of nations alike."*
> —T.R.

MCALLISTER ENTERED MOZART'S obviously bristling with news. That was evident when, all in one swift move, he whipped off his coat, tossed it onto the coat rack and turned to Sage. Sage felt hope surge. Maybe E. J. had learned from Fenton who else might be entertaining an out-of-town guest. If only they could find the mastermind behind the plot. They had to identify that key person, follow him, see who his confederates were–take them all out of action. Or, at the very least, they needed to prevent the leader from giving the signal to that poor deluded assassin.

"May I seat you, Mr. McAllister?" Sage inquired as he stepped forward, a menu in hand.

"Yes, yes, you can, Mr. Adair. There will be three in the party. I am expecting my clients within the quarter hour. But, I came early so I could talk to you. Do you have a minute to sit with me?" There was a definite undertone of urgency in the lawyer's question.

Sage gestured to Horace and asked him to temporarily add hosting to his duties. Then Sage led McAllister to a table for four some distance from the other occupied tables. They waited until the waiter filled the water glasses and left.

"What is it? I can tell you have news," he said.

"Things have heated up at the BCS."

With just those few words, Sage felt his anticipation drain and dread take its place. "Are Mrs. Clemens and Matthew safe? Have you seen them?"

McAllister held up a hand to stop the worrying words. "They're fine. It's just that, apparently, your boy is bound and determined to rescue his young friend whom he believes they have imprisoned in the BCS's fourth floor attic."

"Ollie," Sage said, absentmindedly as his thoughts grabbed onto Matthew's past encounters with other bad characters. Each time, things had gone wrong and they'd had to rescue the boy.

"I don't think that's a good idea," he said.

"It's too late now. The plan's underway and there is no way to get to Matthew and tell him to drop it," McAllister said and described the special dinner party already taking place, Matthew's planned attack on the attic door, his own role in stationing himself in the stairwell and Eich's plan to cart the prisoner to safety.

Sage couldn't fault the plan. As long as the Cap'n, his aide and guest slept off their drunk the next morning, the plan should work and leave Matthew, Mae and McAllister clear of any suspicion.

"What if Matthew gets caught breaking open the door or leading the prisoner down the stairwell?"

"If Matthew doesn't show up at the bottom of the stairs within fifteen minutes, then Eich is going to create a ruckus in the front lobby, I'm heading for the third floor and," here the lawyer looked a little sheepish, "I hope you don't mind but I've enlisted the aid of my friend, Robert Clooney, and a mutual friend of ours. They're also going to be on hand and will rush the stairs if I whistle. If they've caught Matthew, we three will free him, come hell or high water. It's that simple."

At that moment there was a minor commotion at the door as two women arrived. One was a formidable matron with her dark hair neatly divided into two braided buns on each side of her head. She allowed Horace to aid her in removing her coat. As he turned to help the second woman, the first woman gazed around the dining room with pursed lips. Evidently she did not approve of what she saw. Her companion, thin as the matron was rotund, also had a sour frown on her narrow lips. Had she been in the first blush of girlhood, he might have called her a "waif." As it was, with her unruly hair and lined face, she resembled a stiff, disapproving broomstick.

Sage started to rise. "Those two look unhappy. I'd better go help Horace."

McAllister glanced toward the door and chuckled. "Don't bother. Those are my clients. We might as well get this over with."

Before Sage could puzzle out the meaning of McAllister's statement, the two women were advancing in quick long strides like avenging angels. Sage and McAllister both leapt to their feet.

"Mrs. Nora Williams and Miss Rose Trumbull, I'd like you to meet the proprietor of this fine establishment, Mr. John Adair."

The heavyset matron, Mrs. Williams, sent Adair a chilly glance but instead of shaking his offered hand, swept aside her skirts and planted her ample behind on a chair. Her companion swiftly followed her example.

Once seated, Mrs. Williams looked up at Sage, disapproval still writ large across her face and said, "Well, Mr. Adair, if Mr. McAllister insists I meet him here, I might as well make our visit worthwhile. I would appreciate it if you would sit so I don't have to continue to crane my neck upward at such an awkward angle. It is highly uncomfortable."

Sage hastened to obey her command even as he shot an inquiring look toward McAllister whose twitching lips indicated he found the situation amusing. Apparently, the lawyer then felt some remorse because he hastened to explain, "These two estimable ladies are officers of our local White Ribbon Society."

Sure enough, each woman sported a tiny white bow pinned to her lapel. "White Ribbon Society?" he repeated, uncertain what mission that organization might have.

"Well, really, Mr. Adair. I am not surprised that you might be ignorant of our good works. Undoubtably, you are too busy imbibing and purveying King Alcohol to pay any attention to those of us who seek its banishment from the life of our community!" Mrs. Williams said before again pursing her lips shut.

Sage looked at McAllister who grinned at him. Temperance women. These clients of McAllister's were temperance women.

McAllister looked at the two women but his words were directed at Sage, "I have informed my clients that I drink alcohol on occasion but not to excess. One of my conditions to providing them with discounted legal services is that they can only proselytize me on the subject once a month on the 15th day. Additionally, in exchange for meeting here and letting me buy them dinner, I agreed that they could each speak their mind to you about Mozart's serving of wine provided they do so briefly and, only once, before we order dinner."

Sage felt his eyebrows crawl up toward his hairline before relaxing back down into place. He turned to the two women.

"Please state your opinions, ladies. We have some very good dishes this evening and I am sure you are hungry."

Despite Sage's gracious tone, the Williams woman did not unbend. If anything, her nose raised further in the air and she bit off her words with a snap, "Very well, since Mr. McAllister has correctly stated our arrangement, I will proceed."

She paused to stare around the room. Sage looked too and saw that a number of patrons were enjoying crystal goblets of wine with their meals. Light glinting in the ruby and gold liquids gave the drinks a shimmering beauty. He thought it most unlikely, however, that the sight would arouse Mrs. William's esthetic appreciations. He was right.

"I see here that you have invested a great deal of effort and money to make this an elegant establishment," Mrs. Williams said. "Then you ruin it by throwing wide its doors to the evil influence of the demon drink."

"I don't see anyone in this room displaying any indication of being under the influence of the demon drink," Sage said, his tone mild. He could afford to relax since he knew McAllister had promised that this particular confrontation was to be of limited duration.

From beside him, Miss Trumbull spoke for the first time, her soft voice intoning, "'To rise in might and cast the evil out that slays the Christ life.' That is what we in the White Ribbon Society are striving to accomplish."

Sage turned to her. "Please tell me of some of your recent activities."

Her thin cheeks flushed and she said proudly, "Mrs. Williams and I just returned from an evangelistic trip to Wallowa country. We are forming a new chapter there."

Mrs. Williams interrupted, snapping, "Really Rose, Mr. Adair is merely trying to distract us from our mission here." She turned to him. "I officially ask, as the superintendent of the Society's Sunday school and commercial work sections, that you cease and desist from serving alcohol within this establishment!"

Sage scooted back his chair and said, "Ladies, I respect what you are attempting to accomplish. Too many men drown their sorrows in alcohol. Too many women and children suffer pain and hunger because of it. But, I must say, many people responsibly enjoy alcohol periodically without any negative effect on themselves or their families or society. For that reason, I must respectfully decline your request." He started to rise but McAllister gestured him down.

Mrs. Williams sniffed and said, "That is exactly the self-serving, bullheaded response I expected." She turned to McAllister to say, "We may as well order now." Miss Trumbull sent a shy smile toward Sage and her checks colored again when he returned the smile.

"Oh, really, Rose," chastised Mrs. Williams who'd seen the exchange. In response, the timid spinster's blush turned crimson and she looked down at her gloved hands that started twisting in her lap.

McAllister cleared his throat and said, "Ah, before Mr. Adair returns to his duties, Mrs. Williams, I was hoping you'd tell him of your more recent activities about Portland."

She didn't hesitate. "We have decided that the public needs to be educated about the most serious dens of inequity plaguing our working men. The members of our organization have voted to become picketers! We have spent the afternoon creating slogans for the signs. Ms. Trumbull and I have engaged a sign artist who has offered to paint the signs for free–we will supply him with the required materials, of course. We have quite a healthy bank account thanks to contributions from others who seek a sober, God-fearing society." She sat back in her chair clearly satisfied with the Society's new direction and her role in bringing it to fruition.

Sage contemplated the vision–hordes of sign-waving women congregating outside saloon doors, their voices shrill with righteous indignation. He felt a pang of sympathy toward the unsuspecting saloon keepers and the patrons who would soon find themselves having to thread their way amongst the temperance movement's bonneted and gloved foot soldiers. Too bad they didn't put all that emotional indignation to better use, like protesting child labor or starvation wages or the forced overcrowding in Chinatown or. . . ." The idea burst into his brain with the suddenness of photographic flash powder.

"Tell me," he asked, striving to keep his tone mild, "how does the White Ribbon Society feel about child prostitution?" Miss Trumbull's gasp slipped out before she could stifle it with her dinner napkin.

Mrs. Williams was made of sterner stuff. Although two bright spots of red flared on her cheeks, she said briskly, "It is an abomination! Of course, we loathe it! I am surprised that you think you have to ask such a question."

He glanced at McAllister and saw that the other man was grinning yet again–this time with a look of satisfaction in his eyes. The lawyer had already hit upon the idea. That's why he'd brought the women here. The rogue!

Out of the corner of his eye, Sage caught the movement of the kitchen door swinging open. That was nothing new since it swung to and fro all night long as the waiters went in and out. But, unusually, the door had been eased open. This fact alone made Sage turn his head to look more closely in that direction. Fong stepped into the dining room and stood there, to one side of the door. He wore his customary black tunic and trousers but not the apron. Nor was he holding a busboy tray. Clearly Fong was not there to work. But it wasn't the absence of these trappings that made Sage catch his breath. It was the paleness of the other man's face and the enlarged black of his eyes. Something was terribly wrong. Sage fought the urge to jump up. Fong looked at Sage, then up at the ceiling before stepping back into the kitchen.

Forcing his attention back to the table, Sage was aware the women had not stopped talking. He locked gazes with McAllister. From the lawyer's intense scrutiny, it was clear he had also observed Fong's tense state as well. "Excuse me, ladies. There is a pressing matter I must see to." He bowed, saying "Mr. McAllister, I trust that you will be able to carry on the discussion without me?"

McAllister stood and held out his hand for Sage to shake. "You can rely upon that with every confidence, Mr. Adair. I will endeavor to bring the matter to these ladies' attention in the fervent hope of obtaining a satisfactory outcome."

Sage turned back to the two women whose faces expressed mystification at the men's oblique exchange, "Ladies," he said, bowing. "I will send you a contribution in support of your efforts and I will continue to ensure that Mozart's does all it can to discourage public drunkenness." He bowed again, turned on his heel and strode toward the stairs. He had to force himself to mount them at a measured pace when, in fact, every muscle in his legs demanded to be let loose to charge up them, two at a time—which is what happened once he'd passed from the sight of those in the dining room below.

Rushing upwards, he had a dreadful premonition that disastrous news awaited him. Fong's bleak face, so different from its customary placidity, had signaled that whatever news awaited, it was not good.

TWENTY-FIVE

Dispatch: *May 17, 1903, President breaks camp in Yosemite Valley, California.*

> *"A man who is good enough to shed his blood for the country is good enough to be given a square deal afterwards . . . When I speak of 'square deal' . . . I mean not only that each man should act fairly under the rules of the game . . . but I mean also that if the rules of the game give improper advantage to some set of people, then let us change the rules of the game." —T.R.*

WHEN HE REACHED HIS ROOM, Sage threw open the door only to find the space empty. He didn't hesitate but headed for the attic stairs. Once he reached the polished wood floor of the exercise space, he paused to let his eyes adjust to the dim light from a single flickering candle. In that near blackness he saw Fong. The other man was moving through the form of the snake and crane but at a speed that made him a whirling dark blur. Normally, the movements of the snake and crane were slow, studied and deliberate. Fong, however, was a whirling demon, his speed and snap revealing the power of each carefully constructed move. Each thrust, kick and roll back was calculated to vanquish the enemy in at least ten different ways. Then the blur came to rest. Fong crossed his arms in front of his body, separated them and allowed them to float down until his hands were at rest beside his legs. He stood motionless for a full minute–allowing the power of his movement to subside back into calm.

Fong turned, gestured toward the floor cushion beside the low table where the candle sat, its yellow flame, flaring and flowing with the room's faint stirrings of air. Sage sat and Fong also lowered down onto the only other cushion in the room. Fong's face gleamed a rich honey gold in the candlelight. The bleak look still lingered in his dark eyes, but the exercise had returned calm to his features.

"Bad news, I take it." Sage said in a low voice.

The older man's face was a graven mask, pain etching new lines. He said, "Mr. Sage, they catch Mr. Meachum."

Sage let the breath he was holding whoosh from his lungs. "He's dead then?" A wave of grief rushed into Sage's heart carrying memories of Meachum's brave deeds and wise advice. He'd told Sage to find something rewarding to do in addition to saving the world. Meachum shared that he spent his own free time crafting fine furniture. Thanks to Meachum, Sage had come to experience deep satisfaction from the growing of flowers. Sage glanced up through the skylight, glimpsing the flower boxes he planned to tend throughout the summer months. What was he going to tell Meachum's wife and children? And St. Alban? How could they successfully complete the mission? Did they have any hope of saving Roosevelt without Meachum's help?

"I don't think Mr. Meachum is dead yet," Fong said softly.

The relief was immense, Sage felt a smile start across his face but he let it fade when he saw that the other man's face still set in stoic grimness. A thought cross his mind and he spoke it, "Something happened to one of your men, is that it?"

Fong lips tightened and then he said, "Choi Ji was standing guard outside the saloon where Mr. Meachum was meeting with one of his men. Another man was in back of saloon, making sure no one forced Mr. Meachum out that way. When nothing happen for long time, man in back go to front. He found Ji lying behind trash can, knife in between ribs, hands cut and bruised. He fight very hard."

His gaze traveled around the room, but Sage didn't see it. Instead, he saw the body of a young, slender, black-clad Chinese man curled in pain. "Is Ji dead?" he forced himself to ask.

Fong didn't answer directly. Instead he said, "Choi Ji was nephew who recently traveled here from China to be with me. Mother is my younger sister."

Fong's use of the past tense caught Sage's ear. Choi Ji was dead. "Fong, I am so sorry."

His friend didn't answer, merely dipped his head, silently accepting Sage's sympathy. After that they sat silent, each absorbed with his own thoughts.

Finally, Fong cleared his throat, "I think they have not killed Meachum. They have followed him for ten days. They know he has help from Chinese. They know he meet with his own men. They know some other man, you, Mr. Sage, also helping. Before they kill him, they will want whole story," he said. "They will want to know about us."

The coldness in Fong's tone made Sage look toward him. That face was still, expressionless, a distant stare, a warrior's face. Sage stood and began pacing. Fong was right. Their opponents couldn't take the chance that there were still others intent on thwarting the assassination. That meant there was time to discover where they'd imprisoned the Flying Squadron's leader. As for Meachum's team, it was going to be hard to keep them looking for the assassin, the gang of rowdies who were to create a distraction and the one man who'd be in position to trigger the whole dastardly sequence of events.

That thought triggered a question. He hadn't had a chance to ask McAllister if he'd learned any more about who would be present on that platform. Obviously, the man they hunted was one of the attendees. He'd be in the perfect position to signal the assassin when to throw the bomb at Roosevelt. Another thought came to Sage. According to their prisoner, who was now aboard a coastal steamer heading south, the man from back East was supposed to have arrived today. It couldn't be a coincidence that the violence had suddenly escalated into murder and kidnaping.

"What do you think we should do?" he asked, turning to Fong.

"First we need to find Mr. Meachum before it is too late. Also, we must not stop trying to find the assassin. And there is new man in town. I think he is maybe reason my nephew . . . ." Fong didn't continue and that long-distance stare was back.

After a moment's silence, Sage hesitantly asked the crucial question, "Will your men keep helping us?"

For the first time, Fong smiled. It was an arctic smile, one that promised death was in the offing. "More men will help now. I already ask other tongs for help."

"But I thought the tongs warred against each other."

Fong stood and faced Sage squarely. "Tongs many times at war. But I am their peacemaker. For me, they will do as I ask, even make peace so they can fight side by side. China men might battle between selves, but when it comes to white man, we become one, a clenched fist. They already on the streets, asking in North End if anyone saw one man being led by others. Finding Mr. Meachum is their mission. You . . ." here he pointed at Sage's chest, "must go talk to Meachum's men. I sent message that you will be at Slap Jack's saloon at ten o'clock tonight."

Sage pulled his gold pocket watch from his vest pocket. "Crikey, as Matthew would say, I best get cracking." His own mention of the boy reminded him that Fong knew nothing of the rescue planned for the early morning hours. He filled Fong in on the plan and timetable for its execution.

"That boy very determined. He make himself good part of team. I will try to be there tomorrow in morning but I cannot promise. Meachum is much harder problem. Matthew has plenty of help."

"I agree. Meachum is your priority. I'm going to change my clothes, stop and see Solomon at the New Elijah and then head down to Slap Jack's." Sage turned toward the door and took a few steps before turning back. "I am really sorry about your nephew. Nothing can soften the pain of his loss but I do want to help. If you permit, I will send something to his mother."

"Choi Ji departed a warrior. I will tell his mother. Money will also help because he has wife and child in China. His dream was to send money home to buy small farm, make many more children and die an old man with many grandchildren. Now that is lost. All lost." Fong's voice was hollow with grief. He shifted and seemed to square his shoulders, "Can do nothing to bring him back. But I will make sure his killer does not go free. Hurry, we must go."

They left the attic. When they reached the third floor hallway Sage asked, "What did Ji's name mean?"

Fong paused. "Lucky" he said in a flat voice as he slipped behind the tapestry to head down the secret stairwell. Once on the other side, he'd descend three flights of stairs into the cellar and along the tunnel to the outside. Sage would soon follow. First, though, he had to go down to the restaurant and ask Horace to take over its operation.

When he reached the entry way and looked through into the dining room he could see that McAllister and his two guests were nearly finished with their meal though their conversation remained lively. McAllister caught sight of Sage and stared as if willing Sage to communicate by mental telepathy. Sage tightened his lips and shook his head slightly. McAllister got the message that nothing good had occurred.

Sage pointedly looked at the two White Ribbon Society ladies and raised his left eyebrow. McAllister's face relaxed and he raised a thumb to signify success. Sage allowed himself a rueful chuckle as he thought of the slogans the redoubtable Mrs. Williams and the shy Miss Trumbull would create in their effort to kill Lynch's business expansion plans.

Solomon stood behind the front desk of the New Elijah hotel, looking alert and in command. He showed no reaction when Sage ambled through the door, fully outfitted in his "John Miner" role. Not for the first time, Sage wondered how the Carolinian managed to hold down a full-time job, oversee the New Elijah's operation and still remain impeccably groomed and genial as a country gentleman. With a slight head gesture, Solomon directed Sage toward the interior door that opened into his apartment. Once inside, Sage quickly told Solomon what had transpired.

"The young man died with honor protecting Mr. Meachum. That is some comfort to Mr. Fong I am sure," were Solomon's first words.

For a moment Sage got lost in the realization that his friend from China and this friend from the other side of America were more alike than he'd suspected. Life was tough for everybody except the rich in this country. Most Americans fought for survival every single day of their lives. But for the yellow man and the black man, it was immeasurably harder. At any moment they might experience random insults and violence simply because of their skin color. Worse, they had to hide their true feelings every minute they spent outside their circle of friends and family. Not for the first time, Sage was aware that he too hid who he was but with one big difference. He did so by choice, not necessity.

He realized Solomon was looking at him inquiringly. "I'm sorry, Mr. Solomon. My mind was off gathering wool like a springtime shepherd." When the other man raised his eyebrows, Sage explained, "It's an old saying of my mother's. She's got a lot of them and they tend to pop out of my mouth without warning."

Solomon's smile widened as his shoulders lifted in a subtle shrug. "Ah, mothers. Their voices remain forever with us. But I suspect, Mr. Adair, that you are here to ask my help?" Solomon prodded.

"We believe that Meachum is still alive. They'll want information from him. But, knowing Meachum, he'll make them work for it. I don't know how long he'll be able to hold out. We don't think they took him out of the North End here. Also, we can't see him going along willingly. That means they either knocked him out and carried him down the street like he was drunk or stuck a gun or a knife in his ribs and forced him to walk with them. If they did that, they would have walked really close together. Either scenario could be memorable to bystanders. Do you have anyone who could go question some of your folks in this area? See if they noticed anything like that? We've got to find him fast," Sage said, urgency tightening his voice.

Even before Sage had finished speaking, Solomon was moving toward his writing desk. It was an elaborate affair, constructed of neatly filled cubbies and a polished writing surface. When he reached the desk, Solomon pulled out a piece of paper and used his quill pen to scratch out a message. He lifted the paper and gently waved it through the air to dry.

"Consider it done. I have a very sharp man I often rely on. Once he gets this note, he'll round up some of his runners and come here. He owes me."

"Runners?" Sage echoed.

"He runs a gambling establishment here in the North End. Takes bets on various and sundry matters. His runners collect bets and deliver payoffs so they're out and about at all times, day and night," Solomon explained.

Sage pulled a tin watch from his pocket, the cheapest model to be found in local stores. He had only eight minutes to make the meeting at Slap Jack's. The Squadron's men tended toward hotheaded and were fiercely loyal to their leader. If Sage wasn't on time, who knew what they'd end up doing.

Slap Jack's was popular with the hobos and other itinerant workers. They served decent beer and didn't skimp on the meat, bread, cheese and pickles that went along with the beer. Still, the floor tended to pull at the soles of your boots and the musicians belting out a raucous ditty weren't going to be performing at the Portland Hotel anytime during their lifetimes.

The grim faces of the six men sitting around the corner table starkly contrasted with the shouts of rowdy laughter that accompanied the women's theatrical shrieks and curses at each sly pinch. As if by agreement, though, the saloon's patrons kept their frolicking far away from the gloomy group sitting at the corner table. Sage took a deep breath and strode briskly toward Meachum's men.

They'd spotted him and, as one, the six faces took on a hopeful look that lasted only until Sage shook his head. By the time he reached their table, the faces were again grim or, in the case of a couple, angry.

"Hello, men. I don't have any good news as of yet. We don't know where they took him but a lot of people are already out looking for him."

One man's face flushed red as he slammed his glass beer mug down on the scarred table top. "It's you that got him in danger. If something happens to Meach, I'm going kick your tail all over this town!" He half rose from his seat only to be yanked down by the man sitting next to him who growled, "Shut up Chauncy. You know damn well it was Meach who decided he'd let the China men guard him. He wouldn't listen to us." These words came from a man Meachum called "Buddy," his second in command when it came to running the Flying Squadron.

"Before you blame the China men," said Sage, "I want you to remember that one of them died tonight trying to protect Meachum. That man had a wife and child." The men looked shamefaced and all the anger dissipated as one of them said, "That could of been one of us with a knife in the ribs. Likely it would have been. Matter of fact, the way I see it, that China man was one of us."

Sensing that they'd passed beyond the need to place blame, Sage leaned forward and spoke softly. "Fong has raised a search party of over thirty men. Even as we sit here, they are searching the entire underground beneath the North End. They are visiting every Chinese worker in the area, looking for anyone who saw someone hauling an unconscious man, or an unwilling man, down the street. The same question is being put to every black man in the area. We have help from that quarter as well." Sage thought he saw a glimmer of relief in their expressions. Good. Although they were not going to like his next words.

"Men, we have just a little more than three days before they try to kill President Roosevelt. If they succeed, it can mean the end of the labor movement. At the very least it will make all of our lives and missions harder. You don't live in this town. You don't know the North End as well as the people already searching for Meachum. But one thing you all do, very well, is blend in. Only you can find that assassin. It's up to you. You need to keep looking for that assassin and let the others find Meachum."

Once again, Chauncy was quick to roar his disapproval, his voice rising above the others who also opened their mouths to protest. "We don't care about Teddy Roosevelt. He's just like the rest of 'em. Still cuddling up to the corporations and letting us working people live like slaves!"

The others shushed Chauncy. His voice had carried over the hubbub to such a degree that the entire saloon quieted, leaving the band tootling weakly on, the musicians oblivious to the drama taking place in the corner.

This time, Buddy merely put a calming hand on Chauncy's forearm and said kindly, "Chaunce, be still now. You know as well as I do that if Meach was sitting here, he'd tell us to do exactly what Mr. Miner is asking us to do—finish our mission for the Saint." He looked around the table into each man's eyes, his weathered face tightening with determination. "And, that's exactly what we are darn well going to do. We're going to do Meach proud or die trying!"

TWENTY-SIX

Dispatch: *May 17, 1903, President's train leaves Yosemite for Raymond, California.*

> *"Our basic problem . . . is to see that the marvelously augmented process of production . . . be made to administer to the needs of the many rather than be exploited for the profit of the few . . . . The labor struggle . . . is one aspect of the larger social struggle growing out of the attempts to readjust social conditions and make them more equitable." —T.R.*

SAGE OPENED HIS EYES. It hadn't been the customary dream ejecting him from sleep. Nor was it any distant alarming noise down in the street. He was certain of that because his heart wasn't thudding. He lay there, letting his sleepy mind roam. The building and the street outside were still.

Fong too would be sleeping. He'd stayed in his room down the hall last night instead of going home to his provision shop. Thought of Fong's loss landed like a heavy weight on his chest. Gold Mountain had proved an evil place for Fong's relatives. First his uncle and cousins, now his nephew. All dead by white man's violence.

Overhead, the ceiling began to softly creak. Then came a gentle thump, like a graceful cat jumping to the floor. Fong wasn't asleep. He was up there in the attic, his body flowing through the ageless movements of the snake and crane.

Sliding from beneath the blankets to pull socks over his bare feet, Sage knew only that he belonged upstairs. He wrapped himself in a blanket from off the end of the bed, slipped from his room and climbed to the attic. He had no idea what, if anything, he was going to say to his friend, but somehow he couldn't bear the thought of Fong being alone.

Soundlessly, he climbed the steep stairs to push open the door. The light of two candles flickered atop the wooden chest beneath the wall scroll. Fong was there, his obsidian hair in a shining braid down the middle of his straight back. Dressed in a high-collared black tunic over black cotton pants and slippers he called to mind the wheeling ravens of the high Yukon skies. Displaying seamless transitions between strength and suppleness, advance and retreat, the Chinese man's body seemed to ride an invisible current just like those birds.

Stepping silently across the floor, Sage found a pillow and lowered himself to sit against the wall. His western back pained him whenever he sat very long without support. Once settled, Sage concentrated on his breathing, something Fong had taught him to do so that he could release his thoughts and become fully present in the moment. Overhead, raindrops began splatting randomly on the tar paper roof, heralding the fitful weather to come.

Fong did not pause in his movements though his gaze momentarily sharpened, focusing on Sage's face before turning blank once again. That glance seemed both a greeting and a tacit acceptance of Sage's presence.

If asked, Sage could not have said why he was here. His friend Leo had been right–sudden death made words clog the throat like dust. Yet, he hoped that, somehow, his mere presence would comfort.

Sorrow seemed to lay over the man even as he moved, gentle as an underwater frond set swaying by a random ripple. Yet power imbued every graceful gesture. It was as if Fong was immersed in an ancient, timeless pool of strength. As though his skin no longer separated him from the air through which he moved. Sage knew, somehow, that Fong's sorrow had slid into a deeper, wordless place, merging with something larger and more profound than words could describe. As he watched his friend's body manifest and move through grief, Sage's body began responding. His own bones, muscles and tendons began recalling the sensations of each movement. Time passed, its only accompaniment the swish of Fong's clothes and the patter of fitful raindrops.

It wasn't until a draft slipped up the stairway and flowed across the floor that Sage felt the tears upon his face.

Low groans intruded from somewhere beyond the dream. Meachum groggily pondered why someone would be groaning when everything was so peaceful. Fighting the cobwebs of sleep, he made it to a level of consciousness where he knew that he was awake–just barely. Once there, the vibrating sensation in his throat told him that he was the one groaning. He struggled to lift his head, to look around, but gave up–letting go. It wasn't worth the effort. Beneath him, a wood floor firmly resisted his hipbone. Funny how it didn't hurt like it usually would. Where was this place? It was dark. Close by, seagulls seemed to be keening. Seagulls didn't cry at night. Wait a minute, he'd heard them at night. Near that North End sewer outlet, right where it emptied into the river.

Nearer, from overhead, came the spatter of rain starting up. He liked the sound it made on the tin roof. Comforting. An advancing wave of blackness swept over him, edging the world's commonplace sounds away, carrying with it the dream world's vivid colors and fantastic images.

Meachum didn't react when the boot hit his ribs hard enough to bruise. Nor did he hear the voice of the man standing over him when it said, "I told you to go easy on the drops. He's no damn good to me like this!"

❀ ❀ ❀

The hinges on the gate screeched like a cat getting its tail stomped. Sage froze, holding his breath and swallowing a curse as water streamed off the roof onto his head. Once he was certain that only the sound of rainfall filled the night, Sage stepped through the gate and eased it shut. Carefully he squished his way along the side of the house, conscious of every sucking step. Near the back corner, a gray cat crouched atop a barrel, sheltering beneath the roof's overhang.

Unblinking cat eyes stared at him. Sage willed it not to leap off the barrel in fright. So, of course, it did. Its powerful hind legs set the barrel clattering against the house wall. Again, he froze. Again, he endured the downpour while his ears strained to hear beyond its noise. Had the racket roused anyone? Only silence seemed to emanate from the house. No matches flaring, no curtains twitching aside, no cries of alarm.

A few short steps and he had rounded the corner to stand near the back of the house. He studied her window that was, luckily, on the first floor. Reaching into his pocket he found and removed the small pebbles he'd gathered on his way here. He tossed one against the window and waited. Nothing. He tossed a second, a little harder, waited, and saw the curtain move. A white hand reached up, twisted the lock and the window eased open. He stepped closer. Blackness framed her head, a shawl draped her shoulders, and wispy hair floated loose from her nighttime braid. Still her whisper sounded anything but sleepy when she hissed, "Sage, what in the world are you doing here this early in the morning?"

He moved even closer so that she could hear his whisper, "I wanted to make sure you were all right. That you are okay with Matthew's rescue scheme."

Her voice came as a dry drawl, "I should be. It's my plan. There is some risk but I think we can do it and not get caught. Besides I think the Capt'n and his sidekick will be sleeping in real late this morning."

"What do you mean?"

His mother smirked, an unusual expression for her. "I added a little extra seasoning to the soup that Matthew took up to the two of them," she said.

"Extra seasoning?" Maybe he was too tired, he didn't catch her meaning.

"A triple douse of my wild strawberry elixir." Now her smirk became a wolfish grin that was not all that attractive in the dim light. "I expect they had to be up and down all night visiting the necessary," she told him.

Finally it dawned on his tired brain what she had done. She'd overdosed them with the herbal laxative she'd periodically given him as a small child.

She twisted, glancing behind into her room and turned back to hiss, "If you don't close that mouth of yours, you just might drown. Good night, my boy. I hear steps in the hallway and besides, some of us have to get up early and go to work." With that the window slid slowly but firmly down and the curtain was pulled shut. She was gone, leaving him staring at the place where her face had been.

Cap'n Branch slammed the kitchen door open so hard that it bounced off the counter that housed the dry goods and root bins. Mae looked up from where she was paring brown spots off of last fall's apples. Mrs. Wiggit calmly lifted her stirring spoon from the pot and Gussie scuttled into the alcove. The scullery girl shrank so far into the corner she disappeared. At Mae's side, Andy slipped his little butt off the bench and slithered under the table, the oilskin tablecloth hiding his presence unless someone got down on his knees to look. Cap'n Branch wasn't about to do that. Still, Mae tugged the cloth down, making sure Andy would be hard to spot. She noticed, with satisfaction, that the man looked both tired and peaked before quickly returning her attention to the apple in her hand. It wouldn't do to have him see the smile twitch her lips.

Pointing an accusing finger at Mae, the Cap'n spoke to Mrs. Wiggit, "Has what's-her-name been in the kitchen all morning since she got here?" he demanded.

Ms. Wiggit turned from the stove and looked at Mae. Mae held her breath and hoped her face showed only confused inquiry. This was it. In just one word she might find herself in mortal danger. Mrs. Wiggit's eyes narrowed momentarily before she turned to the Cap'n.

"I've been keeping her too busy to be traipsing about. We had all that mess from last night's dinner to clean up and wasn't nobody else gonna cook breakfast and dinner except me and her. If she left, I would have known it."

"What about that new boy, Matthew? You seen him around this morning?"

Putting her spoon down, Ms. Wiggit turned to face the Cap'n. Her voice was loud and firm as she said, "He dropped off some coal like he always does. Good thing too, we didn't have time to fetch it ourselves." The cook spoke the truth, but not all of the truth. Mrs. Wiggit could have also said that, right after Matthew had delivered the coal, Mae Clemens had mumbled about needing to use the "necessary" and disappeared for a good five minutes or more. But the cook stayed silent about that little absence. She picked up her spoon and began stirring once again, as if Cap'n Branch had already left the kitchen. But he hadn't. For one long minute he stood there, glaring first at the cook, then at Mae and then scanning the entire room as if hunting for something. Finally, without another word, he twirled on his heel and exited, slamming the door shut behind him.

Mae relaxed only to stiffen, as an outraged Andy said so loudly that it would have traveled all the way to the back rows of a theater, "Mama lied to Cap'n."

Mrs. Wiggit's shoulders rose and fell as though with a heavy sigh. She turned again from the stove. "Gussie," she said to the girl who'd emerged from her hiding corner in the alcove, "Take Andy outside for a walk around the block, please." This request triggered a scurry of activity around Mae's feet as Andy scooted out from under the table. Gussie quickly helped the boy on with his jacket and donned her own. A mid-morning walk was a treat for both of them. They wasted no time exiting the kitchen.

Mae's shoulders tensed as she watched Mrs. Wiggit carefully move her pot to the cooler end of the cookstove. Then she turned, walked to the table and sat. She silently studied Mae who met the cook's eyes with what she hoped was a steady gaze.

"Well, Mrs. Clemens, do you think I should know what you and that young Matthew are up to or is it better that you just keep me ignorant? 'Cause I have to tell you, if the Cap'n finds out I lied to protect you, Andy and I will have no place to live. You want that on your conscience?"

Eich's cart rolled across Chinatown's cobblestones feeling only a slightly lighter than it had a few hours ago. The boy had weighed so little. Eich had realized that when he'd unloaded Ollie at the back door of the Fong's provision shop. The boy was slender to the point that he was all sharp angles. He'd been breathing but, unconscious, when McAllister had laid him in Eich's cart. The boy's head lolled against Eich's shoulder when the ragpicker carried him inside.

Mae's plan worked perfectly. Eich had stationed himself and his cart at the mouth of the narrow walkway that lay between the high brick walls of the BCS building and its neighbor. Before he had time to worry, McAllister was hurrying forward out of the gloom, a slender body draped across his arms. The lawyer's lips were pressed in a grim line that didn't ease even at the sight of Eich standing ready.

"This is that boy named Ollie," he whispered to Eich from the gap between the buildings. "Young Matthew recognized him." The lawyer's voice was low but thick with suppressed anger.

The ragpicker surveyed the street, saw no one and lifted the tarp. McAllister stepped out of the gloom and settled the boy into the nest of blankets Eich had prepared. Eich quickly dropped another blanket atop the boy and tied the tarp back down.

"I got to get back inside. I need to keep an eye on Matthew. A strange man was wandering the hallways. I get the sense that he's somehow tied to Cap'n Branch's business since I saw him heading up to the third floor where they don't permit others. And no wonder, since that's where they're holding their prisoners."

Prisoners. McAllister was right. Those boys were being kept subdued and locked away on the third floor. That definitely made them prisoners.

Sipping green tea in the Fongs' living quarters behind the shop, Eich had waited for Ollie to regain consciousness. If he hadn't stayed, the boy might have panicked upon discovering himself somewhere in Chinatown, surrounded by Asiatic faces. Given all that had happened to him, Ollie's mind might have leapt to the worst possible explanation, despite the tiny Mrs. Fong's gentle reassurances.

That threat was past. Eich had been right there when Ollie's vivid green eyes had fluttered open. The boy knew that he was now, at last, safe. When Eich had left, the boy had been shoveling down his second bowl of rice, the pink starting to tinge his pale cheeks. In between mouthfuls he said he'd been caught trying to free the other boys on the third floor. He also told Eich that only the Cap'n and his henchman were involved in selling the boys. The citizens who sat on the BCS board seemed to know nothing about the Cap'n's dirty little sideline business.

The ragpicker's cart left the exotic street with its splashes of red and gold behind. "It was a successful mission all and all," he mused. The boy was safe. Matthew, Mae and McAllister were also still safe so far as he knew.

His satisfaction was momentary. A recollection he'd suppressed made its way to the surface. It had been after he'd rolled the cart across the street that fronted the BCS. Just before he'd passed beyond sight of the building, he'd paused, turned and surveyed the scene. Everything had looked normal. As he turned back forward, the corner of his eye caught sight of a dark figure standing at an uncurtained third floor window. Before he could squint to see better, the figure disappeared.

"Unsettling," Eich muttered to himself before softly para-phrasing Shakespeare, "Black, suspicious, threatening cloud." Should he try to get word to Mae right away? Problem was, it was too soon to return to the vicinity of the BCS. The sight of his cart might stir the memory of those who, by now, were hunting for the missing Ollie. He shook off his unease, reaching for another of the Bard's quotes, this time a reassuring one. "'Be not afraid of shadows," he chided himself as he raised his bearded face to the moving mosaic of fleecey clouds were drifting across a deep blue sky.

TWENTY-SEVEN

Dispatch: *May 17, 1903, President's train arrives in Reno, Nevada.*

"In our modern industrial system the union is just as necessary as the corporation, and in the modern field of industrialization it is often an absolute necessity that there should be collective bargaining." —T.R.

"I DON'T GIVE A DAMN ABOUT YOUR PROBLEMS. I have one purpose for being here in this dripping backwater and one purpose only. Your job, my friend, is to make damn sure our mission is successful. I've already had to step in to clean up the mess you made. Lucky for us all, I only had to kill a Chink. If it had been a white man, it could have brought the entire police force down on us. And maybe even all those Dickenson and Secret Service operatives they've got hanging around every street corner."

His companion opened his mouth to protest but the angry flow of words beat him back, "You keep that pie-hole of yours shut and listen to me. We thought this podunk town was so far from D.C. that we wouldn't have to worry about any interference. But no, I get to town and what do I find?"

The other man didn't open his mouth. His double chin quivered and his face reddened with frustration but he kept his "pie hole" shut as instructed. After all, he was staring into the face of a furious killer.

That killer went on to answer his own question. "What I find is, that in addition to the city and state police, Dickenson's and Secret Service operatives, all of whom we expected and can handle, there is also this rogue union group that has somehow hooked up with the Chinese. Why they're involved is beyond me. Roosevelt hates Chinamen." He fell silent, his brow wrinkling as he thought over the situation.

"We've got that Meachum fellow tied up," he went on, his tone less strident. "I bet he knows everything we need to know and then some. You send that sidekick clown of yours down to soften him up. I'll be along later to get the information out of Meachum or make sure he dies from the trying. You got that? You think you can manage to do at least that much?"

The other man nodded and started to relax only to tighten up again when he realized the killer wasn't through instructing.

"And get our hoity-toity friend over here. Tonight. It's about time he earns that gravy he's been getting from our friends back East. They own him. He better show his gratitude and deliver on their investment."

The workmen arrived on the job site just before sunrise. Flames had scorched the upstairs walls and blackened the fresh paint. Their boss had told them that the owner wanted the plaster down and replaced in record time. It was going to be an elegant house once it was finished. There was crown molding, a porcelain-tile fireplace in the downstairs parlor and another in one of the upstairs bedrooms. One funny thing was the great big bathtub. They'd laughed about its size, speculating that the owner and his missus plan to frolic in the suds.

The early morning had brightened into a uniform grayness when they decided to stop plastering and rest their backs. Shambling onto the covered front porch, the workman were astonished at the sight of six women striding back and forth on the sidewalk before the house. Each woman gripped a picket sign in her gloved hand. Of the four workmen on the porch, only the foreman could parse out the words. He slowly sounded them out so they'd all know the messages: "House of Ill Repute Not Welcome, " "Begone Abomination" were just two of the sayings.

The workman chuckled. Well, that explained the oversized bathtub. Portland had hundreds of whorehouses, what was one more? Besides, it was a job and construction jobs were hard to come by what with all the rain that had fallen the past year.

"Men, don't spend your honest labor to further abuse and torment," shouted one of the ladies who, while looking demure in her bonnet, hollered shrill as any fishwife.

One of the men on the porch, shouted back, "Ah, go on. A whore's got to live somewhere." The men all trooped back into the house, laughing at their companion's witty rejoinder.

By noon, the group of six women had grown into a crowd of twenty-five. Without discussion, the four workmen chose to eat their lunch in the backyard while sitting on a stack of old boards they'd pulled from the walls during the original remodel. Even from this distance, they could hear shouts floating over the rooftop and along the sides of the house. Their faces were glum as they silently smoked their hand-rolls, each contemplating the likely loss of their jobs if the protest didn't stop.

By mid-afternoon they couldn't ignore the crowd out front. It had grown, augmented by near neighbors who apparently didn't want their school children walking by a house of prostitution. The increasing numbers and noise outside on the street had the four of them exchanging worried looks. Their worry was justified. From downstairs came the sound of a rock hitting the front window glass and busting it to bits.

"Well, boys," said their foreman. "I guess it's time to find the local policeman and put a stop to that hullabaloo."

They followed him down the stairs and stood in the doorway as the foremen approached one of the women picketers. At first, the foreman waved his arm, gesturing for the group to move on down the street. Then they saw his arm drop and his shoulders sag as if all his bluster had leaked out of him. He turned and looked at his three men whose curiosity had spurred them to the porch edge. The foreman bent his head to ask the woman a question. She nodded vigorously in response, using her gloved hand to sketch an invisible "x" over her heart.

The foreman turned away from the crowd. With a grim face and heavy steps, he advanced along the walkway and up the steps onto the porch. Without saying a word, he jerked his head toward the open door. The men followed him into the dim hallway, wondering what the woman had said to have such a sobering effect on their easy-going foreman. They crowded close to hear his words.

"It ain't your normal whorehouse, fellas," he said. "They plan on selling children here. Boy children. To grown men."

"Mother of God," breathed one of the workmen. In the silence that followed, all four men gazed about the rooms they'd so carefully repaired, adorned with plaster swirls and painstakingly painted.

"I don't want no part of that," said Alfie, the Englishman. He had the most to lose since his wife had just presented him with a fourth child to feed. There was a hushed murmur of agreement. Without another word, the four men trooped up the stairs, gathered up their tools, coats, lunch boxes and headed down again. Along the way, Alfie's boot snagged an open can of wet plaster, sending its contents splashing down the stairs. Another workman's plastering trowel dug into the wall, leaving a deep gouge down its length from top to bottom. Neither man acted like he noticed. Upstairs, an oozing mix of paint and plaster flowed across the tub bottom, soon to clog the drain.

When the four men stepped out onto the porch, lunch pails, tools and jackets in hand, a great cry went up from the crowd that had expanded to include at least fifty souls. The men descended the steps, traversed the walk and entered the crowd of people, each one of whom seemed intent on slapping a workman on the back. The men only nodded, silently making their way through the crowd and heading down the street. Behind them, the house's front door stood unlocked and open.

A block away, standing beneath the concealing bows of a cedar tree, their hat brims pulled low, McAllister and his friend, Robert Clooney, watched the workmen plod past. Although the four workmen did not look happy, their spines were straight and their heads were high.

"That ought to slow the bastards down," McAllister said.

"Let's hope so," responded Clooney.

If it were possible for a day to pass at the speed of a slug's crawl, this one is doing it. Sage thought to himself. Meachum was still missing. Fong's and Solomon's men were scouring the North End for him. For a moment, the scary image of Meachum's body drifting beneath the Willamette River's swirling surface seized Sage's mind. He shook the image off. They wouldn't kill Meachum until they'd forced him to talk. Knowing Meachum, that would take some doing and some time. There was still a chance they would rescue Meachum. He had to believe that.

The boy from the BCS, Ollie, was safe. That was one thing. Mrs. Fong had sent a messenger. Ollie was hidden away in the provision shop deep inside Chinatown. Those monsters at the BCS could never find him there. They'd be afraid to look. Sage wanted to go ask the boy questions. But he couldn't. He was stuck here, performing the role of operator central. Frustration sizzled and his muscles twitched. He wanted to be out on the streets doing something but he knew that would be useless. All that could be done was being done and someone had to be ready to act if something else came up. So, here he was, planted at the kitchen table, helping Ida by chiseling out the eyes and peeling the skins off the potatoes she planned to cook for Mozart's supper hour. As his mother would say, he felt just "like a penny waiting for change."

A rhythmic creak sounded in the alley outside the kitchen door. Eich! Sage dropped a half-peeled potato into the bowl of water. Raising a finger to Ida to signify he'd only be a minute, Sage slipped outside.

The alley's damp bricks glistened in the light of a momentary sunbeam. At the bottom of the steps, Eich dropped the shafts of the cart, rubbed the small of his back with both hands and smiled a greeting at Sage. "This running from one end of town to another is getting a bit hard on the old spine," he said. Despite his words, the ragpicker radiated an air of suppressed excitement as he removed his floppy hat, letting the sun shine warmly on his thinning hair.

"What is it? What have you learned?" Sage asked.

"Well, you know that boy Ollie is safe, I suppose?"

"Yes, Mrs. Fong sent word." Sage felt disappointment. He'd been hoping for some news related to Roosevelt's assassination.

Eich didn't disappoint him after all because he said, "You can cross Mr. Holman's guest from back East off your list of suspects."

"Why, did you learn something about them?"

Eich nodded. "After I delivered Ollie, I ambled my way up to the Northwest. I'd repaired a plate and bowl for a talkative little maid who works at Holman's residence. She and her husband needed a marriage gift for her sister."

Sage nodded his head rapidly, trying to hurry the ragpicker's story along.

Eich smiled, displaying the patience Sage lacked. "I know, I'm getting to the gist," he said. "'Anyways,' as Mae would say, the reason Holman is in a tizzy over this particular guest is that the man is considering giving Holman a lot of money to develop a power plant on the east side of the river. He's traveled here to decide whether he wants to invest in Portland. And, he's a big fan of Roosevelt's apparently so he scheduled his visit around Roosevelt's. An assassination attempt would definitely send this gentleman financier and his money packing. I conclude, therefore, that Holman is not involved in the plot and neither is his guest."

A sigh escaped Sage. "I have to agree. We can eliminate Holman's guest. And we've already decided that it doesn't make sense it could be Fenton's elderly parents. At least the field has narrowed considerably. Of all the trust men likely to be close enough to Roosevelt on that platform, only Dolph has an un-known out-of-town guest. The one staying in the hotel. I'd better hike over there and see if Mr. Solomon has discovered anything about him."

Slapping his hat back onto his head, Eich raised a hand in farewell, saying, "And, as for me, I am going back to the BCS. I intend to hang about outside, like a fly around the dustbin, for the next few days."

"Why, did something go wrong with Ollie's rescue?" Sage asked.

Eich hesitated and, in that moment, a chill traveled through Sage. "Is something wrong?" he asked again, anxiety making his tone insistent.

"No, nothing went wrong. It's just that I thought I saw a man in the window of that building as I was leaving. Now, I find that I cannot shake a vague feeling of unease. I'd feel better if I was close at hand for Mae and Matthew. It's probably nothing," he ended with a rueful smile. But his actions belied his assur-ance since he moved quickly to pick up the shaft, turn the cart and head down the alleyway. "Don't worry," he called over his shoulder.

Sage said nothing as the ragpicker disappeared around the corner. With a sigh, he turned toward the kitchen door and slowly climbed the steps aware that Eich's unease had become his own.

TWENTY-EIGHT

Dispatch: *May 18, 1903, President's train remains in Reno, Nevada.*

> "I speak . . . to those especially personally and vitally interested
> in the labor struggle and yet I speak of this primarily as one
> aspect of the larger social struggle growing out of the attempts
> to readjust social conditions and make them more equitable . . .
> the most pressing problems that confront the present century are
> not concerned with the material production of wealth, but with
> its distribution." —T.R.

PAIN FLOODED HIS DREAMS, stabbing Meachum into dazed awareness, his mind lazily turning over the memory of the foul-tast-
ing water they'd forced down his throat. Funny how the pain
in his ribs lasted only a second before his thoughts began their
drift back into the dream of swirling color and strange looking
creatures.

As if from a distance he heard that voice again, somewhere
above him, bellowing like an outraged god. "By Christ! I told
you, to go easy on the drops." An answer buzzed near his ear but
Meachum couldn't distinguish the words, though he tried. The
angry voice spoke again, "I don't care if you had to leave him

alone. I can't question him if he's too drugged up to do more than mumble!"

Meachum fought to make sense of what he was hearing but his head felt like it was stuffed full of soggy cotton. At last he grabbed onto a single, clear thought. If he wasn't awake, he couldn't talk. His mind chuckled just before he relaxed and let go of consciousness once again.

Sage whipped his long tie into a complicated knot and gave his thick hair a vigorous brush. The last thing he wanted to do this night was entertain Republican bigwigs in the dining room below while everyone else was out combing the North End for the missing Meachum. How could he tell St. Alban he'd failed to prevent the leader of the Flying Squadron from being kidnaped or, worse, killed?

Trudging downstairs, Sage's mood lightened when he saw that Horace, their most senior waiter, had risen to the occasion. He'd pushed tables together so that at least ten people could dine together in the area below the musicians' balcony. The place settings were immaculate. Horace was directing the final positioning of wine and water glasses. Mozart's was at its best, the dark wainscoting buffed and shining under the sparkling glass of sconces and chandelier. Overhead, a trio of string musicians softly tuned up, readying to release delicate, melodic refrains into the air above the diners' heads.

The front door opened. McAllister and his friend, Robert, entered the restaurant, suppressed excitement wafting in with them, along with cool evening air. A searching glance at their faces told him they had news and that it was good. Sage snatched up two menus and led the men to a table. Few patrons dined this early so he could seat them at a table by the windows.

"Good evening, gentlemen," Sage said, using his best host voice before asking, in low voice, "What's happened?"

McAllister reached for a menu, exchanged grins with his dining companion and said to Sage, "Our ladies came through, one-hundred-and-one percent."

"Tell me, man, don't drag it out," Sage said, feeling hope rise for the first time that day. "What's happened?"

Robert jumped in, pride and excitement animating his face as he took over, "By mid-afternoon there was a crowd of at least fifty. When the workmen found out the purpose of that house, they walked right off the job. Left the front door wide open and their full paint buckets behind."

McAllister laughed and said, "I imagine some of those women are scrubbing the paint splatters from their skirts as we speak." It took a second but then Sage got it and joined in their laughter.

Sage abandoned all pretense of a restaurant host. He pulled out the table's empty chair and sat. "Tell me the details," he commanded, a grin spreading across his face.

So they did. "The point is, there is no way that house can open up now. The whole neighborhood is up in arms. Even a reporter from the press showed up just like you said they would, Adair. They'll be forced to find a different location. That will take time. We've bought some time."

A sly smile settled on McAllister's face. "You know, once we save the boys and Roosevelt, the ladies will be ready to take up another cause. I'm thinking that I'll sic them on Lynch's other house. Keeping busy there will give saloon keepers, like yourself, a break."

The three of them shared a laugh. In the silence that followed, Sage felt a spurt of gratitude toward Johnston. The *Journal's* publisher had acted on Sage's message, dispatching a reporter to the address in Sage's note.

Still, they all knew that the women's demonstration had only put a temporary hold on Lynch's plans to exploit the BCS boys. It was a minor success. But still, it was a success. Then Robert's face abruptly lost its good humored glow as he asked, "Do you think they'll keep those boys at the BCS now that they have nowhere to move them?"

Before Sage could even contemplate the answer to that question the front door opened and three men bustled into the restaurant, quickly doffing their hats to shake off raindrops. The Republican planners had arrived.

Signaling a waiter to take care of McAllister and his friend, Sage strode to the door as he struggled to conceal the dark thoughts Robert's troubling question had just raised in his mind. Had their fight against the house of prostitution increased the danger to the boys? Would Lynch ship them out of town to a similar house in Seattle or elsewhere? Worse, would he have them murdered?

Sage took a deep breath and released it slowly. Fong's calming technique. By the time he reached the foyer and stepped forward with his hand outstretched, his lips were stretched in a wide smile. It was a smile he was certain did not reach his eyes.

Minutes later, the table under the balcony became a center of backslapping conviviality. As he had hoped, they invited Sage to join their planning party. Horace, his lined face looking like a genial frog's with its long mouth and meager chin, provided excellent service for the entire table of eight men who'd turned up to put the final touches on their plans for Roosevelt's visit.

Corporate lawyer, William Fenton, had brought along his father-in-law. The genial, older man was a retired doctor. Sage quickly confirmed the man had no ties to the timber trusts. Mills, the investment banker, turned up with his teenage son in tow, no doubt eager to introduce the boy to his birthright place at the center of power. The boy, in his turn, worked at looking blasé but his avid eyes sparked with the excitement he was feeling. By a similar token, Fred Holman, hoping to impress, had brought along his potential financier for the utility expansion. The man was indubitably a Teddy supporter. His interjections of "bully" became increasingly insistent the longer Horace kept the wine goblets topped off. All food and drink are "Compliments of Mozart's," Sage smilingly assured Mills.

Cyrus Dolph, unfortunately, did not bring his guest from the Portland Hotel. And Dr. Harvey was also alone and seemed less lively than normal. By unsaid agreement, the talk was kept light over dinner, with Fenton the center of admiring attention.

"I say, Fenton, I think you singlehandedly stopped that railway union's legislative bill," said Mills. The rest of the group then eagerly explained to Sage how Fenton had defeated a bill aimed at guaranteeing a small payment to railway workers injured by faulty equipment.

"Instead of taking the obvious position of an employer, Bill went at it sideways. He made the railroads out as victims of unequal treatment–arguing that the protections should apply to every workplace. Then he got one of his legislative buddies to introduce a rival bill saying just that–every injured worker should have right to payment. That scary proposition triggered opposition from every piddling little business owner in the state and killed both bills," Mills crowed.

"I tell you what's brilliant," Holman piped up. "Fenton's railroad has announced its providing low-cost 'excursion fares' for 'colonists' who want to move to the Pacific Northwest. My cousin writes that the railroad has flooded the East Coast with circulars and news articles claiming our area is a 'veritable paradise for those seeking employment–good wages, eight-hour days.' They're also touting free dry farm homestead land in Central Oregon. I predict that's going to increase the surplus labor market in these three states by 75,000 in just four months!" said Holman.

Fenton's thin lips twisted into a satisfied smirk as he said, "That's what my bosses think too. The beauty is that a surplus of unemployed men will drive down wages and weaken the railroad union as well as all the unions you boys have to fight. I'm afraid, though, that I can't take credit for the recruiting idea. That one came direct from headquarters. They've got a whole stable of smart fellows dreaming up clever things like that."

Sage struggled to keep his face genial as he eyed his dinner companions. Admiration for the railroad's "clever" scheme shone in every face. He reached for his water glass, taking time to down half of it in measured sips. Just what this city needs, more hopeful men arriving only to find disappointment. And, either these men were ignorant of the real harm the railroad's legal antics would inflict on countless people or, they simply did not care. The unemployed already flooded Portland streets, crowded its jail floor at night, many of them former trainmen who'd lost limb and livelihood due to the railroad's lack of even basic safety measures.

Fenton must have gotten his fill of basking in praise because he turned to Sage and said, "I must say, it is so pleasant to hear classical music for a change. I am sick of hearing that jangly ragtime everywhere I go. It makes a man tired just to listen to it."

"I could not agree with you more," exclaimed Holman's financier. "I just came from St. Louis. A bully place. Claims to be the birthplace of ragtime. Walk into any dance hall in that city and some fool will be pounding the piano keys so people can two-step around like chickens gone loco."

"I've got it even worse than that," said Holman. "Every time they publish another sheet of ragtime music, my wife runs out and buys it. It used to be she'd play sensible Sousa marches and classical airs. Now all she wants to play is ragtime. Says it makes her feel young."

As one, the men turned to look at the Mills boy. He blushed and tentatively offered, "Some of it is fun to dance to."

Once dinner was over, the group got down to business. First, they completed their plans for Roosevelt's overnight stay at the Portland Hotel, which included a no-speeches banquet as the president had requested. Then, they moved on to finalize the various activities taking place on the day of arrival: the greeting program at Union Station when the president arrived, the slow open-carriage procession up the main street, the plan to release the school children to fill the park blocks and, which bands would be allowed to march in the parade. At last the discussion reached the time capsule ceremony at City Park.

Keeping his tone casual, Sage asked, "So which local dignitaries will have the honor of sitting on the monument platform with the president?"

This question turned everyone's attention to Mills, who cleared his throat to say, "Of course, there will be very limited seating on the platform. Its dimensions are only 50 by 75 feet. The head of the Chamber of Commerce, senators, judges and the usual newspaper editors will all be present. And, the governor will be there, of course."

Hissing followed this pronouncement. The governor was a Democrat. Mills quelled the hiss by saying firmly, "His presence is a matter of protocol, the governor must be there as well as a few other high-level Democrats. Roosevelt's secretary, William Loeb, won't have it any other way."

Mill delicately sipped his wine before setting it down carefully, using this theatrical gesture like a professional to strengthen the anticipation and anxiety of those present. "And then, I was thinking that each one of us might invite a guest or two," he added, with a smile.

A collective exhalation of held breath indicated that this was the information the group had been waiting for. They'd been hoping and expecting to have a seat in that place of honor but until Mills rendered his decision they hadn't been sure. "And, of course, Adair, you will be issued an official invitation to join us on the platform."

Sage started, surprised that Mills would include him, a relative stranger. Hope leapt and his mind raced. By being on the platform, he would be in the best position to thwart the assassin. So, his pleasure was genuine as he said, "Why, thank you, Mr. Mills. I'd be honored and pleased to be there with all of you." He raised his glass in toast, "To President Roosevelt, and to the most felicitous greeting he will receive on his entire trip across this great western land of ours."

"Hear, hear," the group rejoined, their glasses high. By the time dessert was over and the last wine bottle drained, the platform guest list for those present was complete. Joining Sage on the monument platform would be Mills, his wife and son, Dolph with his guest from the hotel, Fenton with his father-in-law, Dr. Harvey with an old school friend, and, Holman with his Roosevelt-loving financier. If that man's rosy-faced delight was any gauge of success, Holman would soon acquire the financial backing he needed to begin constructing his eastside power plant.

By the time the party broke up, Mozart's was empty of all other patrons. Sage locked the door behind the last of them and trudged up the stairs. He hadn't seen Fong all evening. And, no message had arrived to say that Meachum had been found. As he shed suit coat, vest and tie, Sage mulled over the fact that there remained only a single unidentified visitor in town as a guest of the trust men. That was Dolph's friend who, more than likely, had ties to the railroad trust that just happened to be the very trust most angry at Roosevelt.

There was some relief in knowing that the investigation as to the trust's assassination leader had eliminated everyone but Dolph's visitor. If they were right, it was that man. He was the only one they had to watch. All they lacked was Solomon's identification of him. Sage felt like he could put that concern aside. He considered whether to tumble into bed or to change into his John Miner outfit and join the search for Meachum. A loud knock rattled his bedroom door, cutting off the debate.

Ida's husband Knute stood in the hallway. His presence was a surprise in itself since Knute usually left before dawn to start his shingle mill job. That meant he always went to bed with the chickens. His explanation was that he needed to be sharper than the two saws that he ran simultaneously. And, indeed, Sage discerned the cotton stripes of the man's night shirt beneath a hastily thrown-on coat.

"What is it?" Sage asked, his voice sharpening with alarm, fear for his mother flooding his head.

Knute went straight to the point, the melodic singsong pitch of his Swedish accent thickened by anxiety. "It's Mr. Fong. Someone has shot him. He is in the hospital."

The news hit Sage's solar plexus and his knees momentarily sagged.

"Is he dying?" Sage voice sounded calm to his ears.

"I don't know." The worry in the man's voice drew the last word out. "I heard a pounding on the front door. I go down and a China man is standing outside. He jabbers and all I can make out is that Fong is at St. Vincent's, shot, and you should come."

Sage whirled, grabbed the coat he'd just removed and followed Knute down the stairs.

"Do you need me to come with you, Mr. Adair?" Knute asked.

Sage paused in his rush long enough to pat Knute's shoulder. "No, Knute. You need your rest. I suspect there's not much we can do. Take care of Ida. I'll send word."

"Tell Mr. Fong our prayers are with him," Knute called softly after him.

❀ ❀ ❀

Fong lay in a darkened ward, other people of color around him. Even in the hospital there was no mixing of the European-types with other races. Fong's face had lost its golden hue and instead shone sickly yellow beneath a white bandage. His wife, Kum Ho, sat at his side. When Sage appeared she rose, her eyes large with worry.

Without thinking, Sage stooped and wrapped his arms around the tiny woman and felt her relax into his hug. Stepping back he asked her, "Mrs. Fong, how is he? Where was he shot?"

She looked at the terribly still figure on the bed. "He shot in head, right here." She touched the upper right side of her head. "They say bullet not stay inside. Waiting to see if it break skull, bleed more into head." She didn't have to say what would happen if there was bleeding inside Fong's head. The bleakness washing across her normally serene face answered that question.

"Where did it happen?"

She shook her head. "You wait here. Man from tong coming to help. He tell you everything." She sat back down in the chair, scooting it closer to the bed so she could lay her hand atop the unconscious man's.

As if summoned by Mrs. Fong's instruction, a distinguished, elderly Chinese man walked through the door. Trailing two steps behind him were two younger men, their faces stern and watchful.

The Chinese man didn't hesitate but walked right up to Sage and said, "I am Li Wu Yuan. Mr. Fong is my friend. I am also the president of the Hop Sing tong. Mr. Fong asked me to help you in the event it happened that he could no longer do so." The man's English diction was perfect, only slightly accented.

Glancing around the crowded ward as he shook hands, Sage asked Mr. Li, "Can we speak somewhere more private?" At the other man's nod, Sage turned to Kum Ho. "Mrs. Fong, I will speak with Mr. Li outside and then return. Will you be all right?" She gave a single nod and the four men stepped into the hallway.

It being so late, the hospital corridor was empty. The four men walked to its end where they were unlikely to be overheard. Before Sage could say anything, Li said. "Mr. Fong has kept me fully informed of your activities related to the president's visit. About the assassination. I also know that many of our tong cousins are searching for your man, Meachum. I will stand in Mr. Fong's stead. After his nephew was killed, that is what we arranged," he added.

The man's black eyes now glittered cold and, for the first time, Sage glimpsed steel beneath the man's courtly demeanor. Sage glanced at the other two men and saw that their eyes were wide in fierce black stares. His next glance was to their waistbands. Not surprisingly, the tops of hatchet blades showed beneath their coats. High binders, hatchet men. The tong's enforcers. Sage felt an odd mix of unease and reassurance. These were the wrong men to have as enemies but the right ones to have on your side. In the days ahead, their well-trained ferocity might come in handy. "Good. Thank you. We need your help," he told the three of them.

He and Li talked a while longer. When they all returned to the room, Sage squeezed Mrs. Fong's arm, momentarily laid his hand on the unconscious man's shoulder and left once assured they'd notify him if Fong's condition changed—in either direction. One of Li's silent guards was remaining behind to guard Fong and to keep Mrs. Fong company. With a heavy heart Sage accepted that there was nothing more he could do at the hospital. Fong was either going to make it or not.

TWENTY-NINE

Dispatch: *May 19, 1903, President's train arrives in Sacramento, California.*

> *"It is my conviction that the ultimate fate of the nation will not depend on the law nor yet upon the high ideals of the nation but only insomuch as these ideals are manifest in the character of the average citizen." —T.R.*

AT LEAST IT HAD STOPPED RAINING, Sage thought as he carefully stepped alongside the building toward the backyard. Not for long, though. Overhead dense clouds scudded across a sky that was rapidly losing its stars. It took three well-placed pebble tosses before the window slid up and Mae Clemens stuck her head out, one hand clutching a shawl wrapped around her shoulders.

"Can you come outside?" Sage whispered.

Surliness momentarily crossed her sleepy face before she snapped awake, sudden alarm taking over. She raised a finger to her lips, pointed toward the privy and disappeared back inside. The window slid down softly and the curtains twitched closed.

Sage entered the outhouse noting that it must have its night soil removed with regularity. Only the slight smell of lime tainted the air. But then, the lid was tightly closed upon the hole. The spring screeched as the door was pulled open and his mother slipped inside. Once the door was shut, they stood, with only inches separating them. "This has to be a first," he whispered, "I've never conducted a clandestine meeting in an outhouse before."

"It's the best we've got. What is it? What's happened?"

He told her about Fong. She gasped and grabbed his arm, her fingers a painful claw. He wrapped both arms around her shoulders, pulled her closer and hugged. Releasing her, he said, "It will be okay. I spoke to his doctor. They are doing all they can."

For a moment, both stood without speaking. The silence was unbroken except for the sound of raindrops trickling off overhead fir boughs to softly pelt the tin roof above their heads.

Sage started to take a deep breath until he remembered where he was. "In the meantime, we have only two days to find out who's behind the assassination. Fong's tong is going to help but without him directing things, I don't know," he said.

"I expect you'll find a way, Sage. You've managed worse situations in the past," she told him. Her warm hand patted his shoulder, her confident voice forestalling any further statements of doubt. "We better head out. Can't imagine how I'd explain this little meeting to my landlady. Scandalized wouldn't be the half of it."

He eased open the door. After the dark of the outhouse, even the clouded quarter moon made it seem bright outside. He stuck his head out the door and then ducked it back inside. "It looks clear, why don't you leave first?"

She pushed him toward the gap in the door, "No way. I get woke up in the middle of the night, I've got to go. You head on out. I need to take care of business before I go back inside."

Sage was chuckling softly as he slipped alongside the house to the sidewalk. He could always count on Mae Clemens to supply a hefty measure of salt to calm the boil of a chaotic situation.

Mae slipped into the BCS kitchen a few minutes late. She hadn't slept well after Sage left and finally, as the first bird started chirping, she'd gotten up, dressed, and taken the early morning trolley to the hospital. Kum Ho had been sleeping, sitting in a chair, but with her head resting on Fong's hospital bed near the injured man's hand. At the foot of the bed, a stern young Chinese man stood at hard-eyed attention. When Mae entered, he'd given her a piercing look but then relaxed when she'd placed a finger across her lips and slipped silently to stand beside the bed across from Kum Ho's sleeping form.

Fong's face looked pale and old and vulnerable beneath the swath of white bandages that encircled his head. Tears filled Mae's eyes as a fizz of fear ran through her. She looked at the silent young man who had slowly shaken his head. This was not mere sleep. Mae gently laid her hand on Fong's shoulder, closed her eyes and wished fervently for his recovery. After which she removed her hand, nodded to the young man and slipped away.

The trolley had overflowed with morning passengers avoiding the discomfort of sloshing to work in the downpour that had started while she'd been inside the hospital. With all the stopping and starting and slow loading of passengers, the delay of Mae's arrival at the BCS had increased with each passing minute. Exasperated, Mae shoved her way out of the trolley and walked the last six blocks in the rain, arriving in the kitchen wearing a soggy coat and squishing boots.

Mrs. Wiggit was hard at work, frying up rashers of bacon and scrambling innumerable eggs. She sent no chastising glance toward the late arrival, merely nodded and said, "My goodness, it must be mighty wet outside since you're leaving a trail of wet across the floor."

"It's a right fine spring shower, that's for sure. I am sorry I am late," Mae said as she shed her outer garments and donned a clean apron. "A friend of mine is hurt bad and I had to go to the hospital early this morning. All the rain, the return trolley was running late. Otherwise, I would have been on time."

Breakfast at last being served upstairs, Mae and Mrs. Wiggit sat at the kitchen table drinking coffee, their tired feet raised onto chair rungs. Behind them, Gussie was swishing the empty porridge pots through water, their tin clattering in the large metal wash basin. Fried bacon still scented the air, which made Mae's stomach growl. Mrs. Wiggit heard the noise, because she smiled and shoved a basket of biscuits and a pot of strawberry preserves across the table toward Mae.

As Mae sliced the biscuit and spread the preserves, the cook said, "I don't know how much longer I want to keep working here." She kept her voice low. "If it weren't for Andy, I'd have packed up and left right after the Capt'n took over."

"How long ago was that?"

"Two years. Two long years," Mrs. Wiggit sighed and stared into her coffee cup.

"What was the BCS like before that?" Mae asked, curious whether the Capt'n was continuing bad practices or whether he had started his own.

A smile lit the cook's face. "Oh, it was wonderful. Mr. Carter was in charge and he was a fine man. Didn't have all the peculiar rules. We could go anywhere in the building. He made us feel like we were part of a family. I like working with the boys, even taught a few of them to cook." Her face turned wistful until bitterness twisted her lips. "But Mr. Carter decided it was time to retire. He moved up to Seattle to be near his daughter. Everything changed when the Capt'n got here. Said he didn't want the boys 'coddled,' that they weren't paying me to help out with the boys and my place was to stay in the kitchen, cooking."

The sight of the door to the basement edging open behind the cook's back diverted Mae's attention. Matthew's face appeared briefly before the door was silently pulled shut. That was her cue. "Something's not right here, I am sure of it," she said to the cook before swallowing the last bite of biscuit and standing. "I'll just head to the necessary and then I best get back to work. The dinner time pies won't make themselves," she said.

Mae stepped into the basement hallway just in time to see Matthew slide into the coal room. She picked up her pace and followed him in, closing the door behind her. He put a finger to his lips and stepped over to the blurry glass of the dirty casement window. Carefully, he twisted the latch and the window silently fell open a few inches at the bottom. He motioned for Mae to stand beside him.

She edged closer. Outside, the rain had stopped. In a shaft of sunlight the courtyard's wet red bricks glistened and tiny water droplets glittered on the moss starting to turn green between them. A scrape of a foot on brick drew her attention to where two pairs of shoes stood just to the left of their open casement window. Mae widened her eyes at Matthew and he leaned forward to whisper in her ear, "The captain. Saw them sidle into the courtyard. Figured we should listen."

She nodded and they both edged closer, Mae slipping her finger into the gap at the window's bottom to open it wider. The men's voices were low but not so low that their words weren't clear to the two eavesdroppers standing inside the dim basement.

"I tell you. I don't like this." The Cap'n's voice sounded higher than normal, as if he was anxious.

"You don't have to worry. It's not you who will be sitting on the platform in City Park. Everything goes as planned, and nobody will ever connect me to the deed or you to me."

"But, what if it goes wrong? Every time I turn around, things are going wrong. That herd of women attacked and ruined the house yester . . . ."

The curt, clipped words of his companion interrupted the Cap'n's whining. "Now is not the time to turn coward. You agreed to help. You took money to help and you damn well will keep up your end of the bargain." The snarl underlying the man's words sent shivers up Mae's spine. "Who?" she mouthed.

"That's his visitor," Matthew mouthed back.

The other man's tone must have worried the Capt'n as well because his tone turned wheedling. "No, no, I'll do what you ask. Besides, it's only two more days before you're gone and things can return to normal. Now, I didn't mean that I don't like having you here. You're a fine guest. No trouble at all. It's just the risk and afterward, they're going to be looking at every stranger in town."

"I'll be gone. That's been arranged. My men rented a place with a small stable. I'll be on a horse and heading out north within a half-hour."

"What about the doctor? How's he going to explain where you disappeared to . . . oh," the Capt'n voice trailed off as if he'd picked up on some nonverbal signal. In a tentative voice, he asked. "Won't they back track where he's been? Find out you stayed here?"

"Who is going to tell them? You?"

"Oh, God, no, I'd never tell. They'd hang me. I'm not stupid. Far as I know, the good doctor only came here to do the boys here a good turn, helping us out by doctoring them for free," the BCS director hastened to reassure.

The creak of a hinge sounded behind Mae and Matthew. The door to the basement hallway was opening. Before they could turn, a garbled childish voice shouted exuberantly, "Goody, goody, I found you. What is out that window? A cat?" They swiveled to see Andy. He hobbled toward them from the open doorway, his face brightly eager.

As one, they turned back toward the window. Outside there was only one pair of shoes and this time the toes were pointed straight toward their window. It took no imagination to visualize the man staring down at the window, trying to see who lurked behind it.

As one, they both rushed toward the coal room door, Matthew scooping up a squealing Andy on the way. They weren't fast enough.

The Cap'n's visitor stood in the hallway, a scowl on his face, one of his hands sliding into a coat pocket. "Put the kid down," he said.

Matthew responded by hugging the now-silent little boy closer to his chest.

The man's hand came out of his pocket. Even in the dim light of the casement window there was no mistaking the metal barrel that extended from the man's fist. Matthew gently set Andy onto his feet. "He doesn't know anything," Matthew said, his voice reverting to the high squeak of an adolescence not completely past.

The man studied the puzzled, twisted face of Andy and nodded. Mae put out a hand and gave Andy's shoulder a gentle nudge. "You go on now, boy. Your mama was looking for you," she said.

Andy looked up at her, indecision wrinkling his forehead. She smiled at him, saying, "You go on now. We'll be along in a bit. We need to talk to this man here."

Andy turned to Matthew. "Can we play tops?" he asked.

For a second, Matthew was speechless. Then he nodded and said, smiling weakly, his face now deathly pale, "Yes, Andy. We'll play with the tops. You go get them ready."

"Yay," the little boy said and he limped away down the hallway. The three who remained behind said nothing, merely waited while he opened the kitchen door, stepped inside and closed it behind himself with a bang.

The stranger gestured with the gun barrel toward the door— the one that opened into the stairwell. Matthew slid one arm around Mae's shoulders and they wordlessly obeyed the silent order. Mae was glad of the strength in that arm, despite the acrid odor of Matthew's sudden fear.

THIRTY

Dispatch: *May 19, 1903, President's train in Sacramento, California.*

> *"Of vital moment is the regulation and supervision of the great corporations . . . as well as securing fair play as between the big man and the little man . . . " —T.R.*

A PAINFUL THROB IN HIS ARM yanked him awake. At first, Meachum's awareness focused solely on the arm. It felt twice its normal size. A hazy sense of urgency kept him motionless and silent. He lay, struggling to put the pain, memories and dreams aside and focus on the reality of the wood floor. It was rough, his cheek felt the sharp nick of splinters while the mingled scent of dirt and manure filled his nostrils Secondary pains radiated from arms tied behind his back and legs trussed together. A gritty rag filled his mouth, wicking spit and leaving his tongue feeling dry and cracked as an old shoe.

Day had come. Gray light filtered through the grimy skylight overhead, pushing the dark into corners. So, he'd made it through another night. Not easily. God, he hurt. It was hard to feel a place not bruised by boot or fist. Last night was the worst. The stranger knew how to target every vulnerable spot on his body and make it scream. Worst of all, the bastard had clearly enjoyed himself. That's what his gleaming dark eyes had said though his tone implied the opposite. The torture had been coldly reasonable, passionless, matter-of-fact. He'd asked his question, paused for an answer that didn't come, and then struck. Satisfaction surged momentarily. He'd told the stranger nothing. Not how much they knew of the plot. Not who was involved in stopping it. Through it all, Meachum kept his puffy lips clamped. And, peering from beneath swollen lids, Meachum had methodically memorized each line, each expression in the other man's face. He'd know the bastard anywhere. His silent resistence had finally yielded the result, he sought. His beater had become infuriated and lost control. The blows had strengthened beyond bearing and oblivion once again had sent him out of reach into a troubling landscape of fearsome monsters and shadowy threats.

Slowly Meachum shifted his body on the hard floor, trying to ease stabbing kinks and sore spots, fearful least his guards catch the movement. He didn't want them summoning that sadist for a return bout. As bad as he hurt, the next round might be the last. A sharp pain drew his eyes to where the knife wound in his injured arm had torn open and was beginning to seep. Blood was soaking what he could see of the filthy sling and ripped plaid shirt. Maybe that was why his head felt light and his body so cold. Was he going to die of blood loss? That would be a fine kettle of fish. And here he'd always thought his end would come swiftly, in the midst of battle or peacefully in bed, at an old age. Meachum's lips tightened in a rueful grimace.

Then, crystal clear, his mind's eye conjured up the vision of the half-finished curio cabinet. He'd left it laying on its side, atop his workshop bench, its tenderly-sanded surfaces gleaming under their first coat of varnish. He could hear his own voice promising Mary he'd be home in time to finish it by her birthday. Tears of regret stung his eyes and the wordless ache filling his chest followed him down into blackness.

❀ ❀ ❀

Sage sat at the kitchen table, palms pushed against his eye sockets, elbows resting on the table, ears registering muted conversation and the stacking of heavy crockery. He hadn't been able to sleep. Every little noise jerked him wide awake, riding a gush of fear. Was it a knock on the door, the one bringing news that Fong had passed? Once alert, he could reassure himself, push aside that particular fear only to have the terrifying prospect of their mission's failure take its place.

Finally, Sage had hauled himself out of bed and into the streets. He found Meachum's and Li's men only to have them report that the night had yielded no positive news. Today and tomorrow, that was all the time they had left. According to the newspapers, Roosevelt had ended his sojourn in Yosemite with that nature lover, John Muir, and made a quick trip into Nevada. The president's train would be rolling across the Oregon border later today. So, day after tomorrow, Roosevelt would arrive in Portland. Within hours their mission would be done, for better or for worse.

Frustration pushed his palms harder into his eye sockets. The would-be foolish assassin remained unidentified and loose somewhere in town. The only concrete information they had was the identity of the men who were to create the distraction in the crowd around Roosevelt. But, those men played only minor roles in the assassination plot. Worse, sight of them had been lost amid the throngs of spectators who now flooded the town from outlying villages and towns all eager to catch sight of the nation's president.

Less than forty-eight hours, Sage told himself with an inward groan. Their failure to find people and answers was going to get President Roosevelt killed. Exactly who was to be the plotters' back-up man on the dedication platform? What man was poised to step in if the duped assassin failed? If they were lucky, it would be Dolph's guest, the mystery man staying at the Portland Hotel. But, Lord, what if it wasn't him?

And it wasn't just the president who might die. Bombs always slew more than their intended target. And, where was Meachum? Was the Flying Squadron's leader still alive? Did the attack on Fong mean that they'd tortured Meachum into giving up information? If so, was Meachum already floating face down in the river? Were they wasting time and men hunting for a man already dead? Sage pushed his palms even tighter into his eyes, as if doing so would force from his mind the awful image of Meachum's silver thatch of hair drifting lazily in a muddy current.

The squeak and rumble of a wooden cart straightened Sage's backbone, his hands dropping away as his ears strained to confirm what he thought he'd heard. Yes! That was a cart in the alley. Sage pushed back his chair and opened the kitchen door. Eich stood there. Seeing him, the ragpicker rested the cart shafts on the ground and stepped forward, concern wrinkling his wide brow. "What is the matter? What has happened? Is Mae alright?" he asked.

Sage stepped out onto the stoop, pulling the door shut behind him. "Must be my worrying is writ large upon my face," Sage thought, but he spoke to reassure Eich, "She's fine. Least she was this morning about one a.m. No, it's Mr. Fong. Someone shot him. In the head," Sage said, before softening the message, "We're hoping it's just a graze. He's still unconscious. I've been waiting to hear from the hospital. Come inside, we need to talk."

The two of them sat at their usual table, deep inside the closed dining room beneath the balcony and away from the curtained windows. Sage absently noted that Horace again was proving himself a fine dining captain. Although it was an hour before opening, Mozart's was all ready. Horace, himself, stood at the buffet, using a clean linen napkin to polish the silverware.

Keeping his voice low, Sage told Eich everything that had happened to Fong. "Herman, I'm at a loss what to do now," he continued. "We've got the problem at the BCS. There are boys locked up on that third floor. And now that they can't use that house, who knows what the Cap'n and his cronies will do to those kids? They've become a liability."

Sage started to speak, paused to gain control over the lump now caught in his throat, and said, "And we haven't found Meachum. I was out at the crack of dawn, talking to Fong's men and they are still looking. But, no luck so far. And since they are looking for him, they can't also be searching diligently for the assassin. I haven't had a chance to talk to Solomon, yet. So, we still don't know if the man staying at the Portland Hotel is the signal guy on the platform. We suspect it's Dolph's guest at the hotel, but what if it isn't?"

Eich remained silent while he digested Sage's litany of woes. When Eich spoke, all he said was, "Do you suppose I might have a cup of coffee? It's a bit chill outside and it might help me think."

Sage jumped up and when he returned to the table, Eich's warm brown eyes were calmly resolute. He sipped his coffee. "Here is what I suggest," he said, "Mae and Matthew are watching things at the BCS. Seems like Mr. McAllister and his friend, Mr. Clooney, could call in there and make sure nothing bad happens to those boys. Maybe we need to give them the assignment of figuring out how to free those young captives. I'll head over to McAllister's office and see if he's willing to take over. I'll also stop by the hospital and see how Mr. Fong is doing. After that, I'll go over to the BCS and let Mae know how Mr. Fong is doing. She must be frantic with worry. I'll also ask her to stand ready with Matthew to help McAllister. Once that's all done, I'll head back over here to let you know how everything will be handled."

"Okay," Sage agreed. The plan sounded as good as any he could come up with. Better. Enlisting McAllister to carry out the boys' rescue just might work. The lawyer had both the ability and desire to tackle the problem. "Still, what about Meachum and the assassin? Mr. Fong was running both search parties using a combination of his tong cousins and Meachum's Flying Squadron men."

"You said Mr. Fong had already chosen Mr. Li to help. Does the man speak good English?"

"Actually, he's more fluent at it than Mr. Fong," Sage said.

"Well, then. You have to trust that Mr. Fong knew what he was doing when he chose Mr. Li as his stand in. How about you go see Mr. Li and Meachum's lieutenant and see how they're doing? After that, go visit with Mr. Solomon. Maybe he'll have good news and you'll at least have the identity of the man on the platform established. Then we can meet back here and see where things stand."

Walking Eich to the kitchen door, Sage realized he felt better now that they had a plan of action. Maybe their efforts would solve none of their problems but there was a small measure of relief in the fact that he'd shift at least some of the heavy weight onto the ragpicker's willing shoulders. Sage stood in the open door, watching the cart as it trundled down the alley and out of sight around the corner. Eich was right. They may have lost two of their most important warriors, but they still had a sizable complement on the battlefield.

The man from back East stood at the window, glad that his was a corner room. That way, he looked down upon both of the streets fronting the BCS building. Alertness was important. This morning had proved that point. Damn Cap'n and his disgusting little sideline. Had he known of it, he'd never have arranged to stay here. Still, it remained a good place to hide out. Better than one of the hotels. He just hoped that, when the Cap'n did as promised and "took care" of those "loose ends" upstairs, the fool wouldn't make the situation worse.

He lit a cigar and allowed the smoke to dribble out slowly. A little more than two days, he'd be out of this backwater burg. He examined the skinned knuckles of his right hand. Damn, next time, he'd wear gloves. He'd underestimated the man. Lost his temper. Yes, indeed. Next time, gloves. And there would be a next time, he promised himself. There was at least one more opportunity before day's end to question Meachum. If Meachum didn't deliver then, well, it would be too late for Meachum. There'd be no reason to keep him around any longer. Hell, who was he kidding? Deliver or not, this was definitely Meachum's last day. That thought sent grim satisfaction rippling through him. Meachum's little followers were about to learn a lesson. In fact, Meachum's death would be a very good object lesson in exactly what happens to nosy union men.

The mercenary stiffened, an inarticulate alarm sounding inside his head. What was it? He scanned the scene down below, outside the window. Nothing on the main street. He peered up the side street and he saw it. A wooden cart being pulled down the street by that shabby old ragpicker. He'd seen that cart before. The day that boy had disappeared. That was the Cap'n's mess. None of his. Still, now was not the time to have more problems in his vicinity, that's why he'd taken care of the woman and the boy.

He stepped to the side of the window so that he could watch without being seen. The ragpicker paused outside the kitchen door down below. He dropped the shafts of his cart and stepped into the courtyard. When he came back into view, the man carried a few items that he tucked beneath the cart's canvas.

The mercenary relaxed. Just a typical ragpicker rooting in the BCS's trash bin. No connection. He waited for the cart to roll away down the street. That didn't happen. The man didn't leave. Instead, the ragpicker stood on the sidewalk, looked up and down the street and even up toward the building's windows. The mercenary didn't draw back. He knew he wasn't visible because sunlight had broken through the leaden layer of cloud and was shining in the ragpicker's eyes. The ragpicker didn't move on. Instead, he stood there, staring at the kitchen door, as if waiting for it to open.

Above him, the mercenary swore and stepped away from the window. He flung the lit cigar into an ashtray, snatched up his jacket and strode toward the door as his fingers made sure his gun was secure inside its leather holster. He paused, returned to the table and plucked up the razor sharp knife. He slipped it into his leg sheath. The ragpicker didn't look like he could put up much of a fight but it didn't hurt to be ready for anything. That's why he had survived as long as he had.

Uncertain what to do, Eich stood beside his cart, hoping the kitchen door would open and she'd be there. Mae always wandered out whenever he'd entered the courtyard to rummage through the BCS's dustbins. He didn't think she'd left already. She and Mrs. Wiggit should be racing around the kitchen preparing the evening meal. He'd meant to come earlier so he'd miss that rush but it had not worked out. He'd ended up staying at the hospital a long time. Fong was still unconscious but Mrs. Fong had needed some things from her home and wanted to send their guard to get them. The guard refused to leave her alone. Apparently, he had orders. The only solution had been for Eich to stay while the man made the long trip from northwest Portland down to that area of Chinatown that sat east of downtown, right near the river.

It had taken over an hour but Eich hadn't minded. He'd formed a friendship with the petite Kim Ho when she'd nursed him back to health following a near fatal attack the previous fall. Looking strangely small and defenseless, Fong hadn't stirred from his coma despite all the strong encouragement Eich mentally sent his way. He'd left the hospital reluctantly. He would have preferred to stay at his friend's bedside, caught up in the foolish notion that his presence could hold Death at bay.

His subsequent visit with McAllister had also met with delay. The lawyer hadn't been in his office. The note on the door said he'd return at 4:00 p.m. Rather than leave and return, since the fitful weather was reminding him that he was not getting any younger, Eich had rolled his cart into the gap beside McAllister's building and gone inside to wait in the warmer stairwell.

Finally, he heard McAllister and his friend Robert Clooney enter the lobby. As they rode the clanking elevator to the second floor, he'd climbed the stairs so that they'd met in the dim hallway outside McAllister's office. It hadn't taken long for McAllister to grasp the situation and agree to take charge of the BCS rescue.

Eich heaved a sigh. After checking again to make sure no one was watching him from the building's windows, Eich stepped to the kitchen door and knocked sharply. He heard rapid shuffling steps and the door was pulled open. Andy stood in the doorway. His eyes were red from crying and Eich felt a tug at his heart. "What's the matter, Andy boy?" he asked.

Andy snuffled a bit and said, "Matthew never came back to play tops with me like he promised he would." Then the boy was jerked backward, his mother shoving him behind her skirts. "What do you want, ragpicker?" she asked, her voice was sharp. Eich studied her face and saw fear in her eyes. Before he could answer, she was pulled away and the door opened wider.

"I think our ragpicker friend needs to go about his business," a cool voice said and a well-groomed man stepped in front of the cook. Eich looked down to see the black hole of a revolver's barrel centered on his own chest. The man held the gun so that the cook couldn't see it from where she stood. The man said pleasantly. "I am sorry, sir, but we cannot have you interfering with our cook's work." Even he spoke these words his eyes were ice-cold and he was using the gun to gesture Eich back. Eich stepped back onto the sidewalk and the stranger followed, pulling the kitchen door shut while never taking his eyes off Eich's face or lowering his gun.

THIRTY-ONE

Dispatch: *May 20, 1903, President's train arrives in Ashland, Oregon.*

> *"It is a question of the control and regulation of those great corporations. I see them as great efficient economic instruments that need to be regulated and controlled to subserve the economic good." —T.R.*

SAGE MET WITH MEACHUM'S MEN for the second time that day. It had taken Sage a while to find Meachum's lieutenant and then more time for the two of them to meet up with Mr. Li. The Chinese man radiated the calm assurance of an experienced leader. His men had spotted one of Meachum's attackers and Meachum's men were trailing him. Li expressed confidence that it was only a matter of hours before his men narrowed the Meachum search to just a few buildings. Once that happened, they planned to rescue the Flying Squadron's leader.

More problematic was the idea that the duped assassin had gone to ground and might be hiding until it was time for him to appear and throw what he thought was a smoke bomb at Roosevelt. They confirmed the deployment of their combined forces. One team would continue to hunt for Meachum while the other would continue the search for the assassin. At ten men in each team, surely there were enough men on the hunt. Sage hoped they'd be in time for Meachum.

Back at Mozart's, Sage expected to find Herman Eich waiting at the kitchen table. Ida said she hadn't seen the ragpicker since his morning visit. Sage finally got tired of waiting for Eich's return. Maybe there'd been bad news at the hospital and Eich had decided to stay with his friend. But no, Mrs. Fong had promised to send word of any changes and no word had come. Maybe the ragpicker had been forced to wait for McAlister to return to his office. Or, maybe Mae had found it hard to pull away from the kitchen to talk to Eich.

Sage gave himself a mental shake. As his mother would say, "Bedeviling maybe's in the head help as much as matches in a twister." She was right. Action was what he needed, not working himself into a tizzy over every "maybe" that might never happen.

Talking to Mr. Li and Buddy Kendell had taken longer than expected so he'd skipped stopping by the Portland Hotel to talk with Solomon. Given the ragpicker's delayed arrival, though, he might as well head out and complete that task. See if Solomon had determined whether it was Dolph's friend at the center of the scheme. Slapping a hat on his head, Sage grabbed an umbrella and slipped out Mozart's front door. He exchanged an absentminded greeting with some customers entering for dinner. They sent him puzzled looks. Usually Mozart's host was pleasantly obsequious. Sage noticed but didn't care what they thought. He was busy adding to his mental list of things to do and wondering whether McAllister had agreed to mount a rescue of the boys. And, if he had, exactly when that rescue would take place. As he strode through a sudden spring downpour, Sage peered up and down every street he crossed, hoping to see the unmistakable figure of the ragpicker and his cart.

Solomon's deep brown eyes lacked their customary sparkle when they met Sage's. Tension gripped Sage's gut and grew as he watched Solomon seat a couple and pause to exchange pleasantries with them before making his way back to the dining room's entrance podium. The scene itself was serene beneath the steady wash of the hotel's electric lights. When the hotel had been erected in 1890, this electrically illuminated dining room was considered one of its greatest attractions. Personally, Sage found the light cast to be cold, much preferring the warmth of Mozart's flickering gaslight.

Sage studied the approaching man, looking for some indication of whether there was good news. The confident stride said nothing. That slightly bemused lift of lips remained in place. Yet, there was concern in those features. Then Solomon was upon him.

"May I seat you, Mr. Adair?" he asked. "We have a lovely dessert of Neopolitan three-layer cake this evening, if you are not staying for a meal."

That was his cue that the news was not good and Sage would need to act on it immediately.

"No, Mr. Solomon. But I'd appreciate a cup of coffee before I head out back out into the rain. I've become somewhat chilled."

Solomon's news was short and to the point. "Dolph's guest is not your man," Solomon told Sage. "He left Portland today, on the train. Some emergency back East sent him packing."

"Maybe it's a ruse. Maybe he moved to another hotel," Sage said, unwilling to lose his only hope for finding the man who would be on the platform to signal the assassin.

Solomon shook his head, the severity of his look showing that he knew how exactly how bad this news was for their group. "I took the precaution of having my co-worker trail the man to the train station to make sure he got on the train and that it left with him. It did. We also have a porter on the train keeping an eye on him. If he deboards before the train crosses the Rockies, I'll receive a telegram."

Leaning closer, Solomon said in a low voice, "Also, the maid searched his room for me after he checked out." Solomon stretched out a hand and, his body blocking anyone else's line of sight, he laid a folded up paper on the table. It was the dun color of a telegram that had been first crumpled, then smoothed out and re-folded. Solomon stepped away from the table, motioning to a waiter that the empty coffee cup at the top of the table setting needed filling. Then he was gone.

The waiter came over and silently filled the cup. Once he had left, Sage reached out and picked up the piece of paper. He moved tentatively, suspecting that once he read its words, all hope in that direction would be lost. Unfolding the piece of paper, Sage's foreboding was confirmed. "Come at once. Stop. Father dying. Stop." Sage felt hope crumble. "Somehow," Sage thought, "I doubt a cold-blooded assassination plotter would take himself out of the plot this close to the end. And certainly not because his father was dying." Sage crumpled the note in frustration before burying it in his suit coat pocket. He left without touching the coffee.

By 7:00 p.m. Sage had given up on the idea that Eich was going to return to Mozart's. He donned his overcoat and headed out into the growing gloom of a rainy dusk. Of his four major worries, Fong, the assassination, Meachum and the imprisoned boys, it was the latter situation that remained unsettled in his mind. He needed to find out whether McAllister had agreed to rescue the boys.

He was in luck. He found Clooney clacking away at a typewriter in the anteroom while McAllister intently paged through a heavy black book in his office. Clooney looked up and smiled. "I thought I'd give E. J. a hand since he stubbornly refuses to learn how to type with more than two fingers," he said.

The two men told him that they'd met with Eich and were heading over to the BCS after dinner. They figured that would be the easiest time to find Matthew and learn how best to free the boys imprisoned on the top floor.

"Now, I'm a bit worried, " McAllister said. "When Mr. Eich left here at least two hours ago, he said he was just going to let Mrs. Clemens know we were coming and then head over to meet with you. He said nothing about stopping anywhere else. He should have been there by now."

Alarm rippled through Sage. "You certain he didn't say any-thing about going somewhere else before heading to Mozart's?" he pressed.

McAllister responded by standing up and donning coat and hat. Clooney did the same. McAllister said, "I am positive that Mr. Eich was going straight to your place once he'd seen Mrs. Clemens. He was anxious about getting there because he said he was already late. We'd better get going."

They moved quickly along the damp, dark streets toward the BCS. Sage's eyes scanned all the nooks and crannies along the way. Portland's dark alleys had proven to be potential hiding places for thugs. His effort yielded a reward but not the one he wanted. About a block from the BCS, Sage spied a familiar shape inside the narrow, dark gap between two buildings. He stepped into the gap and then gestured his two companions over. "Tell me that isn't Eich's cart," he said, lighting a match and holding it close to the contraption knowing, even as he did so, that no such assurance would come.

"It is his cart!" Clooney exclaimed. "I recognize that stained patch on the canvas. I walked him down to the street when we were finished talking and I saw his cart. That's it. I'm certain." All three men stared at the cart, dread now thickening their silence.

"I think we better get moving," McAllister said. "Robert and I will go in the front and see what is happening. I am afraid, Mr. Adair, that it will be up to you to confront Mrs. Wiggit in her kitchen. Let's meet in an half-hour at that saloon across the street."

❀ ❀ ❀

Sage stepped down the single outside step to the kitchen door and rapped on it with his knuckles. The door swung open and a small boy, his face streaked with tears, nose running and mouth lax, looked up at Sage.

"Andy," Sage thought. His mother had talked fondly of the boy and told Sage of his affliction. Sage knew from her that Andy was much smarter than he looked and sounded.

"What's the matter, fella?" Sage asked, his voice gentle.

The boy gulped, his eyes filled with tears and he mumbled what sounded like, "Matthew didn't come play with me like he promised and Mama hit me."

Before Sage could respond, Andy was yanked away from the door opening and shoved behind the skirts of a wide woman who also sported reddened eyes. Sage's gut clenched but he tried to keep his voice light and steady. "Greetings, ma'am. I am here to see Mrs. Mae Clemens."

The woman shot a look behind her and her face, when she turned back to him, was a mix of fear and suspicion. "And, just who might you be?" she demanded.

"I am a friend, and you are Mrs. Wiggit. Mrs. Clemens talked about you. She said you were a good person and ran an efficient kitchen."

Sage thought he detected a slight weakening of the woman's defenses and sure enough, after one more glance behind her, she opened the door further. "You'd better come in, sit there at the table," she commanded, pointing toward a large oilcloth-covered table in the center of the room. The oilcloth was so large that its red-checked expanse hung all the way down to the floor. He did as she ordered and took a chair. The woman picked up another kitchen chair, walked over to the inner door that presumably led into the rest of the basement and push the chair against it. She then picked up a child's picture book from the table, tucked Andy under her arm and carried both to the chair. She put the child in the chair, put the picture book in the child's hands and told him softly, "Andy boy, you sit right here and listen very carefully for any sounds on the other side of the door. If you hear anyone coming, you call out 'Mama' okay? This is very important." The boy gave a solemn nod, his eyes big in his face.

Mrs. Wiggit paused at the cookstove to slide a pan farther from the fire box before she sat down across from Sage. "I hope to God you are truly a friend of Mae's. If you're not, then I guess Andy and me will be out on the street before nightfall. It doesn't matter. I can't stay here any more. Too many bad things are going on and today is the last straw," she declared even as a tear escaped from her eye. Her work-reddened fingers impatiently flicked it away.

She didn't wait for Sage to respond. Instead, she leaned across the table. "First thing you need to know. If Andy there tells us someone is coming, you and he are going under this here table. You understand? I expect you to protect him as best you can. Dangerous things are going on and I won't have my boy hurt. So, you scoot under here," she pointed, "and keep yourselves quiet as a house mouse when the cat's around. Andy knows how, God knows Andy boy's had to do it enough times. The Cap'n doesn't like the look of him."

Sage could only make an inarticulate murmur of sympathy. He didn't trust himself to find the right words in light of the strain this woman had must have endured from the rejection of her son and the continual need to shield him from her employer.

She must have seen his compassion in his eyes, because, for the first time, her face showed both resolve and a lightening of misery. Her backbone straightened, she twisted to look over her shoulder toward a small nook where Sage noticed, for the first time, a young girl slowly swishing water across crockery. "You might as well get your fanny in here, Gussie," the cook called, "I know your ears are flapping out big as an elephant's." The kitchen scullery let the dish slip to the bottom of the basin and was soon sitting alongside Mrs. Wiggit at the table. Her eyes were enormous in a pale, wan face. From the look of them, she too had been crying.

Mrs. Wiggit studied Sage a moment before her substantial bosom heaved and her breath whooshed out. Her face bleak, she said, "Well then, Mr. Friend-of-Mae's, I don't know where she is, but wherever she is, it's not good." With those words, the woman's chin wobbled and her backbone sagged once again.

THIRTY-TWO

Dispatch: *May 20. 1903, President's train pauses in Eugene, Oregon.*

> *"This country spurns the thought of inflicting wrongs upon the weak."* —*T.R.*

McALLISTER AND CLOONEY WORE GRIM FACES when they finally entered the saloon. Although his watch said Sage had been waiting only fifteen minutes, it had felt like half a day. He'd been nervously rocking his empty beer glass on the table until he realized his fidgeting was attracting the bartender's attention. Next, it had been his right leg jumping under the table. He'd had to quash that as well.

All three stayed silent until the beers they ordered were sitting on the table before them. Once the bartender was out of earshot, McAllister leaned forward over the table. "It doesn't look good," he told Sage. "How about you? What did you learn?"

"The cook says Mae went to use the restroom and never came back. Instead, the Cap'n came in and told her he'd found Mae in the main building. He claimed he fired her on the spot. Said she wouldn't be coming back."

"Do you trust what the woman told you?" Clooney asked.

Glumly, Sage sighed. "'Fraid so," he said and repeated what he'd learned from Mrs. Wiggit. After she'd repeated the Capt'n words, the cook had pointed toward a row of coat pegs and said, "I know Mae didn't leave this building of her own free will. It's nippy cold outside and that hat and coat are hers. No way she'd leave them behind. They ain't fancy, but they're well-mended and warm." Sage, Mrs. Wiggit and Gussie silently stared at the peg where Mae's long black coat still hung, her small-brimmed hat on the peg beside it.

Sage had cleared a throat suddenly constricted by a fear. "Um, Mae has a friend. A ragpicker fellow. Gray-haired, with a beard, boots to his knees. I don't suppose you saw him today?" he asked.

Mrs. Wiggit started saying, "He was here but left . . . " when Gussie's piping voice sounded for the first time, "I did! I saw the ragpicker! He was out in the courtyard. With that other man."

"What other man?" Mrs. Wiggit asked sharply.

"Why, that friend of the Cap'n's. The one staying upstairs. The one who came into the kitchen and told the ragpicker to go away. They was in the courtyard and the Cap'n's friend had ahold of the ragpicker's arm. It was kinda funny. The ragpicker looked mad and so did the other man. But the other man was sorta helping the ragpicker inside."

"Inside?" Sage asked.

"Yeh, he led the old fellow inside this building that we be sitting in right here. They was walking real close together. And kinda fast."

"And, that's about all they knew," Sage said. "It looks like they must be holding Mae and Herman somewhere in the building. I suspect Matthew is a prisoner too since he didn't turn up to play with Andy and Matthew would never disappoint the boy like that." Sage stopped talking and gulped half a glass of the tepid beer without tasting it.

McAllister and Clooney exchanged somber looks. McAllister softly hit the side of his fist against the table. "It all fits," he said. "The Cap'n and his conspirators have Mrs. Clemens and Mr. Eich for sure. And, we suspect they also have Matthew.

Between us, Clooney and I managed to look in every room accessible to the public. No Matthew. Nor were the other two anywhere in sight. When we tried to search the third floor, we found the stairs guarded by the Cap'n's henchman, Grindstaff. No way he was letting us go up there. That means the Cap'n has imprisoned our folks with those boys up on the third floor. We must act soon."

Clooney shifted in his seat, leaned closer and spoke softly. "The Cap'n has to be getting desperate. He knows his game is about to be exposed. Ollie's escape told him that. He also has to realize that it's only a matter of days before those picketing women get the whole town in an uproar. The house Lynch bought in Northwest Portland is useless for their purposes now. I'll bet the Cap'n thinks every witness to their wrongdoing is locked away on the BCS's third floor. It's guaranteed that he's going to try to get rid of those witnesses and soon."

Sage put his elbows on the table and held his head in both hands, overwhelmed by all they had to accomplish in the next twenty-four hours. On one hand, those BCS miscreants needed to be stopped and all their captives freed before harm came to any one of them. But the BCS conspiracy was separate and apart from the assassination. They still had to rescue Meachum, find the duped assassin, identify the second assassin on the platform and prevent harm to the president, all of it without Fong's help.

Gradually, he became aware that McAllister was speaking. He lowered his hands, "What did you say?" he asked.

"I said that Robert and I, we intend to mount the rescue tonight. After the Cap'n has gone to bed. We devised the plan while we walked over here. You do know, don't you, there's more men than Robert and I who want to stop the Cap'n's trade in young boys? Right?"

He wasn't sure where the lawyer was heading, but Sage was beginning to see a glimmer of hope. He felt his shoulders straighten.

McAllister continued, "So, we propose getting everyone to immediately converge on the BCS. We figure it will take about a couple hours to get everyone in place. I'll go round them up while Robert checks in as a guest to keep an eye on things. If we keep the place hopping and full, it might stop anything bad from happening until we're ready." Sage saw the wisdom of the plan. The Cap'n was unlikely to murder three people when the building was full.

The lawyer continued to lay out his plan. "The group of us will stay there until closing with Robert staying overnight. He'll let the rest of us in the alley door near the swimming pool after the Cap'n closes up and goes to bed. We'll probably end up having to give a few of the Cap'n's men a thumping but we figure, because of sheer numbers, we'll be able to overwhelm them before they know what's happening. Besides, we're going in armed. Once we've taken control, we'll search the third floor, free whoever we find and spirit them away into hiding."

"But, you said Lynch and his buddies threatened to expose you. Make it so you can't practice law anymore. They can still do that." Sage reminded him. "And they can hurt all your friends too," He glanced toward Clooney.

McAllister grinned, "You know, Adair, there is a heck of a lot more to life than being a lawyer. And, when matched against the loss of Matthew, Mr. Eich and Mrs. Clemens, and the horror those young boys face if we don't act tonight, I conclude that the exchange is worth both the risk and the damage if it comes to that."

A glance at Clooney showed him to be gazing at McAllister, with pride and hell, might as well acknowledge it, with love. He thought of Lucinda, felt regret and then let it go. Now was not the time.

Sage looked down at his hands gripping the beer mug. He hated to relinquish leadership of the BCS rescue effort. It was his mother, after all, who needed rescuing. But the determination on McAllister's face, as well as the man's proven intelligence, had to be enough. He had to let go and focus on preventing the assassination and finding Meachum. Time had nearly run out.

It was galling that not everything Roosevelt did favored working people. He was still too close to the big corporations that owned Congress. And he belonged to that score of politicians who were trying to save the capitalist system through regulation of its inherent greed. Regardless, Roosevelt's death at the hands of a duped union member would be disastrous for the union movement. That act would reverse what little progress working people had made toward economic justice. Roosevelt's murder would vindicate the corporate overlords and strengthen their ability to enact more anti-union legislation. The tiny progress Roosevelt had made toward empowering ordinary citizens would be set back for years, maybe decades.

"All right," Sage said with a sigh, "I'll leave the BCS rescue in your hands. I have to find Meachum before he's murdered and the assassins before the president's train pulls into Union Station tomorrow morning. And, first, I have to go check on Mr. Fong."

The hospital ward hummed with mingled sounds of cutlery clattering against tin plates and subdued visitor hubbub. Fong's bed, however, seemed enclosed in a thick bubble of silence. The Chinese guard, leaning against the wall, looked relaxed but his watchful eyes glittered as they constantly swept the room.

Kim Ho sat slumped in a bedside chair but she managed a weak smile when he approached. She shook her head, her dark eyes wide with worry, her lips pressed tightly together as if to suppress their trembling. Fong was still unconscious.

Sage advanced to look down at his friend. Fong's eyes were closed, his face haggard and exceedingly pale below the stark white of the bandage encircling his head.

"No change then?" he asked.

"He same," she responded in a sorrowful voice.

"You've been here the whole time?" At her nod, he asked, "Who is watching your provision store?"

"Cousin," she responded. Not for the first time, Sage thought about how fortunate the Chinese were to have their fraternal tong connections that were, seemingly, as strong as family bonds were among the various European nationalities. Probably stronger. He supposed the tongs were one of the benefits of the

Chinese culture–an intelligent response to the extreme adversity the Chinese encountered in America. Of course, all was not perfect in the Chinatown. There were, after all, those bloody tong wars. As he gazed down at the still face, he pondered whether the tong's negative aspects would go away if the adversity lessened. Would the tongs evolve into social clubs once the Chinese had better economic opportunities and the right to bring their wives and families to America?

"You too young to make such big wrinkles in forehead," came a hoarse whisper from the bed.

Sage started. With a sharp little cry, Mrs. Fong leapt from her chair to her husband's side.

Fong's eyes were half-open as they moved between the two of them. "Head really hurts," he whispered, before closing his eyes.

Kim Ho took Fong's limp hand into her small one. Sage tarried just long enough to see his friend's fingers tighten around hers before he hurried off to find a doctor.

Leaving the hospital an hour later, Sage's step was lighter, and not just because he was heading downhill. The doctor said that it was a very positive sign that Fong had regained consciousness already and appeared to have retained his "marbles." Not exactly a precise medical term but Sage had managed to convey its meaning to Kim Ho, causing her face to brighten. Fong had awakened one more time and stayed conscious long enough for them to tell him he'd been shot. Just before his eyes closed, he'd asked whether Sage and Mr. Li had met. Upon being reassured that they had and were working together, he said, his voice weak from the throbbing pain in his head, "Happy to hear. Good you not going it alone." After which he smiled slightly and closed his eyes.

Sage waited only a short time in the fragrantly-scented Chinatown noodle house before Mr. Li and Meachum's lead man turned up. Both men looked like they hadn't slept in days.

Meachum's man, Buddy Kendall, was much younger than Sage, but tonight he looked ten years older and he hadn't changed his clothes in days. The Chinese man, on the other hand, was impeccably dressed, Western style. Dark smudges beneath his eyes were the only sign he showed of strain. The hunched shoulders of both men relaxed upon learning Fong would recover.

"That is excellent good news. He is a very important man in our Chinese community," Mr. Li said, smiling for the first time since Sage had met him. Mr. Li raised a hand, barking out instructions in Chinese while gesturing at the three of them. Within a minute, each of them had a bowl of seasoned noodles before him. Not until Sage took the first bite did he realize that he had not eaten since very early that day. The noodles were delicious. From the way he shoveled in the food, it was evident that Buddy Kendall had also forgotten to eat.

Mr. Li waited until his companions were nearly finished before saying, "My men have narrowed the search down to two empty warehouses in the North End, by the river. I have put guards on both. They will tell us if they see anyone going in or out."

"I don't think we can wait," Sage started to say before Meachum's man jumped in.

"They will kill Meach before tomorrow. I say we raid the two places tonight and see if he's there," Kendall said leaning forward, his hands clenched and white-knuckled atop the table.

Sage remained silent, waiting for Mr. Li's response, because he happened to agree with Kendall. If Meachum wasn't already dead, he soon would be. The Chinese man nodded thoughtfully. "I think you are right, Mr. Kendall. It is better we act tonight, right away. Tomorrow we will be too busy stopping the assassination. And, I also think the danger to Mr. Meachum is now most serious." He glanced over at a wall clock. "It is ten o'clock. I will round up all the men I can and meet you in one hour inside the rail yard across from the Slap Jack saloon. You do the same. Maybe, in the meantime, the guards will learn more and we will not have to search both warehouses.

❀ ❀ ❀

It was Meachum's own groaning that once again sent him back into consciousness. He lay there, cataloging each pain beginning at his feet and working upwards. His ankles, from the rope. Legs and buttocks and back from the kicks that had landed on them as he tried to protect his front from the sharp-toed boots. His ribs, the ones that hadn't escaped, felt broken. Each time he shifted or took a breath it felt like a knife point stabbed between them. And his privates. Despite all his efforts, a few well-placed kicks had left him aching. He tried to imagine what his beat up face looked like. He'd never thought of himself as any beauty but Mary had always called him striking, saying she loved the "ageless strength" of his face and his vivid blue eyes. He cautiously opened those eyes now, one at a time. Testing. Yes, he could still see out of each one, despite the fact they were swollen nearly shut. That was a relief.

There was the rattle of a padlock being loosed and the metallic sound of a tin door slapping shut. His captors were back. He closed his eyes and quieted his breathing. From behind slitted eyelids, he watched the light brighten as one of them approached, paused and then kicked him hard in the back. Meachum bit the inside of his lip so he would not react, trapping the cry of pain in his throat.

With a "humph," his attacker strode away, saying in a voice that Meachum knew he'd never forget, "Still out. We're supposed to send word when he wakes up. The boss wants one more go at him. Then we take him for that little boat ride."

Meachum shivered at the thought of that cold, swollen river bisecting the city. If they took him into the middle of the Willamette and dropped him in, with his hands tied, that would be the end. The spring rains had raised both the river level and the current's speed. His body would probably end up somewhere down the Columbia River. Hell, he might even make it to the ocean. He'd never wanted to go out on the ocean. He was a mountain man by preference, preferring to leave the seagoing to those who liked water.

Carefully wriggling around, Meachum was able to watch his captors from beneath his lowered eyelids. The men sat on wooden crates around a kerosene lantern. Luckily, the lantern's pool of light was not large enough to reach Meachum. He could study the enemy from relative safety.

There were three of them. One of them was a new addition. Meachum had not seen nor heard him before. He squinted as he strained to hear what they were saying. He'd always had sharp hearing and, as of yet, their blows had not damaged his ears.

"It's a real brave thing that you are doing, my friend," said the man who'd done the kicking.

The new man's voice quavered, "I have to make a statement. It's important to make a statement. Roosevelt has to realize he can't ride roughshod over union men and get away with it. A union shop is a union shop."

"That's right!" agreed the kicker. "Now, you might get shoved a bit but, when all is said and done, it will be worth it. Teddy will know he can't take a man's job and not pay some price, even if all the smoke bomb does is make his face turn redder than it already is."

"You sure, now, that this smoke bomb isn't going to do any more than just make smoke?" the new man asked, reaching for the lantern and moving it closer to a brown, twine-wrapped package sitting on the floor at his feet. For a brief moment, Meachum saw him clearly. The man was so thin that, if he turned sideways, Meachum wasn't sure he'd be visible in the gloom. He had short black bangs cut square across a bulging forehead, a narrow nose and a receding chin that lent him a fearful, timid look. Not a man who would stand out anywhere–not even in his own mirror.

"Yup, I'm positively sure. It'll just smoke and raise a God-awful stink. That's the worst that's going happen." The response sounded suspiciously hearty to Meachum but, then, it would, since Meachum knew the package contained a real bomb, not a smoke bomb. Meachum wanted to warn the dupe, and would have, but the gag in his mouth made that impossible.

"Tell me again what I have to do," the new man said.

"Well, first of all, you want to carry this package under your coat, tucked tight into your armpit. And, you have to be real careful. You drop it and you'll spoil every thing we've put together. Second, you get up to City Park long before Roosevelt arrives and find a place right near the front platform edge. Once Roosevelt gets there, we'll have a man on the platform. He'll give the signal when you should toss the package at Roosevelt's feet. That will break the glass ampules, the chemicals will mingle and phew! Folks will be leaping off that platform to get away. In the confusion, it will be easy for you to escape."

"How will I know the man on the platform? What signal is he going to give?"

"First, he's going to start coughing. That means you should push forward to the edge of the platform. Next, his coughing fit's going to be so bad that he'll have to leave the platform. As soon as he stands up to leave, people will be looking at him. That's when you throw. The smoke bomb will start up as soon as it hits the ground. Since Roosevelt is traveling with a passel of reporters, the whole world will know what happened here in Portland, Oregon."

"And afterwards? How's Roosevelt and the reporters going to know why I threw the smoke bomb at him?"

"'Cause as soon as you've gotten away, we're going to send every reporter a note telling him exactly why you did it. Roosevelt shouldn't have let that union-busting fellow keep his job at your expense."

Seemingly reassured, the duped assassin took up the package, shook each man's hand and accepted their claps on the back before heading out the door.

The other two men sat in silence for a few minutes, apparently waiting to make sure the other man was truly gone. Meachum felt himself slipping from consciousness. Fighting to stay alert, he heard only one more exchange between his captors before the blackness closed in once again.

"He sure is one stupid dodo bird," said the other man, who'd remained silent up until that point.

"Yup, 'stupid' is definitely the word. If the bomb don't get him and the police don't shoot him immediately, we'll have to do it ourselves. Just think, they'll call us heroes."

"What if the bomb doesn't explode or Roosevelt gets shoved out of the way?"

"That happens, the boss said he'll take care of Roosevelt personally. That's why he's there in the first place. He's back-up. Just in case the dodo screws everything up."

THIRTY-THREE

Dispatch: *May 21, 1903, President's train pauses in Salem, Oregon.*

"There is no proper place in our society . . . for the rich man who uses the power conferred by his riches to oppress and wrong his neighbors." —T.R.

AFTER BINDING HIS WRISTS BEHIND HIS BACK and marching him up three flights of stairs, Eich's captor had opened a door, shoved him across its threshold and slammed it shut. As Eich fought to maintain his balance, his mind registered the snick of the doorlock being turned. The room was windowless. The dirty transom glass above the door provided the only light.

"I'd be a tad more cheerful about our rescue if you weren't trussed up like a wild turkey heading for the oven," came the wry, distinctive Appalachian drawl from somewhere further inside the room.

"Mae Clemens, your voice might be the most glorious sound I have ever heard in all my long and varied days," he said, shuffling forward, widening his eyes to adjust for the lack of light. There she was, sitting on the floor, her legs stretched out, her arms behind her back. Stretched out beside her, lying along the wall was the still figure of another person. Matthew, no doubt.

"I've heard tell that the hearing goes afore anything else," she said, but he could see her grinning in the gloom.

"Mae, are you okay? Did they hurt you? And Matthew?" By now he could clearly see the pale oval of her face.

"He's got himself a snoot full of that opium drug but he's still breathing," she answered.

"Opium?" Eich wondered why they'd drugged only the boy.

She must have read his mind because she explained, "Matthew took a bit of exception to them treating me rough, silly boy." Despite her words, her tone was tender. "They held his nose and made him swallow it."

"Ha! Little did they know you were the one they needed to worry about," he said and received another grin.

Eich stepped to the wall, turned his back to it and slid down until he sat next to her. Her body was warm and lightly scented with the clean leathery smell of carbolic soap. "How long has he been like this?" he asked.

"A pretty long time, but he's been twitching and moaning so I expect he's about to come out of it."

Wriggling his fingers, Eich tried to gauge the thickness of the ropes around his wrists.

"Don't be bothering," she said, her voice now gloomy. "That varmint who tied us up knew what he's doing."

"Humph," Eich responded and twisted away from the wall, angling so that his coat pocket gaped open. "He isn't nearly as smart when it comes to searching a fellow," he told her. "If you can wriggle around a bit, I got a folding knife in my coat pocket here. It'll take some work but I expect we can use it to break free."

Mae immediately sprang into action, scooting forward to face away from him, the fingers of her hands groping until they found the knife handle. She carefully pulled it out and began inching the knife loose from its leather sheath.

"You want to do the sawing?" she asked him.

"I'd better. I'm used to the knife and your hands must be numb by now."

They scooted until they sat back to back, and she passed him the knife. He gripped it firmly. "Now comes the tricky part," he said, as his fingers began fumbling over the rope binding her wrists, feeling for an opening big enough to accept the knife blade without slicing her skin. Once he found it, he inserted the knife point slowly.

"Ouch!" Mae said forcefully. "How about you try a bit more to your left? That knife point feels a bit sharpish on my palm."

He moved the knife blade to his left and began slowly sawing up and down against the rope, praying his sweaty hands wouldn't drop the knife.

He worked steadily, pausing only when she said softly, "They're fixing to kill us. Keep us locked inside here and then set the place afire to get rid of the evidence–meaning you, me, Matthew and those poor boys. Sometime before sunrise, I heard the devils say."

Carefully stepping through the dry grass, Sage's feet felt for unseen potholes. He was familiar with this stretch of ground alongside the railroad tracks. He'd stumbled his way across it only the summer before. Back then, some very bad men had been chasing after him and another fellow.

The dark forms of Buddy Kendell and his five men from the Flying Squadron stood about ten yards into the weedy lot. Just as he reached them, Mr. Li and a group of black-clad Chinese men seemed to materialize at the field's edge. Only Mr. Li wore Western attire. Catching Sage's appraising look, Li explained, "I am here to coordinate my men and perform the job of respectable lookout."

Sage quickly counted the strength of their invasion force. Ten men strong plus the respectable lookout. He doubted that the opposition had those numbers guarding Meachum. The worry was the bad guys' weapons. But, maybe that wouldn't be a problem. As his eyes adjusted to being away from the gaslights outside the saloons and bawdy houses, he began to discern the telltale curve of pistol butts peeking out of waistbands and coat pockets.

Mr. Li seemed to notice the focus of Sage's gaze because he said. "Yes, my men carry firearms but I told them no shooting unless there is no other choice. They also have knives. Knives are better because they are silent." The Chinese leader smiled. "I have two pieces of good news. Mr. Fong sat up and took a drink of water this night. Second piece of good news is that we believe we know exactly which warehouse is Mr. Meachum's prison. It is down near the river."

The group divided, setting off in two's and three's. A large, combined force of Chinese and European men would attract unwanted attention. Only Sage and Mr. Li stayed together. They received curious looks from those they passed but no one made a derisive comment. Sage wondered whether it was their intensity that kept passersby silent.

No moon brightened the sky and the scuttling clouds hid the stars. Every once and awhile a wind gust would deliver a shower of fine droplets sufficient to sodden a man's coat. The organizers of tomorrow's welcoming celebrations were likely bustling around trying to make sure the president would stay dry. The on-again, off-again weather was always a problem for those who came from climes where the weather was predictable. Pacific Northwesterners, however, knew to layer their clothing and took the changeable weather in stride. Sage smiled, remembering how he used to approach the city's weather with resistence. Now, he was learning to appreciate the sweet freshness of the air and the fact that every day brought variety. He must be turning native. Next thing he knew, there would be webs growing between his toes.

A scuffle of boot on sidewalk pulled his thoughts out of fantasy. He glanced at the man walking beside him. Mr. Li's face was impassive except for intent eyes scanning the sidewalks ahead. For a moment, the absurdity of the situation hit Sage. Here he was, an Appalachian hill kid who used to squirm on his belly beneath a coal face to gouge out dynamiting holes. Now, he was strolling down a boardwalk in the far West, with a distinguished

Chinese man at his side. Never in his wildest dreams could he have imagined the twists and turns that had delivered him into tonight's exact situation. An involuntary chortle rose in his throat, to be smothered by a discreet cough. Whimsical thinking was not appropriate given their current situation all around. Probably his nerves were going for a gallop, as his mother would say.

A quick sideways glance told him that Mr. Li was smiling. For an instant, Sage thought the man had read his mind. But the Chinese man merely observed, "It is good the night is dark and that it has begun raining. If they are watching, it will be hard to see us approach. And, the rain on the tin roof should drown out any noise we make. We are nearly there."

The brick sidewalk became a wooden boardwalk as the street changed to cobblestone, bordered by packed dirt. They were approaching the river and the buildings around them were mostly warehouses or small manufacturing. The river's tang mingled with the smell of wet horse manure. Down here, the manure scoopers had trouble keeping up. Mornings, this street overflowed with drays and wagons of all shapes and sizes, each pulled by a manure-producing horse or two. The frequent rain showers further hindered the clean-up efforts, because the mix of water and hooves quickly mashed the horse plops into the mud. Still, the barnyard odor signaled that it was a place of lively commerce and, for that reason, a place of hope for countless unemployed men.

Glancing around, Sage saw that men lay everywhere. Their sleeping forms curled up in doorways or snugged against warehouse fronts, taking advantage of the sidewalk awnings erected to keep the boardwalks dry for deliveries. Each man along this street hoped to be first in line to obtain the next day's work loading and unloading goods. They'd awaken, clothes grubby, bodies chilled, empty stomachs cramping at the first stirring of commerce. And, they'd count themselves lucky if they were hired to earn a single dollar for a day of backbreaking work.

"There it is, that building straight ahead." Mr. Li spoke softly, nodding his head toward a tin-roofed warehouse at the block's end. It was small, old and stood apart from its neighbors. Age had greyed its fir-planked sides. A sturdy padlock secured the two doors tightly shut across an opening large enough to admit wagon and horse. Another man-sized door was in the front wall. It was likely secured from the inside since the door hasp hung open and its padlock was missing.

They approached the building and strode back and forth, since the lack of windows meant observation from inside was impossible. Sage stared glumly at the narrow gaps alongside the building. "Any windows in the back?" he asked Li, who shook his head.

That didn't look good for a sneak attack. Evidently fearful of robbery, the warehouse builder had provided only high windows at the top of each side and probably skylights in the roof for light. Sage paused to study those side windows. One good sign was the faint guttering glow behind the grimy glass. Someone was inside.

The windows were frustrating. They were wide enough to admit a small man but far too high to peer through. At least ten feet above ground. He supposed they could hunt up some crates, stacking them like steps against the building's side. But that was risky. One misstep and the element of surprise would vanish.

He turned toward Mr. Li only to see that the other man was engaged in a whispered conversation with two of the tong "cousins." Before Sage could say anything, the two slipped into the gap beside the building and stopped below one of the windows. He watched, amazed, as one man quickly slipped from his boots and jumped onto the thighs of other man's bent legs. Like acrobats in a circus, the first man catapulted onto the shoulders of the second man, whose shoulders rested against the building. Very slowly, the bottom man straightened, the effort silently raising the first man's head above the window frame. "My God," Sage breathed, "that is incredible."

"Those two are specialists. Performers. They carry head of the largest dragon during Chinese New Year celebration," Mr. Li said softly. His explanation conjured up a memory of the tall, brightly-colored paper dragon, its many-legged body advancing up Second Avenue through the swirling smoke of exploding fire-crackers. The crowd gasped and cheered whenever the dragon's fearsome head reared up to tower above everyone else. Now Sage knew who was responsible for that dramatic effect.

Unencumbered by the immense dragon head or the need to move, the bottom man held rock steady while the topmost man raised on his toes and looked through the window. After a moment, he slowly reached out and pushed a finger against the window. Sage saw it slant inward. Good. That window, at least, was unlocked. A minute later, as silently and swiftly as it had been erected, the two-man totem pole collapsed with the topmost man landing neatly atop his waiting boots. He slipped back into them, tied up the laces and both men returned to the boardwalk.

The four of them moved away up the street, away from the building. Li and the two acrobats paused to hold a whispered exchange in unintelligble Chinese. To each side of the warehouse, small groups of men–their men–leaned casually against build-ing fronts out of the rain. Since there was no street activity this time of night, any passerby would think their presence odd. But that was unlikely. Apart from the sleeping itinerants and a few foraging dogs, no one else was abroad.

Beside him, the conversation stopped and the two acrobats stepped off up the boardwalk only to melt back into a doorway close to the warehouse.

Expectantly, Sage turned toward Li who said, "Street door is fastened shut with a simple hook. There are two men sitting around a lantern, back near another door on the river side. That door is barred but it is made only of weak tin. Also, another man is lying on the floor, all tied up, by the wall under the window."

Relief flooded Sage. Meachum had to be alive if he was tied up. Before he could say anything a third Chinese man slipped up to speak to Li. Once they had spoken, he too melted back into the night that had darkened with a thickening of clouds. No lon-ger did hazy patches of a star-studded night sky dot the canopy overhead. Instead, a lowering mass of sullen gray obscured all night light. "Good. The darker the better," Sage thought.

Mr. Li spoke. "My men say that earlier tonight they heard shouting and cries from inside. Then before we arrived, another man knocked on the street door and they let him in. He left the warehouse maybe one half-hour ago." Li didn't have to say any more.

"Do you have men watching the river side?" Sage asked. It would be horrible if those two inside opened the door and heaved Meachum into the water before a rescue was launched.

"Yes. There are two men there on the back wharf. My best swimmers. They are also ready to fire a gun and drive the bad men back inside." Li responded, showing that he too recognized that Meachum was in imminent danger given the river's proximity.

"Let's move down the block a bit and meet with our men," Sage said. "We need a plan that won't get Meachum killed during its execution." At Mr. Li's nod of agreement, they moved northward along the boardwalk, signaling to the other watchers that all should follow.

THIRTY-FOUR

May 21, 1903, President's train readies to leave Salem, Oregon.

"Because of enormous changes in cities and industrial practices, the wage earner can best use his individual will and power if he unites with other wage earners." —T.R.

IN THE END, THEIR RESCUE PLAN WAS SIMPLE. The Chinese acrobats were key. Sage, with Meachum's right-hand man, Buddy Kendall, at his side stepped down the dark street. When they reached the latched warehouse door, they exchanged a look. Their part was easy, unless the galoots inside let fly with a few bullets. Sage nodded at Kendall before raising a fist to bang on the building's front door.

"Hey, Gus, it's Elmer and Casey, open up!" he shouted, his words slurred. "We got us a bottle of that thar Scots firewater you like so much." They kept up the racket, pounding and shouting like two happy drunks out on a binge and seeking companionship.

Immediately, a querulous voice shouted back from within. "There ain't nobody here called 'Gus.' You men have the wrong warehouse. Move along."

Sage looked toward the remainder of Meachum's men. They stood at the right front corner of the building. At his nod, they quickly slipped out of sight, trailing each other down that side of the building, heading toward the dock at the back. There they were to wait.

It was time to step up the racket. Now both Sage and Kendall started pounding on the door in earnest and shouting at the top of their lungs. It was crucial that both of Meachum's captors move to the front of the building, away from Meachum and the rear door. Sage grinned at Kendell when the second captor's voice sounded from a point just inside the door, "Shut the hell up you fools. We don't want no whiskey!"

Sage raised his hand and Mr. Li stepped from under the awning of a neighboring building. He signaled to his two acrobats who were waiting beneath the high side window.

If all went as hoped, that signal would propel the Chinese acrobat onto his partner's shoulders once again. Once Sage and Kindell had the two men inside sufficiently distracted, the topmost acrobat would ease open the window and drop to the floor inside. From there, he was to race over to the rear door, unbar it and return to protect Meachum.

Buddy and Sage stepped up their assault on the tin door, Sage kicking it with his heavy boot, Buddy pounding on it with the butt of his revolver. All the while, both of them shouting, keeping up the pretext of being friendly drunks eager to share their bottle. That friendliness was the only thing keeping the two men inside from firing their guns straight through the door. Once they realized they were really under assault, bullets would pierce that thin metal door easy as hot knives through butter.

Sage's ears strained to hear over the racket he and Buddy were making. Mr. Li, who had moved to the building's lefthand corner, was peering along its side. Suddenly Li raised a hand and circled his index finger in the air. The acrobat had dropped into the building. Sage instantly stepped up the noise and began to pry at the door, hoping to spring the latch.

"There ain't no damn 'Gus' here! You git away from that damn door or I'm going start . . . . " came a yell from inside before it abruptly cut off. A distant clamor and a sharp whistle sounded in the night air. Both signaled that the rear door was open, the team had entered the building. Sage and Buddy, as one, slammed their shoulders into the flimsy door. Their reward was a metallic screech as the nails anchoring the inside metal hook tore loose from the wooden door frame.

It was dim within, the only light being a kerosene lantern flickering near the rear of the building. Still, even in that feeble light it was clear that the assault was over. One of the thugs was clutching his shoulder, blood pouring from between his fingers, as he struggled to steady the hilt of a deeply sunk knife blade. The other thug, his rheumy eyes wide and glistening, stood like a frozen statute with his hands high in the air. He was not a total fool. The muzzles of six guns were pointing at him.

All Sage cared about was reaching the side of the warehouse where the acrobat had reported seeing Meachum. Buddy was already kneeling beside his boss. As Sage reached his side, Buddy looked up, his face pale and wide-eyed with fear. "He's breathing mighty shallow, he's hurt bad," he said. Meanwhile, one of Li's men knelt at Meachum's back, sawing at the unconscious man's bonds. As Meachum's hands fell free, he gave a groan but his puffy eyes remained closed in a face that was barely recognizable.

"Let's find something firm to carry him on. He might have broken bones. We'll take him over to the hotel. Angus is expecting him. I sent word ahead," Sage instructed. Two of Meachum's men rummaged around the warehouse and returned with a door. They laid their coats atop its surface before gently sliding the injured man onto it.

Swiftly, they headed out, Sage trotting behind. As they exited the building, he saw Mr. Li standing in the cluster of his men. Sage raised his palms to signal Meachum's chance of survival was unknown. Li nodded and gave a slight bow before he and his men turned away to head down the street.

Sage paused. Without Fong's Chinese "cousins," Meachum would not have been found. He would have died for sure. Sage wanted to yell out his "thanks" but decided they'd made enough noise on this street. Someone might have called the police. He pulled out his pocket watch, tilting its face to catch the faint light. It was twelve-thirty in the morning. In just eleven hours, the president's train would chug into Union Station. To the sound of marching bands and cheering crowds, the assassination team would slip into place. A mix of anger and fear surged up from his gut. He reluctantly turned back toward the warehouse and the two captives. Above, the sullen clouds loosed a spate of spring rain, its light, well-spaced droplets vanishing circlets in puddle surfaces.

Matthew was still groggy but he'd shed most of the opium's residual effects. Enough so that he was able to comprehend the whispered discussion between Herman Eich and Mae Clemens.

"We can't wait for rescue," Mae was insisting. "Sage has his hands full already. We aren't even sure that anyone knows we're missing!"

"But, if we do get Matthew out that transom above the door, he still has to get himself past Mister Growl who's guarding the stairs. Why, he could drop down right in front of the fellow. I say we wait until they open the door and we jump them. They won't be expecting us to have our hands free."

"Don't you realize they could set fire to the building without ever opening the door? And, they took away the damn door key. Do you really want to be trying to break open that door from inside when the hallway's in flames? They made it clear as springtime rain that they're going to act and soon." Mae was adamant, fear hissing in her whisper.

Matthew cleared his throat, "I agree with Mrs. Clemens, Mr. Eich. From what they said, I think they plan to burn us up tonight and soon. It must be getting near morning. They wait any longer and too many folks will be up and about. At least, if we . . . ." Matthew didn't get to finish his point.

"Shh! Listen," commanded Mae.

The three held their breath as they strained to hear whether something was happening outside their prison. Then they knew. Faint illumination brightened the transom window over the door. Their eyes, already adjusted to pitch black, had no trouble discerning the terror on each other's face. As one they moved toward the door and listened even harder. In the end, it wasn't their ears but their noses that answered the question foremost in their minds. All three knew the smell. Everywhere in the city small, gas-powered generators ran workshop stitching machines, printing presses, harness makers, electrical plants and a host of other equipment. It was the chill, chemical smell of gasoline that now slithered beneath the door to fill the room.

Mae and Herman looked at each other, their initial terror replaced by thin-lipped determination. Herman bent down, putting his hands onto his knees so that his back formed a table. At the same time, Mae grabbed Matthew's arm, saying, "You crawl out that transom, boy. If you can, run on down to that room where the other boys are kept and free them. Lead them down the stairs."

"But, you'll be trapped inside here. There isn't even a window!" Matthew protested, even as he grabbed the door frame to steady himself while he climbed atop Eich's back.

"There's nothing that can be done about us, boy. They took the key out of the lock. It would take an axe to break down this door and there isn't time to find one and do the job. You told us that they leave the key in the other lock. You go see if it's there. Find a way to free those boys, now!"

Matthew reached up, shoved open the transom window, and extended his forearms into the hallway. "All clear" he said, fear making his voice loud. At that, Mae grabbed hold of his legs and with a grunt, she shoved the boy upward, propelling him out. There was a thump as he landed on the hallway floor.

"Oh, God," he whimpered, "the rug is soaked."

Eich straightened, a hand on the small of his back. "Do what Mae said, Matthew," he called. "Free the others. Lead them out. Go for help. We'll be fine."

They heard the thud of his feet as he ran down the hallway in the direction of the room where the Cap'n had the boys imprisoned. Overhead, the transom window hung slightly ajar. The odor of gasoline grew stronger in their prison. Mae and Herman stepped to the farthest corner of the room. As they stood there, their backs pressed against the windowless wall, Herman slid an arm across Mae's shoulders and pulled her tight. She slipped her arm around his waist and hugged him back. "Regrets?" he asked, his lips touching her hair. He felt her head shake "no" and tightened his hold. "That's the girl," he whispered.

"Hurry, hurry, hurry," Robert Clooney's voice was a near squeak as he shooed the waiting men through the side door into the BCS's stairwell.

McAllister paused, "What took you so long?" he asked even as he noted that Robert's face was dead white and more tense than he'd ever seen it.

"The Cap'n's been running all over the place, shoving things into suitcases. And his two henchman have been guarding the stairwell all night long. They've got the damn front door blocked shut with a desk. I tried to move it and made way too much noise. They almost caught me. I had to hide in the dining room under the table."

"What's happening right now?"

"The Cap'n and that guest of his just fled out the kitchen door with their suitcases. The two thugs are up on the third floor with gasoline cans."

As if on cue, gasoline vapor flowed down the stairwell. The four other men with McAllister yanked revolvers from their coat pockets and rushed toward the stairs. McAllister paused to say, "Robert, go outside and keep watch. We'll take it from here."

"Like hell you will," Clooney said, pulling out his own revolver before charging past him up the stairs.

McAllister followed, fear and admiration giving such strength to his legs that he was soon back in the lead.

The mercenary leaned down to wipe his knife blade on the deadman's clothes. "It's a good thing I keep my friend here sharp," he thought to himself. "Damned hard stabbing a man through a heavy coat and all those layers. The fool must be wearing his entire wardrobe."

He reached down and picked up the Cap'n's bulging suitcase. "Nice little bonus this. Mighty obliging of the fool to gather up all his valuables for me." There was the clank of metal on metal. He smiled to himself. The BCS's silver was heading to a new home.

When he reached the alley mouth, he looked both ways. The street was empty of any life except for a passing dog, sniffing his way along the gutter. No human was abroad at five o'clock in the morning. Glancing over his shoulder, the mercenary looked down the street toward the BCS's third story. In minutes, maybe only seconds, there'd be that satisfying whoosh followed by an orange flicker behind the window glass. That glass would eventually explode outward, cries would sound and the fire truck would rumble toward the conflagration. A sight to see but one he had to forego this time.

The mercenary turned and strode away in the direction of the livery stable. Heavy suitcases in each hand, he marveled that the Cap'n had been so stupid as to think he would still be alive at the end of the operation. Despite the lack of sleep, his steps were lively. Anticipation coursed through him as well as satisfaction. Both were sensations he liked but rarely felt. In the end, and after a few problems, everything was proceeding as planned.

Meachum was dead by now. Too bad there hadn't been one more opportunity to teach him a lesson. The rocks he'd told them to put in Meachum's pockets guaranteed that his body wouldn't surface for some days. Meanwhile, a rented buggy sat waiting at the livery stable. He planned to stash the two suitcases behind its seat. He'd instructed the livery owner to have the horse harnessed and ready to go at five p.m. sharp. He'd be on his way within minutes after the job was done. South to Salem. There he'd catch the train. He'd be out of Oregon before nightfall, hours before the chaos died down. He smiled to himself, imagining that chaos. Everything would happen just as planned. The police force, that do-gooder chief police, the extra detectives and even that strange combination of chinks and union bums couldn't stop him. President Theodore Roosevelt, the so-called "Rough Rider" hero, would lead no more assaults up piddling hills or get his picture taken with the carcasses of animals he'd shot.

The mercenary's step on the cobbled sidewalk quickened. He was meeting with Destiny, this drizzling, miserable May morning and he could not be late.

THIRTY-FIVE

Dispatch: *May 21, 1903, President's train enters Portland, Oregon*

> "*It is essential that there should be organization of labor. This is an era of organization. Capital organizes and therefore labor must organize.*" —*T.R.*

SAGE LIMPED TOWARD MOZART'S, hampered by a painful "hitch in his git-along" as his mother would say. The warehouse's flimsy-looking tin door had been stronger than it looked. He tried to relax his face because he could feel it scrunch into lines of worry. The two men in the warehouse hadn't told them much of anything. Not that the scoundrels seemed to hold back anything. A few punches into one of their guts and they spilled everything they knew. Turned out, they were just two drifters, hired to guard a man and forget everything they saw. Neither would admit what their instructions had been with regard to the union leader once the "stranger" had left. But the snick of their eyes to one side when questioned about their plans for Meachum confirmed Sage's suspicions. Murder was the intended outcome. As for the stranger who'd beaten Meachum—they said that he'd pulled his hat brim low and made them stay at the far end of the warehouse whenever he'd questioned Meachum. Sure, they'd heard the blows and Meachum's cries but not what the stranger had said to Meachum since he'd pitched his voice too low for them to hear.

The two captives remained behind, guarded by Meachum's men. Once the president had left the city and things settled down, he'd deliver them to Hanke. Sage spent the next six hours dozing fitfully in Solomon's plush parlor chair, just steps away from the unconscious Meachum. The healing hands of Solomon's friend, Miz Esther, had ministered to the injured man throughout the pre-dawn hours but he never regained consciousness.

Finally, Sage could no longer remain by the injured man's side. He had to get back to Mozart's so he could change his clothes and join the president's Republican welcoming committee at the train station. The street he walked along was not on the president's parade route but still, parade goers were everywhere, streaming westward, eager to find a viewpoint from which to watch their country's leader pass. Overhead, the sky was the mild blue of May, fleecy white clouds scooting before a stiff breeze aloft. He hoped that breeze would not catch up any rain clouds. But this was the Pacific Northwest and its spring weather was so erratic it defied accurate prediction.

Fortunately, the street in front of Mozart's was much more thinly populated. He was glad of that. He reached the alley trapdoor without being observed and had soon found his way to the bathtub on the third floor. When he entered his room, Sage saw a folded note sitting against a vase of early hydrangeas. His mother's handwriting had scrawled Sage's name across its front. Sage snatched up the note to read her terse message, "Matthew, Herman, and I all safe. So are BCS boys. Thanks to McAllister and friends. Know something about assassination. Definite platform is location. Meet you there!"

Suddenly Sage understood what it meant to feel weak in the knees, because his legs gave out and he had to fumble for the chair. Sitting, he read the note again, noticing that unshed tears of relief were blurring the words. She was safe. Herman and Matthew were safe. Fong was conscious and had his "marbles." Only Meachum's outcome remained unknown. "To hell with the president. Today is already a success," Sage exulted.

He mentally shook loose of that celebratory excess. This was no time for exuberance. Not today. And, Roosevelt's life did matter. Not just because he was more progressive than most politicians but, also, because the plotters intended for his assassination to deliver a death blow to the union movement.

Within an hour Sage was thoroughly cleaned, groomed and dressed in his most formal suit—specifically, a "hand-tailored, jet-black, German-worsted, double-breasted, Prince Albert suit, complete with silk-lined vest." The haberdasher had almost sung the suit's attributes while making his sale. A tall silk hat and black wool overcoat completed his meet-the-president ensemble. A bit of blackening to polish up the shoes, a nod to the gnome-like Horace who was still ably maintaining Mozart's operation and Sage headed back onto the streets.

This time he mingled with the crowds walking the parade route. For a moment all his concerns were pushed aside as he got caught up in the excitement that had seized hold of the city. Authoritative adults were herding chattering clusters of school children, dressed in their Sunday best, toward the park blocks on the west side of downtown. One of the key events planned for the president was a meeting with the children of the city. When Sage reached the Portland Hotel, he saw that a mass of color had transformed its east courtyard. They'd arranged the flags of many nations in large clay pots. Multitudes of red, white and blue American flags and bunting hung from every window, with an enormous, slightly tattered old glory spanning the area above the entry door. This was a special flag, having been the one first raised inside the city of Manila after its surrender in 1898. It was here, at the Portland Hotel, where the president would dine, once the time capsule ceremony at the monument site was over. "If he's still alive," Sage cautioned himself.

Lengthening his stride, Sage headed north toward Union Station. Throngs of people filled the space between building fronts and curbs on either side. Sage was forced to walk in the street. Overhead, bunting and flags fluttered from lampposts and from wires strung across the street. Intrepid young men, high up the power poles, perched with one leg wrapped around the pole arms, just like sailors in ships' rigging. The buildings along the route sported bunting, flags and flowers. People crowded every window from the second story up, shouting and waving to those who stood below.

The street in front of the railroad station was even more crowded than the sidewalks along the parade route. Uniformed soldiers, tootling bands, prancing horses hooked to open carriages and scores of police officers made walking a challenge. Eventually, Sage spotted the well-dressed welcoming committee gathered to one side of the station doors. Just as he reached them, a distant roar sounded in the east. Sage knew that masses of men, women and children stood vigil on the bridges crossing the river, hoping to catch an early glimpse of the president's arrival. Their faraway cheers were the first indication that the presidential train was approaching the city proper and right on time. Next came the boom of the twenty-one-gun salute from cannons arranged on the bluff top across the river. This signal meant that Roosevelt's train was on the bridge and crossing the Willamette's waters. A hoarse cacophony of lumber mill whistles, shrill riverboat wails and exultant toots of steam locomotives parked in the nearby rail yard joined the din.

Near the train tracks, a battery of cannons began to roar, spurting fire and huge puffs of smoke as they recoiled backwards. Nimble soldiers deftly reloaded and fired them again and again in perfect unison until the air around the station turned milky white from the drifting smoke. All around the station the crowds began cheering as the president's steam locomotive rounded the final curve and began to decelerate as it pulled into the station. At its windows, passengers peered out at the scene. The crowd pressed forward, the din increased. By then, the welcoming committee was passing through the station's ornate wooden doors heading toward the platform.

Sage stepped back. He was not part of those select few designated to actually mount the train steps to greet the president. They numbered only three, Senator Mitchell, Mayor Williams and, of course, as chair of the planning committee, banker Abbott Mills.

Searching the crowd for Sergeant Hanke, Sage finally spotted the big policeman near the archway out of which the presidential carriage would advance. Sage sidled up next to the tall policeman, who acknowledged him with a nod even as his eyes continued to scan the crowd for trouble.

"We found out where they're going to try for certain," Sage said, just loud enough for his words to carry to the sergeant's ears without anyone overhearing. Hanke's eyes ceased scanning and he looked directly at Sage. "Where?" he demanded.

"Just as we figured. City Park, during the time capsule dedication. When the president's on the platform."

Hanke's attention was fully riveted on Sage, such that he was totally ignoring the din and activity boiling around the two men. "Who? What do they look like, man?"

"Well, that's still a problem at present," Sage said. "But, I think Mrs. Clemens will be there at the platform to identify one of them. The other, the one tossing the bomb, I don't know. We never found him. No one has seen him. Except maybe Meachum."

"Jesus Christ, man, ask Meachum what he looks like!" Hanke's voice was tight with checked panic. They both knew that a thrown bomb could travel far. In the crush of the crowd that was sure to be surrounding the platform, a bomber could stand anywhere.

"Can't. He's beat up bad. Unconscious . . . " Sage started to explain when interrupted by a sudden commotion at the station's side. A U.S. artillery captain gave a sharp command and eighty mounted soldiers lined up, facing each other, forty to a side. The crowd stilled and in that silence, the captain issued a second sharp command. In response, the soldiers whipped out their sabers and angled them to form an open arch. Brazen bugles blared the President's March, heard for the first time in the city's history. Slowly, the president's carriage rolled forward between the raised sabers. Sunlight struck Roosevelt's ruddy face, glinting off his wire-rimmed spectacles and catching on big white teeth beneath his bushy mustache. The president was grinning widely as he raised an arm and waved vigorously.

As the crowd roared, Hanke jumped into action, raising his own arm to signal his men to take their places. He cast a final look at Sage who mouthed, "See you up there," as he gestured in the direction of City Park. The sergeant nodded and then waded off through the crowd.

The president's open black carriage was elegant but unadorned, except for a single thin gold stripe. The papers had reported that he'd ordered that neither flowers nor bunting festoon the carriage or its horses. Riding with the president was the mayor, Governor Chamberlain and the president's secretary, William Loeb. As it passed the soldiers, they sheathed their sabers, wheeled their horses and began moving alongside the carriage in two columns. Spanish–American war veterans next took up their honored places, forming two additional columns to the inside, on either side of the carriage. They raised their battle flags in the air and their feet kept time to the small band that marched before the carriage. Sage spotted solitary, stoic-faced men standing on the streets, atop buildings and perched in overhead windows, their wary eyes watching the crowds. Hanke had been right. The parade route, with its layers of participants and protectors, made it too hard for an assassin to get close enough to throw a bomb accurately.

Leading the parade was Police Chief Hunt, striding at the head of a tight formation of city policemen. Hanke was one of their number. Behind them came the parade's grand marshal, General Beebe, who raised a staff into the air and stepped out. The procession began to move forward. Eight carriages trailed the president's, all containing dignitaries and a select few of the city's notables. Following them came a series of musical bands—including those representing the Italians, Letter Carriers Union and even a band of American-born Chinese. Uniformed aides raced back and forth along at each side, undoubtedly for the purpose of carrying the messages necessary to keep the procession orderly. For a brief moment, Sage allowed himself to experience a swelling of pride at the good show being put on by his adopted city.

Sage watched until the last band passed and then he slipped through the crowd, seeking a less crowded street away from the parade. He intended to reach the platform long before the parade did. And that would be awhile, maybe an hour-and-half to two hours. The delay was inevitable. Along the route there would be more bands waiting to perform for the president. At different locations, various organizations and their members would be waiting, all wanting to be acknowledged by the head of state. The presidential pause in the park blocks to speak with the city's children would also be slowed by the scores of people who waited there to join in the parade, including a large contingent marching as a "human flag."

Although Abbott had promised Sage a seat on that platform, the enormous turnout of notables threatened that plan. The best way to guarantee that Sage would be close enough to the president to save him, was for Sage to stake out his position on the platform well in advance.

Overhead, the sun began flirting with the plump gray clouds even as a stiffening breeze began to push more clouds in from the west. Not a good sign. Sage buttoned his top button, raised his coat collar and lengthened his stride.

THIRTY-SIX

Dispatch: *May 21, 1903, 3:30 p.m., President speechifying in Portland, Oregon.*

> *"My fellow citizens, I think I shall not refer, while in the western portion of Oregon, to the subject of irrigation. The proprieties of the situation would seem to call for remarks by the Secretary of the Navy." —T.R.*

PEDESTRIAN TRAFFIC CROWDED THE SIDEWALKS near City Park. Apparently, Sage wasn't the only person intent on arriving early to stake out a good spot from which to view the ceremony.

The long, steep street into the park split into a "T" just below the flat terrace where the platform stood. The platform was where an obelisk, dedicated to the Lewis and Clark Expedition, would eventually stand. Sage considered what he'd learned about the event from reading the newspapers. He knew that it was from this platform that Theodore Roosevelt would deliver his major speech of the day. The president would also place into a hole in the platform, a copper box containing Oregon memorabilia. Finally, he would use an ivory-handled, engraved silver trowel to smooth the cement around the stone covering the box and thus conclude the ceremony.

The city's monied elite intended for today's event and the obelisk to kick off their scheme to promote a 1905 Lewis and Clark Centennial Exposition. The purpose of that extravaganza was to attract new residents to Portland, thereby lining the pockets of those who had the financial means to exploit those new residents–the exposition's promoters. All over the country, other expositions were being launched with the same intent–additional wealth for the already wealthy. Sage wondered whether any of them would ever have enough. Probably not. Greed was one ravenous beast.

Joining the crowd hurrying up the steep Washington Street toward the platform, Sage thought about how none of them knew of the dire threat hanging over today's festivities. Yet, somewhere, in this press of people, other people were intent on putting the president's life in grave danger.

Sage's heartbeat quickened at that thought and he stepped up his pace. He had to get on that platform. Already, the street was closed to all horses and people filled the sidewalks on both sides of the street. He saw a smattering of Chinese men but not Mr. Li. He searched the crowd for the sight of his mother or McAllister or Meachum's men but there were already too many people.

When he reached the platform, a tall policeman in a shiny-button, double-breasted coat and beehive helmet blocked his access. Sage pulled out Abbot's engraved invitation. The policeman studied it before saying, "This looks fine, sir. But, they've issued way too many invitations. We don't think the platform is big enough to hold everyone invited and the president's party too."

A moment of extreme panic swept through him. It must have showed in his eyes because the policeman's face softened. "Well, seeing's how you are just one man and you came early, I'll let you on. But stay inside the ropes," he gestured to the three-rope fence strung along each side of the platform, "Don't leave, sir. If you do, they won't let you back on."

"Thank you!" Sage said and squeezed past the man who quickly stepped forward to block anyone else's access to the platform. Sage noticed that, on each side, a line of white-gloved policemen buttressed the rope barrier that encircled the structure's base.

The platform was just a simple concrete foundation. Later, they would clad it with granite slabs upon which they would install the actual obelisk. Sage quickly found a place to stand near the hole where the copper box would be placed. Sitting on blocks, next to the hole, was the platform's central granite slab that would be lowered atop it and cemented in. The city spread out below them. In the far distance, the craggy, solitary Mt. Hood stood bathed in sunlight. But, to the northwest, a cloud's dark underbelly was roiling eastward. It was high and thick enough to eventually hide the mountain.

With nothing left to do but watch and wait, Sage surveyed the scene. There was little room to move on the platform. Men and women in their best clothes occupied all available chairs while those of lesser social importance stood elbow to elbow. Across the platform stood the Republican planning committee: Fenton, Abbott, Dolph, Holman and Doctor Harvey were all there. He nodded to them but did not cross to speak. He didn't want to lose his spot because it was closer to the speaker's podium. He saw that only wives accompanied Abbott, Holman and Fenton. Dolph had his daughter in tow while a well-dressed man, who stood apart from the group, seemed to be accompanying Dr. Harvey. Clearly this was a stranger. Sage narrowed his eyes at the thought. A stranger? But Harvey couldn't be the one. He had no connection to any of the Trusts.

Before he could ponder the meaning of that discovery, a blast of trumpets began a lively marching tune just as the presidential procession turned the corner at the bottom of Washington Street and advanced up the block. Sage turned, as did everyone, all eyes seeking the first glimpse of the president's carriage. As he did, a stiff breeze swept across the platform causing all to clutch their hats.

Sage turned to look toward the west, into the breeze. The cloud had solidified into a wall of dense blue gray, rain a dark curtain slanting downward from its leading edge. He glanced at his watch. It was already ten minutes after three. He wondered whether the rain would be upon them even before the president arrived.

Jostling against his side interrupted these thoughts. A flood of dignitaries from the parade swept onto the platform, further crowding those already present. The newcomers were likely the governors from the neighboring states with their entourages. Sage fought to maintain his position against the press of bodies. A familiar voice sounded at his back. "Now, sirs, please do not crowd. Let's move over this way," Hanke spoke with the perfect mix of respect and command and Sage felt the pressure against his back easing. He turned and caught the sergeant's eye. Hanke raised a questioning eyebrow but Sage could only shake his head. No, he had not spotted any of the assassins. Hanke's brow furrowed and without another word he moved toward the front edge of the platform to gaze across a crowd that was packed tight as canned salmon.

Sage tried again to view the area around the Republican planning committee but the platform crowd had grown too great. He did spot a bobbing tall hat that he thought belonged to Dolph but he could see nothing of the rest of them. Probably because they were occupying the few chairs allowed on the platform. Once again, events overtook his search as the band and then the president's carriage came to a halt. A fanfare of trumpets accompanied Roosevelt's mounting of the platform. People surged forward, eager to get closer to the president.

"Will it happen now?" Sage wondered but dismissed that idea. No, it was too crowded. The press of bodies were shielding the president and none of them looked remotely like an unemployed, disgruntled printer. These were Portland's elites, the rare few privileged to be close enough to clearly see and hear the president.

Below the level of the platform, many faces stared upward. With a start, Sage recognized that of his mother. She wore somber black, dress, boots, hat and coat. Her face was pale and strained. On either side of her, stood E. J. McAllister and his friend Robert Clooney, with Eich at her back. He stared at Mae, willing her to notice him. She did. A quick smile spread across her face and he grinned in return. She truly was safe.

With one hand, Sage gestured toward the platform and raised both eyebrows. She shook her head. So, the man she knew to be involved in the assassination was not visible from where she stood. She said something to McAllister, who swiftly extended his arm to give her support as she clambered atop a small flower planter in the northeast corner. Sage winced at the sight of her boot crushing red pansy plants. Still, her new vantage point could only help. Holding on to McAllister's shoulder she raised up onto her toes and scanned the platform. Finished with her search, she again shook her head at Sage before lowering herself back down onto her heels. She kept her perch in the planter, however, one hand resting on McAllister's shoulder. Sage saw Robert Clooney push up to her other side and then hold his ground like a determined guard dog. Those men weren't going to let any harm come to Mae Clemens.

Meantime, Roosevelt was shaking hands with the architect of the monument, the Oregon governor and a few other notables, all of whom were rosy with pleasure. They showed a copper box to Roosevelt. He nodded and gestured toward the wooden podium standing at the platform's center. Then he shook his head, gesturing toward the front of the platform. As if on cue, the clouds overhead let loose a deluge. From the crowded platform and the crowd below, there came gasps of dismay and the hurried unfurling of countless black umbrellas. Cries accompanied this uniform movement as the newly opened umbrellas smacked and poked.

True to his reputation, Roosevelt appeared neither dismayed nor discomforted. Apparently remaining intent on rejecting the planned podium, he pointed emphatically toward the front of the platform. It was obvious that he had realized that none in the immense crowd below the structure would stand a chance of hearing his words unless he moved closer to them. And, that s what he did. A phalanx of secret service men scurried along beside him as he strode right to within a few feet of the platform's front.

The rain strengthened, hitting the umbrellas and pouring onto the ground that swiftly became a mire. A voice called for an umbrella but, when one appeared, the president waved it away. At last, a solider's rubber poncho appeared. This seemed to be acceptable because Roosevelt good-naturedly allowed two secret service men to drop it over his head and settle it around his shoulders. The crowd laughed along with Roosevelt when the men's efforts knocked his wire-frame glasses from his nose.

Sage tensed. This was it. Out of deference to the speaker, the platform crowd moved back. For the first time since mounting the platform, the president stood alone, isolated. Sage was vaguely aware that the president's opening remarks had elicited roars of laughter and cheers but had no idea what the man had said.

It was the perfect time for the assassin to attack. A frantic scanning of the crowd behind the president at last yielded the sight of the planning committee members. And there was the doctor. And there, to his side and slightly behind, stood the stranger. Sage studied the stranger's face. Its expression differed from those of the surrounding people. The man's eyes were narrowed, his lips compressed. He looked tense, like he was unhappy about being there or seriously irritated at the rain. And he wasn't looking at the president, who cleared his throat and began speaking in his high, cultured voice. Instead, the stranger was eyeing the crowd standing around the base of the platform. Suddenly, he raised an arm, grabbed his hat and shook it as if to rid its brim of rain. Was that some sort of signal?

That gesture sent Sage's attention spinning back toward the crowd below. "Damn, damn, damn," he cursed under his breath. The open umbrellas made it almost impossible to see faces or even movement. But then he caught sight of a man rising onto another's shoulders near the southeast corner of the platform. Unlike most of those present, the lifted man wore a workingman's grubby clothes, battered hat and sported white bandages over most of his face. The man was looking at Sage and waving. With a start, Sage realized the waving man was Meachum. Simultaneously, there was another disturbance behind Meachum. It appeared a fight had erupted. The fracas ended almost immediately. At the far edge of the crowd, a cluster of men broke free. Sage squinted. Four white men were being forcefully marched away by a group of much smaller Chinese men. Sage smiled. The cousins had found and ejected the men who were supposed to create a distracting disturbance.

That left the two assassins, one an ignorant dupe, the other coldly determined.

He looked toward his mother. She still stood in the planter even though that vessel had filled and water was lapping at her boots. A drenched black feather drooped down from her hat brim and stuck to her cheek. She rose again onto her toes, her neck stretched out, her eyes straining to see those on the platform. Meachum too was searching from his perch atop his friend's shoulders. The injured man's attention, however, was focused on the people standing directly below the president. Damn those umbrellas. Hanke's postured stiffened as he spotted Mae. The sergeant looked toward Sage, who felt his breath stop. Something was about to happen but he didn't know what, where or who. Sage pointed two fingers toward his own eyes, and then pointed toward Meachum, mouthing, "Watch him!" Hanke understood, because he turned his full attention on the bandaged man. That left Sage free to divide his attention between Mae and those on the platform.

Ignorant of his danger, the president continued speaking. He ignored the rain now steadily dripping off his hat, sliding down the rubber poncho and pooling at his feet. Roosevelt's grand gestures and exhortations inspired cheers from those close enough to hear his words. Those cheers were picked up by those who could not hear the words, the sound moving in a rolling wave down the street. The wind strengthened, blowing sheets of rain sideways. To the east, Mt. Hood had completely disappeared behind billowing pewter-gray clouds.

THIRTY-SEVEN

Dispatch: *May 21, 1903, 3:45 p.m., President in City Park, Portland, Oregon*

> "Our fight is a fundamental fight against both of the old corrupt party machines, for both are under the dominion of the plunder league of the professional politicians who are controlled and sustained by the great beneficiaries of privilege and reaction." —T.R.

SAGE'S BODY TENSED and his blood began racing, filling his ears with a rushing sound. The umbrellas below the platform undulated forward and back as people pushed through and broke free of the crowd to shove against the police lines. The rope barrier sagged and then seemed to give way as people clambered onto the platform's edge. Soldiers rushed forward and shoved them off the platform. The line of policemen re-formed and held.

Moving closer to the president, Sage's gaze swept in an arc between those standing at the base of the platform and the stranger who stood next to Dr. Harvey behind the president. That man's narrowed eyes were scanning the crowd in front of the platform.

Looking to where he'd last seen Meachum, Sage saw that his friend was no longer in sight. There was only a smattering of small boys perched atop shoulders so they could see but no Meachum. The patter of heavy raindrops hitting umbrellas was now nearly loud enough to drown out Roosevelt's words. Despite this, he continued without pause, his speech precisely enunciated in the manner of an educated, eastern elite, his right hand jabbing the air to emphasize points, his big body twisting left and right to capture his listeners' attention.

Directly below the platform, Mae still stood in the same flower box but now she was rigid, tense as a bird dog eying its target. Sage followed her look and, sure enough, her gaze was fixed on the man who stood beside Dr. Harvey. Sage began edging around behind the president, amid angry hisses and elbows in his ribs as he blocked first one person's view and then another's.

There was a disturbance in the far right-hand corner of the platform. The bandaged head of Meachum appeared and he clambered onto the structure. As the soldiers moved to shove him off, Hanke stepped forward and interceded. Meachum remained in place. He and Hanke exchanged whispers before, as one, they both turned to search the crowd bunched before the platform.

He had to get closer to the stranger standing next to Dr. Harvey. Sage took a step only to freeze as a sequence of events began unfolding before him. He saw Meachum move forward and point downward. At that same instant, the stranger on the platform began coughing violently and a man lunged out of the crowd to the platform's edge. The president's shouted words, the rain patter on umbrellas and the cheering crowd meant the actions of Meachum, the coughing stranger and the lunging man went unnoticed by everyone else–a riveting three-point pantomime Sage could only watch in horror.

Movement ahead of Sage snapped his attention back in the direction of Dr. Harvey's companion. Sure enough, the coughing fellow was sidling backward while keeping all his attention fixed on the man who now stood at Roosevelt's feet.

Where was Hanke? Didn't the sergeant know the president was in peril? And then, Sage saw him. Hanke had slipped off the platform into the crowd. He'd shed his helmet and was pushing in the direction Meachum had pointed. Small cries of irritation wafted up from beneath the umbrellas as the big policeman shouldered his way through.

The man at the president's feet stared upward at his target with wide eyes. His lunge forward had knocked the hat from his head and rain was plastering dark hair onto his scalp. For a moment, the president paused and glanced downward, as if on some level of awareness, he sensed danger. "Instinctual, just like one of those animals he likes to hunt," a part of Sage's mind commented. But then, Roosevelt seemed to shake off his internal warning because he resumed speaking, his voice loud and firm.

Horrified, Sage watched the assassin began to raise his right arm, a brown, paper-wrapped, parcel clutched in his hand. The bomb. It had to be the bomb! Sage saw Meachum start forward along the platform's edge, moving toward a point forward of the president.

Sage also began moving, his goal Roosevelt himself. He had to catch the bomb. Abruptly, his movement was checked as a secret service man whirled to face him. Roughly shoving him back, the man gripped Sage's upper arm and held on. The strength of the hold meant that Sage was going nowhere without a fight. Even as his mind raced through Fong's instructions on how to break such a hold, Sage realized that it was too late. He couldn't reach the president in time to shove him outside the bomb's arc or deflect the bomb. In fact, all his leap toward Roosevelt had accomplished was to distract one of the president's protectors.

A silent flurry of activity erupted at the front corner of the platform. Over the shoulder of the man who held him, Sage watched two other secret service agents spring into action but in the wrong direction. Just when Meachum was only five feet away from being between the bomber and the president, two agents seized his arms and lifted him off his feet. They quickly walked him backward to the platform's side where they unceremoniously shoved him off the platform into the arms of waiting policemen who quickly carried a protesting Meachum away. Damn it!

Sage watched in horror as the man at Roosevelt's feet began to raise his arm higher, making ready to throw the package he gripped in his hand. That hand, with its deadly object, reached shoulder height. Panic seized Sage, he fought for release. That bomb was about to fly!

Absurdly, Roosevelt himself had raised the emotional pitch of his speech to such a high level that its intensity seemed to echo the fear gripping Sage. Sage opened his mouth to scream a warning. But, even as he did so, he saw a white-gloved hand reach around the assassin and grab the man's forearm, jerking it backward. Hanke's face appeared, floating behind the assassin's shoulder, his big face grimacing with effort as the two of them struggled over which of them would possess the bomb.

Chaos erupted below Roosevelt as police officers abandoned their duty at the rope and rushed to help subdue the assassin. Hanke's hand reappeared, gripping the brown, paper-wrapped parcel. He watched the big policeman carefully pass the bomb to a colleague, lean over to issue some instructions and then begin to push his way toward the platform.

During this minor melee, Roosevelt had continued speaking. From the angle of his head, it was clear that the tussle at his feet had not escaped the president's notice. Apparently, the expressions on Sage's face, as he watched these events take place, caused the man holding Sage to release his grip and turn back toward the president. Sage immediately moved in the direction of Dr. Harvey. He noticed the stranger had stopped coughing and stepped forward. Now he stood close to Harvey's right side. One side of the stranger's mouth twisted in a slight, rueful smile. For the first time, the man's attention was focused on Roosevelt. Then his eyes flicked toward Sage. Like a snake the man's right hand whipped under his coat and emerged with a small gun. Without taking his eyes from Sage's, he shoved the gun beneath his left arm, aiming its barrel at the doctor's ribs.

"What is happening?" Sage's mind shouted. In answer, the man's eyes narrowed as a sharp report sounded. Harvey cried out and began to fall. Shrieks and shouts erupted even as Harvey's body fell. The stranger didn't hesitate. His attention switched to the president, who stopped speaking. The gun began to raise. Sage glanced over his shoulder, saw Roosevelt start to turn his body toward the commotion at the rear of the platform. Sage's mind was shouting, "The bullet, stop the bullet!" Sage jumped forward, his arms outstretched. A word roared out of his mouth, "Noooo . . ." even as a corner of his mind coldly calculated the distance and gave him a less than even chance of intercepting the bullet.

The man's gun hand swung forward in one smooth move. Just as it aimed at Roosevelt, a loud report sounded, cutting through the pattering rain and crowd noise. In the sudden hush, Sage's airborne launch sent him slamming down onto his side. As he fell, his eyes locked on those of the stranger. Next he saw that the man was falling too and, that those pale eyes were widening with shock. Then a forest of legs quickly surrounded the man, cutting the link between them.

A frantic hand grabbed at Sage's shoulder. His mother's voice, almost a keen, was saying his name over and over. Sage breathed deeply, realizing that, other than where his hip had collided with the concrete, he felt no pain. "I'm fine, Ma, really I'm fine," he told her.

He heard her shaky intake of breath before she said, somewhat sharply, "Well then, haul yourself up. The president is still on the platform. You're making a spectacle of yourself."

Hauling himself onto his feet as ordered, Sage was vaguely aware that Roosevelt was again speaking, this time calming the crowd, assuring them all was well. Of course, all was not well. Dr. Harvey's sightless eyes stared up into the rain. Nothing would be well for him ever again. Before Sage could dwell on that maudlin thought, his mother's voice snagged his attention. He looked toward her. Her hat was askew, she had a bloody scratch along one cheek and she was missing a few buttons from her sensible black coat. She had obviously fought her way to her son's side. She wasn't looking at him, though. Instead, her gaze was also fixed on the dead doctor. "Hmpf, well, good riddance to that wicked creature," she said as she straightened her hat, flicking its feather off her cheek.

THIRTY-EIGHT

Dispatch: *May 21, 1903, Evening, President Roosevelt remains in Portland, Oregon.*

> *"It is essential that there should be organizations of labor. This is an era of organization. Capital organizes and therefore labor must organize. My appeal for organized labor is two-fold; to the outsider and the capitalist I make my appeal to treat the laborer fairly, to recognize the fact that he must organize that, there must be such organization, that the laboring man must organize for his own protection, and that it is the duty of the rest of us to help him and not hinder him in organizing."* —T.R.

SUDDENLY SERGEANT HANKE APPEARED before Sage. "Mr. Adair, please come with me, quick like," he said, his voice urgent as he pulled at Sage's sleeve.

"Why?" Sage asked. He didn't want to leave. He wanted to make sure Roosevelt was really safe.

"The man that got shot. He's on his way to the hospital but he says he wants to talk to you. One of the doctors in the crowd said the shot's fatal. There's not much time."

Sage exchanged a glance with Mae Clemens. Her face mirrored his own mystification at the request. Why would the stranger want to talk to him? Curiosity propelled him forward and he meekly followed in Hanke's wake as the policeman's large form cleared them a path off the platform. A two-seater phaeton awaited them, the horse sidestepping in its traces, no doubt made nervous by the press of the crowd and the heightened excitement.

Hanke untied the horse and over the objections of the buggy owner, they climbed between the large wooden wheels to sit on its tufted seat. Hanke snatched up the reins and clucked the horse into action. The crowd stepped aside to allow them passage. The buggy rolled up the through the park to intersect with a back road that descended into the Burnside canyon. The wind snatched the ceaseless rain and flung it sideways so that the buggy's leather top provided no shelter.

"Did you shoot that man?" Sage asked once they were clear of the crowd.

"Nope, it was the secret service man that had a hold of you for a while. You made such a scene that he turned in time to see that man shoot Doc Harvey."

"You and Meachum saved the president. You grabbed the bomb-thrower just in time," Sage said, casting a glance at the policeman.

Hanke said nothing and his profile looked stern. Finally, he said, "If it hadn't been for Meachum and what you all were doing, they would have succeeded. Even if we'd spotted the bomb thrower, we would have missed the man on the platform. I can't take much credit. We had all that extra help and every one of those galoots slipped right past us." Hanke's voice was glum.

Sage said nothing. The sergeant was right. Despite the secret service, the Dickenson agents, extra detectives from all over the West and intense effort by the city's police, two assassins and their cohorts had managed to sneak into Portland and get within killing range of the president. Still.

"You will never know how many assassins you discouraged with your efforts. And, besides, you had the good sense to believe me. You had the good sense to make sure Meachum stayed on the platform. You got there before he threw the bomb. You singlehandedly overpowered the assassin. Give yourself some credit," Sage said.

The big policeman sighed, "I guess," he said, but his mood didn't lift.

Milling police, reporters and others crowded the hospital lobby, everyone there caught up in the excitement of the attempted assassination. Hanke plowed through them all, Sage in his wake, until they stepped through swinging doors into the hallway. A white-jacketed doctor stood alone beside an open door. "This the man?" he asked Hanke. At Hanke's nod, the doctor gestured toward the door, "Make it quick, he doesn't have much longer."

They stepped into the room. A uniformed policeman sat in a chair by the bed. Charles Hunt, the police chief, stood with his back against the wall. Both men's eyes were on the man in the narrow bed.

Sage looked at him too. His face was almost as white as the bandage that encircled his mid-section. The man's eyes were closed and for a second, Sage thought they'd arrived too late. But then, the injured man's eyelids raised and he looked directly at Sage. "Get them out of here and I'll tell you what you want to know," he said. The effort of speaking made his voice a near whisper.

"Now you listen here," the chief started to protest but the man's voice, now stronger, cut into the protest, "You leave or I die and you don't learn a damn thing. Your choice."

The chief hesitated then jerked his head toward the policeman and Hanke, gesturing them to exit the room.

Sage grabbed Hanke's arm, stopping his departure. "The sergeant stays to take notes or I leave," he told the man in the bed.

His statement elicited a weak chuckle. "I guess the sergeant has earned that honor. You're the one who grabbed the bomb, aren't you?" At Hanke's nod, the man said, "Okay, he can stay. But nobody else. And shut the door."

They waited while both the chief and patrolman left the room, closing the door softly behind themselves as they exited. Hanke pulled a pad of paper from his breast pocket along with a stubby pencil. He licked the pencil and waited in silence.

The man looked at Sage. "You're the one who engineered my failure," he said as a statement rather than a question. When Sage nodded, he said. "I didn't expect it. Once we found out that St. Alban knew, we figured on having some trouble with Meachum. But Chinks, a ragpicker, a boy, a cook's helper and you–some fancy gentleman with access to the platform? Who could have anticipated that?"

"You shot the Chinese boy and Mr. Fong?" Sage asked.

The man grimaced, "I did. I had to. My men told me about the Chinese so I watched. Killed the boy just to see what would happen. Looked to me like your Mr. Fong was the leader. Had to take him off the board, so to speak."

"You killed a boy just to identify Fong?" Sage didn't bother suppress the disgust he felt toward the man in the bed.

The other man smirked and Sage wanted to drive a fist into that face but he held back. There was more at stake then the opportunity to vent his own emotions.

"We all die at one point or another. The boy, Fong, me and you too, eventually."

It wasn't possible to resist taking a stab at the man's overbearing ego, "You failed. You're the one who lost, despite taking Fong 'off the board'. But that is only temporarily, I might add."

Sage's retort elicited only a mild smile. The man shifted in the bed and a gasp escaped his pale lips. "Oh yes, I guess you could say I lost in at least one way."

"What do you mean? Roosevelt wasn't touched. The unions won't be blamed. Black Hawk failed, pure and simple."

The man's face slackened, as if Sage's knowledge had taken him unawares. Good, Sage thought. At least that smug look is gone. He didn't expect us to know their code name for the assassination.

But Sage was wrong, because the man's voice was only questioning, "Black Hawk?" he repeated.

"Yes, the code name for your plot," Sage answered.

Once again, the man chuckled until pain cut it off and the man raised a feeble hand to press against the white bandage wrapped around his midsection. By now, his face had drained of all color and his eyes had sunk into his face alongside a nose turned bonier. The blue-veined eyelids descended over those pale, staring eyes. Was this assassinating mastermind going to die before they learned who was behind the plot?

Sage leaned forward, "Tell me who were you working for," he insisted, putting his hand on the man's shoulder and giving it a shake.

The eyelids flew up and the man stared at him. "Not 'Black Hawk,' you fool. 'Black Drop'."

Stepping back, Sage's mind flailed. What the hell was a 'black drop'?" Then it hit him. "Opium," he breathed out, almost to himself. "The pharmaceutical companies. But, in God's name, why?"

"Hmpf, you think only about the labor movement. But Roosevelt plans to outlaw the opium trade in the Philippines, all of Asia and here at home too. He's planning to appoint a commission. It's only a matter of time."

"Why are you telling me this? I'd think you'd protect your masters."

"They aren't my 'masters.' I am my own man. I am a specialist for hire. Besides, I can't stand that pompous little Austrian bastard."

Sage glanced toward Hanke, who nodded. He was recording every word. "Give me the name of the Austrian," he ordered the dying man.

For the first time, Sage encountered resistance. The man weakly shook his head from side to side on the pillow as he said, "Well now, that's for me to know and for you to still find out. Wouldn't be professional to tell you that." He clamped his lips shut and turned his face away. He was clearly finished talking.

Sage again looked at Hanke, who shrugged and began stowing his writing pad and pencil in a coat pocket. Sage turned toward the door. Then a thought stopped him. He turned and stepped closer to the bed. "What did you mean when you said I 'lost in at least one way?' Do you think you won somehow?"

The head turned on the pillow and the man was looking at him, his pale eyes shining with a manic gleam. "My name is Rudolph F. Flammang. Unlike your name, mine will live forever in the history books. The assassination attempt may have failed but my name will go on for as long as men read history. Your name, on the other hand, will be lost to memory. Probably within a few years of your death. No memory of you will remain behind except for your moldering bones and a few words carved into granite. And both of those will also disappear over time." Contempt laced those last few words. Once again, the killer shut his mouth and turned his face away but not before Sage glimpsed the smirk curving those dead white lips.

THIRTY-NINE

Dispatch: *May 22, 1903, President's train leaves Portland, heading for Seattle and from there, turning home toward Washington, D.C.*

> "*A man must, in the last analysis, be the architect of his own fate. We need high ideals, and we need the power to fashion them practically.*" —T.R.

HERMAN EICH INSISTED that their mission end where it had begun. So, Sage stood outside the ragpicker's lean-to, thinking how crowded it was going to be inside its small confines. He'd taken his time getting there, his steps dragging, matching his mood. He should be happy. After all, they'd been successful. Seven days after the ruckus on the dedication platform, Roosevelt was alive. Today, his train was chugging across the expanse of the Midwest, heading toward Washington D.C. and the end of its 14,000-mile journey. And, the BCS boys were safe. Yet, it seemed like he remained trapped in that hospital room, his mind's eye ensnared by that sardonic smile on the assassin's lips.

Sage sucked in a breath and let it whoosh out. Darn it, he should be feeling joy: at their success, at the soft spring day with its celebratory blossoms, at the gentle blue sky, at the heavenly light, sweet air.

He stepped to the edge of the ravine to look down at the creek through the bright green growth that now blurred winter's naked branches. Another month or so and the neighborhood children would be down there, splashing in the trickling creek, its raging winter flow only a distant memory.

A sound made him turn. Mae Clemens stood in the open door of the lean-to, a slight crease between her bold brows. Their identical dark blue eyes met and he saw a question in hers. "I'm coming," he told her and moved away from the ravine's edge. As he walked to the door, he noticed a small evergreen someone had planted in a tin bucket. He leaned closer, curious to see what kind of tree Eich had decided to display beside his entrance-a redwood maybe. Next, he spotted a large mason jar holding white chrysanthemums. They had to be specially-grown hothouse flowers because it was too early in the season for them to bloom.

Crossing the threshold he saw that they were all there. In deference to his size, Hanke sat on the tall workbench stool. Eich, Mae and McAllister perched like a row of alert birds on the edge of the cot. Fong and Matthew straddled chunks of unsplit firewood. Meachum, his head still bandaged, occupied a scarred, ladder-back chair, one softened by one of Eich's bed blankets. Sage took the only unclaimed wood chunk. As he did so, Eich stood and walked to the potbellied stove where the small flames flickering behind its mica window took the damp chill out of the room. With solemnity, the ragpicker carefully poured tea from a tin pot into a variety of cups, no doubt some of his dustbin "treasures," and passed them around.

Sage looked at Fong. The Chinese man's face was still pale, a dark scab marked the wound in the shaven patch above his ear. He wore a pale blue ribbon wound around one arm. A sign of mourning, Sage thought and his sadness deepened. He raised his gaze and exchanged a wordless look with his friend. Fong's eyes seemed subdued by grief and acceptance. They'd not been entirely successful. A young man, barely started in life, had crossed the ocean full of optimistic dreams only to die. Poor Fong, he'd lost his only blood relative living in America. And, his sister had lost her son. What a hard letter that must have been for Fong to write.

That thought seemed invasive so Sage, instead, surveyed the shed. When first he'd seen it, cracks in the walls were channels for the cold wind and its roof provided no more protection than a sieve when it rained. Not any more. Another young man, Daniel, had turned his skilled hands to making it tight and dry. He'd done so to repay Eich's kindness. He'd done it secretly, as his final act. Daniel had died too.

Hanke's voice broke through Sage's maudlin thoughts and he was glad to let loose of them. "Flammang died of his wounds. He never told anyone the names of the men responsible for hatching the plot. But his talking about the pharmaceutical companies and an Austrian, left enough of a trail for the secret service to follow. The fellow they tracked escaped just ahead of them on a liner back to Europe. They're working with European police to intercept him. He won't be coming back."

"Hmpf, I bet we could of caught the rascal," Mae said.

Hanke's chuckle was wry, "I don't doubt that, Mrs. Clemens. I think all of you can do anything you set your mind to."

"It's 'we', Sergeant Hanke. And that 'we 'includes you," Sage said, a genuine smile on his face for the first time that day.

"I did what you asked, Mr. Adair. Once again, I kept my trap shut about everything you and the others did to save the president. But, I have to tell you, I don't like it one little bit," Hanke said, the sincerity of his unhappiness evident from the shame in his face.

Speaking for the first time Fong spoke softly, "Sergeant, you understand. If you tell, then everyone will know and we can no longer do our work. And we need you. Without you, we have no way to make sure that problems we discover come to light. You take risk every time you help us."

The big policeman blinked rapidly and quickly raised his cup to his lips, its tilting rim concealing his eyes.

Eich cleared his throat and changed the subject, "Personally I feel a tremendous gratitude to E. J. here and his friends. Without them, the three of us and those five boys would not be alive to-day." Mae and Matthew murmured in agreement.

Eich turned to Meachum and Sage. "Those miscreants poured gasoline over the upstairs floor and if McAllister and his friends hadn't burst through the stairway door when they did, they would have burnt all of us, those poor boys too, to a crisp."

McAllister spoke eagerly, "It's Robert who was the brave one. He stayed inside the BCS all that night, creeping around, trying to locate where they had the three of you imprisoned. Two times, they nearly caught him." His pride in his friend was evident.

"Where is that wonderful man, anyways?" Mae asked. "I want to thank him again."

McAllister said, without any sorrow. "Gone back to Boston." Before Sage could wonder at the man's lack of concern over his friend's departure, the lawyer grinned and continued, "He's actually decided to close up his business back there. He says I'll need some help if I am going to be the best damn crusading lawyer in the West." As if anticipating an unspoken question, he was quick to add, "Angelique has found him a place to live close to our house. Says I've made her and her children happy and that she likes him and she is glad to see that I now have a chance at happiness. She's a wonderful person. But then, I've always known that."

Sage smiled, but even as he did so, a sobering thought hit him accompanied by the memory of an old man sitting on a park bench, his voice bitter as he chided Sage, "Terrible situation all right. So let's see whether you just walk off from it. Wonder how long it will take you to forget how bad you feel right now." The sight of those pale boys sitting on those steps leading to that damnable red door. That had really been the beginning.

"What about that house on the other side of the ravine? The one where those poor boys work?" Sage asked.

McAllister laughed. "The victory at the house in the Northwest emboldened the ladies of the White Ribbon persuasion. Somehow, word of that house in Lair Hill reached their ears," he paused to wink at them before continuing, "Even greater numbers of them turned out to parade and picket. As you know, that is an activity in which they surpass all others. Lynch moved himself out, turned the boys back into the BCS. No doubt he's expecting it to be a temporary hiatus." McAllister smiled. "Unfortunately for Lynch, that will be hard since his house burnt down the night before Robert left for Boston." McAllister looked anything but sad. "And, as an extra incentive, a certain lawyer," here he brushed his fingernails across his lapel, "filed a lawsuit on behalf of the boys for false imprisonment. A certain banker friend of mine," here he cocked an eyebrow to let them know what kind of friend, "made sure that Lynch's funds became unavailable. Last I heard, he was on a train heading south." He seemed to sense their next question, "Don't worry, I made sure that the particulars of our Mr. Lynch traveled ahead of him. Telegraphs are a fine thing, don't you think?"

Matthew asked a question, his shaking voice letting them know that his was a burning question. "What will happen to those boys? The ones in the house, you know. And the ones they kept for so long on the top floor of the BCS?"

The tone McAllister used was calculated to reassure the boy. "Seeing as how the Cap'n is dead, there isn't any danger to them from his direction. And those two clowns of the Cap'n's are going to prison for attempted arson. There's a new man in charge at the BCS. Folks will watch him closely. Besides, my temperance ladies intend to make sure those boys get the best of care. Once weaned off the opium, they will have the chance to go to school or learn a trade. They've also obtained a guarantee from the BCS board of directors that women will have access to the entire building. Still, it won't be easy. Every one of those boys is addicted to the black drops. That opium is a vicious mistress. So, it will take time for them to get their feet back under them."

"I can see how somebody would like to drink that stuff," Matthew mused, the dreamy quality in his words riveting their attention on him. He raised both hands to stop any admonition, "Don't you worry," he assured them, blushing so red that it overwhelmed his freckles. "One little go around with those black drops was enough for me. If I ever want to see things that ain't there and have the whole world turn swoopy, I'll dive head first off'n a roof."

The room rang with laughter that mixed relief at his earnest declaration and amusement over the comical expression on his face.

It was Mae's turn to contribute. "You'll all be happy to know that Mrs. Wiggit has a place at the BCS for the rest of her life. I went to the chairman of the board and explained how she'd saved our lives, at risk of her own and Andy's. I made him promise." She said the last four words with that determined upward tilt of her chin Sage knew so well.

"And, what exactly did you threaten him with?" Sage asked teasingly.

She didn't look the least embarrassed as she said, "I told him I was friends with the publisher of the *Daily Journal* and, if he didn't want to see the whole story of the Cap'n's doings at the BCS in that newspaper, he'd better sign a paper giving Mrs. Wiggit a job for life or for as long as she wants to stay there. Plus, a raise to make up for all her suffering since the Cap'n was put in charge." She smiled as she looked around the room and said, "E. J. here, helped me write out the promises. He says it is 'air tight'." Satisfaction surrounded her like a warm cloak as she sat back, arms crossed and chin raised. Eich patted her shoulder and, when she turned to look at him, her smile flashed extra bright.

"Hmm, I wonder what happened in that room when those two thought they were about to die?" Sage thought.

Meachum shifted on his chair, grimacing at the movement. It would be awhile before he'd ride the boxcars again as a hobo. In fact, he'd be riding the cushions back to Denver where his understanding wife would surely nurse him back to full health. "I feel kind of bad for the unemployed printer. He had no idea that was a real bomb he was fixing to throw."

Hanke turned toward the union man. "Mr. Meachum, what you told the prosecutor was real helpful to Obediah Perkins's situation," he said. "I don't think he'll be doing very much jail time. It would be different if you hadn't heard them talking to

him and telling him lies about it being a smoke bomb. I heard
Roosevelt isn't even mad at him. We're hoping his testimony will
help us convict the real culprits–if we ever catch them."

For a moment, silence fell on the eight people crammed
into that little lean-to. Sage looked at the faces of his companions, each one different, each one having reached this moment
together after traveling a different path. And yet, they were all
here. For a moment a powerful, thankful awe overwhelmed
him.

The ragpicker and Chinese man exchanged a glance and
Fong nodded. Eich stood and said to all of them, "Sometimes,
people need a ritual to recognize how their life has changed or
made a difference. You probably wondered why I asked that we
meet here, rather than at Mozart's where we would have drunk
our tea in much greater comfort. The reason is that Fong and
I have devised a little ritual. We're hoping that each of you will
honor us with your participation."

Fong stood. As Meachum struggled to his feet, Matthew
leapt to his side to help. Again, Sage felt grateful that they'd come
to know such a fine young man. It would be one of life's great
pleasures to watch Matthew grow into manhood. "That is, if he
doesn't get killed getting there," came the cautionary thought.

When Eich opened the door, they filed out into the yard.
Eich picked up the pail holding the twig tree. Fong grabbed up a
shovel and the mason jar holding the flowers. With a small bow,
he offered the jar to Mae to carry. She looked pleased and carefully took it into her work-worn hands. Eich then led the way
along the path that ran beside the ravine, heading toward the
bridge. Eich and Fong were in front. Mae and McAllister behind,
followed by Hanke and then, Meachum and Matthew, the latter keeping a strong grip on the injured man's arm. Sage walked
alone, the last in the parade.

Sage hesitated momentarily when they reached the bridge,
remembering how it had swayed and dipped the last time they'd
braved its buckled and broken timbers. But, today, it seemed
sturdy. And, indeed, it was. As a carriage rattled across its wooden

planks toward them, its passage causing only a slight vibration in the structure.

He looked toward the other end and suddenly realized the intended site of Eich and Fong's ritual. The remains of the house where Daniel's wife and baby son had died were gone. Only a square of charred earth remained, springtime grasses beginning to blur the blackness on the ground.

They reached the place where Daniel's shrieks of despair had soared heavenward as his home turned into a blazing inferno, one impossible to enter. Sage had not seen the fire but Eich had vividly described the horror of that night.

They stepped off the bridge and stood before the vacant lot. Just steps from the road, someone had dug a foot-deep hole in the ground and ringed it with the smooth spheres of river rock. To one side was a small mound of soil. Far beyond, to the east, the snowy pristine peak of Mt. Hood rose into a pale blue sky, the fading sunlight washing gold up its flanks.

Eich set the pail down and straightened. He turned to them. "I spoke to the property owner and he agreed that we could plant and tend this small tree in honor of those people who died because of this place. And, Fong and I, we wanted a place to honor Chou Ji, a good person who also died too young, never to fulfil the promise of his life." He gestured toward the twig in the pail. "You are looking at a redwood tree in the making. It is the most majestic of trees and a fitting symbol for the enduring beauty of the human spirit. In one hundred years, deeply grooved bark will clad its soaring trunk and many small creatures will call it home."

They gathered around, silent as Eich carefully took the tree from its pail and placed it in the hole. Once it stood straight, he used the shovel to drop dirt into the hole, then kneeled and used his hands to spread and pat the dirt around the tree. Standing again, he motioned that they should do the same. Each, in turn, shoveled, knelt and used their hands to scoop dirt around and over its tiny roots. Each patted the earth firm before standing.

Fong stepped forward, a slight breeze catching the pale blue ribbon around his arm, lifting its ends into the air. He carefully withdrew the chrysanthemums from the mason jar and gravely, handed each of them a flower, keeping the last one for himself. Turning toward the tree, he knelt and poured the water from the mason jar around the tree. As he did so, he intoned words that none of them understood but all of them felt. Standing again, he looked down at the tree before gently tossing his flower at its base. After a moment's hesitation they all followed suit, each one in turn, with Matthew the last.

Eich's spoke softly saying, "As a boy, I grew up in a house surrounded by ancient English chestnut trees. Those trees were my playground, my shelter from the rain. Their roots knew my tears of sorrow and joy. Those who planted them were gone long before my birth. They probably never saw those trees in full growth. I will never see this tree in full growth. It does not matter. Actions shape one's life. And, it is really only a man's or woman's deeds that live on. Good or bad, the deeds are their only lasting legacies to the future. The planters of those trees around my boyhood home could not foresee how the twigs they planted would comfort and teach a lonely Jewish boy. They only knew that planting those trees was a deed that would continue to live on beyond their time."

The ragpicker paused and looked at each of them carefully. "We, each of us and all of us together did the best we could. Roosevelt lives and will continue to exercise his presidential powers–however he chooses. Because of our efforts, those BCS boys, as well as future boys, will have a different life, hopefully free of degradation and offering them some degree of choice. We don't know if, in the end, the eventual outcome of our deeds will be good or bad. What we do know is that we did what we believed to be the best thing to do and that our actions came from the heart of human compassion."

Those words first landed like a blow to Sage's stomach. But, that sensation passed quickly. Replacing it was a growing flicker of joy. He was a part of something good and right. It was a feeling that he'd lost when Flammang had spoken his final words and smiled that sneering smile. "Flammang was wrong," a voice within Sage seemed to sing. A name is nothing more than letters on paper—a flat thing. It does not contain the essence of the human being. Like a whisper in the wind, old man Compton's challenge echoed in his mind. Did that wizened old man know Sage hadn't walked away? Did Mr. Compton know how instrumental his words had been in bringing about those boys' salvation? Sage wanted to think so. And, in his heart of hearts, he believed so.

He reached out for his mother's hand to find it already seeking his. Like a wave, that reaching out continued until they were all linked, one to another, hand in hand. A spring breeze, laden with scents of early rose and lavender, washed across their circle. At their feet, the newly planted twig jittered and the flower petals lifted.

FORTY

Late Summer, 1903, Washington D. C.:

Pursuant to Act No. 800, President Theodore Roosevelt appoints the Surgeon General, Major Edward C. Carter, to the chairmanship of the newly-formed Opium Committee.

The committee is to visit Japan, Formosa, Shanghai, Hong Kong, Saigon, Singapore, Java, upper and lower Burma.

The committee is charged with informing itself "concerning the law governing the importation, sale, and use of opium in force in those countries and cities, the operation and effect of the laws in restraining or encouraging the use of the drug, the estimated number of users of the drug, the total population, the amount of opium consumed, the price at which it is sold, the value of the monopoly concession, if there is such a concession, and its increase or decrease year by year and the causes therefore, the amount of opium smuggled into the country or city, the method of its use, whether by smoking, eating, drinking or hypodermic injection, the effect of the use of the drug on the different races, and, in general, all the facts shown by the experience of the government of the counties and the cities named above, a knowledge of which is likely to aid the commission in determining the best kind of law to be passed in these islands for reducing and restraining the use of opium by its inhabitants. The widest latitude is given to the committee in making such investigation as may seem best to the committee. The result of the investigation will be embodied in a report, together with the evidence . . ." William H. Taft, Governor General of the Philippine Islands, Manila, August 8, 1903.

THE END

Historical Notes

1. The quotations at the beginning of each preceding chapter were not selected to provide a balanced view of Theodore Roosevelt's stances on the issues of his day. He held a number of beliefs and positions that current progressives would find repugnant. That said, when viewed in the context of his time, he was an enlightened progressive in many ways. Those are the quotes that were selected. Some of the quotes were in the speeches he made during his extensive 1903 train junket. Most are not because, by the time he'd given a number of such speeches, he'd honed them down to a single speech that he thought was the most effective for the tour.

2. Roosevelt wrote, after the severe backlash against Booker T. Washington's dinner at the White House, "The only wise and honorable and Christian thing to do is to treat each black man and each white man strictly on his merits as a man." Contrast that sentiment with the one expressed by South Carolina's senator, Ben Tillman, who said of the Roosevelt dinner invitation to Mr. Washington, "The action of President Roosevelt in entertaining that nigger will necessitate our killing a thousand niggers in the South before they will learn their place again."

3. Despite his open-mindedness toward Afro-Americans, Roosevelt was deeply prejudiced against the Chinese. This may have come from his close association with Jacob Riis. An immigrant from Denmark, Riis helped shape social history in a positive way by publishing a book of photographs depicting the poor of New York City entitled *How the Other Half Lives*. While his sympathy for the downtrodden was evident, the captions beneath the photographs made it clear that his compassion for the poor did not extend to the destitute Chinese.

4. President Theodore Roosevelt feared that the unrestrained greed and thirst for power among the day's most successful capitalists was resulting in too much social and economic injustice. He feared a revolution. To save the capitalist system he advocated increased government regulation and the adoption of certain aspects of the progressive and radical agendas. The more short-sighted of the capitalists and their congressional supporters resisted his efforts.

5. With the intent of building up overwhelming public support for his goals, Roosevelt took his message to the people in a cross-country train tour. He visited Portland, Oregon, on May 21, 1903. Thousands lined the streets to greet him and watch as he inserted a time capsule into a hole in the platform that would support the Lewis and Clark obelisk. That monument still stands at the entrance to Portland's Washington Park. The descriptions of the measures taken to protect the president came directly from newspaper accounts of that day. After this book was drafted, it was discovered that a mildly deranged man did lunge toward Roosevelt on the dedication platform. He was wrestled to the ground and taken off to jail. It was later determined that the strange object he carried contained only spectacles.

6. The description of Theodore Roosevelt's arrival in Portland on dedication day faithfully tracks contemporaneous

newspaper accounts of the event. The only exception is that the reception committee meeting the president's train did not include Abbott Mills.

7. Fenton's tactical blocking of legislation aimed at protecting injured railway workers is an accurate depiction of his legislative lobbying on the issue. Accurate too, was the railroad company's false enticements to Easterners seeking more opportunities out West. Finally, another accurate report is that setting forth the facts about Abbot Mills' appointment to the city's franchise commission and the "honest graft" tactics he used to steer city-related business to his bank.

8. Police Chief Charles Hunt was in charge when Theodore Roosevelt came to Portland in 1903. It was Hunt's second stint as Portland's top police official. He lost the office initially because of his efforts to root out corruption within the ranks. Nine years later, he was reappointed and once again he attempted to clean up the police force. This proved nearly impossible because of the monied elite's successful campaign to shrink the city's tax base. Thus, although the city's population doubled in eight years, the city's entire budget had been cut by $23,000 to $75,000. As a result, police officers were grossly underpaid, overworked and thereby highly susceptible to bribery.

9. The medicinal properties of the opium poppy have been known and used for millennia. It was the activities of the Europeans, however, that ushered in the problems of widespread, worldwide addiction. Their cornering of the shipping trade and insistence, at the point of a sword, that Asian countries accept importation of India's opium, meant that by 1900, there were 13.5 million addicts in China consuming 39,000 tons of opium annually–with fully 27% of China's men smoking the drug.

10. Worldwide opiate use has declined significantly since 1903 when it was ten times higher than it is in the present day. Citizen reformers and Theodore Roosevelt were key to this reduction. Following the Spanish American war, the United States took control of the Phillippines. With that control came 190 legally-sanctioned and taxed opium dens that collectively sold 130 tons of opium each year to their addicted customers.

11. The deliberate addiction of the Europeans and their European-American cousins was more insidious. European pharmaceutical companies manufactured laudanum, or "black drop." This liquid opium preparation was odorless, easy to procure and easy to hide. Local apothecaries carried the substance. Over time, laudanum became a key ingredient in over-the-counter patent medicines used to break tobacco addiction, suppress coughs, stop diarrhea, reduce chest congestion and relieve various aches and pains. It also offered the pleasures of opiate intoxication without the social censure.

12. The 1900 census reported that eighty million Americans spent a total of $59 million each year on patent medicines. These tonics, elixirs and syrups contained up to eighty percent alcohol and often had morphine, cocaine or the heart stimulant, digitalis, as a basic ingredient. Naturally they sold well. *Paine's Celery Compound, Burdock's Blood Bitters, Doctor Pierce's Favorite Prescription*, and *Colden's Liquid Beef Tonic* promised to cure maladies ranging from a baby's fussiness to cancer. Many people considered these nostrums to be an inexpensive alternative to visiting doctors. Even church publications carried their advertisements.

13. In 1898, the Austrian Bayer pharmaceutical company introduced heroin as an over-the-counter, non-addictive alternative to opium. Bayer introduced aspirin the next year but dispensing of aspirin required a doctor's prescription.

14. By 1903, the equally addicting derivatives, morphine and heroin, augmented opium's impact on society. America had three kinds of opiate addicts: those who frequented the opium dens, parlor tipplers of patent medicines and children whose cries of hunger and other discomforts were treated by nostrums like *Mother Bailey's Quieting Syrup*. By 1900, patent medicine was a $250 million annual business–that would be $1.6 billion in today's dollars. Advertising dollars and sales profits kept the media and others silent on the issue.

15. Common journalistic bombast of the day, particularly on the West Coast, resulted in stories about the Chinese and their purported use of opium dens to seduce white women. In fact, surveys conducted at the time concluded that 56% to 71% of all opium addicts were white women. Few of these women, however, ventured into the company of the Chinese or their opium dens. Instead, they were addicted to over-the-counter pharmaceutical company nostrums and laudanum.

16. Early in 1903, President Roosevelt began to talk about the need to curtail opiate use in Asia and the United States. He established the U.S. Opium Commission and appointed various individuals to investigate and make recommendations. Companion to this effort was Roosevelt's determination to enact national pure food and drug legislation. He intended to force pharmaceutical companies to list the opiates and other ingredients contained in their patent medicines. The eventual result of his efforts, internationally and nationally, was a marked reduction in the use of those medicines–and enormous financial loss to the international pharmaceutical corporations. The official declaration that forms the book s final chapter is a verbatim presentation of the document that initiated those efforts at the international level.

17. As noted in the earlier Sage Adair story *Timber Beasts*, a Christian aid society did sell boys into prostitution. It is

unknown how long that practice had persisted but, when it was discovered, it created a great scandal. That scandal, however, broke after the time of the events in this story.

18. Portland's local temperance league was called the "White Ribbon Society." Its membership was generally comprised of upper-middle-class women who subsequently became the powerhouses behind many of State's progressive social reforms. The Society was active in Portland at the time of events in this book. Its members did, in fact, travel to the Wallowa area in order to form a chapter.

19. The character of E. J. McAllister is based on an actual Portland attorney by that name. He did represent unions, temperance women and others who were relatively power-less. He was also an effective and successful advocate in the effort that amended Oregon's constitution and granted citizens the right to initiative and referendum. Other than those facts, everything attributed to him in this story is pure fiction. The real E. J. McAllister lost his license to practice law when it was discovered that he was a homosexual. He left Portland to live in Myrtle Creek, Oregon, where he died of a stroke twelve years later. His obituary stated that "He was a man who had many friends and was highly respected by all who knew him."

A selection of the original source documents that partially inspired *Black Drop* and other Sage Adair historical mystery stories can be found at: www.yamhillpress.net.

About the Author

S. L. Stoner is a native of the Pacific Northwest who has worked as a citizen change agent and as a labor union and civil rights attorney for many years.

Acknowledgments

Once again, I want to start by thanking the readers of this series. Their enthusiasm and support has encouraged Sage to keep adventuring and fighting the good fight. I hope he returns the favor.

To the extent this series accurately reflects history, that is due to those who have done their best to preserve the past. In particular, I want to thank the staffs of the Oregon Historical Society, the Portland City Archives and the U.S. Congressional Library. These folks and organizations deserve our gratitude and support.

This book in the series received special assistance from Joel Rosenblit, Helen Nickum and Sally Ann Stoner. Many heartfelt thanks to each of them, particularly Helen who read every single word with such great care and red pen in her hand. Helen is greatly valued, not only for her grammar skills but also for her kindness and her joy of life. That said, any remaining errors are solely my own.

Family members, friends and my colleagues in the labor movement, both old and new, continue to be the loving foundation of this series. While it is not possible to name everyone, I do want to especially recognize Monica Smith. She was everything a labor lawyer should be and more.

I also want to acknowledge the contributions of the E. J. McAllisters of the world. Despite being given a very "hard row to hoe," as Mae Clemens would say, people like him manage to give more, and do more, for their fellow humans than most of us. In his short tenure as an Oregon lawyer, McAllister played a key role in bringing greater justice and direct democracy to Oregon. And, despite the adversity he endured at Oregon's hands, he did not abandon us. It is comforting to know that he was appreciated by the people in his final home.

But, most important of all, I must acknowledge George Slanina. He has been here for the good times but even more for the bad. Without him, Sage Adair never would have got out of the Klondike. George's unwavering support, kindness and always pithy but, right-on, observations make this series possible.

Request for Pre-Publication Notice

If you would like to receive notice of the publication dates of the fifth Sage Adair historical mystery novel, *Dead Line*, please complete and return the form below or contact Yamhill Press at www.yamhillpress.net.

Your Name: _____

Street Address: _____

City: _____ State: _____ Zip: _____

E-mail Address: _____

Yamhill Press, P.O. Box 42348, Portland, OR 97242

www.yamhillpress.net

Author Contact: slstoner@yamhillpress.net